MERKER'S OUTPOST

BLUE FEATHER BOOKS, LTD.

To Peace

ALSO WRITTEN BY I. CHRISTIE AND AVAILABLE FROM BLUE FEATHER BOOKS:

- Queen's lane

COMING SOON:

- Murder on the Beach
- Arnica

www.bluefeatherbooks.com

MERKER'S OUTPOST

A BLUE FEATHER BOOK

BY

I. CHRISTIE

MERKER'S OUTPOST

Cover design by Ann Phillips

A Blue Feather Book
Published by Blue Feather Books, Ltd.
P.O. Box 5867
Atlanta, GA 31107-5967

www.bluefeatherbooks.com

ISBN: 0-9794120-1-3

First edition: April, 2008

Printed in the United States of America and in the United Kingdom.

Acknowledgements

I would like to thank my beta reader and great supporter of my writing, Martha Elser. For all that she has going in her life, she still takes time to proofread my stories. Namaste.

I would like to thank Ken Kimura, who gave me more than a few hints about what he felt would work and what wouldn't. Namaste.

From my heart to yours, all the readers from the Athenaeum (www.xenafiction.net) who have read this story enough times to earn it an Honors Award. I am very proud to have written a story so many of you enjoyed. Namaste.

To the Webwarriors of the Athenaeum, Namaste.

Note

For the interested reader, there is a glossary and list of characters at the end of the text.

Chapter 1

Were they trying to get rid of her by posting her to this sorry excuse for a space freighter? Maybe permanently? Lieutenant Commander Harriet Montran turned the idea over in her mind, not for the first time. Maybe they meant to bore her to death. Her lips curved into a wry grin as she waited for the Gleanean to take his turn at the gaming table. At least the contest engaged some of her senses, and no one else seemed bored. In fact, the *Spinner's Tale* mess hall was packed with tension as thick as the goop from the freighter's shunt gate. Bets had been halted and silence settled uneasily in anticipation of the next move. A dozen figures, of various species but dressed alike in grubby work fatigues, pressed around one of the tables. Even the few that were there for other reasons waited, pausing in mid chew or conversation, watching the backs of their fellow crewmembers.

The Gleanean, hulking over the gaming table, finished his bonus point move. Montran held his gaze with a hard unblinking look, and once again, he seemed uncertain. With obvious hesitation, his eyes moved back to the game board. He wrapped his large hand around the control and moved his wizard's servant unsteadily into the castle hall, past a dead troll dog.

"Bleep, bleep."

Crewmembers jumped at the pager's signal, and Montran's hand was a blur as she slapped irritably at the acknowledgement button on the back of her wrist comm band. Careful not to touch the board or its controls, she stood and let the parting crowd direct her to the communicator on the unevenly faded, two-toned painted hull. Her wrist comm, as with most equipment on the freighter, was old and not up to spec. Typical of the way Fermin and Sons ran their woebegone fleet.

"This better be a 'Hello, hope you're enjoying some time off,'" she grumbled to herself. Every species needed some downtime, and she was no exception. "Bridge, this is Commander Montran," she said in a low tone.

"Report to cargo bay seventeen, Commander." The order was crisp and unnecessarily loud. With difficulty, she held back an angry retort.

"I'm off duty for another twenty stan hours, Ensign Desoto."

She imagined a smirk on Ensign Desoto's blue face to match the amusement he was undoubtedly feeling. His fourth antenna was probably twitching, too. It irked her that his status wasn't based on battle or academy training, but either way, she still outranked him. No matter whose space they were in.

"Those are your orders, Commander."

She hit the wall communicator with more force than necessary. After taking a few deep breaths to calm herself, she turned and threaded her way back through the restless crowd.

"Back on duty." Again, she made an effort to keep her tone even and noncommittal. She used to be able to emotionally detach from annoying things like this, but her time aboard this freighter was changing her.

The computer-run Gaming Master announced, "This game is closed. One player is BOD. Game two thousand four-four is ruled a draw. This score will be sent to the Gaming Center of the Galactic Committee of Families and Communities." An audible click locked the score into the Gaming Master's system to preserve it for the GC.

Sounds of outrage mixed with jubilant voices from some of the crew rose to a loud din as Montran stepped through the hatch, grateful she would not have to break up the fistfights that were sure to ensue. She would have enjoyed punching someone herself. Someone like Lord Chaney, the committee member responsible for her "emergency drafting" back into GCFC service and for sticking her on this disaster-waiting-to-happen tub.

Quickly, Montran strode away from the noise, hoping to outrun her temper.

She'd been caught by the ADSW—Active Duty for Special Work—clause, a typical political loophole in the Rue Despario Agreement, which was supposed to be a courtesy concession between two galactic egos. No one had ever used it before, but she couldn't fight it, and she'd spent three miserable months of solitude on this freighter.

She had intended to rendezvous with her cousin, Lord Hadrian DeMonte, on Z3, a small but busy outpost near a jump gate used primarily for switching shuttles. From there, they were to travel to their home planet aboard his private liner, the *Alborak,* a ship that had enough armor and weaponry to fight off pirates and any other trouble short of a swarm.

Why had Hadrie sent for her? It wasn't for military or political reasons, otherwise Admiral Hailbrun would have told her something.

As head of Collective Space NetSec, Admiral Hailbrun had an extensive web of informants, and his intel included all the gossip in both GCFC and Collective space. He had been Montran's CO for seven years, and he would never knowingly send her into danger unprepared.

What did that leave? A family reunion?

She had sent Hadrie a brief telepathic image of her emergency draft orders. His answering thought puzzled her.

She grasped the red harrier, the pole that would allow her to drop quickly to the next deck without using the stairs.

He knew she couldn't figure out feeling messages. She needed an image. Why all this secretive stuff, when a simple communication call would have been fine? Or would it? What could possibly be so important that he sent a thought? Maybe it was just habit, from when they were kids, always keeping in touch via thought. It was so much more personal. When had they stopped doing that?

Her boots thudded solidly on the lower deck, jarring her. With a slight pause and a curse muttered under her breath, she continued toward the hatch, trusting the sensors to open the hatch covering before she reached it.

This assignment was supposed to last less than one stan month. But by Hydra's breath, three months had passed and she was still here, along with the cursed toxic gasses she was supposed to be watching over.

She rotated her shoulders and took a deep breath, trying to ease the ache in her head.

The comm call couldn't be about docking preparations. There were no docking possibilities in this part of space that she knew of. No exchange of freight at all, unless some passing ship was suicidal and wanted to link for supply transfers.

What service compartment needed her to squirm into it and fix what malfunction her reactivation of the ship's diags had found? Or what virus might be running through the systems that their own officers couldn't nail and purge?

The hatch swished open.

A party of twelve, dressed in their A'mort Environmental Garb, or AEGs, was assembled around a pile of covered crates. Montran nearly tripped over someone's gear, heaped carelessly in the entranceway. Annoyance flashed through her. She had been drilling the crew since her arrival on the proper handling and storage of life-sustaining equipment. But after three months, with her own health deteriorating from long hours, little exercise, and poor food, she was no longer interested in saving the crew from themselves.

Commander Martinez, the only member of the group not dressed for outside work, looked her way just long enough to gesture at the heap. "Dress up, Commander."

She picked up the upper part of the AEG and read her name across the back. So, they had gone into her quarters and snagged her suit. That was too considerate. She hoped the joints and packs weren't damaged from lying on the deck. These AEGs were the oldest version the ship could legally carry.

Commander Martinez had focused his attention back on the group moving the unmarked crates onto the transport pad. If they were at a legal toxic dumpsite, Montran would be hopping with joy that her pseudo-official duty was completed. Now, she studied Martinez's body language in her peripheral vision.

Martinez raised his voice, turning her way as though checking her whereabouts. "Put some more speed into it, Commander."

"Aye, Commander." By now, she was used to suiting up without assistance. She snapped the fasteners, ran sensitive fingers over the lips, cinches, and connections to ensure the suit was secured, and tapped the wrist gauges, more out of habit than for any remedial reason. Covertly, she studied the crew in the room—identifying them, ranking and classifying them by their known specialties—and came up with a group ill-suited for any away mission she could think of. For that matter, no one on *Spinner's Tale* was qualified for any ship duty, and that had been her assessment after only a few days on the freighter.

"When the commander's ready, move out. I don't have all day, so brief her." Martinez turned on his heel and walked out, going past her without a glance.

Montran snapped her utility belt in place and pulled a sidearm from the secured weapons locker nearby. Her hands were steady and her movements smooth as she went through the routine, but her insides churned with foreboding.

"First group, prepare for descent," Chief Petty Officer Decker said into his helmet mouthpiece, bypassing her in the chain of command for debarkation.

Ignoring the insubordination, which she had become accustomed to coming from the crew on the freighter, Montran continued to look for something out of place that might have given rise to this uneasy feeling. It was highly unlikely, but for a moment she hoped it was the cursed toxic canisters they were removing—and then quickly changed her mind. Her aging AEG might not withstand exposure to toxic substances should there be a breach, and it would be safer to shuttle the canisters to the dumpsite rather than move them via the molecular transporter.

"Where and what are we transporting, Chief?" Montran asked. By the tic reaction in the chief's shoulder, she knew he had heard her, but he continued to order the next group into position alongside more unmarked boxes and canisters. The second group was ready and assembled on the pad, waiting, while she remained to the side.

"We're taking supplies to an outpost planet," Decker finally replied, speaking in a churlish voice.

Montran noticed he had not named the outpost or addressed her directly, but it appeared her presence was required, because they were waiting for her. Suddenly, it dawned on her where they were dropping.

"Merker's Outpost?" Curiosity replaced irritation. What was *Spinner's Tale* doing taking supplies down to a supposedly deserted planet? And what kind of supplies?

The chief's lips curled up, giving his visored features a grotesque look. He had a rather unpleasant face to begin with, Montran thought. His sarcastic voice came over her speaker. "I only obey orders, Commander."

As was her habit with anything this crew did that involved her safety, Montran checked their work. She moved to the transporter console to verify the settings and made one minor adjustment, unnoticed by the crewman who was busy at the monitor. Then she stepped into the spot that had been left for her.

* * *

The usual disquieting sensation of being moved in molecular form from one place to another paused in the midst of the transportation process. Montran felt momentary fear, but then the restructuring continued. When the transportation sequence finished, she stood surrounded by open space, alone and with nothing to grab onto as a heavy blanket of weight settled over her body. She bent her knees to keep her balance. She could hear the suit kick in to compensate for her out-of-kilter bios. Taking a deep breath of air, she choked as it burned her lungs. If the increased gravity weren't so difficult to move in, she would have let herself fall.

"Don't panic, Harriet. This is workable," she whispered to herself. As a Centurion officer in the Collective, she had experienced this gravity load before in military training exercises. However, at that time she had reliable equipment, and support in case of a problem. She pushed that thought out of her mind and concentrated on the immediate task—surviving.

Dragging her left arm up, she looked at the life support status gauges on the wrist of the suit. Everything read normal.

"Can I be so lucky?" She stifled a cough. "Hail to *Spinner's Tale*. This is Commander Montran."

This time the cough caught her by surprise, and her chest constricted in a cramp. Now would be a good time to cast away caution and use the meds. She felt along the suit controls for the emergency medical packets, but nothing happened when she pressed the button. Alarmed, she looked in the pockets for a first-aid kit. Nothing. She activated her water refresher. Nothing.

"Commander Montran to *Spinner's Tale*, come in," she said, her words coming thickly and slowly. Was she out of her mind? They were the ones responsible for her being in this situation.

Looking closer at the gauges, she noted her communicator had failed to register her voice. Saved from her own foolishness.

She mentally reviewed the transport coordinates. How could this have happened? She had reset the coordinates to be behind the crew, not out of sight of them. Helios fires! She should have checked the calibration for the planet's harmonics.

Montran tried to focus her eyes on the view before her.

The sky was azure, but thin streaks of gray appeared only inches above the horizon line. She turned slowly, seeing the same flat land in all directions. Squinting against the reflected light that managed to get past the visor screen, she strained to see something more then studied the red surface, letting her eyes adjust to the different lighting. What had happened to the crew?

Was Merker's Outpost above ground, below ground, or both? Because of the atmosphere's density, her best guess was below.

No landmarks or any other distinguishing features caught her eye, except a dark line that lay along the horizon in one direction.

She would head that way. Slowly, she pushed her legs forward, her efforts barely lifting them above the dull red ground. She was already tired from her long shifts on the freighter.

She wouldn't think about that. It was self-defeating. She needed to move her feet forward, and make a plan. What did she know about being dropped in a hostile environment with a faulty suit and no supplies, and with air that smelled faintly of contaminants?

Step one, look for her shipmates. She laughed to herself at the dark humor of the thought. She would skip that part. Two, look for shelter. Completely flat land, no obvious markers for access panels. Finally, yet most importantly, step three: wait for the Auto-R to rescue her. So, where was the Auto-R? Did Merker's have underground living spaces? It had to, if the crew were taking supplies planetside. They couldn't survive in this atmosphere. So…

She gave a small sigh and moved another few feet.

I'm here alone... no back up... What do I do?

She would have to think of something to take her mind off how miserable she felt. But before she could censor her drifting thoughts, a subject she had been avoiding for over four stan months came to her attention. Sharon.

By now, Sharon should know of the change of beneficiary on the life insurance policy… the one she had insisted Montran take out.

Montran heaved a great mental sigh. Thinking about her personal problems was not going to help her out of her present misery.

She realized she had stopped walking. Automatically, she ran a mental check on her physical condition. Slight tremors ran up and down her legs. Sweat trickled down her neck, and she imagined her clothes were soaked. The AEG was laboring, and the visor was collecting condensation on the inside. Determinedly, she started forward again.

Even as her eyes fixed on the distorted view through her visor, Montran's world went careening at an odd angle and her faceplate smacked down into the dust. For what seemed like a long time, she lay where she fell, letting the tremors in her legs diminish. Then she started the arduous process of getting up. Rolling onto her hands and knees took an immeasurable amount of time, effort, and racking coughs, as if the atmosphere both inside and outside of her suit were working against her. Stabbing pain radiated from her lungs through her chest and back. She closed her eyes and braced herself, giving her heart time to stop pounding so hard, and savored the victory of getting up as far as her hands and knees.

She was thirsty.

The inside of her helmet was weeping with condensation, and the outside was covered with fine, iridescent dust. She coughed again and wished she could hold her head as the throbbing pain increased.

She sat back on her haunches and lifted a trembling arm to wipe the exterior of the faceplate. The faceplate acted like a magnet to the glittering flakes. Now it wore streaks from her dust-covered glove, making her view worse.

She avoided the temptation to shake the dust off her gloves, since she knew she couldn't raise enough vigor for any real effect. Besides, the jolt would only make her head ache more.

She slowly leaned forward again and patted the ground around her knees. She felt the unmistakable form of a cylinder. A maintenance pipe, which should lead to an access entrance.

Angling her helmet for a better view, she saw two bright arrows stamped on the pipe, one larger than the other, pointing in opposite directions. She went in the direction of the smaller arrow. Minutes later, crawling on her hands and knees to keep the pipe in view, she came to the lip of an elevator plate, a standard maintenance entrance that operated by detecting weight distribution. Crawling gratefully into the center, she pulled out the control bar and moved it into the "on" position. Small lights lit up around her, and with a noticeable jerk, her descent began. She remained on her hands and knees in the center of the plate, exhausted and laboring for breath. A noise sounded from the overhead plate encapsulating the elevator, and the pressure around her body eased. Was the air breathable now?

Her fingers shaky, she released the faceplate safety. She didn't have much choice. Her suit was out of air. Gulping, she filled her lungs with the fresh, clean air and then began coughing, expelling the toxins she had taken in. As the coughing lessened, she leaned weakly into a sitting position against the wall. She noticed that the air that cooled her face was scented. Her throat and lungs were sore, but she was now able to breathe deeper and without as much pain. She removed her gloves and then wiped away the sweat running down her face. Tired, she remained against the wall, trying to gather her strength.

* * *

Startled green eyes shot open. How long had she been out?

The muted light in the pale blue elevator was easy on her eyes, but they still watered. A soft tone sounded, and she could hear seals release. She rose unsteadily, using the wall for support. If she had to defend herself, she was going to be a real disappointment to anyone looking for a challenge.

A movement in the air from behind had her turning unsteadily to the opened door. Holding onto both sides of the elevator doorframe, she looked out before committing herself. A softly lit waiting room with three corridors leading from it—right, left, and forward—was before her. In the center of the room, couches were arranged around a sculpture. It appeared to represent a pair of polo players riding their mounts toward an imaginary goal, one trying to steal the ball from the other.

Cautiously, she leaned out to get a better look around the room. The light in the waiting room brightened as the center corridor lit up, and the scent in the air became stronger. She released her grip on the doorframe and stepped completely out of the elevator. The door swished closed behind her.

Now that she had a better view of the room, she saw that, like most waiting rooms, there was a water refresher tucked into a corner. She wondered if it would work. Her throat was parched. She tottered over to it, leaned against the wall, and pushed the small activation button. The green light came on and a stream of water arched into the bowl. She sniffed it for contaminants, but then her thirst got the better of her and she sipped, then gulped, her fill. It tasted a little like lemon water.

Straightening up, she wiped the back of her hand against her lips, studying the room once more, looking for other familiar conveniences. To the left she spotted the EC, the emergency cubby, usually found near elevators.

She pushed a button, which turned on a small indicator light.

"Your shuttle is charged and ready to go. Press X to release it from its space," a genderless voice said.

She pushed X, the wall panel slid up, and a cart moved out. A light flashed on its console. Ah, it was voice activated. Montran sank into the seat gratefully. "Take me to…"

"Destination is Guest Quarters on Green Deck Alpha O Zeta. Please place both feet flat on the floorboards in order for shuttle to become active."

Montran quickly complied. How did this thing know what room to take her to? Did that mean all the others had been taken there? Was this some kind of hotel?

Pictures, paintings, and sculptures decorated the hallway, giving her the sense she was in a well-cared-for private art gallery. She couldn't see a speck of dust anywhere.

The cart moved at what she would have called a fast jog, faster than a cart should move in a crowded corridor, but there was no crowd, only her. It slowed and then stopped in front of a room. The door slid open with barely a sound.

It looked like she had arrived at her stop, and a good thing, too. She was fading out.

Everything went black.

When she opened her eyes, she was lying on a couch. A bot leaned back, removing an oxygen mask from her face.

"Guest Lieutenant Commander Montran has recovered consciousness. Recommendations are for a full night's rest after a soak in an herbal bath of remedial salts to rebalance her bios and to remove the last of the toxins from her system. Have you any questions, Guest Commander Montran?"

Montran peered at the bot. "Who are you?"

"I am the medical assistant assigned to these quarters."

"Where am I?"

"Guest Quarters on Green Deck in Alpha O Zeta."

Montran blinked a few times. "I don't feel so good," she whispered.

"Guest Commander Montran's bios…"

She blacked out again.

* * *

Captain Montran of the GCFC Spartan Force was shaken awake to bright sunlight and a pounding headache. Oppressive heat bore down on her. Her eyes felt raw and her mouth was swollen from heat blisters. She was tied, as the others were, to the bar of a cross, waiting her turn to be tortured to death.

As the bright sun dropped below the horizon, Captain Montran struggled to open her swollen eyes to see who was still alive. She could make out three, but there could be more somewhere out of her view. Thirst was just another torment. Fire burned through her shoulder joints. Barely conscious of the effort, she struggled to bring her feet underneath her to bear some weight, only to realize that she couldn't feel her feet. A punch to her broken ribs brought her eyes open again. Before her, a figure dressed in ceremonial garb held something out to her. Once he had her attention, he stepped up to Corporal Wen and ran the wand over a portion of his body, starting at his neck. She realized he was naked—they were all naked—and as the wand moved over his body, his flesh started to seep blood. They were skinning him alive. Wen's cries were no louder than a whimper. Staring at him, horrified, she realized they had broken most of his bones, and that the bindings holding him fixed to the cross were the only things keeping him upright.

Captain Montran wanted to close her eyes at the horror, but each time she glanced away, she was beaten.

"Gods, hear me!" she screamed silently. Delirious with pain, she felt a part of her reach out for someone from childhood... a mentor who had sacrificed herself for the continuation of her species' evolution.

Then Kela stood before her. She fluffed her feathers and then laid them down smoothly.

"Well, my child, what are you going to do about this?" she asked, as if it were a glass of spilt milk that needed cleaning up.

"I can't do anything."

"Of course you can. Step back and look again."

"Please, Kela, help us."

"I'm doing my best, child, but you must, too. What does this situation need from you?"

Montran didn't dare think of anything violent, for the DeeNaJa of AltaLa were not a violent species. They were mentors for young empath adepts who were learning to sense various life-forms, on many levels of awareness.

Through blurred vision, she could see Corporal Wen's spirit hovering near his physical form, looking confused and lost. The ceremonially dressed figure must have seen it, too, because it smacked the skinned body and shook something at the spirit. Montran reached out mentally to the spirit and whispered a prayer of guidance to the young soldier, so he could move on without being caught up in the angry violence these people were creating. Montran felt something slap her own body, bringing a fresh wave of pain. Her eyes opened wide in startlement, and she lost the concentration she had been focusing to help Corporal Wen find a peaceful end.

"They don't want you to help your charges. They wish to trap the unhappy souls and use the anguish, fear, and hate the energy

will generate to continue their wars against their neighbors," Kela explained dispassionately.

Montran refocused on Corporal Wen's spirit. The spirit was ready to let go, but it was afraid to with so much violence around it.

Another figure, dressed in garb similar to that of the first, carried a many-stranded whip. He slashed Montran across the face with it, breaking her concentration again. Whatever the strips had been soaked in, it was meant to burn and, if the victim survived, to scar.

"Kela, what can I do?" she pleaded in anguish.

"Love."

What other advice would a wise teacher of the DeeNaJa give, a part of Montran asked. Another strip of skin was torn off the corporal's body. It was difficult for Montran to open her heart with the violence heavy in the air around them.

"Help me, Kela." Montran felt the love her mentor had for her, and as it filled her, she seized it and sent the same love to Wen. Montran was beaten unconscious.

When she came to, she found Corporal M'summa was next on their captors' list. The realization that they wanted her to witness the tortured death of each of her soldiers made her determined to help them the only way she could, by wrapping them in love and helping them to escape the violence of their deaths.

Days passed. Montran would never know how many. The two running the torture show were furious that they weren't able to prevent her from touching the souls of her soldiers. When only Sergeant Cooo was left, they cut off her limbs while Montran watched. The sergeant's eyes were locked on Montran's as her body parts were hacked off. Her spirit didn't stay long. Perhaps because of the prolonged torture of the others, she was more than ready to leave. When Cooo died, one of the enemy soldiers delivered a blow to Montran's jaw that broke it.

Her days of pain seemed to go on forever.

Slowly, she came to the awareness that she wasn't hanging in the sun, and that whatever she was lying on was hard and cold. It surprised her to notice discomfort that was on the outside of her body, because the wounds inside her were raw. She forced herself into a black space where she would feel nothing.

Images weaved in and out before her. A droning became loud and then stopped. Montran opened her eyes, conscious that she felt no pain.

"It is good to see you," an elder of Clan Montran greeted her.

"Where am I?" she whispered.

"Not Mutteyalamma, the Land of the Dead," he said, and then added softly, "though you probably wish you were. You've been rescued."

She closed her eyes, not knowing if she could believe what she was seeing and hearing.

"We're on our way to a hospice. You're on the mend physically, but you'll need a lot more than that, Captain. Take it nice and easy." With that, he rose, and another took his place.

* * *

Montran opened her eyes slowly. There was no pain. It was just another bad dream. Rising slowly from the couch, she studied the room.

Beside the couch were two matching armchairs and a knee-high, oblong table within fingertip distance of them. A corner held bookshelves and a workstation, and throughout the room, artwork hung on the walls and sat on occasional tables.

She sniffed the air. It was scented, but not from recent occupation. And all this space! Even a kitchenette with a bot. It was downright decadent. In all her time in uniform, she'd never been quartered in such a nice room. Whoever had decorated this room had good taste.

A bot that was about her height became active at her movement and awaited her acknowledgement. If it was more than a service bot, Montran was in no condition to do anything but surrender. The time she had spent unconscious had only taken the edge off her exhaustion, and she was still feeling ill from the bad air in her AEG.

"Where am I?" she asked the bot.

"Greetings, Commander Montran. I am Bach. You are in an area called the Lair. Would you care for some tea and a light snack before your bath?"

Montran stifled a snicker. "I'll take some tea. And crackers," she added, not trusting her stomach to accept anything else.

Keeping the bot in sight, she peeked into the adjoining room. A bed moved out of its wall storage and settled quietly over the carpet, leaving plenty of space around it. The thick, off-white carpet looked tempting to walk barefooted on. She stepped to the bedroom control panel and checked out the available options then whistled softly.

Besides the usual bed size adjustments, the panel had mood settings. It even offered time periods. You could choose the season and on which planet. She guessed whoever lived here hadn't had much chance to travel off-planet.

An ankle-high bot emerging from a wall station caused her to look toward the doorway. A trail of glittery particles led right up to her boots.

"Chair," she ordered. The expected chair materialized from the wall next to the bed. Gratefully, she sank down, the chair forming a comfortable bench that allowed her the maneuverability to remove her AEG while sitting. The small bot moved forward and helped pull off her dusty boots. As she struggled to remove her suit, it extended itself to assist her. She had forgotten what it was like to have help with simple things. The bot folded the discarded suit into its proper configuration and waited.

"That suit doesn't work, so if you've got something that works better, I'll swap with you," Montran said. "If not, I'd be grateful if you could repair it."

The bot rolled to the wall where a compartment opened, set the clothing in it, and then rolled back into its wall space. Handy to know where things were kept.

She looked down at her feet, buried in the thick carpeting, and wiggled her toes in delight.

"Okay, let's check out some of this." She pulled the small console on the chair closer and studied the controls. "This must be for the closet." She pressed the icon.

Large double doors folded back, revealing an empty closet with plenty of drawers, a full-sized mirror, and an automated butler. Once the doors had completely opened, the butler came out and the chair, unbidden, moved so that she faced the new bot. She and the bot studied each other.

"Nothing to unpack," she said, holding out her arms. After a few moments, the bot returned to the empty closet and the doors closed. She returned her attention to the buttons and pressed the icon for the bathing room.

"Your tea and crackers, Commander Montran."

Bach's genderless voice startled her. Just as quickly as her thoughts focused on the voice, the chair turned and she had to grab the armrests so as not to be unseated. Suspiciously, she glared at the bot.

"How did you know my name… you and the medbot?" Her voice faded as she spotted the layered crackers. Her mouth watered and her stomach grumbled again.

"Your name was on your uniform."

"Oh, right." If it were possible to be embarrassed by a bot, she would have been, but her attention was on the refreshments. She took the tea and crackers from Bach with unsteady hands, and her face creased into a smile at the familiar name of Estabol stamped across the cracker face. She took a bite and let it melt in her mouth, giving a hum of satisfaction.

"Is there anything else I can get you, Commander Montran?"

Another bite of the cracker. Her thoughts were focused only on the mouthwatering taste. She shook her head.

Sweet on the outside and tangy on the inside. Highly nutritious. What a life. Maybe she would try those dials for mood settings. She wondered if the accommodations came equipped with a metradame companion. Companionship from someone who knew how to carry on a nice conversation and give a good back rub sounded enticing. Just like any other stopover for a weary soldier, huh?

Abruptly, she turned to see where the earthy and fragrant smell of blossoms was coming from. A doorway had opened to a tropical forest.

She jumped up from her comfortable seat. What was this place?

"Whose lair is this?" she asked Bach.

"You will learn more later."

Good enough. She gulped the rest of her tea and handed the cup to Bach. Feeling more energized, she walked around the bed and peered through the doorway.

Most wilderness areas she had visited hadn't come equipped with a shower and toilet. If this was a dial-a-mood, it was the best she'd ever seen.

She gently touched a leaf on a vine near the entrance. For a moment, she believed she felt the life force from the plant, and then she quickly discarded the sensation as imagination. The plants looked like they'd been there for a while.

A long, two-sink counter separated the shower area from a trellis that supported scented flowers and blocked the view of the other side. She walked slowly toward the trellis, looking around for anything that might resemble wildlife. The plants didn't appear to be carnivorous or poisonous, but she wasn't a botanist. On the other side of the trellis stood a large tub.

"It's big enough to have a bathing party. Sharon would like this."

A small bot hovered expectantly in front of her. “My name is Ald. Your bath has been drawn, Commander Montran. Is it to your liking?”

Montran stared open-mouthed at the bot and then clamped her jaw shut.

I take back anything nasty I said about the emergency services of this planet. It’s too unbelievable to be real. Am I dreaming?

She sniffed the air appreciatively. “What’s in the water?”

“Elesa balm and oil. Good for refreshing depleted cells and mind.”

Clearly, the medbot’s diagnosis had been programmed into the bathing room attendant bot. The fragrant aroma that filled the air eased her headache. Looking around the bathing room, she noted a door a few steps on the other side of the lattice that surrounded the tub. Another room?

She stepped up to the door to test its sensors, but nothing happened. Walking back to the shower, she stripped down and tossed her uniform and other articles of clothing into a pile, which Ald quickly picked up and seemed to scan. Sizing her up for something? She disregarded the thought and stored her sidearm in a niche in the shower wall.

After scrubbing herself clean, she padded across the warm, cobblestone floor to the steaming tub. Kneeling at its edge, she sniffed cautiously, alert for any caustic elements. She risked dipping a finger into the swirling waters to test the temperature. Satisfied that the water was nothing more than what it appeared to be, she stepped into the bath. Sliding down until the water was up to her neck, she held her breath for a moment as the heat went from hot to warm. She closed her eyes and let out an audible sigh.

Glorious.

Idly, she caressed the surface of the bubbling water.

Is this why Spinner’s Tale *is using this place as a stopover? It’s not on their charts for stopovers. No. It has to be something else... like smuggling.*

Imagining the crew of *Spinner’s Tale* capable of smuggling brought a snort that turned into a snigger.

Not that group of misfits.

Sighing, she ran her fingers through her damp hair, massaging her temples.

“Would you care for a back massage, Commander Montran?” Ald said.

"Please, and thank you." She rose to her feet and leaned forward, holding on to the rim of the tub. The sound waves from the bot started at the small of her back and gradually moved up.

"Ohhh. Yes… that really is sore." The pressure shifted, and she heard a small pop. She sighed at the immediate relief. From now on, she was not going to accept service on any ship that didn't have a bot that gave massages. Or even a person. That would be even nicer.

"Ald, are there other residents here? Guests or visitors?"

"Here in this compound, you are the only resident."

"There are other compounds?" She sat back down and turned in the water to face the bot.

"Yes."

"Where are they located?"

"I have no information on them. The information you wish may be accessed from the computer in the sitting room."

That's just what she would do. Right after a nap.

She leaned back, closed her eyes, and let her body and mind relax.

* * *

A small beep startled her. She lifted her dripping fingers and, from their puckered appearance, decided that she had soaked long enough. Standing up, she grabbed the rim and hoisted herself out of the tub. She dried off quickly with the towel Ald provided, and headed back to the bedroom, fully relaxed. The bed covers were pulled back on the left side, ready for her to slide in. Sleepwear, consisting of shorts and a brief top, lay at the foot of the bed. Enough to give the appearance of modesty, should she receive a visitor, but nothing she would get tangled in if she slept restlessly.

How did they know she slept on the left side? It wasn't as if her sleeping quarters of late had been big enough to make that determination.

Not really interested in the answer at that moment, she crawled into the inviting bed and fell fast asleep. Three months of poor sleep had finally ended.

Chapter 2

"Hey, Cadet! Wait up."

Cadet Montran cringed inwardly, struggling to keep a polite smile on her face. She stopped and turned to face the civilian-clad figure of a man she detested.

"Alan. I thought diplomatic classes were on semester break." And that by now, he would have been long gone on his vacation.

"I have some business to finish up." Even in the dark, his eyes were disturbing. He looked at her briefly and then glanced around. "Where've you been? I checked your quarters and you weren't there." He looked back at her then took another quick look around.

Montran withheld her first, indignant, reply. "Now that you've found me, what do you want?" Who had let Alan Fermin into the women's quadrangle? Or for that matter, onto academy grounds? Montran shuddered at Alan's physical nearness. Even at this distance, she could feel his animosity.

"The problem with you is that you're too impatient."

"Just tell me what you have to say, so I can continue my quiet walk back to the barracks—alone," she said, hoping her voice didn't give away her apprehension.

"I want to see you."

Even in the dark, she could see his smirk. Fear, of a strength she had never felt before, nearly paralyzed her legs.

"I want you to come over to my place for some socializing, a drink, and a bit of talk... on family politics."

"No!" she blurted, surprised.

"What, am I not good enough for you?" His voice was low and menacing.

"I'm not interested. Period. End of conversation. Now let me by."

Alan remained blocking her path, his hands resting on his hips.

"Get out of my way, Alan."

Suddenly, heat radiated from the center of her forehead. A link shot out to her Dancer. A soul... a warrior's soul... a woman with so much passion, it burned her very essence.

Images she had once witnessed of a tall, athletically built woman dancing under the moonless night came back to her. The dancing woman's eyes had been dark and expressive. They had only seen each other once in the light. It was in the bar, over the heads of a crowd, and then she was gone.

Alan! Her thoughts quickly flashed back to the man before her.

"Don't panic," her Dancer imparted to her. "You can get by him."

But Alan wasn't alone. Where had they come from?

The other men, all larger than she was, stood on either side, blocking any escape. Distracted, she missed seeing Alan's fist heading toward her face. He had moved without warning and so quickly that she failed to defend herself. Then a stunner immobilized her, and someone slammed her face onto the hard ground. Only partially conscious, she felt more than one set of hands pulling at her and dragging her off. She remembered no more of the attack... or of her rescue.

* * *

Montran woke briefly, trembling and in a sweat. Another nightmare. Why had they been plaguing her lately?

What was done was done. Let it go, she implored herself. Her heart beat rapidly and her breath was shallow with fear. Mumbling something unintelligible, she rolled to her other side and quickly dropped into another dream.

Harriet read the brochure on metradames. Her eyes scanned down the manufacturer's glowing descriptions and exorbitant claims for its product. The bottom of the brochure listed the name of her life insurance company as one of the backers of the metradame model she was looking at. Turning to her lover, she nudged the woman. "Sharon, look at this. Why would a life insurance company invest in a toy only a few people can afford, when anyone can go to a House of Aphrodite to work off their sexual energies?"

"Not all metradames are for sale, nor are they toys to be played with!"

Harriet closed her mouth with a snap. Sharon had never been so defensive before. And what did she mean? Didn't she think it odd that a life insurance company would get involved with sex toys?

Chapter 3

CPO Decker of *Spinner's Tale* shifted his bulky shoulders in the AEG. He planted his feet squarely to hold his balance in the heavy gravity. The inability to move freely irked him, as evidenced by the beads of sweat that rolled down his face. More times than he could count, he turned to look back toward the entrance to the underground city, making sure it was nearby in case something should happen.

He was being blamed for Centurion Commander Montran's disappearance, and it incensed him. To his way of thinking, either the ship's equipment had failed, or someone had kidnapped her—that someone being the smugglers or the Spartan soldiers—to make him look bad. His suspicions leaned toward the Spartans, and he made sure his boss, Alan Fermin, knew that. So there was no reason for someone of his status, a chief petty officer, to wait outside the city for transmissions from the search teams or from the ships circling above the planet. The two rabbits could relay the necessary information. But his fear of Spartan Captain Miller, captain of the notoriously tough Black Rose squad, was stronger than his irritation and discomfort, so he remained at his station.

A bleep sounded, followed by the voice of Captain Largo, from *Spinner's Tale*.

"Decker! Did they find the body yet? Where are the hourly status reports? They've been at it for seven stan hours with no updates."

"Captain Miller has no updates," Decker replied defensively and then added, "sir." His tone was just short of being insolent.

"Get one now or you're going to be out there for another day. Out."

"Fricking officer," Decker said. "Getting in a panic about nothing. I told him her tank doesn't have enough air for over one stan hour, and it's already been eight. Idiot doesn't know how to do the math."

If Miller's Spartans knew he meant to hand Montran, ex-Spartan captain of the Degas squad, over to Alan Fermin for delivery to a metralab, they would probably freeze him out. But they would get over it, after a few weeks of extra duty.

The chief glanced at his timepiece. He had signaled Captain Miller five stan minutes ago, and still no response. Decker had also tried the leaders of the search parties, but they were ignoring him, too. Obviously, Miller didn't care about updating Captain Largo. Fermin was no doubt heating up Largo's feet for news.

Captain Miller's curt message, eight stan hours ago, was that he would let Lord Chaney know if he found anything.

The Black Rose squad was here by Lord Chaney's order. Some members of the GCFC considered it part of their right to deploy squads for their own personal business. It helped if they were in a position to influence the Galactic Central Command that oversaw the GCFC military, which Lord Chaney was.

Rather than think about those over whom he had no power, Decker turned his thoughts to solving a more important problem: how to get back into the underground city without anyone noticing. Since most of the resident smugglers were out looking for the be-damned Montran, there should be no one but his people in the city. But there would be consequences if he were caught returning without a direct order. He needed an excuse to be in the city. Irritated that he couldn't think of something good, he cursed the person he felt was responsible for this predicament—Lieutenant Commander Harriet Montran.

"Where in the bloody moon did she drop to?" he asked himself. "I hope one of those cursed windstorms blew her right off the face of this stinking planet."

He looked around nervously, worried that Montran was nearby, waiting to take them out. Before becoming a Centurion, she was the captain of a Spartan recon group that had dropped behind enemy lines. They took out lonely sentries, one by one. "Once a Spartan, always a Spartan," a small voice taunted him.

Startled, he looked at his companions, wondering if they'd heard it. They seemed focused on their suit equipment, monitoring for messages. Because of their substandard AEGs, they weren't out scouring the desert for Montran, whose suit was just as ill equipped to handle this harsh environment. If he'd had his way, they would be inside playing in the game room, or…

That was it!

He switched on his mic. "Move inside," he said. "There's an auction broadcast to get ready for, and we need updates on the situation there."

If he were to use the excuse of the broadcast for leaving his post, then it had to look like work was being done. Normally the smugglers didn't like outsiders involved with their business, but most of their members were out planetside, looking for Montran, and Decker knew the broadcast had to go on as scheduled. He would offer his two rabbits as helpers.

As the outside hatch swung shut and locked, an alarm sounded in their helmet communicators and inside the small chamber they were in. But they couldn't respond to the unknown problem until the chamber filled with breathable air.

Crowded in the small area with two too many people and bombarded by the shrill alarm, Decker's anxiety level rose. His suit functions kicked in to handle it, but before the suit blinked red, the all clear light came on and the inside hatch unlocked. Decker pushed roughly past the two men and recessed his helmet into the suit collar, taking deep breaths to quiet his rapidly beating heart.

Ignoring the panicky voices that flooded the suit's comm link, he focused on his own fear—that Montran had been spotted inside the city. He pulled out his illegal sidearm, ready to fire at the first sign of anyone with orange hair, indifferent to the warnings that firing his weapon in the complex's atmosphere would cause more harm to him and those in his proximity than to his target.

His hand trembled as he pointed his weapon from one corridor to another. Seeing nothing, he straightened up and breathed a sigh of relief.

"Shut up, all of you!" he shouted into his comm. "What's going on? Turn off those cursed alarms."

"We… we don't know, Chief," a hesitant voice said. "It may be that one of the rooms was gassed, or something…" The voice faded out and the alarms stopped.

"Where is that butt, Nixon? I left him at the command center's console. He should check out what set off the alarm."

"Maybe that's where he is, Chief."

"Where did you last see him, you moron?"

"We left when Master Alha Bahna ordered us to help prepare the cargo in Alpha C for the auction, Chief."

"Since when do you take orders from a smuggler? You work for Fermin. Who took Nixon's place at the console?"

"No one. We've been getting the merchandise ready. Everyone else is out searching for Commander Montran, and—"

"She's trouble, even in death." He turned to the men, who waited nervously just out of his striking range. "Well, what are you two waiting for? Do I have to do everything myself?"

Without waiting for a reply, he stomped up the corridor to the room Nixon should have been checking out. The two men trailed behind him. Decker stopped in front of the room. The indicator light was amber instead of green, but he pressed the controls anyway. Nothing happened.

"Who's got a sensor?"

Neither crewmember said anything. Like Decker, they had left their heavy utility belts in the command room.

"Get a COR, Sams." The COR sensors from *Spinner's Tale* were ancient, but the only ones available.

The heavy tread of boots hurrying away soon faded to nothing. Minutes passed and the amber light flickered to a bright red.

"Blasted light." Decker slammed his gloved fist against the panel. He realized almost immediately it was the wrong thing to have done. The door beeped and the hermetic seal hissed. Frantically, he and Edison scrambled to get their faceplates back up before the door cracked open.

Fluorescent green gas surged out of the room. Edison's collapsing body slumped heavily against the back of Decker's legs, knocking him forward a few steps. His helmet bounced against the partially opened door, and he cried out in fear as his hands frantically sought solid support from the wall or door. The green gas dissipated around him. His heart raced wildly at how close he had been to his own death. Then it occurred to him that he could turn this to his benefit.

His story would be embellished, of course, but there would be no one to refute his version. He gripped the doorframe until he was sure his voice and nerves were steady.

"All hands, now hear this!" His voice deepened with self-importance. This was going to be his moment. "We have a broken seal in the main passageway. Secure all hatches. I'm going to have a look inside," he declared grandly.

Master Alha Bahna's voice boomed in his ears. "What's going on there? Where's the cargo I ordered to be—"

Disdainfully, Decker shut his communicator off. No one was going to steal his moment. He took a deep breath and held it briefly then let it out in a puff. He wondered what he was going to do next.

Uncertain, he peered through the crack in the door, but couldn't see anything in the darkness within. Firming his resolve, he gave a halfhearted push on the lever to manually open the door. No response.

He took a step back as if to leave, the relief giving him a rush of energy, but then, with a sickening, high-pitched whine, the door opened farther, enough for him to fit through. He could see only inky blackness inside. The light from the hall went no farther into the room than the length of his boot.

I have to get in there. They'll know if I didn't.

He forced one foot into the room.

Come on, moron, get the other foot in there.

He dragged his leaden leg beside the first one.

Almost in. A little more, you coward. Move!

He was now completely out of the light. A part of him was detached, so to some extent he felt safe. That part watched far enough away from the AEG-clad figure that there was no danger of being hurt. Dispassionately, he viewed a physical body that he didn't even identify as himself, standing unmoving in the darkness. Then, suddenly, he was back in his body, betrayed by some unknown curse and forced to experience his fear intimately. He could feel the blackness as though it were a physical entity, crowding and pushing against him.

What if he bumped into something? There was no telling what was in this room. What if it was a trap?

Something was in here. He could feel it.

He backed frantically into the corridor, bumping against the partially opened hatch in his haste and stumbling over his crewmate's body.

As he stood shaking, his back pressed up against the wall, he realized that if he had moved farther into the room and the hatch had closed behind him, he would have been trapped in complete darkness with whatever was in there. The AEG made small whining sounds as it worked hard to keep up with his runaway bios. His faceplate had fogged up, obscuring his view of the outside.

As he moved, a whiff of what his fear had done to his bowels and bladder assaulted his nose. With jerky movements, he somehow managed to get up the hall to safety, using the wall to guide him. Salvation was before him: the door to the command room. The gripping sensation around his chest eased. It took him a few moments to register that the hatch wasn't opening. Did Sams lock him out? He'd kill him when he…

The hatch isn't going to open until that room is sealed! Of course. That's why that idiot Sams hasn't reappeared.

All he could see was the inside of his faceplate, covered with condensation from his rapid breathing, and that increased his panic. He flattened himself against the wall as the flashbacks started, and his almost nightly dreams replayed.

He stood in front of the tall, dark-haired, lean-muscled Black Rose Spartan, ready to stun her into submission, when the room went dark. Just as he had staged it. But she was laughing at him. She said she knew of his plan and found him incredibly stupid and a pitiful example of his species.

He had the upper hand. He had brought the weapons and the night vision goggles. He was the smart one.

However, once the treacherous darkness engulfed them, he felt the agonizing pain of each strike her hands and feet delivered before he could reach his goggles or his weapons. His salvation had been the light that came back on, but by then he was no longer conscious and his broken body lay in a heap.

As the flashback ended, bile rose in Decker's throat and rage filled his thoughts. He screamed silently at the cocky grin his nightmares kept replaying, and now, even his waking hours were being taken over with her face. A cool, dispassionate voice broke through his darkness, replacing it with a different type of fear. "Captain Miller here, CPO. What did you find?"

"Captain… no light… to see… anything." He gulped, struggling unsuccessfully to keep fear out of his voice.

A member of the elite Black Rose Spartans, the captain wouldn't take carelessness lightly, especially when a life was lost. If Miller knew Decker was responsible for unsealing the door to the contaminated room, he would find himself abandoned surfaceside. His last moments of life would be facedown, looking through a visor crusted over with the shimmering dirt that he had been introduced to on his first transport down to the surface.

The memories of that humiliation—falling on his face in a screaming panic when the unfamiliar weight descended upon him—overlapped his fear of abandonment. His knees shook so hard he slid down the wall.

"We've sealed the room from the other side of the maintenance panels," Miller said. "The corridor should be breathable in about twenty minutes. How's your air?"

Decker slid to the floor, the bump jarring him into alertness. Automatically, he lifted his arm to check his gauges but couldn't read them through the fogged faceplate.

The captain paused two heartbeats. "As soon as the corridor is secured, I'll send a team to you. Out."

Decker knew that if he were one of Miller's Spartans, he would have found a way to bring him a fresh tank. He was determined that Miller wouldn't see him die from this mess.

* * *

When the hatch finally opened, Captain Miller, accompanied by a small group from Security, found Decker lying on his back. According to his gauges, he was still alive.

"Get him back to *Spinner's* sickbay, Sergeant. Corporal Anders, check on the other one up the hall. Corporal Drewer, call the teams in. We have some damage control to do before the auction."

"Yes, sir. Sir, Commander Martinez is on his way down to the planet for a conference with Lord Chaney."

"Thanks for the information, soldier." Captain Miller returned the salute and walked back into Com-C, the Command Center, to look over the control room one last time. A smug smile formed on his lips. Some of the recent developments were fitting nicely into his plans, while others were moving up the deadline for achieving his own agenda.

Chapter 4

A cold, stiff breeze blew from the direction of the tall mountain spires blanketed with snow. It sent Alexandra's long orange tresses, the ones that weren't currently weighted with beads and ribbons, into her face as she turned her head to listen to the faint sounds of chanting. With practiced skill, she caught the wayward strands of hair with one hand and held her position on the rock with the other. Her grandfather sat next to her.

"M'dearie, now pay attention. This is very important," he said to her.

But Alexandra continued to look for the source of the chanting.

"All right then, Alexandra, listen ta the music, but focus on the sound in here, m'dearie." A finger touched her below her navel, at her dan tien. *Warm energy vibrated through her from the point he touched and up her spine and then shot out through her head. It took her breath away.*

"Breathe deep, m'dearie. Ye need ta breathe deeper." His fingertip touched points on her stomach, her chest, her throat, and her forehead and then rested gently on her head. A painfully bright light flashed between her eyes, and a loud popping noise sounded in her ears. The earth moved beneath her, and she lost her balance.

Montran awoke instantly, throwing her arms out to stop the fall. The room light brightened as her bios leapt from sleep to wakefulness. Disoriented, she lay for a moment with her arms splayed and her body pressed firmly into the bed. The intense humming in her body receded to a tingling in her fingers and the soles of her feet. As awareness of her surroundings penetrated her sleep-fogged mind, she remembered she was on Merker's Outpost. Rising on one elbow, she glanced at her timepiece. A little over eight stan hours had passed. This was the longest she had slept in ages.

Slept! She was on a strange planet, alone, and she went to sleep? She was lucky she hadn't awoken to a weapon stuck up her nose.

Reluctantly, she let go of the self-recriminations. She stretched, and her muscles absorbed the rush of blood, giving her a charge of energy. She lay still for a few moments and let fragments of her dreams turn over in her mind. Sighing, she rolled over and got up.

"Store the bed," she said and then added, "Open the bathing room door." She would enjoy smelling the healthy vegetation as she resumed her morning workouts. On *Spinner's*, long hours and lack of sleep had kept her from her usual daily exercises.

Standing very still, she used her breathing to center herself then opened her eyes and moved slowly into the first pose, greeting the spirit of *Qi.* She was halfway through the *Qi Quong* breathing meditation when she felt another's presence.

Was it next to her? No, it was all around her. Sensing no danger, she accepted its light touch. The consciousness had the feeling of constant flux, chaos, and she was dimly aware that it monitored, maintained, and—

It was the consciousness of the planet.

She had not done this for a long time. Too long. Breathing in deeply, she greeted the presence. She felt a gentle greeting in return, and then it was gone.

Montran moved into the next stance, breathing slowly and deeply. Thirty stan minutes later, she had completed a shortened version of her usual routine and her legs were trembling from the exercise.

Her prayer mantra marked the end of her meditation, followed by five breaths, during which she remained still. Slowly, she opened her eyes to the jungle in the bathing room. Again, she breathed in the smell of the moist dirt and blooms. She had been living on ships and space stations for too long. For all of their elaborate gardens and ecosystems, biospheres couldn't provide a connection with the living spirit of a planet.

For the next stan hour and a half, she tested her stamina, balance, and flexibility, moving from one degree of kata to another in a more rigorous workout that called for strikes, kicks, and spins in the air. She was disappointed that she was out of breath before she got to the eighth degree, her muscles burning and tight.

"Oh, joy." She bent over, panting. Three months of inactivity and her stamina had faltered. Commander Nelson would have her running with the new recruits. And she bet those greenies would be dying to embarrass a flag officer.

She used the toilet facilities and, taking a quick shower, planned what she needed to do.

Clothes and food, then I'll check this place out closer. I need to find out who runs this nice hotel and thank her, him, or them. Then find out just what Spinner's Tale *is doing here. It can't be legal. Oh, and contact my CO and let him know I'm not AWOL. And tell him what? That I've been kidnapped? That I crash-landed on a deserted outpost and don't know when I can get back? I bet he's never heard that excuse. And if he asks what the conditions are, do I tell him my quarters are the equivalent of a luxury room in a seven-bud-rated hotel? I think not. Best leave that part out.*

Ald handed her a towel as she stepped out of the shower.

Back in the bedroom, she eyed the apparel the butler held up for her.

"So, that's what all the sizing me up was about, huh, buddy? I sure hope you only did it for clothing and not for a tree-suit or any other unpleasant surprises that I might find confining." She reached for the gray material, so sheer she thought it would tear if she didn't handle it carefully.

"This is a Second Skin and is to be worn while you are here on Merker's Outpost," the butler bot said. "It will act as an emergency blanket until help arrives, should you encounter a breach without wearing an outersuit, or if the suit you are wearing becomes damaged."

"How do you know this is going to work for me? I just arrived and you already have something?" She gingerly held up the pants, letting the light shine through them.

"The faulty equipment you discarded was analyzed, and your bios have been monitored and anatomized since your arrival. This is a bioengineered suit made specifically for you. Breaches are a possibility, therefore all guests are issued a suit of their own until they depart the outpost."

Bioengineered? Breaches were serious anywhere that the exterior environment was alien to one's own. She certainly agreed with that precaution. And they wanted the suit back. Souvenirs limited to toothbrushes and slippers, if they had any. What was this place? She loved this bot service.

She thrust her foot into the Second Skin and wiggled her toes into the slots provided for them. The skin seemed to pour around her toes as if it were liquid. Amazing. When she had the skin on, she could feel a sudden rush of energy, though nothing overpowering. Without effort, she picked up differing scents from plants in the bathing room, the dirt, various herbs, and other smells she couldn't identify but knew were there. She could also hear the butler's movements and the rustle of clothing as it was removed from the closet.

"Second Skin, huh?"

Regarding herself in the mirror, she wasn't pleased to see that her three month stay on *Spinner's Tale* had left her looking too slim. Their menu was sadly lacking in her idea of palatable nourishment, so she had eaten little. Damp orange hair curled around her face, emphasizing her dark green eyes. Impatient with her own scrutiny, she pushed a curl off her forehead.

I need a haircut.

"I sure hope it's not going to be a hassle when I have to relieve myself," she said to the butler when it returned with another layer of clothing.

"Your biological waste is recycled by the skin, sustaining your energy without nutritional supplements for a standard day. However, it is not advised to wear the suit for more than a standard week at a time without removing it. It is better that the body not rely too much on artificial means of regulating itself. In your species, your gender experiences a monthly cycle of menstruation. When that time comes, the suit will absorb the discharge of old tissue and recycle it into energy. Furthermore, due to the excess of energy, you should be feeling more energetic than normal. Remember to adhere to your species' observances of that time."

"Women of my species who spend a lot of time in space don't ovulate much." Her lips tightened at the reminder of why *she* wouldn't be menstruating again. She shook her head to rid herself of unbidden images and a few tears.

She took the dark green two-piece suit and boots that the butler held for her. The pant legs fit snuggly into the boots. The boot ankles were padded, the toes were tough, and the heels were hard enough to hurt someone if she kicked backward.

Her growling stomach told her that the Second Skin didn't take care of everything. She picked up her sidearm and carried it with her into the kitchenette. A bowl of steaming cereal was waiting for her, along with cinnamon and chopped apple. A beverage sat beside it. Her stomach growled again.

Bach produced a chair for her. "Is the breakfast selection suitable, Commander Montran?"

"Yes, quite. Thank you." She laid her weapon on the table within easy reach.

Someone on this planet had a profile on her. Just how worried should she be?

She ate quickly, as was her habit, keeping her eyes moving around the area, searching for anything that would indicate she was being monitored. Without an HR, a hand reader, it would be difficult to really know. She didn't even bother thinking about the antiquated Catu's Ortual Rstr, CORs as they were called, that *Spinner's Tale* carried. As a veteran soldier, she knew that having the most up-to-date equipment to read and translate the environment and to diagnose and prescribe treatment for an injured person was a life-and-death necessity. Maybe freighter crews were more expendable than soldiers.

When she finished her meal, Bach removed the empty dishes. Montran decided to make a closer inspection of her quarters before venturing out into the rest of the structure. She eyed the farthest corner of the room and decided to start there.

Real books. She pulled one out and turned the pages. She wondered what the pages were made of. Would they turn yellow with age, or just disintegrate after a calculated time?

With sensitive fingers, she felt the cover, even sniffed it. It reminded her of her uncle's library, which contained information from all over the galaxy, stored on tapes, discs, books, and holographs. His books didn't smell like this one, nor did the pages feel as fragile. She slid the book back onto the shelf and perused the rest of the titles. A wide variety of subjects, from authors with differing views, filled the shelves. The collection offered a compelling study for someone who had a lot of time on her hands. She laughed to herself.

Wouldn't that be a joke, if the only way she could leave this place was if she gave a summary of each book? But then, so far this place wasn't so bad.

Pausing at the knee-high table, she admired the detail. Beneath the transparent top, the base displayed a carving of a wilderness scene surrounding a small village. In the village, seven different species worked and played together.

Now that was a flight from reality. If any one of those seven species got so much as a whiff of the other, they would break out weapons without even thinking about it.

In one corner of the room sat a detailed porcelain statue of Quan in her meditative state. Both palms were open, one holding the holy measures and the other empty, representing another world. Quan sat on the flower of Pa with her eyes half-lidded, focused on the unknown. The holy flower rode on ocean waves, surrounded by the twelve holy leaders from the time of the Empress Ges. It was unusual to see Quan depicted with her eyes open. Her clothing was the ritual garb, down to the knotted sash and the way it was tied. At one time Montran knew what each knot represented and the prayers that went with the knotting. Or were they called spells?

Her gaze moved to a painting of the sun, setting the tops of trees and mountain peaks ablaze with light. Quickly, she glanced around at the other art pieces. Even the animals in the art depicted serenity.

How nice it would be to have the time to gaze at these works and enjoy them for their aesthetic qualities, but she had things to do. She settled in front of the monitor. The chair adjusted its shape to fit her form, and when she was comfortable, the screen activated.

"Your request?" a neutral voice asked. No hologram appeared beside her. Usually room communication centers were personalized to suit the resident. She noted from the icons on the screen that the personal hologram option was turned off.

"Show me the history of this workstation's use."

"The history has been cleared. This station is awaiting your input for preferences, Commander Montran," the voice said.

"Where are other life-forms, like me?"

"In Century City. Would you care to contact anyone there?"

"No!" Wherever Century City was, she couldn't take the risk of letting anyone know her whereabouts. That could certainly ruin her stay here. "Pinpoint their location in yellow, and mine in green." She hoped they were not on the other side of the elevator.

Onscreen a planet appeared, overlaid with hexagon shapes that quickly faded. Then on one side of the sphere, a yellow light flashed. The sphere then revolved until a blinking green light appeared.

"Show me the entire planet and any other cities."

The image continued to revolve slowly, giving her a view of the entire planet and of underground structures that looked like separate cities.

"Show me viable habitation for my species and others of like bio-makeup."

Century City appeared in three colors—green, red, and gray. Her location on the other side of the planet was in two colors—green and gray. The green portion of Century City covered a larger area than where she was. The green was enclosed in a thick red barrier, and the area beyond the red was in gray.

Okay. Century City was some distance away. Green was livable, gray was not activated, and red was what? Not negotiable?

She studied the other grayed-out cities. One was just a ghost of an outline, as though it had been erased.

"Give me a detailed engineering image of my location, with entrances and exits marked in red."

A three-dimensional image detached itself and became a hologram. A pulsating red dot was labeled as her level location. For a few moments, she studied the levels, noting that each, except the seventh, had access to three elevators from the surface. The seventh level had only one elevator, giving her the impression that it was a secured area.

Looking back at the third level, where the red dot was pulsating, she saw two entire corridors were green and one ended at a Command Center, labeled Com-C. The other corridor she had noted upon her arrival was closed off and gray. She could either exit back the way she had entered the underground city, or head over to Com-C. Any other place she wished to visit would require an AEG, and hers was nonfunctional, to say nothing of the fact that it hadn't been returned.

For a few more moments, she studied the planet, frowning. "I wonder how I got here?" she said, more to herself than the computer.

"The emergency system was activated."

She blinked at the unexpected answer.

"How does the emergency system get activated?"

"When a life-form that is within the influence of Merker's Outpost, this planet, is in danger, an alert is sent to Guardian. Guardian determines what action to take."

"Who is Guardian?"

"The Keeper of Merker's Outpost."

"What is Guardian's gender and location?"

"Guardian is not a biological entity at this time. Guardian's location is everywhere."

It sounds like a supercomputer has been left to care for the outpost. Not unusual.

"What business goes on in Century City?"

"I don't have that information."

"Where could I get that type of information?"

"In the Command Center. It is the last room at the end of the next hall." A holographic image of her walking to Com-C appeared.

"Does Guardian protect the outpost from hostile or unauthorized occupation?"

"Guardian oversees the protection of Merker's Outpost and its inhabitants."

Montran rose from her chair and took one last sweeping glance of her luxurious quarters. When she stepped out into the hall, the lights came on, indicating the direction she was to go.

As she walked briskly toward her destination, she looked at the continued display of paintings and sculptures and noted the number of rooms she passed. Taking in a deeper breath, she checked for the usual stuffy smell of an artificially maintained habitat. There was none.

When she was five strides from the Command Center, the door slid open with a sibilant swish. Lights came up slowly, revealing a typical Com-C room. She stopped just short of entering and peered around the circular room, cautious and curious. Four sets of steps led up to a second level. Monitors covered the majority of wall space. From the ground floor, she could look through the transparent floor of the second level and see a similar scattering of video screens. All Com-Cs in both Collective and GCFC territories were designed pretty much the same, both civilian and military. In the center of the room was the Command Chair. The Command Chair exuded an energy of its own, which the person who sat in it became part of. It was an interactive connection between computer, people attending to the monitoring, and the person in the chair.

She sensed that this chair wasn't on.

She walked around the dais, and her gaze swept across the inactive consoles and blank screens. Like everywhere else she'd been so far, the place was free of dust or smells of biological occupation. She inspected corners and tested closed doors. Nothing yielded to her inspection, other than the room she was allowed to enter. Warily, she looked again at the Command Chair.

Montran hadn't been in a Com-C since she was a cadet, but she was sure their basic operation hadn't changed much, or she would have heard about it. That meant she had to sit in that chair if she wanted the power on. It looked like she was in for a new experience, one of those "druther not" types.

As she stepped one foot onto the dais, a light above the chair came on, making her pause before she turned around and cautiously sat in the chair. The form of the chair slowly fitted itself to her, and a panicky feeling sent chills along her arms and a shiver up her spine. But other than that, nothing further happened. She let out an exasperated breath of air.

"Now what?"

"You must sit back," a voice near her elbow explained.

Montran leapt out of the chair and spun around in a low crouch, coming face to face with another bot. Her hand went automatically to her sidearm, and found none.

What a time to go slack! Where did that bot come from? How could I have missed something that bright?

Before her was a bot striped in brilliant colors, with more appendages than she could imagine it would ever need. The bot didn't look like a few hand chops or well-placed kicks would knock it off balance, much less put it out of commission.

"My name is Charles. I tend the Command Center and Guardian. To engage the chair and communicate with Guardian, you need to sit back with your head on the headrest and relax. Guardian wishes to communicate with you."

"Yeah? Why don't you just relay the message?"

The appendages gestured at the consoles. "My connection would not bring up the monitors you wish to view or give you access to the information you need."

That was a sorry explanation. And how would a bot know what she needed?

Images came to mind of the bed being turned back on the left side, where she normally slept, and of the breakfast selection she would normally choose. She glanced at the chair, then the monitors, and then back at the bot. With great reservation, she sat back down in the chair, keeping an eye on Charles. The moment her head rested on the back of the chair, the video screens came to life and the chair moved to the left, giving her a view of the first row of screens.

Her awareness expanded into… it was difficult to describe, since she had no basis for comparison. However, her eyes focused on the first monitor, and within her mind, she was immediately in the scene with the soldiers and civilians, standing next to them as they moved around cargo crates.

What was in those containers? It… they looked alive. She leaned down to get a better look. Intelligent eyes stared back at her. Startled, she straightened up.

Since when had cages become the standard for detaining prisoners? The Galaxy Charter would have had to be changed, and everyone would have heard of it.

Something wasn't right here. She knew if those idiots from *Spinner's Tale* were involved, it would be illegal.

With a blink, she broke from that scene. When her eyes moved to the next screen, the chair adjusted to her gaze, and as she stared, she again became like an unseen spirit moving among the people. She recognized a few of them from the freighter.

She studied the unit patches on the left shoulder of the Spartan uniforms. Another screen showed a group dressed in military issue AEGs, weighted down with full weapon trappings, looking every bit like a group on a hunt-and-destroy mission. Unlike *Spinner's Tale*'s equipment, these suits were the latest in technology. She looked closer at the patch on one AEG. Her awareness jerked her back to Com-C and the bank of monitors before her.

What were Lord Chaney's pets, the Black Rose, doing here? Were they still sponsored by him? What was going on? Was this a new GCFC outpost? She thought the planet was marked on maps as privately owned. Did Lord Chaney own it? No. GCFC members couldn't own planets. Was someone trying to take over this place?

"*They are trying*," she heard a voice say inside her head.

That didn't come from her. The timbre of sound and thought was way off from what she was used to hearing.

"Who are you?" she asked cautiously, suspecting it was the main computer, or Guardian.

"*I am.*"

"What's that?" she asked, not quite understanding.

"*I am who you think I am.*"

"Guardian."

"*Yes.*"

Her hand waved at the monitors. "What are all these people doing here?"

Feelings and thoughts flooded her mind in answer, upsetting her stomach. "I don't quite understand," she said, more to herself than to Guardian. Her mind struggled to make sense of what flashed by her. "You mean everyone is here for different reasons?"

"*They are here for more than one reason.*"

"Is any of this business legal?"

"*No.*"

"So, this *is* a thieves' or smugglers' den," she said excitedly. "Who owns Merker's Outpost?"

Before her appeared an image of a young male Copoc, characterized by his species' multiple arms and legs. First dressed in a business outfit and then older looking, wearing a lab coat. The next image was of another person pointing a weapon at him. He collapsed to the floor in a laboratory as the perpetrator turned and ran. Then the image flashed back to that of the younger version of the Copoc, smiling at her.

Montran's breath caught in her throat as her thoughts imagined the Copoc's brain being part of the computer. "You're Guardian?"

She leapt out of the chair. Guardian was a dead person. She had heard about experiments carried out with the brains of highly respected scientists after their deaths. But the idea of commingling with someone, or something, without any idea of what she was touching—or what was touching her—gave her the shivers.

Rather than get back into the chair, she stepped closer to the screens, trying to distance herself from Guardian and regain her composure.

Civilians were feeding the captives in the cages. In another room, a small group of soldiers and civilians were eating, sitting separately, with more than space distancing them. Pursing her lips in thought, Montran shook her head ruefully at not being able to put her finger on just what was so familiar about this situation. Instead of struggling with it, she continued moving slowly along the row of screens. She pointed at one screen. "Who's that?" she asked Charles, who was trailing her.

"Maud, on an assignment," Charles replied.

"Who's Maud?"

"Guardian's assistant."

"What's she doing?"

"I don't know. It's Guardian's business. If you wish to ask him, you must sit in the Command Chair."

"What can you tell me about Century City?"

"I only know about this area, and that information is limited."

"But you identified Maud."

"She visits here often."

"Is she a bot, a human, Guardian's rabbit? What is she?"

"She is not quite like you," Charles said.

"What do you mean?" Montran was getting impatient. She felt an urgent need to do something. Her adrenaline rose and her heart pounded as though she were getting ready to jump into action.

Hold on. Why this urgent need? Where was it coming from? Military training, or influence from sitting in the chair? Or was it just because she needed to do something?

Deciding it was not a manipulated impulse, she turned her attention back to the figure, which had stepped out of the dark tunnel and was now in one of the well-lit city corridors. She was wearing an unfamiliar suit that covered her from head to foot.

Montran realized Charles had continued to speak. "What did you say about Maud?"

"She is composed of the basic bios as are you. However, she is different. What the specific difference is, I don't know."

She looked back at the chair. She needed to separate from her fear.

There was no way she was going to let a dead person into her brain.

As something came to mind, Montran glanced back at one of the monitors. She slapped her forehead in exasperation.

Admiral JoCastao has a detachment of the Tanjmi forces searching for a group of smugglers that escaped from a raid about two stan years ago. They were involved in a slave trade ring. Is this part of that group? It would explain why the containers are holding these people.

A familiar aroma caught her attention, and she turned to the brightly decorated bot.

"Perhaps a cup of tea would help?" Charles said. "Maud usually has one when she has things to think about."

All right, so Maud was not a bot. She was able to think for herself.

Montran accepted the tea and continued to study the screens, counting the number of personnel in Spartan uniforms and how many different company patches they wore.

"I'll bet they're rogue Spartans," she muttered. But the Black Rose? There were enough here to make up a healthy squad. She had never heard of a Black Rose involved in this type of outlawry. But a lot could change in seven years.

Lord Chaney. His name sure had been coming up a lot lately. He had signed the orders that dragged her back into GCFC service and onto that run-down freighter.

Montran took a deep breath to stop her anger from building. She drained her tea, handed Charles the cup, and stepped back onto the dais. She sat in the chair with her head pressed firmly against the headrest and her fingers curled over the arms so tightly that her knuckles were white.

"Are you still upset with me?" a soft voice spoke aloud.

Her eyes widened. "I just find it uncomfortable to have a computer in my thoughts."

"I do not think that is all that is bothering you, but we shall move on. What is it you need?"

Montran distrusted the change in the computer's approach, though using verbalized words rather than subliminal images from a dead person was more within her comfort zone.

"I would like to send word of my whereabouts and of this business to my commanding officer, Rear Admiral JoCastao on the Collective flagship *Ziggy*."

"What *word* would you like me to send?"

Montran let out a short laugh. "Multin, and the message should be marked for her eyes only, from Lieutenant Commander Harriet Montran."

"Ah, Multin. A code name for an operation in the Collective's sector. It took place two years and four standard months ago, and was the cause of the smugglers' unwanted company here."

"So," Montran spoke softly to herself and then louder to the computer, "you heard about it from the smugglers?" *How did they know the code name?*

"I heard about it through the rumor mills, here and there, and from the smugglers. The Tanjmi operators hunted them out of Collective space, and they fled to neutral territory—here."

"I thought Multin was classified information."

"So it is. I have access to many places, and a 'classified' label does not impress me much."

"Did you hear whether *Spinner's Tale* is involved?"

"They deliver supplies to my uninvited guests and give the ship's owner a reason to snoop into their business. The agents for this smuggler group deal in rare commodities. Anything you desire can be purchased from them if you have the fee, usually at a private auction. Some of those people in cages are headed to private zoos, and those tagged red have been selected for the metralabs. Does that answer your next set of questions?"

"Yes. Thank you." She tried to figure out just where her private interview with Guardian was leading, and what she was going to do about the smugglers. Maybe it would help if she knew what Merker's Outpost used to be. She had never heard of it as anything other than privately owned. Guardian had been wearing a lab coat in one of the images he had flashed for her; she guessed he was a scientist. "So, this planet used to be a research facility?"

"Merker's Outpost was designed to function as a research facility."

"Just what kind of research did you do?"

"The Second Skin you are wearing is one of the products from my laboratories. Perhaps you are more familiar with MLL."

Montran's eyes opened wide. Was Guardian the CEO of MLL? Maybe not, because the company was doing well on the galactic stock market. If anyone knew the CEO was a brain in a computer, it wouldn't be seen as a legitimate company, would it?

"I've heard of MLL. It's one of the few corporations that won't create anything intended for warfare. But I haven't seen anything like your Second Skin on the market."

"It was not my intent to put it on the market. I created it for my staff and their families on this outpost, so they could move topside and throughout the various cities without worrying too much about a breach."

"I'd like to have your Second Skin on a ship."

"That would require a different composition, which does not interest me these days. My interests have changed since I have taken up residence in a computer."

"I guess they would," Montran said. Thinking back to the planet's diagrams, she remembered only two small sections out of all the cities that were still active. "What is Merker's used for now?"

Montran blinked in surprise at the amusement she sensed from the computer.

"Besides a haven for smugglers? A refuge for those fleeing their enemies."

Had he just told her that anything else regarding this planet was not her business? "What happened to the guy who shot you?" she asked. "Did he steal any of your secrets?"

"We did not get a chance to find out from him. He died of natural causes before my agents could question him. Until two years ago, no one knew what was on this planet. I keep the location of this laboratory secret."

On one of the monitors, she spotted Maud securing a hatch in a rail tunnel.

"I notice you are interested in my assistant, Maud. She could use some help. She has no military training, and Sheila, a metradame, is proving to be more than she can handle."

"A metradame?" Montran's interest was piqued. "What's Maud doing?" She wondered just what problems Maud was having with a metradame. Metradames were procured for sexual pleasure by those with lots of credits.

"To the first question, Sheila is a metradame trained to be a personal bodyguard to one of the smuggler chiefs. To the second question, Maud was able to free a few of the abducted, but that was easy because they were quite sick and did not have guards around them. She has moved them to a secured infirmary on the other side of Century City, which the interlopers have not been able to breach. Our aim is to rescue all of them before the smugglers can ship them to their new owners. I am sure that with your training, you can create believable diversions while Maud frees the remaining prisoners."

"Our aim? Just Maud and you? Aren't there any more of your people in the cities?"

"I have only you and Maud."

He didn't offer an explanation as to why there were so many cities and no residents. Maybe they were new cities, not yet inhabited. Montran frowned. She shook her head, trying to stay focused on the important point—rescuing the abducted victims. What did a metradame, and a bodyguard at that, have to do with this?

"Before I get involved in this rescue operation, I would like some more information on just what's going on here."

"You mean you are only hearing one side of the story, and would like to make sure I am not the outlaw."

Montran glanced at the monitors. "If you created those scenes just for my benefit, you've done a darn good job. But why the hurry to get me involved? If you know so much about Admiral JoCastao's special forces, why not just wait for their arrival? One person is not as likely to make a successful rescue as, say, two dozen trained units."

"Based on your past experience with smugglers," Guardian said, "what are the chances that they will be gone and these captives scattered to their new owners by the time the rescue ships arrive?"

"All right, you have my cooperation. But I'm not going to risk my life creating diversions against this kind of force unless I have some intel. If it's possible, I'd like profiles on the smugglers, soldiers, and anyone else helping run this business. I want to know what kind of weapons they have, a detailed plan of your facilities..."

Her mind took off as she continued making a wish list. As a flag officer on *Ziggy*, Admiral JoCastao's flagship, she worked at the war table, planning raids on outlaw hideouts and strongholds. Here, she was going to be the diversion. This would be a first for her, running interference in a two-person operation. Who said old war dogs couldn't be retrained?

And the metradame? That made for an interesting image of foreplay. She couldn't prevent a smirk, which had her shaking her head to clear her thoughts. She really needed some shore time.

"What's that?" she asked, startled. She had missed a remark from Guardian. It also occurred to her that she needed to be careful of her thoughts while linked with the computer.

"I was about to brief you with background on my unwanted visitors. At the moment, the smugglers and soldiers have two priorities. One is to locate you, and the other is to prepare for the private auction."

Montran was surprised at first and then nodded. Though she doubted she could do much damage on her own, the idea of a lone wolf on the loose could give the smugglers enough cause for concern that they'd hurry their business. If they had to break camp sooner than they wanted to, their contraband wouldn't have a destination other than their next base, thus creating heavy traffic to a supposedly secret site.

"Judging by these scenes, it doesn't look like they're too concerned with security."

"They feel safe with the Spartans acting as security. Right now, there is a storm above their part of the planet, so the hunt for you has been called to a temporary halt. When the winds abate, the smugglers will start the auction and the military and any available smugglers will resume their search for you, nearly emptying the city. Captain Miller of the Black Rose is head of their security. He is also the son of the ex-employee that shot me. He is using the topside excursions to search for other entrances to my cities."

"So that's how they knew of the cities here."

"Not from Captain Miller. He has not shared what he knows of the outpost with his employer."

"Just what does Captain Miller have in mind for your cities?"

"He is a treasure hunter. So far, I have only allowed them one find, Century City. I let my curiosity get the better of me and allowed them in. Maud has not quite forgiven me for that lapse in judgment."

"He's known for two years? I'm surprised he hasn't blown your city wide open looking for others. The Black Rose get messy when they don't get what they want. Persistence and patience are two different qualities, and the latter is not something they keep in their kit."

"If he wanted to share his knowledge of the other cities, I'm sure he would have tried that tactic, but any explosion would attract unwanted attention. There is a major trade route nearby."

"Secrets." She smiled. A tool that could be put to some use. "I wonder what would push them to mass mutiny?"

"Unpredictable environment," Guardian said promptly. "The only ones that haven't been rotated out are the Black Rose group."

"How many personnel on this outpost?"

"About five hundred."

"That's a lot of personnel to rotate, and makes it pretty tough to keep a secret. It says a lot for their loyalty." She was quiet for a while, wondering if the location of the outpost next to a popular trade route was the only reason the smugglers had chosen this site to establish a small base. "About this metradame. What do you know about her programming, and who does she guard?"

"Lord Chaney."

"Chaney!" She jumped up from the seat in dismay. Quickly collecting herself, she sat back down. "Naturally, since the Black Rose are here." She took a few breaths. "So, my being here is not a coincidence."

Was she meant to be a pawn? Against whom, Hadrie? Admiral JoCastao? She shook her head, perplexed.

"No. As soon as I discovered your name and rank, I tapped my sources of information, and believe me, they are galaxy-wide. I learned your assignment to *Spinner's Tale* resulted from a personal vendetta. You are here because Lord Chaney could not get rid of you during your tour of duty as captain of the Degas squad. He started out doing it as a favor for the Fermins, and when you refused to die, you became *his* personal issue. Alan Fermin wants you as his personal metradame, but not quite in the same role as Lord Chaney's Sheila."

"What? What are you talking about? Alan?" *I'm gone for seven years and I walk into this? What's been happening around here?* "Wait a minute. A metradame? Me? They're not real. All they're used for are sex toys." A shudder shook her frame at the thought of being touched by Alan.

"You have been misinformed. Metrapeople are people who have had behavior modification chips implanted, their faces changed, and their original personalities suppressed. They are remodeled to fit into roles their new owners have chosen for them for the rest of their unnatural lives. Sheila is a trained bodyguard who kills, maims, or tortures, as her owner orders. Not a toy, in any sense of the word."

Guardian flashed Montran pictures of many faces. Some looked familiar, but the pictures were going too fast for her to consciously identify them. She knew little of metrapeople, and she couldn't remember anything that mentioned they were... well, recycled people. A small residue from a bad dream surfaced, and her insides turned cold.

"It is not something you would find in their advertisements," Guardian said, "but two life insurance companies are behind the body collecting. They say they are using the bodies for medical research. The people who donate their bodies for the large premium do it to give their beneficiaries a better life after their own supposed deaths. The beneficiaries might hesitate if they knew the donors were still alive. The programs are aimed at people of lower socioeconomic status, and they would have little or no resources to investigate, even if they did suspect something was amiss."

Finally, Montran's speechless shock turned to outrage. "That can't be! The Galactic Scientists' Union and the Galactic Science Academy would prevent anything like that from happening. It was outlawed eons ago, when one planet forced chip implantation on all its citizens."

The memory of signing a life insurance policy made her suddenly uncertain. Tightening her lips, she said doggedly, "It's not ethical or legal, any more than slavery is. Slavery is certainly not necessary in Collective and GCFC space. Even the new settlements have rules against selling people, or using them against their will."

Even as she was saying it, she knew it wasn't totally true. Chips were implanted in violent criminals so they could be put to productive use in their communities, and law enforcement found some families selling their own members for one reason or another, as well as poor people indenturing themselves rather than starve on isolated settlements.

Taking a deep, steadying breath to find her centering point, she asked with less intensity, "What proof do you have of this?"

"If you would like, I will give your room console access to my library, and you can research it for yourself."

"Yes. I would like that." Hadrie would hit the ceiling if he heard of something like this, to say nothing of the Collective's response.

Guardian continued. "Because of the customer base of the metrapeople business and the security around the business of producing them, we have to move slowly with our investigation."

"'Our' refers to whom?" Montran asked.

"Naboth's Vine, of which I am a member. I am sure you have heard of them. They work to change the mindset of the—"

"Yes, yes. Hadrie once told me about them," she interrupted impatiently. "Totally unrealistic. Unless the GCFC's Ethics and Rules Committee get back their teeth, there isn't going to be any peaceful change. GCFC members consider themselves above the law."

"Unless we catch them red-handed, so to speak."

Montran cast back in her memory for the meaning of "caught red-handed." *Ah, caught in the act of slaughtering someone else's cattle. Ugh.*

"Them?" she asked.

"Yes. A dozen or so of the GCFC members collect these intelligent species and add them to their private zoos."

Disgust pulled Montran's lips into a thin line, and her eyes darkened to black.

"So, you catch them bidding on forbidden goods in this auction," she said slowly, "then what? The GCFC has too many members that are reluctant to censure their own, either because they've been coerced or because they're apathetic. They won't point fingers, and since you're into euphemisms, remember that 'for the one that is pointed forward, there are three pointing back,' give or take a digit or two. None of them wish to have their business aired in public, or to risk suspicion of wrongdoing."

"Yes, yes. Very good. I have not heard that expression for a while. The information will be telecast to major stations, reaching every planet that receives transmissions from the INet Corporation." He sounded smug.

"Ah, a public outcry." Her tone was cynical. "I don't put too much trust in citizens who are only likely to get involved in policy change if they're directly affected, and then only because they're afraid of making their life worse than it is now. And what then?"

"There is an understanding between the GCFC and the Collective that when it concerns the closed planets, planets whose populations are not mature enough to be allowed to travel in space, the highest authority, the Council of Rings, will judge the case. Over half of the occupants in those cages are from closed planets.

That is what makes possession of them desirable for those who have everything… or wish to have something before a competitor has it."

She didn't believe that those who had enough influence and credits to break the galactic law would face a court hearing, but who was she to pop the bubble of a group of idealists?

"Okay. So, this is the plan: The auction proceeds, and before they ship the captives to their new owners, I create diversions while Maud releases the captives. Did I leave anything out?"

"That is the plan, unless you have an alternative."

"Until I get to the staging ground and see what the situation is, I think that's a plan we can start with."

"I will monitor the whereabouts of Sheila, Lord Chaney, and the Black Rose, and keep you posted concerning any other danger heading your way." There was a pause. "As I have said earlier, Lord Chaney considers you a high-level threat, and does not believe you are dead. He has ordered his smugglers and Spartans to take you alive. From my recent monitoring of communications, however, I am not certain what the Black Rose or the other Spartans will do, should they find you. There is this code of membership where they mete out justice to their own, and I do believe they consider you part of their membership."

"Just what type of justice do they believe I'm due?"

Guardian made an audible noise, as though clearing his throat. "I believe they see you as a hero, and they have reservations about turning you over to the smugglers or to Lord Chaney, in spite of his orders."

"A hero?" Montran was now thoroughly alarmed. "And what do they plan on doing with me?"

"On the individual level, I do not believe any of them know."

"Well, if I create trouble in their neck of the city, I guess we'll find out." She paused for a moment.

"In addition to the layout of Century City and pertinent information on the personnel over there, I'd like to know how you've been handling them since their occupation, as well as how they've been reacting to whatever you or Maud have used against them. I also want to make something clear here. If I think Maud and I are in more trouble than we can handle, we're out of there. I'm not a hero, nor am I suicidal. We'll wait for reinforcements.

"I'm agreeing to stir the pot because if you and Maud have been doing it for two years and you're both still around, you must have an advantage." She cocked her head and asked, "Has there been any loss of life on either side of this occupation?"

"Their side only, and that because of equipment failures or lack of judgment. We have what you might call the home court advantage. Not only do we have intimate knowledge of the planet, but my equipment is specifically designed to be used here."

"That's a plus, given your lack of players."

"I have a subliminal of the information you need to know. I believe in the military it is officially called MDL, Mission Download."

Montran shuddered at the idea of getting information stuffed in her brain while she was in a drug-induced trance.

"I do not employ the same brutish methods of downloading information as the Spartan military." Guardian's tone sounded outraged. "And my profiles are detailed and precise."

"I didn't say I don't trust you. Just don't feel you need to fill my head with the personal hygiene habits of the smugglers or Spartans unless it's something I can rattle their world with. It will be a change to amuse myself, instead of ordering someone's injury."

"I have found them entertaining. I've had excellent suggestions from various behavioral scientists on tests to put them through to see their reactions."

Montran sat up suddenly. "Wait a moment. They're study subjects?"

She felt like she had just been sold on a mission. Perhaps she was being a bit too trusting again. Was Admiral JoCastao really going to be notified? She should demand to speak to her in person.

"It is by their choice. They choose to break into *my* city and wreak havoc among *my* bots, shooting them for fun. They did not leave when asked, but rather they shot my messenger."

The energy behind his anger made Montran's hair stand up.

There was a long pause as both took a moment to recover from the outburst.

"Even without the plethora of scientists that once resided here," Guardian said, "this is a scientific outpost, so I do have whatever is needed to run experiments, and safe ones. No one has died as a result of anything I have done."

"The scientists that have you running these tests, what do they say?"

"They do not know where these tests are being conducted."

"I'm not going to be part of this mental game of—"

"Of course you are, just by being here," he interrupted soothingly. "You truly are rescuing those people in the cages, and this truly is a smugglers' den, and Maud truly does need assistance, and so do I. I am simply taking advantage of the situation. Occasional annoyances may be presented to unwelcome visitors, but the purpose is to make them go away. I do not take lives, and I do not use anything that will maim them. Any psychological discomfort is of their own making."

Montran pursed her lips and wondered how her plans for a vacation with her clan had gone so wrong. That seemed a lot longer than three months ago. "What's showing on those screens is RT, actually happening at this moment, and not staged by you or anyone else?"

"It is real time. I am recording what is happening. That is not to say that I do not take measures to protect my planet and those under my care. I just do not use violent methods or intentionally take lives."

"Two years is a long time for this group to stay anywhere. You're not running subliminals to keep them here, are you?"

"It is their choice to remain and be miserable. And do not forget, those who left were replaced by others, so they have not been miserable for two years. Even the Black Rose leave for R&R. However, hiding stolen goods is not the same as auctioning off abducted persons or victims of unethical barter. It has become imperative to end this operation. I've spent two years studying them and their responses to various circumstances, and the data will be put to good use, and also made available to you."

Montran raised an eyebrow at the generous gift. "When did they start bringing in the live cargo?"

"Two stan weeks ago. The Tanjmi made a surprise raid on their main base in Horkio Mau."

Montran's lips curled in triumph.

"Your Admiral JoCastao's Special Forces," he acknowledged. "There was not even a ripple about the raid in the rumor pipeline. They estimated only a quarter of the smugglers escaped, and most had spotters on their tails. Lord Chaney is not happy, nor are his customers. Since this base is near a jump gate, and a heavily traveled corridor, the smugglers were able to elude their tails and deposit their expensive cargo where they already had a small operation going. They need to proceed with this auction to settle the nerves of their suppliers and customers, to say nothing of Lord Chaney's stockholders. He is also losing credits, shipping his live cargo around."

"Stockholders? I hope Lord Chaney has a list of them, because I want a copy."

"Maud has just reminded me not to spend so much time socializing, as there is work to be done. Make yourself comfortable. My method of downloading subliminal information is passive, so the information is slower in making its way to the surface of the mind. Therefore, Maud will be making sure you do not shoot yourself in the foot, so to speak."

Closing her eyes, Montran slipped easily into the necessary beta state.

Chapter 5

Delorita was born to Yeva, in the Healer's House of Jeborhara, on Velta V. Delorita's father was the nefarious Lord Chaney of Dlephae. He had raped her mother, Yeva, who was an empath. In her shame and fear, the seventeen-year-old Yeva changed her name to Masha and scrubbed floors in the Healer's House, terrified of leaving its protective environment. Eight months later, Masha dedicated her newborn daughter to the House of Athena, to become a warrior who could avenge her mother's forcible deflowering.

Yeva's empathic abilities had intensified her desire for retaliation against Chaney, and she spent agonizing years wishing vengeance on him. Delorita learned her lessons of recompense well and was determined to fulfill her mother's expectations. When Delorita was only ten, her mother took to her deathbed, and in a profound reversal, removed the obligation from her young daughter's shoulders and died in a state of peace. Masha chose the name Leor to pass through the lighted gate of Amattas and find peace with her ancestors.

Relieved from vendetta and therefore devoid of purpose, Delorita was adrift.

Delorita's second mother, Aglauros, redirected Delorita's energy into athletic training for the Galactic Games. Until her sixteenth year, the year of her first menses and thus her welcome into the House of Women, Delorita found contentment in this world of discipline and camaraderie. At sixteen, her coming of age naming, she chose to be called Zohra, disdaining the name Delorita and the burden it had carried.

At seventeen, her life took on added meaning as she prepared for her Vision Quest. At eighteen, she had her Vision in the Sacred Temple of Hekate. In that dream-like state, her life purpose unfolded, and those whose web of life she would touch were revealed to her. Her guide wrote it out on parchment made from the sacred Trees of Ossark. A week out of the Temple, Zohra lost the clarity of the vision.

She was initiated into Hekate's Inner Circle and ascended to the next level of Athena's warriors. Her guide, teachers, and mentors steered her toward the training she would need to help her in her future lessons and tasks. Traveling under the guise of a competitor in the Galactic Games, she met many teachers who gave her lessons to work on that were more arduous than her competitions in the games.

At nineteen, Zohra enrolled in one of the galactic academies that trained space and infantry officers for the GCFC. During her first year at the academy, the Brothers of the Shadow approached her and a few of her sisters with an offer to join Naboth's Vine, an undercover operation formed to undo the abuses of the GCFC.

Her Shield House cleared it, and she joined.

* * *

Cadet Zohra looked over the grounds of her new home, where she would live for the next four stan years. Her athletically trim figure threw a long shadow behind her, down the deep blue grassy slope, shading some of her fellow cadets. They were at ease, laughing and comparing notes. They had been at the academy for three stan months, and were still adjusting to their new life before the academic regimen went into full swing, which was a stan week away. The returning upper cadets, the Pugs, had taken over most of the training and recreational facilities, and as Plebes, the first year cadets found it safer to remain out of their way.

Zohra's dark eyes scanned the group of buildings, looking for the flight training tower. She heard Cadet ChaTak approach before she felt a long, thin finger tap her shoulder.

Though ChaTak, one of her roommates, was not at all like anyone she had grown up with, Zohra had connected with her immediately. No matter a person's species, within a quarter of a stan hour she was usually able to read them, mostly through their body movements, voice intonation, and eyes. She had made a game of it during her competitive years as a galactic athlete. But ChaTak gave nothing away about herself, which made her a curiosity Zohra wished to explore.

ChaTak nodded toward the short row of buildings to their left. "The elder said that is where the simulators are."

Cadet ChaTak and Cadet Zohra were to report there in the early morning hours for testing of their piloting abilities. ChaTak, to Zohra's amusement, could undoubtedly teach the academy staff more than a few tricks, but she knew ChaTak would do only what the task required.

Finally, they were going to do something other than slog through the mud, lugging enough equipment to supply a village.

Zohra shaded her eyes as she studied the low buildings. So, the flight training tower wasn't a tower after all. Four entrances, two exits, and a lot of traffic even now, before classes had begun. The classrooms must be underground.

"We should get there early," ChaTak said. "Many others will want practice time before the testing begins."

Zohra glanced at her, dark eyes glinting with humor. "Early by your time or mine?" ChaTak shrugged her shoulders. "I shall be there at 0600 hours, standard academy time," Zohra told her firmly.

ChaTak grinned, which was uncharacteristic for her species. She had picked up the gesture from her interactions with her expressive roommate.

* * *

Zohra's first year at the academy was difficult, as she tried to adjust to the strangeness of a permanent residence and unfamiliar regimes. She missed traveling around the galaxy and the tough physical workouts of an athlete. The camaraderie was different, too. The athletes' presence and support of one another came without emotional ties, whereas at the academy, cadet friendships required constant care, something she was reluctant to give. The only exception was ChaTak.

To alleviate the edginess caused by her new restrictions, Zohra had found a glen to practice in on the other side of a small hill, in the midst of a forest that surrounded the academy and insulated it from its neighbor, another finishing school. Here, she practiced her more rigorous exercises late at night, enjoying the privacy as well as the physical exhaustion that followed.

When the first year ended and classes broke for three stan months, a taller and more mature Zohra returned to her Shield House. Her Shield Mother was pleased with the changes and sent her for advanced training with Naboth's Vine. Zohra's three-month break was spent honing skills she had first learned as a child. The old heat and obsession gave way to the challenge of mastering them.

In Zohra's second year, another type of challenge came her way—Cadet Jaymai. The curves showing under Jaymai's normally genderless cadet uniform would make any roving eye stop for a second glance. And once fixed on Zohra, her slate gray eyes seemed to become wary of anyone around her target who might thwart her goal of ownership. For the stern-faced Zohra, Jaymai became a passionate spot in her otherwise studious life.

The relationship became intense, and for two long months, Zohra contemplated committing to Jaymai. Her strong sense of obligation to the Vine was her anchoring point, and much to Jaymai's apparent consternation, Zohra stayed silent on the subject of commitment. Tension grew between them, and Zohra was looking forward to the three-month break, when she would be able to get some relief.

* * *

"What are you doing out here alone?" Resentment tinged the familiar voice.

Zohra turned reluctantly from her view of the double moons. She had heard Jaymai's noisy approach but had hoped to remain unseen in the darkness. It was *her* nightly ritual, not Jaymai's.

"I'm watching the moons," Zohra replied, stifling her own resentment at having her private moment disturbed.

Dressed to accentuate her figure, Jaymai moved in front of Zohra, her hands taking possession of what she clearly considered her property.

"How romantic. Moonlight and two interested parties." Jaymai growled seductively and pulled Zohra's face down toward hers. Her kiss was deep, hungry, and rough. She ran sensitive hands over Zohra's slim, muscular form and tugged her body urgently against her own, igniting Zohra's passion. They sank to the ground behind the tree, where Jaymai aggressively showed Zohra how the two moons affected her.

* * *

For the next few weeks, Zohra attempted to distance herself from Jaymai by volunteering to assist cadets who were struggling with their class work. Jaymai simply redoubled her efforts on other levels, and Zohra was unable to stay away for long.

As the sexual tension between them increased, Zohra found herself awake at night, mentally practicing parts of the sacred Dance of Attraction. The more Zohra thought about the Dance, the more her body needed to feel its rhythm physically.

The Teachers had warned that if practiced in any form, the Dance would generate the sacred *Qi* for passion and life bonding, but until now, Zohra had thought they were exaggerating.

Zohra's only escape from Jaymai's influence were her studies, which the senior cadet was wise not to interfere with.

* * *

It was the night of Elwin's second moon, when the two moons were on the other side of the planet. The night was pitch dark, so most of the cadets carried lamps while walking outside. Zohra planned to practice one segment of the Dance under the glitter of stars to release some of her pent-up energy. Jaymai was off-planet on the student ship, *Quasar*, for an exam, and Zohra's friends were keeping their distance from her and her prickly moods.

The glen near the school would be empty of others for at least two hours; it was enough time. And as long as Jaymai wasn't around, Zohra didn't have to worry about making the mistake of connecting with her. With Jaymai gone, it was as though a miasma had lifted from her. She laughed at herself. Was this all it took to influence her?

Feeling better already, Zohra relished the pull on her legs as she climbed the slope, walking carefully so as not to run head-on into a tree. She carried no lamp, for fear that its light would intrude on the peace of the environment.

The glen was unusually still. Pausing at one of the trees that surrounded it, Zohra touched its rough bark and felt a slight change of energy in its life force. Then she stepped fifteen paces into the glen, which would give her enough room to move.

Inhaling slowly and deeply, she stilled her thoughts. Breathing in again, she concentrated on bringing the breath to her *dan tien* and then releasing it down her legs and into the ground. Her silent mantra began within her heart, expanded as a pulse throughout her body and then settled into a steady throb. Every cell in her body vibrated. She focused on the energy swirling about her, letting it build before bringing it back to focus in her heart. Inhaling, she connected with the planet's *Qi* through the soles of her feet.

The night was no longer still, as she felt all levels of living things around her pulse with consciousness. The dampness of the air, the vegetation, the richness of the dirt… all were sharp and clear to her senses. She took another deep breath, and her fingers began to tingle—it was time to begin.

Calling the Guardians of the Dance as witnesses, she prayed for rightness of mind, attraction, and attachment to the one with whom she was meant to bond. She reminded herself that this was only a brief exercise to get rid of the energy she had inadvertently built up.

Respectfully, Zohra made her bows to the guardians in each of the directions they ruled. Finished, she brought her outspread arms slowly up above her head, palms facing each other, and then drew them down over her heart as she thanked all the powers who surrounded her. Breathing deeply into her lowest chakra, she held her breath for the appropriate length of time and then released it. She breathed in and out, studied rhythms meant to build strength, while holding her hands in a mudra pose.

There was another presence. The sense was faint, but it was there. Her Watcher. It was this presence that gave the Dance its purpose.

Slowly, she stretched out in the first movement, feeling arms and legs extend, hold, and adjust to the position. She moved to the next step exactly as she had done in her mind and then gradually lessened the rests between each movement, knowing intuitively where the ground rose and where it dipped. Intoxicated with the changes the Dance was causing within her, she continued into the next segment.

At some point, Zohra felt her Watcher's spirit join hers, just as it was intended to do. Zohra could feel her Watcher's excitement, curiosity, and a strange sense of familiarity. Their commingled energy gave her a rush of exhilaration, indescribable and beyond her wildest imagination. Excitement and desire burned in her body as they moved into the last half and the differences between her and her Watcher blurred.

In the final leap, suspended for a moment in time and the air, stretching her arms high overhead as if to pluck out a star from the night sky, the dancers were intimately aware of each other. Zohra dropped back to the ground, finishing in a perfectly executed spin, held the pose for a moment, and then went to her hands and knees, bowing in respect to all who witnessed the Dance.

Zohra held this position, as the Master had instructed, allowing the throbbing energy to dissipate into the ground and giving her heaving lungs a chance to oxygenate her body. The pulsing in her veins, loud in her ears, beat against her yoni, bringing her to a sweet climax, one like she had never experienced before, even under Jaymai's skilled attentions.

Zohra knew her Watcher shared these feelings and was weak from her own release. In that instant, she understood the power of the Dance. Still connected with her Watcher, she felt their shared realization that this meeting was more than coincidence.

Was this their destiny? Was her soulmate to be her lifemate, too?

The sound of approaching voices broke the spell, and the link abruptly dropped away. Her sense of acuity faded immediately, leaving her blinded. Zohra moved behind a tree and used its rough texture to ground her. Her Watcher was gone, but Zohra's desire for her wasn't fading. Questions of "who" and "where" crossed her mind as she waited for her legs to become steady enough to walk back to her quarters. She took a deep, shaky breath.

Lifemate? Here?

As she walked back to her quarters, she felt curiously light, and she realized she had been carrying a heavy load on her shoulders. Jaymai hadn't been making her feel edgy; it was the energy of her lifemate being nearby. For the first time in three years, Zohra enjoyed a welcome sense of calm.

That meant her lifemate was either a senior or a junior, like her. She would have laughed aloud, except for the lateness of the hour. Instead, she felt a smug look spread across her face.

As children, before their first menses, she and the other students had danced the first Dance in class under the supervision of their Teacher. It was intended to open them to the energy of their soulmates. Smothering her nervousness, she had danced it only because everyone else did. She remembered how she had been terrified for months afterward, thinking that some person would drop out of nowhere and claim her, and that her life would again be subject to someone else's vision.

Who are you? You can't hide from me now, anymore than I can hide from you. Zohra was happier than she had ever known she could be. *She's here! Goddess! I feel... different.*

* * *

For the next stan month of Cadet Zohra's third year, whenever the twin moons were on the other side of the planet, she dreamed of her Watcher. On dark nights, she stood at the edge of the glen, looking up at the sky's canopy of sparkling stars and feeling the connection with her Watcher vibrate especially strongly. Once, she had tried to compel her to show herself, but her soulmate resisted.

Jaymai's influence over her dissolved, and their contact ended when Ensign Jaymai left the academy for her first tour of duty, on an outpost near the jump zone in Juan sector. Zohra stood at the door of her room and watched her go, feeling more relief than anything else.

Megan CuDas tapped her on the shoulder. "Get moving if you're going to join us at the bar," she said, her stomach rumbling its need for food.

"I'm with you," Zohra said.

She and her friends were laughing as they walked into the bar. Zohra felt the presence of her Watcher the moment she entered the room. Her heart paused and then resumed beating at a quickened pace.

Clea's stories kept the group laughing as they found places to sit, but Zohra's attention was elsewhere. She scanned the room, her senses heightened as she felt her Watcher tentatively link with her. The Watcher was surprised and hesitant.

Zohra felt responsible for her Watcher's reservations. If she hadn't insisted on seeing her, if only in thoughts, her Watcher wouldn't be this cautious now. But why was she reluctant to meet, now that they had found each other?

Laughter from the other side of the room seemed to become louder as the sounds in her immediate vicinity faded out. Her eyes locked on the dark green eyes of her Watcher. Both were aware of the strong desire to connect reflecting in their eyes.

A shy smile appeared on the woman's face, but then she broke the connection. The cadet casually, or nervously perhaps, tossed her cascading orange hair back over her shoulder in what looked like a well-practiced gesture. Others moved, blocking her from Zohra's sight.

She's beautiful.

Conversation at Zohra's table stopped, unnoticed by Zohra.

"That's Lady Harriet Montran and her friends," CuDas said, with a disdainful sniff.

CuDas, Zohra had found, didn't like the upper class of any society.

Zohra knew this wasn't the same feeling she'd had with Ensign Jaymai—thank the Holy Guardians. This was her soulmate, and they both knew it. But what a dilemma they faced. They were on different career tracks.

Two nights later, Zohra and her group passed the same pub, and Zohra found herself drawn to enter. She could feel Lady Harriet's presence, and wondered how to talk her friends into relaxing there instead of at their usual place.

"Looks like some of our friends are here. Why don't we stop in?" ChaTak said.

Zohra gave ChaTak a grateful smile. Clea, however, didn't pass up the chance of teasing her. "It can't be because of the brew, because they don't carry Zohra's favorite. But then again..." Clea and the others, with the exception of CuDas, laughed.

They glanced at the party going on in one of the back rooms then moved to a table when another cadet waved them over.

Zohra's gaze found Lady Harriet, who was sitting quietly near the back of the party, looking as if she didn't want to be there. Zohra felt that her mood was distracted, and she wondered what caused it.

"Well, Zohra, is it the ale or is it something else you intend to order?" Clea said, taunting.

"I'm not in the mood for a drink, but..." Zohra rose as she caught sight of Lady Harriet moving to leave.

"Hey, you just got here," CuDas said.

"Zohra, she's from a different class. She'd only brush you off politely," another cadet told her.

"You need to concentrate on your studies. You just got one airhead out of your—"

"Come on," Clea said as she dragged a reluctant CuDas to her feet, "we're not leaving her alone. She may say something that gets her in trouble. Wait up, Zohra!"

For a few moments Zohra thought she had lost her soulmate, and she walked quickly toward the barracks, assuming that was where Lady Harriett was headed.

"There she is. Can we slow down now?" Clea asked.

"Isn't that Alan Fermin, that jerk, with her?" CuDas said.

People like Fermin were part of the reason some cadets despised those in the higher socioeconomic classes. They had all heard the rumors that Alan had been expelled from the academy for being physically abusive to his girlfriends, but his father's credits had gotten him enrolled in the Diplomatic Corps next door. How ironic.

Zohra's adrenaline surged and she was suddenly afraid for Lady Harriet. Their link was vibrating with terror.

"She's in trouble." Zohra broke into a run. She heard her friends' voices questioning her, but they followed hard on her heels. When she saw Alan and a few others dragging a collapsed Lady Harriet between two buildings, Zohra cried out the cadet call to arms. The others echoed her as they descended on Alan's cronies, who looked surprised and then fearful. They held their weapons up hesitantly, but Zohra and her friends overwhelmed them.

"Zohra, no!" ChaTak grabbed Zohra, and Clea assisted as they restrained Zohra from pummeling the now unconscious Fermin to death.

The cadets' response had been fast, but not fast enough. Lady Harriet had been beaten so badly that her features were unrecognizable.

Zohra cradled Lady Harriet's bloodied head until the medics arrived. Her face became unreadable as her fury against the Fermins increased.

ChaTak squatted near her friend with a supportive hand on her shoulder.

* * *

For the next week, Lady Harriet was the main topic of conversation. Zohra withdrew from her friends. She spent every spare moment working out alone, trying to rid herself of the rage that was burning a hole in her soul. At the end of the second week after the attack, she got a glimpse of Lady Harriet at the court hearing for Alan Fermin.

Zohra was shocked by the change. As Lady Montran stood before the court and removed her cap, many wept at the loss of her long hair. Her face was grim and tight, her eyes dark and cold. The change gripped Zohra's heart painfully, adding to her resolve to bring the Fermins down.

With the added testimony of Alan Fermin's associates, the court found that he had willfully assaulted Cadet Lady Harriet Montran with the intent of inflicting bodily harm and death. The stunner found clutched in his hand confirmed that he had physically immobilized her, leaving her conscious while he assaulted her. The extent of the brutal beating confirmed his desire to kill his victim. His background of assaulting women was exposed as further proof that a mere reprimand was not only inappropriate, but would fail to address the danger to his future victims. The court ruled that his actions were a heinous crime against the GCFC Charter.

A wealthy psychopath had been convicted of attacking a member of one of the oldest and most respected clans in the galaxy. News agencies had a field day.

Demands by the public for his immediate exile to Hinterwield, stripped of personal belongings, fell on the deaf ears of the criminal hearings board. While the DeMonte and Montran clans were powerful, the votes had already been purchased, by means of blackmail. Zohra's only consolation was that Gustaf Fermin, Alan's father, had planned to use those markers for a different purpose, and now they were gone.

All Gustaf Fermin had bought was time, and one more chance, for Alan. He would be sent for reeducation at the Adjustment and Distillation of Disturbed Minds facility, also called the ADDM. The wealthy could afford to pay for the four stan years of behavior modification, along with chip implantation to enforce the behavior program. Medication was administered to enhance or lessen the effects of the chip, as necessary. The goal was to produce a rehabilitated, productive member of society.

Zohra didn't believe the ADDM would help Alan, and she wondered how long it would take the GCFC to realize that. Naboth's Vine would be keeping an eye on him.

The day after the hearing, classes broke for the summer.

* * *

Returning from her three months of summer training at the Naboth's Vine Compound, Zohra heard that Lady Harriet had switched her course of study from bridge officer to a more physically demanding track—infantry training.

Lady Harriet's tanned and hardened features indicated to Zohra that she had spent her summer working hard to catch up with the level of the other cadets in her track. Zohra understood the need to physically work off the fear of being rendered powerless. She was relieved that Lady Harriet's room was moved near the guardroom. Naboth's Vine was undoubtedly aware that a vengeful Gustaf Fermin might well hire an assassin.

Zohra kept her distance from Cadet Montran and avoided linking with her. Though they were both in the same track now, Zohra's classes were more advanced, so chance meetings were unlikely.

At the end of their senior year, Second Lieutenant Zohra left the academy and disappeared. She had been placed immediately into covert operations, and her appearance, as well as her name, was changed.

Thus was born Jina Gari, or JG. At first, her cover identity was that of a bodyguard to a politician's family. Then she was formally transferred as a noncom into a Spartan infantry group. JG was promoted quickly from corporal to sergeant and then was reassigned to the target group, the nefarious Black Rose.

Ironically, her unacknowledged father, Lord Chaney, who was also the alleged head of a major smuggling band, sponsored the Black Rose and wielded power over them.

Now and then, news of Lieutenant Montran filtered through the Spartan grapevine, keeping JG informed of her well-being. When Harriet Montran was promoted to captain and put in charge of the misfit Degas squad, JG's alarm bells went off, but she couldn't pinpoint why. Years later, when word came that Montran had left GCFC space, JG felt relieved.

Chapter 6

"Captain on deck!"

"At ease, soldiers. Gather around." Captain Miller looked at Lieutenant Ninian, whose nod meant that the area had been cleared of any monitoring devices.

"Our comrades aboard the *Spinner's Tale*—" He paused as jeers and catcalls echoed eerily through the cargo bay. "As I was saying, the *Spinner's Tale* crew was actually given an important job by Lord Chaney. They were ordered to kidnap and deliver a live package to Merker's. True to form, they screwed it up.

"We're being asked to assist in locating and delivering this person to Chaney, who has been visiting Merker's while we were on leave. Chaney thinks she's still alive."

"Since when does Lord Chaney get personally involved with kidnapping people?" Sergeant Vanstar asked.

"Yeah. Usually his goons handle it," another soldier said.

Another voice came from the back. "That's not showing too much sense, counting on the *Spinner's* crew to kidnap someone."

Laughter and rude comments followed again.

Captain Miller hesitated and then spoke. "Chaney's got it up his butt that as a living, breathing, freely moving citizen, Commander Montran is bad for his reputation. He wants her abducted and brought to Merker's for some fun and games at the hands of his metradame, before he turns her over to kid Fermin's metralab people."

He waited. This was where the members of his squad were going to recall that Harriet Montran was a hero among Spartans. As a captain in the force, she, along with her squad, had survived two years of no-return deployments. Chaney seemed bent on using his power as the Black Rose sponsor to destroy her, and his actions didn't sit well with any Spartan group. The Degas squad hadn't survived its final death assignment, but Captain Montran had. And because of her testimony, the military high command had been reformed. Though there were still illegal doings going on—they were themselves a testament to that—they weren't done on such a broad scale or as openly as before.

Captain Montran was a survivor against all odds, making her an unofficial Black Rose member who merited a toast when fallen comrades were remembered. Once a Spartan, always a Spartan; once a Black Rose, always a Black Rose. Even unto death.

"Captain?" Sergeant Major JG said.

"If we find her, we'll treat her as we would any other Spartan." Silently, Miller cursed Chaney for his arrogance in ignoring military culture and his ignorance of the Black Rose squad that he claimed to value so highly. Then again, that lack of understanding was why they were there, which was an advantage for him and his goals.

"If she's alive, what do we do with her?" JG asked cautiously.

"We'll deal with that when, and if, we run into her, Sergeant Major." Miller looked over his squad, studying them closely. He tapped his sidearm, making the familiar sound that told them he wanted their attention. "This also gives us a good reason to search on the other side of the planet without Chaney becoming too suspicious. All right, Lieutenant, let's move out."

"Sergeant Major, you heard the captain. Let's move out," Ninian told her.

"Yes, Lieutenant. You heard the orders! Mount up, you roughnecks!" JG hollered. "Markson, Henderson, Roberts, Bandio, Scout, Guilfo, Rogers, Carson, Smitson, Gino, Vanstar, Varsity, Clovus!" Each one slapped their chest as their name was called.

"Clovus," Miller said.

"Yes, sir."

"I want you to remain aboard *Spinner's*. Nose around."

"Yes, sir."

They all grinned. Clovus liked to sniff around in other people's business, and *Spinner's Tale* had an easy system to break into.

* * *

One of the frequent windstorms that blew across the planet's surface brought a halt to the Black Rose deployment on the far side of the planet. The team's recon tactical specialist had pinpointed that location as the most likely place for Captain Montran's disappearance. For the storm's duration, Captain Miller had his team return to quarters and rest. The alarms sounded two stan hours later, waking everyone up.

Sergeant Major JG scattered the squad to secure and lock down the city access doors, and Lieutenant Ninian monitored damage control. Captain Miller was aboard *Spinner's Tale*, involved in an unsolicited and unwanted call from kid Fermin.

* * *

Alan Fermin paused in the middle of a one-sided argument with Captain Miller. The alarm on the captain's communicator was buzzing annoyingly. "What's going on?"

"This conversation is over and out." Captain Miller ended the comm transmission with a satisfied thump of his fist on the table. His voice command deactivated the link, bringing up the Fermin business logo and then *Spinner's Tale*'s registry ID, signifying that the link was indeed broken. He turned off the alarm on his communicator and waited for the communication link between planet and ship to sync.

As he waited, he stretched his long legs and eased the tension in his shoulders. The conversation with kid Fermin had not been a complete waste of time. Miller could tell from Alan's posturing that he was not yet aware of Chaney's presence on the outpost, which meant that his spies were not as informed as he would have the captain believe. Miller detested the immature, pretentious youth, and therefore would never rise to any formality of address other than "yeah" or "what do you want?"

His lips curled in the snarl he had managed to suppress when the kid had ordered him to make sure no Spartan participated in the search for "that Montran witch."

Captain Miller hadn't wasted his time pointing out that Alan had no authority over anything pertaining to the outpost and, most of all, over him. He had no worries about Alan loosing his small army of metrasoldiers on the base. So far, in every confrontation with Alan's army, the Black Rose had won. That had a lot to do with the kid not wanting to give up any control over his little minions, so when a situation called for deviations, the kid's army kept to its original battle plan. Alan had no business leading military people. In any battle to the death, he would lose all of his expensive toys.

Miller snorted in disgust. People with too much money should be given babysitters who could keep them from interfering with people who have something to do in life. He had warned Chaney many times that the kid was too unstable to associate with, but Chaney liked to play with fire.

His communicator indicated the sync was complete. Miller smiled grimly as he tapped in his code for a secured communication link to his staff on the planet's surface. A bubble surrounded him, blocking out any interference or unwanted listeners.

He sighed as he assessed what Alan's meddling would do to his own plans. Alan wasn't getting what he wanted, which was the undisputed ownership of Captain Montran's remains. Miller hoped that with both Chaney and Alan distracted, he would have more time to reach his own objective.

Impatient, he watched the indicators on his communicator display the progress setting up the encryption. A soft tone announced that the connection was open.

"Lieutenant, report."

"Lieutenant Ninian here, Captain. That slimy cretin Decker opened a contaminated room into the main corridor. All rooms feeding into that corridor have been successfully locked down and secured. We were lucky. One casualty, a crewmember from *Spinner's Tale*. Sergeant Major JG checked on Lord Chaney. His metradame reported that he was sleeping and didn't want to be disturbed by anything that wasn't important. Since the broadcast for the auction should be commencing soon, we need to move out of the compound."

The news wasn't surprising. The smugglers, a suspicious and jealous lot, didn't want the Black Rose squad around when they did their business, as if they were rivals. Technically speaking, they were. However, Miller's pulse jumped when he grasped the underlying message, which was that the winds had finally died down over their target site.

Intuition, refined by years of survival as a Spartan, convinced him that the missing Montran was not only alive and well, but had found the entrance to another city. He hoped it was the city he was looking for. With the luck Lieutenant Commander Harriet Montran had shown in the past, he was putting his credits on her.

"Understood. Have the team geared up and ready to move out when the shuttle lands. Out."

* * *

The Black Rose team assembled in their shuttle, *Queen Bee*, quietly waiting for the officers to join them. Captain Miller and

Lieutenant Ninian, under the guise of checking out Decker's disaster, were searching for Lord Chaney's exact whereabouts. Sergeant Major JG and her team had verified that, regardless of what the metradame Sheila had said, Chaney was not in his quarters.

After a stan hour, Miller and Ninian entered the shuttle, geared up in AEGs and wearing grim expressions. They determined that Chaney was up to mischief and had left Sheila behind to deflect any suspicions. Chaney rarely went anywhere without his bodyguard, which was undoubtedly why he'd left her behind as a ruse. According to Miller's informant, Chaney was negotiating a new deal with a rival smuggling group, to exclude and eliminate one of his partners.

The atmosphere on Merker's Outpost had become dangerously volatile. All it would take was Alan's arrival for the outpost to become a war zone.

"Take her up, Sergeant," Lieutenant Ninian ordered, once both men had secured themselves.

"We'll pick up where we left off," Miller said. "Sergeant Vanstar and Corporal Guilfo will monitor the winds. They're more frequent on this side of the planet, so keep sharp, Sergeant." He suspected his anxiety was showing. After two years, they all knew the weather on this planet.

"Any hint, start the pick up. This is it. No going back. Sergeant Major, do you have the sensor deflector in place?" Miller asked.

"Yes, sir. Windstorm readings in this area, with an occasional window of clearing. Life readings are being sent out regularly that place us on the Southern Rim."

"Good. If any of you find your seals or equipment failing, don't hesitate to call in. I don't want any preventable accidents happening. Got that?"

"Yes, sir," the group responded.

"Sergeant Vanstar and her crew will monitor the equipment and fill the tanks as they come in."

* * *

The team fanned out and worked until the sun dropped below the horizon, leaving them in total darkness. They had replaced their tanks too many times to remember, and even with breaks for rest and food, they were exhausted.

"Call them back in, Lieutenant," Miller said, disappointed.

"Right, sir."

The comm came to life before Ninian could speak.

"Rosebud to *Queen Bee*, come in."

"*Queen Bee* here," Miller answered.

"Markson here, sir. Sergeant Major stumbled on something. She's out of range from your position."

"We're starting the pick up," Miller said, excitement evident in his voice. "We'll be right there with the rest of the squad. Tell her to stay put."

"Sarge, get 'er up," Ninian ordered.

"I'm on it, Lieutenant." Expertly handled, the shuttle rose and skimmed the surface, picking up the scattered squad of soldiers.

"Sergeant Major? JG, come in," Ninian called as they approached her position.

"Here, to the left of you, sir."

"She made good progress in this heavy atmosphere," he said.

Miller nodded. "She's a Sergeant Major, through and through."

JG used her handheld light to direct the shuttle to her position.

"All right, Lieutenant, you're with me. Everyone else, stay here and rest," Miller said.

Ninian and Miller were out of the shuttle the moment the *Queen Bee* stabilized, and they followed the shuttle's outside lights to JG and the lump by her feet.

"Will you look at that?" Ninian whistled and then knelt heavily near the pipe. "What do you think the arrows mean?"

"Have you identified it?" Miller asked JG.

"Yes, sir. It's an old maintenance pipe, but it's in good shape."

"What's your reading, Lieutenant?"

"She's right on. No signs of wear. Amazing, considering the winds that blow through here."

"Good work, Sergeant Major. Let's mark this place and get back to the shuttle. We'll rest and then come back to this." They headed back to the shuttle, Miller already planning the next day's activities.

Back in the shuttle, Miller described JG's find and outlined their next assignment.

"In about five stan—"

"Eight would be better, Captain," Ninian said softly.

"Right, right. In eight stan hours, then, we'll split up into two teams, each following the pipe in opposite directions. Now get some rest."

Miller didn't sleep for long. While the others were still asleep, he went over his plan repeatedly, looking for flaws and trying to find alternatives if one thing or the other didn't work, all the while keeping a wary eye on the weather indicators. He rubbed his face tiredly.

When is Chaney dealing out Alha Bahna? He'd better make sure he kills that guy. Alha Bahna doesn't like to be outsmarted, which means he probably has something planned to get rid of Chaney. It's got to be big because winner takes all, and chances are they'll have a small empire left when the smoke clears.

Chaney has kept the operation here for quite a while. Does he know what I'm looking for? No. He probably thinks we're looking for entrances to the other cities so we can loot them. We've got to find the space portal before Alan gets here. Once that idiot arrives, who knows what he'll stir up? This place won't be safe for tourists and too hot even for soldiers.

He had been right to tell his soldiers that this had to be it. Once the auction transmission was finished, the hunt for the missing Montran would be accelerated and the maps of the planet's surface Miller had been working on for the last two years would have to be turned over to Chaney. Then, it would be only a matter of time until the smugglers, if not Chaney himself, found the other cities Miller's father had told him about. No, Miller would find them first. Surely the hidden space portal would be in one of them.

The electromagnetic storms and heavy atmosphere prevented most of their equipment, including weapons, from working properly. Miller had directed his men through two years of slow, methodical searching, hampered by the unpredictable weather topside and the unbreachable computer that kept them confined to a small part of the city. It also took some doing to keep a low profile and avoid stirring Chaney's naturally suspicious mind. Then, this ridiculous abduction of Montran, an ex-Spartan celebrity, had ended life on the outpost as they knew it.

He grunted softly. What made him so sure she was alive? Was it instinct? No. It was something very simple. Logic.

He doubted that anyone who could survive Chaney's relentless pursuit, and for so many years, would die easily. Miller believed that Montran had telepathic abilities that had helped her and her squad to remain alive as long as they had. With this addition to her military expertise, she was able to bring her squad of misfits back from purposely staged fatal deployments. That they were staged was obvious, considering they hadn't been provided with the proper gear or working weapons.

A smile crossed Miller's face. He was going to finally meet Chaney's demon. He tried to conjure up what she would look like today. He had an old picture of her in her Spartan captain's uniform, but it showed little of what she was like personally. He had met her cousin once. He was of average height for his clan and had no special physical attributes, aside from his orange hair. But when you stepped into his sphere of influence, you could feel his magnetism.

At the appointed time, Miller woke his squad to continue the search. Those following the larger arrow found an elevator plate eight cubits from the mark. The group reassembled in the shuttle, replacing seals and loading up on extra air tanks. They left Vanstar and two crewmembers to monitor the weather and the activity of the five ships hovering above the planet.

They all crowded together on the elevator plate, and Miller activated the lever for descent. The only light in the elevator was from their lamps until the elevator stopped and a green light came on above the doorway.

As the elevator's door opened, two soldiers quickly moved out with the others fanning out behind them, raider style, advancing three cubits at a time as they scanned the entire surface of the corridor. Eventually, they came to another elevator. There on its door was a homing device, just like the one Sergeant Major had left on the elevator in which they'd arrived.

"Hold up, everyone." Miller's voice, sounding aggravated, crackled through their helmet comms. He checked his HR, just as everyone else did. It showed they were moving forward, and yet here they were, back at the elevator. It was another annoying trick of the outpost's computer.

"Captain?" a voice inquired, after a considerable time.

Miller said, "My father told me something about a corridor with no doorways. It just went around. This is it. That means that the laboratories are just above here. Let's go back over this corridor and look for any tiny crack that might go to a maintenance tunnel. They're all over the city, so I'm sure they're here, too. You know the drill. Find one."

After a brief interval, Corporal Roberts called, "Sir, I found it." The others quickly gathered around his kneeling form.

He was looking at a faint line. As Roberts leaned against the wall to change position, a faint click was heard and the crack opened into a crawl space for maintenance personnel.

"Right," Ninian and Miller said together. Ninian shone his light through the opening. It looked like a maintenance crawl space on a ship, except that it was high enough for the shorter members of the detachment to walk upright.

Miller took charge. "All right, everyone, listen up. Check air and temp."

Everyone did and gave the signal they were RFJ, ready for jump.

"Roberts and Bandio, forward position. Sergeant Major and Henderson, remain here. Let's move!" Miller followed behind Roberts, giving him and Bandio plenty of distance to check for surprises. They made a complete circle and found themselves back at the service entrance, facing the drawn weapons of JG and Henderson.

"Sir, it's time to change over to the second tank," JG said.

"Right."

The group climbed back into the corridor where they could change comfortably. While they each switched to their second tank and shed the bulk of the empty one, Miller turned to JG. "Go check with the shuttle, Sergeant Major."

"Yes, sir." She returned to the elevator to go topside.

JG knew Miller wanted a complete report from Vanstar on what was going on topside, and he didn't trust any of the other grunts to remember or know what was important to relay to him.

"How's the weather holding?" JG asked.

Vanstar consulted the console. "Looks fine for the next two hours."

They glanced at the two crewmembers who were busily repairing the valves of emptied tanks. From long habit, the men worked quickly and efficiently. The banter between them reflected the competitive relationship they had and gave JG and Vanstar good cover for a private conversation.

"Most of the tanks are worthless now. I'm having to strip down others for replacement parts," Vanstar said.

"I'll send up our discarded tanks," JG said.

"Let's change yours since you're here. I can see a seam already forming at the stem. Check the others when you get back, will you? We don't have any more replacement stems, so the whole valve unit will have to be swapped out."

As they switched JG's equipment, Vanstar continued speaking. "Lord High and Mighty is upset about something. Sent word he wants to see the captain when he returns from his inspection. Said to check with his staff for his whereabouts."

Both women smirked.

"If Lord Chaney didn't despise his partner so openly," JG said, "Alha Bahna wouldn't be spending so much time plotting to knock him off, and we wouldn't have to play this shell game of 'where's Chaney?'"

"A sudden windstorm over the city caught some of the search groups topside," Vanstar said, "so they were picked up and delivered to two hovering freighters. We have a second windstorm forming over the rim. It should hit here in two days. I don't want to stop your party, but nothing will be safe surfaceside. I'll have to move the shuttle."

"Well, this time we have an elevator to hide in instead of a cave."

JG's descent back into the city was quiet, and she used the time to review her own plans. When the elevator door opened, the others gathered around it.

"Where are the other two?" she asked, worried.

"Placing a charge in the tunnel," Ninian said. "Captain, why don't we wait in the elevator and give our equipment a rest?"

The captain nodded and they crowded onto the elevator to run checks on their equipment. The elevators were the only places the computer didn't threaten them. It had become a standing joke that elevators were the neutral zone. While they waited, JG passed on her information to her CO.

Corporal Roberts, meanwhile, had found a place to wedge the charge. As he and Scout, his partner, hurried back down the tunnel, they could see the exit panel closing.

Scout cursed. "Carson should be keeping that thing open."

The two pushed frantically all around the panel area, looking for something that would reopen their exit. The blast, set with a five-minute delay, would blow them out of their suits if they were caught in the tunnel.

Angrily, Roberts slammed his gloved palm on the corner of the panel and then fell through the sudden opening into the corridor. Scout scrambled over him, grabbed his wrist, and hauled him to his feet. They had to get around the corner, away from the backdraft. The last sound they heard was the muffled explosion. The force of the blast knocked them into the wall, leaving one stunned and the other unconscious. A green gas cloud flamed out of the tunnel, the tendrils curling up into the air vents. Then the empty canisters next to the tunnel exploded.

The elevator shook from the explosions as each canister burst. The group in the small space activated their visors reflexively in response.

"Everyone secured?" Miller asked.

JG tapped each helmet quickly, getting thumbs-up responses. "All secured, sir."

Ninian pushed the button to open the elevator door. The flames had receded, but bits of metal were strewn about the floor and a burnt object was stuck to one of the walls.

"The metal's from an air canister, sir," JG reported from the readout on her HR.

The others also had their HRs out. No one mentioned the two missing soldiers.

"The charge must have hit something. Look at that green gas." Ninian shone his light toward the ceiling as Miller stepped into the corridor. The lights in the area immediately came on. There was scattered shrapnel, but no other damage. The walls seemed unaffected. Cautiously, Miller walked out of sight of the others as he inspected the corridor up to where he believed the panel had been located. The others followed him.

"It's probably from the canisters," Markson said quietly in his helmet, to no one in particular.

"Don't step on anything," Ninian said. "You two, go on up the hall and see what you can find. Stay away from that green gas. I've never seen anything like it before."

Miller knelt in front of the service door, careful not to let the gas cloud touch him. Some of the chemicals the computer used ate through their equipment. His light revealed nothing except the tendrils of gas, dissipating before they reached the ceiling. As the last of it curled upward, he stepped into the tunnel. He was too close to give up and return to the ship, and time was running out. Ninian followed right behind him.

Once in the tunnel, Miller hurried down the passage, sweeping his light along the walls, ceiling, and floor, looking for something to indicate where the charge had been set.

"Ninian, there's an opening here in the ceiling." Preoccupied with his discovery, he failed to notice the silence over the comm link. He tried to move some hoses in the space between the ceiling and the floor level above and saw that two of them were leaking something.

"Get one of the others to help," Miller said.

Not hearing the order, Ninian stepped up to help Miller.

Outside the service panel, JG realized their communicators were malfunctioning.

"It's the computer." Markson wrote his words on a pad.

JG nodded, indifferent to Markson's tendency to give the computer mystical qualities. She motioned two of the Spartans to stay near the elevator and then directed Markson and Bandio to check out the tunnel. Henderson remained with her at the service tunnel opening.

Markson and Bandio found the captain and lieutenant trying to push up a trapdoor above the ceiling. At Miller's direction, Bandio squeezed in and lent his muscle to the task. The trapdoor inched up, opening a space big enough for their gloved fingers to pass through. Ninian gestured for a charge, but Miller shook his head in a vigorous "no."

Markson was relieved that no charge had been placed. Roberts and Scout had laid a charge, and now they were nowhere in sight. He shone his light farther up the tunnel and thought he saw a movement. He motioned with his arm, but nobody paid any attention. Curious, he went to investigate. Ten steps into the tunnel, his heart nearly stopped and a scream that only his ears heard filled his throat. His light revealed two yellow eyes before him. They blinked. He dropped his light and ran frantically back to the others.

Miller and Ninian stopped their attempts at conversation when they saw Markson frantically waving his arms at them, his tethered light swinging wildly around his legs. Ninian caught him by the arms and tried to calm him down, while Miller picked up his light and flashed it down the tunnel to see if there was anything behind them. He saw nothing out of the ordinary.

Markson's faceplate was forming condensation as he babbled on, unheard. Miller reluctantly signaled a return to the elevator so that they could hear what Markson had to say.

At the maintenance access panel, JG helped Markson out of the tunnel and they all retreated to the elevator. When the elevator doors sealed, and their scanners read that the air was breathable, they retracted their helmets.

"What is it?" Miller said.

"Eyes! Two yellow eyes, staring at me." Markson struggling to get his breathing back to normal.

"I didn't see any life-forms in my readings. Not even a Miller said. They hadn't met any other living species on th in the last two years. He didn't want anyone to panic wher so close to finding the entrance to another city. Especially the one that held the portal. "Check your breather mixture."

It was the first thing to do when something like this ha in order to rule out hallucinations.

Miller knew Markson had already done so before ente tunnel, and the mixture had been just fine.

"They register an imbalance, sir."

That was to be expected, since Markson had overtaxed with his hyped up bios. But Miller wanted Markson to stay and keep his fears to himself.

"There you go. You were hallucinating from an unev You should know the drill, Markson."

The others seemed to accept that explanation. Miller rundown of their situation, and the conversation turned to wh should do about the jammed trapdoor.

"You're right, we can't blast another hole. We don' what's in those hoses," Ninian said.

"What do you suggest?" Miller asked him.

"Wedge something in there to pry it up. It feels like need the right leverage."

"I agree." Miller punched his gloved fist into his open p think it's ready to give."

JG pulled a short metal bar from her leg pocket. It was open stubborn doors and such. It was also a handy weapon. " this?" Miller and Ninian both grabbed for it.

"Let's go back and try." Miller looked at Ninian "Everyone check your gauges. Lieutenant Ninian and I will g up the tunnel. Corporal Markson, how are your gauges?"

"They're still off their mark, sir."

"If they don't clear up in a quarter stan, return topside and get new equipment. It could be a bad stem." Miller looked at his watch. "Sergeant Major, if we're not back in an hour, get fresh tanks for everyone and bring us replacements. Three light flashes mean we're in. We won't need air once we're through the city entrance, in fact we won't need air anywhere within any of the compounds. That computer will have to take care of us."

He looked around and received nods. He needed at least four people to make a bid for possession of the city entrance, and he had them.

"All right, gear up."

The soldiers reactivated their helmets and waited for the doors to open. The light for the hallway read green, but they ignored it.

As the door opened, no one moved. A light powder had settled onto the ground, and there was an unmistakable smudged trail leading from the elevator to around the corner.

"It's us." Miller was relieved. "Those are our footprints."

"The comms are working, Captain," Markson said.

"Then let's move out."

Markson and Guilfo kept watch on the elevator and corridor, while Henderson, Bandio, and JG followed the hurrying officers back to the service tunnel. Miller and Ninian reentered the tunnel with Henderson, leaving Bandio and JG to guard the tunnel entrance.

"I almost thought Markson's friend with the eyes was here," Bandio admitted to JG when the officers were well on their way into the tunnel. A dark, unreadable gaze turned his way, and Bandio held his breath. JG's helmet barely moved in a nod. Markson's voice, sounding far away, interrupted the silence.

"Go see what he wants, Bandio. If he goes topside, stay with Guilfo."

He nodded and shuffled off. The sergeant major gave him chills, though he certainly valued her as a soldier. She was good, and she made a point of getting her group out of combat situations, whether on the battlefield or in a bar, with minimal damage. Unless she was irritated with you because you were the cause of the problem. Then she would pummel you, and you would think twice before you did something stupid again.

As Miller and Ninian made their way into the service tunnel, they found that the hoses and partially opened ceiling panel were repaired and back in place.

"Can you hear me?" Miller asked.

"Yes, I can."

"It's the maintenance bots. That's what Markson saw. With all of us in its small space, it probably went back into its cubbyhole to wait until we left. It's a wonder the explosion didn't leave any marks or cause any life support breaches."

“Uh-huh. That green stuff is gone, too.” But neither man deactivated his helmet.

Three lights shone on the ceiling area they had surveyed earlier. They wrestled it back open to a crack until they could slide the pry bar between the panel and the floor above them.

In the main corridor, unseen by any of the group, a wall panel opened and three small robots came out to clean up the dust and debris, sweeping away traces of anyone’s presence.

Markson nodded to Bandio, who was coming to relieve him so he could have his equipment replaced. Bandio’s appearance was a relief for Guilfo. He was getting jumpy about the place and didn’t want to be stuck there alone when Markson went topside.

While Markson went up in the elevator, the two guards moved up the corridor in the usual patrol sweep pattern.

Markson had no problems on his lift back up to the surface. The filled air canisters were lying near the shaft, with a note attached that said Corporal Clovus had called Sergeant Vanstar back to the ship.

“Runt to Pack Leader, come in,” Markson called, after dialing the link Sergeant Vanstar had left.

“Pack Leader to Runt. How’s the search?” Clovus replied.

“Well, you’re no pack leader,” Markson said.

“I’ve got it, Clovus. Go help out.” Vanstar’s voice was heard in the background, and then she came on the link. “What’s happening, soldier?”

“Markson here, Sarge. Search is still going on. My equipment’s damaged, and I was ordered up for a spare.”

“Secured here, Markson. Clovus has been sniffing around *Spinner’s* systems, wondering how the present we left was doing. Seems someone cleaned up the place and reinstated safeties.”

“I’ll let the captain know when I see him. I thought we hid them good,” Markson said.

“It’s not a bad thing. It made it easier for us to find the goodies they’re transporting to their next stop at some smugglers’ base near Rhion. Brand new, state-of-the-art AEGs. Enough for us, plus spares. Sure would bring a bundle on the underground market. Tell the captain they look like they’ve been tested, but not under live conditions. I’ll bring them back with me. We can use replacements.”

“I’ll tell him.”

“I should be back within an hour, if not sooner. Out.”

"Check that. Out." Looking at his timepiece, Markson marked the time. On the elevator, he replaced his own air canister. By the time he reached his destination, most of his helmet was cleared. He wondered what the new AEGs looked like. He also wondered how they were going to show up in them if they were not even on the market yet. Maybe they would wear their old ones out to this side of the planet and then change into the better ones. What a lot of trouble.

When the elevator doors opened, the hall lights were off. Thinking Bandio and Guilfo were scouting around, Markson hesitated. He shone his light around the hall, not seeing any debris from the explosion. Cautiously, he stepped out. The lights came on, and the entire corridor was clean, as if they had not been there. For a moment, he was worried that he was on the wrong floor, but then he saw the device the sergeant major had left on the outside door. More housecleaning by maintenance bots? He was mortified to think that bot eyes were probably what had scared him.

He decided against moving the air canisters into the corridor, in case there was another explosion.

"Sergeant Major, come in." There was no return signal to indicate an open receiver. He walked toward the maintenance panel that gave access to the tunnel, but found no one. Returning to the elevator door, he looked again at the homing device, and touched it to reassure himself. He was on the right floor, so where was everyone? He stepped back into the elevator and decided to wait inside with the canisters.

JG saw a signal flashing from inside the tunnel. They had found something.

She signaled back and hurried to the elevator to let the others know. The status light indicated it wasn't available.

Markson probably had gone topside to get fresh canisters. He had better remember to bring down spares for the rest of them, or she'd have him waiting mess tables to teach him not to forget his team. The other two must be doing their inspection.

One of them should have remained in sight, in front of the elevator door. They were all getting sloppy.

Irritated, she glanced at her gauges. Just over half full. That meant Captain Miller and Lieutenant Ninian must be near reserve. She hurried back to the service door, expecting to see Guilfo and Bandio coming from the opposite direction. She encountered no one.

"Guilfo and Bandio, report," she called impatiently over her comm.

Nothing. Not even a return signal. The computer must be messing with their communications again.

She changed channels. "Captain, this is Sergeant Major JG, come in." There was no voice response and no return signal.

She headed back to the maintenance panel and climbed into the tunnel to chase down the two officers and see what they were up to.

That's all she was, a damned babysitter for this squad, JG thought disgustedly.

She found them. Ninian was pulling on JG's metal bar, which he had wedged between the ceiling and a trapdoor in the floor above. Her comm light went green.

"Where's Henderson, sirs?" she asked, shining her light down both ends of the service tunnel.

"Went to look for a bot," Miller said.

"How's your air, Captain, Lieutenant?"

"I'm on reserve," Miller said.

"Me, too," said Ninian. "Let's go back and get a fresh supply."

"If we leave it, the bot will come by and close the panel again." Miller sounded frustrated.

"Sir, I think you're going in the wrong direction." JG looked up at the panel. "In the room we accessed through a ceiling in the city, the floor panel above moved down and tucked itself under the floor space, leaving an opening."

"What? When was this? Why wasn't I informed?"

"It was in a report Sergeant Vanstar prepared. She and Corporal Roberts went to the east side—"

"Yeah, yeah. I remember the scenario. I just don't remember reading her report," Miller replied testily.

"We departed for leave right after they filed their report. You haven't had a chance to review it yet," Ninian said.

The men each tried to move the panel back down.

"We can go get new tanks and then come back and start with a new plan of attack. Let the bot fix this like it did last time," Ninian said.

"Do you remember how she opened the panel?" Miller looked at JG.

"She said there was a switch at boot level."

They started flashing their lights around the floor.

"I've got it. It's a push plate." Miller kicked the plate a couple of times, but only the ceiling panel closed and opened. The floor panel to the room above them didn't move.

"Captain, I'm going to get my tank replaced," Ninian said, and started back up the corridor.

Miller glared at the plate, then followed him. JG still had plenty of air, so she stayed, hoping to see the bot and Henderson. A noise behind her had her spinning around, weapon drawn and ready to fire. Before her, a bot with a yellow warning light blinking was fixing the ceiling panel. That had to be Markson's scary eyes.

The bot tucked the hoses back into their space. With the ceiling panel closed, the bot's light stopped flashing. It reversed its direction and moved back down the tunnel. JG moved to the ceiling panel to mark it so they would be able to find it again.

All right, now let's go see what the others are up to.

Jogging down the service tunnel, she looked for the exit panel. There was no opening anywhere.

Shining her light on her gauges, she studied the readings. She was losing too much air.

As she moved down the corridor this time, she looked more carefully for the opening, but was still unable to locate it. Leaning against the wall, she could hear her suit laboring.

Have to get to that upper room. The sensor read that it has good air. I sure hope it's not another one of the computer's tricks.

She trotted back down the tunnel, hearing only her heart as she moved in the dark passageway. She concentrated on finding her marker.

The boot plate moved easily as she pushed it with her foot, and surprisingly, both panels above her opened. The energy field that surrounded her was like the ones they had encountered in the city. An air bubble enveloped whoever was within its area, to prevent contamination in one level from spreading to another. Still, she left her helmet on.

Vanstar had said there was a switch for stairs next to the floor panel. JG lifted it, and a set of stairs dropped smoothly. Cautiously, she climbed them.

Peering into the darkened room, she hoisted herself up and then promptly fell forward as a painful cramp in her lungs told her she was out of air. The stem on the breather must have ruptured for her air to go that fast.

Her eyes blurred and she rolled onto her back, dragging her arm up to release her helmet as she passed out.

A shadow in the corner of the room detached itself, and before the fresh air could revive her, an appendage reached down and put a small patch on her neck.

"Sweet dreams," Charles's soft voice said.

Lieutenant Ninian was good with spacing, and he knew he had passed the exit.

"Ninian, where's the exit panel?" Miller asked, irritated.

"I don't know. It's back this way, though. We didn't come this far, I'm sure of it."

Miller started to cough. Checking his suit's regulator, he tapped the gadget, but the low reading didn't budge. He was at the bottom of his tank. Rather than waste air talking, he gestured to Ninian and they carefully examined the wall for the opening.

Miller collapsed against the wall just as Ninian's light showed a crack. As Ninian pushed against the exit panel, he, too, started to sink to his knees. Holding his breath, he pushed the panel open and climbed out. He pulled Miller's unconscious form out of the tunnel and left him near the panel. He thought he could make it back to the elevator, but staggered only two steps before he slumped to the ground, unconscious.

Bots rolled out of the walls and deactivated the helmets. They placed patches on the necks of the unconscious forms and dragged them through a large door that appeared on the opposite wall. Then the bodies were put into separate cells and stripped of their clothing. As luck would have it, the floor they were invading was used to incarcerate unruly visitors.

Chapter 7

Five-year-old Alexandra felt a cool breeze on her face as she watched the birds on AltaLa glide effortlessly in the stiff breeze. Occasionally, one would dive into the water and reappear yards from its entry point. It would then bob on the water while it ate its catch. Sometimes a companion would swoop close and try to grab some of its meal. When they were successful, a chase would ensue. Their swoops and sharply angled turns were exciting to watch, for they had large wingspans that created drafts and noise when they passed. The birds had no fear of spectators and would fly close to them as they tried to evade their pursuers. Drops of water would slide off their naturally oily wings, falling on the spectators as the birds flew by.

Alexandra spread her arms, mimicking the gliding movements of the birds as the excitement of the chase ran through her small frame. She felt the wind as it pressed against her feathers, and the slight movement of her wing tips that changed the dramatic plunges into effortless glides. The joy of each bird she touched, whether chaser or chased, sent shivers of exhilaration through her. It was a game for all of them. The birds, referred to as the DeeNaJa, were not given to violence or outbursts of anger. The DeeNaJa were the willing partners of the Monks of Hela in teaching untrained empaths how to use and develop their gift.

Alexandra Harriet Montran, adopted daughter and third child of the High Lord and Lady of the Sacred Isle of LeLore on AltaLa, was in her second year of training at the monastery. Her mind touched the young bird thief who, like herself, was but a child.

Kela continued her swoops, for she was used to Alexandra. The child came often and joined Kela in her playful antics as she teased her serious father. He was fishing for his new hatchlings. Soon, she would also be ready to bear eggs and care for her own nestlings, while her spouse provided food for her and their young. But for now, she enjoyed her freedom.

Alexandra didn't feel her older cousin's protective arm around her waist as she leaned into the stiff wind, ready to take off and follow her telepathic connection.

Montran became aware that someone was demanding her attention. Tedious. Her thoughts returned to AltaLa and her last visit.

She was on her way to start her first year at the nearest space academy, just two days after her eighteenth birthday. Kela had died four years ago. The DeeNaJa lived less than ten stan years, and Alexandra found the loss of her friend and mentor unbearable. She closed the door to her telepathic and empathic side and, refusing to use her student name of Alexandra, left behind the monastery and its teachings.

Harriet turned to face the stiff wind and watched another young bird playing the same game young Kela had played with her father. The piercing pain resurfaced, and she began to cry. She wanted to enjoy the play of the DeeNaJa without feeling the loss. She needed to take something positive away with her when she left her beloved LeLore Isles to join the AltaCom Academy for officer training. She might never return to AltaLa.

Lady Harriet, soon to be Cadet Lady Harriet Montran, went to the rock where Kela had waited, an easy meal for a predator. To honor Kela's memory, she relived her death, seeing again the predator pouncing on Kela's form, shredding and mangling her body.

Harriet picked up her flute and played a song in Kela's memory. She had thought her throat would be too tight to play, but she surprised herself. The music soothed her, echoing eerily and drawing the attention of some of the large birds. A profound sense of peace settled on her, something she had not experienced for a long time. After the last of the notes died away, she carefully packed her flute. Lifting her head, she paused and listened to the wind. It sounded as though Kela's voice caressed her in the breeze.

Alexandra.

She had not been called by that name since she had left the monastery.

Montran's thoughts moved to another level of consciousness. A message kept reminding her to pay attention, and she finally yielded to it. Faces from personnel files flashed through her mind. Some of the Spartan soldiers were recognizable, but from where? The information didn't match her memory.

Later.

The images moved on to Lord Chaney, Sheila, and Captain Miller. She recognized Sheila in the metradame faces the computer had flashed. One face out of many. Then there was Captain Miller. Where had she read about him?

Later.

Gradually, the images and information slowed down, and then there was only the silence... and the scent of Rotilla.

Sharon's favorite tea.

Montran's eyes fluttered open to see the colorful Charles standing before her, holding a steaming cup of tea and a plate with a sandwich on it.

"Did you have a nice nap, Commander?" He handed her the tea and the plate, not releasing either until she had a firm grip on them.

"Yes, thanks," she whispered, feeling mentally and emotionally weary.

"It is the equivalent of Rotilla," Guardian said, as she breathed in the tea's steamy vapors before taking a sip. "It is from our own garden, so it may not have the exact same taste with which you are familiar."

"It tastes good." Montran blinked a few times as her eyes focused on the screens. Groups of soldiers and civilians were hurrying through the corridors, looking nervous.

The sensation of visual events overlapping with the download of information she had just received gave her a unique view of reality. She knew the people on the screens intimately, but then again did not.

"What's happening?" she asked.

"Your admiral's response to the message I sent her was 'Geomatria.' Commander Montran, can you explain that word to me? I have not been able to locate it in any of my searches."

"It's a slang word we use that combines, 'Good to hear you're fine' and 'hang on, the troops are on their way.' Or, it could mean, 'tough it out, because we're kind of busy here.'"

"Ah. A bit confusing if the receiver is depending on a clear message. Let us hope it is the first meaning. When you were busy getting your update, Maud created some trouble." His voice sounded pleased. "While the soldiers and smugglers were topside searching for you, she was able to free a roomful of captives."

Montran sat forward. "We won't get that opportunity again. The Black Rose will be dispersed throughout the city to keep an eye out for any more surprise visits."

"The Black Rose are not in the city. The windstorm is preventing them from returning to their base. However, there are enough Spartans and smugglers to prevent Maud from rescuing the remaining four rooms of people."

"Are you saying that to make me feel needed?"

"You *are* needed."

"Tell me about this metradame who's been trained as a bodyguard. Just what kind of a threat is she?"

"You find this hard to believe?"

"I was wondering what her skill level is." The image of a seductive bodyguard appeared in her mind's eye, and she had to struggle not to leer. The idea of taking something from Lord Chaney that would cause him a great deal of inconvenience to lose strongly appealed to her. However, the only information she had about metradames were sexual images from advertisements. For a moment, she frowned as she remembered Sharon's anger when she had found Montran reading the ad. No, that was a dream. They didn't have metradames in Collective space.

"Dr. Sharon Teal." Guardian picked up the vivid image of her previous lover. "She is one of the few who went through the metradame labs and was able to override the program."

A long, quiet moment passed before her brain kicked back into gear. *Sharon, a metradame?* "You have the wrong Sharon Teal," she told him. "The one I know is a respected scientist, and she isn't in GCFC territories. Metratoys haven't caught on with the populace in Collective space."

Guardian flashed an image of a young woman on the screen and then recreated her with an older woman's face. She looked just like Sharon.

"I don't believe it. How would you have tapes on something like that?"

"Security recordings at the metralab. I am disclosing this information to impress upon you that metrapeople are real people, programmed according to someone else's agenda."

"Sharon was real, is real. She's not one of those."

"They are all real, as you call it. And that, Commander Harriet Montran, is what you must remember when you meet up with Sheila, Lord Chaney's bodyguard."

"What?" She tried to focus on Guardian's message. "Are you afraid I'll kill her if we get into some sort of skirmish?"

"No. I want you to know that metrapeople are living, viable, although imprisoned, beings. I have faith in the effectiveness of your retraining in the Collective's less aggressive methods, otherwise I would not be asking for your assistance."

"How do you know so much about me and Sharon? And for that matter, about what's going on outside of Merker's Outpost? Naboth's Vine isn't in the habit of letting every member into the nuts and bolts of things."

"I am a scientist in a computer. I gather information, extrapolate what I need, experiment to prove what I have theorized from my data, and store it all. It is a hobby, something to relieve boredom. Naboth's Vine finds my hobby useful, and my beliefs on the use of nonviolence are in line with their charter."

Montran's attention went back to the screens, watching the "enemy" as they went about their lives.

Until I get into the kind of fight where instincts take over, we'll all be wondering if my retraining worked.

The real problem was that her backup consisted of one civilian, so whatever Montran did, it was going to have to be just enough to keep the smugglers off balance and her from getting caught.

I hope Admiral JoCastao sends reinforcements soon.

"Lord Chaney had Sheila trained at one of the best bodyguard schools, Bodshiva Avante Guard. However, I understand that in your new job in Collective space, you were trained by one of their ex-instructors, Ewep De."

Montran looked startled. "Ewep De was a bodyguard instructor?" In a flash, she realized it could very well be true, considering what he taught. "I don't believe any of the students knew that about him, at least not in my track." She frowned for a moment, remembering how many of the young officers grumbled at having to take his class in "Awareness," thinking it was superfluous.

"The class was difficult to pass, but it was interesting." A lot of good it did her when she let those jerks from *Spinner's Tale* remove her from the shuttle without so much as a whimper.

Montran handed her empty cup to Charles. "Everything has more than one weakness." She had faced adversaries that were better armed than she was, and had managed to survive, if not triumph. However, that was a long time ago, and right now, the enemy's sheer numbers nullified any edge she might have.

"Charles," Guardian said, "can you get the Commander her new environmental suit and communicator?"

Charles handed her a communicator. It consisted of two patches, each smaller than the tip of her finger. One was placed on the bone behind her left ear and the other on her throat.

"It can only be heard by someone with my equipment," Guardian said.

The environmental suit was a dull brown, nearly the same as the walls of the room they were in. Once sealed at the neck, the suit lay on her clothing as if it were part of it. When she activated the helmet, her bioreadings flashed on the visor, under her left cheek. As she moved her head, she noted that four new screens came up on the wall.

"As the screens are showing," Guardian said, "the suit gives you a panoramic view, as well as displaying your bios. If you want to know what is behind you, the small viewer to your lower left can be activated by asking for a view—left, right, fore, and hind. For bios, simply ask for vitals. For a reading on someone near you, hold your palm out toward the subject for a few moments, or give the direction and distance, and ask for a reading. This suit was originally designed for monitoring my researchers. For the last two years, I have been modifying it for defensive uses, for Maud. For example, it imitates the texture of whatever it leans against. When you have more time you can study the extras. Know, however, that that particular ability is not something to be used lightly."

Montran looked up at the hologram in surprise. "You mean I would disappear?" she said into the comm. To test this, she leaned against the wall and looked at her hands. Nothing changed.

"Say 'blend on.'"

"Blend on."

She glanced at the screens and found she wasn't visible. She moved away from the wall, and her form reappeared on the monitors.

"Now this is something to play with. But, you're right. It's too valuable a tool to give away its existence."

"Yes. I am glad you see it that way. Maud has been using it to great advantage. To deactivate it, simply say 'blend off.' I had thought of other words to use, but as Maud pointed out, the simpler the better. The suit will protect you from heat, most explosions, and some weapons fire."

Charles handed her an unfamiliar sidearm that fit snugly into her palm.

"This weapon," Guardian said, "is adapted for this planet's atmosphere and will work only for you. It does not kill, nor does it give pain. It can render a person unconscious, or if you want him or her conscious but noncombative, change the selector on the bore to the other color.

"Now you are ready. Charles will show you to the lower level, where the tube will take you to Century City. Maud will meet you at the other end. The trip takes about one stan hour, traveling at a very high rate of speed, so do not try to step out or slow it down. By the time you reach your destination, the subliminal information should be completely assimilated and at your disposal."

Charles was already out the door. At the doorway, Montran turned back to Guardian. The room was already darkened.

"Good-bye and good luck, Alexandra," Guardian said in a warm voice.

Alexandra? Montran paused and then turned to hurry after Charles.

How did he know her by that name? Ah, she must have thought of it while hooked up to Guardian. She would not fall asleep in Guardian's chair again, or even sit in it. No telling what information he was gathering from her for his games.

In the other room, the polo players were in another pose, still hard at play. Charles was waiting at the elevator, and its door slid open as Montran approached.

"It is best to engage your helmet from here on. Guardian keeps the uninhabited sections of the cities on minimum life support. I will leave you here and wish you well with your journey and task." With that, Charles wheeled around and disappeared back down the darkened corridor.

As she had suspected on her arrival, the elevator had more than one exit. This time it opened to the side, instead of directly behind her. She was delivered to what appeared to be a small waiting room, with comfortable couches against the walls and chairs set around small tables. She slapped one of the chairs. No dust, dirt, or signs of wear. Of course, no one lived here to wear them down. But there were people in Century City.

The thought of her trip to Century City gave an extra lift to her steps. For the last seven years, she hadn't been on any away missions that weren't simulated.

She continued to another entrance that had a railcar icon on the door. Though the interior was dark, the view from the helmet revealed a typical transportation station. Lights in the floor flashed in the direction she was supposed to go. Further help came from a soft light on the inside of the vehicle itself, whose door had opened invitingly. Two seats on each side faced each other, with enough legroom between them to make any Copoc comfortable, four legs and all. Montran sank into one of the seats. It was soft, and the moment she settled in, a cushioned restraint slowly descended, securing her from movement in any direction. Lucky she wasn't claustrophobic.

Guardian's voice sounded in her communicator. "It is a very fast ride with a sudden stop, which necessitates padded restraints. I do not want my passengers peeling bits of themselves from the interior. I will be in touch with you at all times, so if you need anything, I am just a whisper away."

Numbers changed on the visor next to her left cheek, showing her bios as they escalated with the pressure from the car's acceleration.

While the small car sped to its destination, Montran closed her eyes to escape the sense of confinement and review her plans.

Bits of information on Century City began to make their way to her consciousness. She knew what the tube station looked like and where its five emergency exits were located.

Montran's adrenaline was flowing, and she felt the excitement of a drop into enemy territory, along with an intense will to survive and beat the odds. For a moment, it reminded her of the drugs low-ranking Spartan soldiers were given before each skirmish, which gave them a false sense of invincibility. Sergeants and lieutenants had to keep a close watch on themselves and their teams, so as not to take unnecessary risks under the drugs' influence.

She pursed her lips at the disagreeable memory then moved on to more immediate concerns.

I can't shut down the smugglers here, but like Guardian, I can make their lives miserable. Maybe, if they get a false reading of me somewhere on the surface, it would slow them down. Surely the entire surface of this planet isn't flat. Climbing would really wear down the small parts on the suits as well as the wearer. Montran started to chuckle at the idea of some of the overweight soldiers and smugglers struggling in the dense atmosphere.

"Ah. I see you are already beginning to enjoy the adventure." Guardian's soft voice startled her.

"Are there any slopes or terrain that would overtax their AEGs?"

"Yes. There is a place the Spartans refer to as the Southern Rim. The Black Rose have been scouting and mapping that area for almost a stan year and have covered only half of it."

"Do you have a city there?"

"Yes, Ilo. Once it was a busy spaceport, but it is closed to outside access now that the cities have been emptied. The Black Rose have been primarily scouting the edge of the cliffs. They get bored easily and find climbing a challenge."

"I think a sighting of their missing quarry over that way would give them a new burst of excitement."

"It could. I will have one of my transponders send out the signal that was set on your AEG."

"Sounds like the beginnings of a good, old-fashioned phantom hunt." Montran closed her eyes and considered other possibilities to divide the groups. "Guardian?"

"Yes, Commander Montran?"

"Why did you call me Alexandra?"

"I am most sorry to have addressed you with such familiarity without asking."

"It's a name I don't use anymore."

"My apologies. I did not mean to offend."

There was a short silence, in which Montran could have sworn she heard the disembodied Copoc thinking.

"It is a rather strong name. Perhaps in the future you shall feel comfortable using it again."

"Maybe." Taking a deep breath and then releasing it, she concentrated on the current problem with more resolve.

The Black Rose. I would never have thought they would throw in with smugglers, even though Chaney is their sponsor. They've had some pretty memorable skirmishes with smugglers, leaving a lot of bad feelings on both sides. At least, seven years ago they had.

Then there's the metradame. If she trained with the Bodshiva group, she's going to be dangerous.

I'm curious to see just what my worth is under fire, and where my skill level is. This is my proving ground. A one-woman assault team. Her lips curled up in humor.

She would worry about the other Spartans as she met them. She had trained many grunts during her two years as a Spartan captain. Although she played down her empathic ability, she was better than most at reading people and gauging their value. Her combat skills were fairly broad, too. Commander Hayes, her immediate superior in the Centurions, had made sure she kept up her infantry skills, probably to see how much of her Spartan impulse training was intact. She shifted uneasily in her seat. She closed her eyes, and her thoughts wandered.

Sharon.

Hesitantly, her thoughts turned to pleasant, loving memories. Why had they separated? Why had she let Sharon go?

Loneliness threatened to engulf her, and her thoughts shifted a little, not quite leaving the subject of Sharon.

A metradame?

What does a metradame feel like?

In all her years of soldiering, she had never indulged in the use of a metradame, preferring abstinence to a short liaison. To her knowledge, she had never come into contact with one.

Could they be dangerous? Just how real were they?

Sharon was real.

She was my safe harbor.

Montran blushed at that admittance. Did that mean she had used Sharon? Maybe it did. Montran had been looking for peace of mind, and Sharon had been devoid of violence. She was ordinary and… safe. Was that what a metradame did? Made one feel safe?

But Sheila wasn't safe. She was trained to kill.

That brought her attention back to her plan for harassing Guardian's unwelcome visitors. Scenarios were reviewed, but without the schematics of the city, they seemed useless.

"I wish I had a map."

"I have just completed downloading the information into your taxi's map service, but you have reached your destination," Guardian said.

"I thought downloading would be relatively fast and easy from one computer to another."

Sudden deceleration pressed her into the restraints. On the lower left of her helmet, numbers appeared, monitoring her bios. Now that really was convenient to have within sight.

"Normally, the download would have been instantaneous, but this car is newly reacquired. It was running on bare operational services in case the Spartans or smugglers appropriated it for their own use. It takes some time for it to update when it is back in use."

"You mean, something like not being able to talk and eat simultaneously?" She laughed. "This helmet will be a best seller. Much better to have the bio information in the visor."

"How is the suit doing?"

"I'm still assessing. I'm getting some of the subliminal stuff on what it can do. Some of this stuff is—oof!"

Guardian was right. The stop was sudden.

The door to her car swung open. Montran leaned back into the seat as the restraint released. She looked out the door and saw a pair of feet wearing boots similar to hers. Peering up, she spotted her welcoming party of one. Maud nodded her helmeted head, as if encouraging her to step out.

"Lieutenant Commander Harriet Montran, welcome to Century City. Are you going to sit in there for long?"

The voice in her comm sounded familiar.

"This area is not secured from Spartan or smuggler patrols." Maud turned to walk away.

The way she carried herself was also familiar. Where could they have met? Montran had started to follow Maud when a sound from behind made her turn. The car she arrived in disappeared into the darkness.

"The car will wait out of sight in a side area. When you are finished here, you can summon it and it will take you back to the Lair." Maud waved her into the service tunnel.

Montran stepped before Maud into the tunnel.

"Do I know you from somewhere?" Montran said.

"Why do you ask?" Maud secured the panel behind them.

"You seem familiar."

Maud turned back toward her. In the dark, Montran's helmet gave her a different view. She could see trace elements and energy from living forms, but little color. The tunnel was high enough for them to walk upright, but not wide enough for two people to walk side by side, so when Maud stepped past Montran they were helmet to helmet. Montran's breath caught as she gazed into the helmet and saw a shadowed version of herself.

Guardian's voice came through her intercom. "Is there something wrong?"

Montran imagined her bios were going off the scale, but her attention was focused on Maud. She gripped Maud's wrist, holding her immobile as she removed the light from her utility belt and shone it into Maud's faceplate. Its surface darkened to block the light from Maud's eyes, and Montran moved it to the side of the helmet.

"We do look alike. Is that what you're looking for, similarities?" Maud asked in Montran's own voice.

"You... your voice."

“I was remolded to look like you,” Maud said.

“Why?” Montran asked, aghast.

Guardian’s voice answered. “I had promised Lord DeMonte that I would do all I could to protect you. You are too important to lose, yet too important not to use. Besides, you would not have remained uninvolved. Providing another image of you seemed a good way to confuse our adversaries.”

“Yes, but... what if she gets hurt because they think she’s me?”

“It is a chance Maud has agreed to take.”

“You agreed to put your life in danger for me? You don’t even know me.” Montran was upset. She had experienced enough guilt-ridden nightmares to recognize the makings of another one. “This is not a good idea.”

“I’m in danger for as long as Guardian’s unwelcome visitors are on this station. It doesn’t matter whether I look like you or someone else. I couldn’t go back to looking like I was before, because then they would know that I was not disposed of as I should have been, and someone very valuable would be in danger.”

Still close to Maud, Montran peered into the darkened helmet, seeing the all too familiar look of determination. She even had her expressions down. She released her hold on Maud’s wrist. “You’re exactly like me?”

“That would be an impossibility. We must move, Commander Montran. We have prisoners to rescue.” Maud turned and started quickly up the passageway.

As they moved along the dark maintenance passage, parts of its schematics surfaced in Montran’s consciousness, giving her a sense of familiarity. Maud stopped and accessed a ladder. An energy envelope engulfed them.

“We are entering the first level of living quarters. The energy you feel surrounding you is sealing the air, so that if a breach occurs, it doesn’t endanger lives on any other levels,” Maud said softly as she climbed up into the next level.

When Montran joined her, Maud signaled her to remain quiet.

“...another time.” An excited voice reached their ears through the walls.

An angry voice overrode the first. “I don’t give a wild hornet’s nest about what happened. Right now, I want the first group set up. We’ll worry about the rest of the problems after the broadcast.”

“Yes, sir, but this may be important.”

“If you don’t get yourself and your crew to their posts, *now*, I will personally execute you.”

"Sir!"

She could hear two sets of boots leaving.

"Idiot," a different voice said. The sound of footsteps going at a slower pace moved in the opposite direction.

After five more minutes of quick travel, Maud stopped and pointed a device at a hatch covering. "They're in here," she said. A soft tone sounded from Maud's device, and the hatch slid open. Light shone into the service tunnel. Stepping into the room, both women deactivated their helmets. An Almadarin's blue face was the first thing Montran caught sight of, its eyes opened wide. Without their helmets on, it was difficult to see a difference between Maud and Montran.

Appearing unconcerned, Maud went to the center of the room and pushed on the floor. A hole appeared as the panel she had pushed descended and tucked itself into a space under the floor, leaving an opening in the middle of the room.

"I have a train waiting in a transportation tunnel one level below the one in which you arrived."

Maud looked at the opened space and then dropped into its darkness. As if it had been prearranged, the Almadarin lifted a member of one of the smaller species, who appeared to be injured, and handed it to Montran. Montran stepped into the floor space and lowered the rescued being into Maud's waiting hands. This shuttling continued until only the Almadarin was left. Montran stepped out of the space to let him descend.

"Someone's coming," Maud whispered, her voice coming from Montran's communicator.

Montran quickly hopped down into the opening, and standing on the top rung of the ladder, pushed the button that would put the floor back into place. Quickly, she went back into the service tunnel and sealed the hatch through which they had entered. She fumbled in the dark for the button to reactivate her helmet as she proceeded down the tunnel. Now it was time to do her thing.

"There it is again!" the same voice she had heard earlier shouted excitedly on the other side of the wall.

Was she going the wrong way? She accessed the schematics on her visor and found her location. She was headed toward the crew quarters, just where she wanted to go.

"You've got to let it go," another voice said. "It's probably another ghost reading. Wait until after the broadcast then give it to Captain Miller."

"And let the Black Rose take the credit for these findings? No way. I told you there were other life-forms on this planet. Look at the readings. They aren't lying. This is for real." The voice rose in excitement. "CPO to Security. I have a red alert in Sector Mim. I repeat, red alert in—"

A voice answered. "What are you getting hysterical about now, Chief?"

"I've got those strange readings, and a life sign, too, sir."

"Burn your soul in Agasta!" the translator said politely. "You go looking for trouble at this time? Were you not just sent back to your quarters? Security!" the voice bellowed, without waiting for a reply.

"Security here."

"Where is that captain of yours? Where is he?"

"By your request, on the other side of the planet," the voice said.

"How many people do I have available to block off that area and flood it with concussion bombs?"

"None, Alha Bahna. With all the time personnel have spent topside, the ship's sickbays are full, and we have equipment failures, so anyone without a working suit stays aboard ship. What you have now is what you get."

"Which is nothing. Chief, get out of that area now. I want it flooded with acidic gas within twenty minutes."

"Gods almighty!" The CPO sounded panicked.

"You seal that end and I'll do the other," his companion said. "You do know how to lock the seals on the doors don't you?"

"Yeah, yeah. I'll see you back at Com-C."

Montran jogged down the dark passageway, her boots thudding softly as she moved away from the rooms to be gassed. Her mental picture of the occupied city indicated the Spartan living quarters were one level up.

She found an access ladder easily enough. Carefully, she crept up the ladder, looking for any traps or trip wires at the entrance to the next floor. She wasn't disappointed. Once they were deactivated, she entered the long tunnel that serviced Spartan barracks on one side and Black Rose Spartan barracks on the other.

At the end of the service tunnel were T&T, traps and trip wires, set in a standard pattern. Nothing tricky or impressive. It was simply meant to slow down any intruders, and made no attempt to hide the fact that it had a motion-sensitive audible alarm. By the time the intruder got into the room, someone would be waiting on the other side.

"Are you sure you want to go into that room?" Guardian's voice whispered in her ear.

"Why?" she whispered back.

"It is Lord Chaney's room."

A smirk appeared on her face. "Can you tell if he's inside?"

"He is on his ship with Sheila. I will let you know when he returns. Maud is busy attending to our guests, so she cannot join you at this moment." There was a pause. "What do you intend on doing?"

"Mischief. Isn't that our business? Your profile on him says he's very particular where he puts things. He's going to be an easy one."

She spied a service bot entrance to the bathing room. Well, it looked possible. She slid into the tight opening, realizing suddenly that if she needed anything from her utility belt, she was out of luck.

"Guardian?"

"Are you stuck?"

"How does the panel open? I don't have access to the directions."

"There is a beam that the bot trips about two of your hand widths from the panel door."

She continued squirming toward the panel, and as her fingers crossed the beam, the panel opened into a darkened area. Cautiously, she looked around before entering. The place looked clean. "Can you see any snoops?"

"No. He has placed none in his quarters. He has them outside of the service panel and the door to his quarters."

Her eyes studied the many bottles and packages sitting on the counter, all precisely arranged.

He had enough bathing products to stock a harem. She could tell he wasn't used to quartering in crews' digs. *Look at all those different hair colors. Who dyed their hair—Chaney or his metradame?*

Montran remembered a school prank of putting dye in the shower spout. She wadded up a sponge, dumped black dye in it, and stuffed it in the shower nozzle.

Finished, she shuffled his bathing room articles around, including what appeared to be personal toys, and then reactivated Guardian's monitors, which Chaney had shut down.

Next was the bedroom. It held a bed and a cot. The cot must have been for the bodyguard. She decided to short sheet both. Finished with that, she moved to the closet. His clothing filled over three-fourths of the closet, and it was carefully arranged by color. She intermixed what was in the closet, pulled out the contents of the drawers, and dropped them into the shoe storage locker. More surveillance cameras were reactivated. Guardian would certainly have his interlopers well watched from now on.

She was feeling very satisfied with herself. Next was the sitting room.

"Commander Montran, you will have to end your fun. Lord Chaney and Sheila have entered the city," Guardian said. "They will be delayed about thirty stan minutes. His habit is to check the status of the city before returning to his quarters, and he will most likely ask about the progress on the search for you."

"I'd like to hear that report, just to know where I stand on remaining inconspicuous."

"That is unlikely to happen. They have blocked my devices in their command post."

As Montran squirmed into the bot access port and pulled herself back into the larger service tunnel, she decided to hit a few more rooms for good measure, notably those of the Black Rose Spartans. She needed more information on them, for personal reasons as well as for strategic planning.

"What about the Black Rose? Are they still outside the city?"

"They always leave the city when a broadcast is being made. The smugglers get too edgy with the Black Rose around," Guardian said. "Usually, the other Spartans guard the city while the Black Rose make expeditions to other parts of the planet."

"No bots?"

"They did not bring any of their own, and they used my few for target practice when they were bored."

"Maybe they didn't like being spied on," Montran said dryly.

The first two rooms she visited were smaller than Chaney's, but they were still larger than what soldiers were usually billeted in. The difference was that the shared quarters each had their own cozy sleep area, and there was a separate sitting room. No decorations or personal effects marked the places as being lived in. She only knew they were in use because kits were neatly stored in the closets. Perhaps the Black Rose's stay on Merker's was intended to be short.

Knowing the strong feelings Spartans had about their belongings being found in someone else's kit, she decided not to go that far. Not yet.

The third room was a different matter. This person didn't share, and though it was as big as Lord Chaney's room, there were motion T&Ts set about, with an alarm outside the service exit.

These were the sergeant major's quarters. All sergeant majors had the same tough attitude. The obvious was not going to disturb this person, Montran surmised. Her eyes roamed the bedroom, looking for inspiration.

She undid the fastenings of a few shelves, switched the hot and cold tubes in the shower, but didn't activate cameras, hoping to trick the occupant into thinking there was another plant somewhere.

Geez, this woman was really a control freak. All her uniforms hung exactly two fingers' width apart. Or maybe this was her way of knowing when someone had looked through her stuff. It certainly made it easy to rig the bar to drop when anything on it was moved.

The sound of someone trying to open the door into the sergeant major's quarters had her looking frantically for a place to hide. "Guardian?"

"I cannot see who it is. However, it is not the occupant. The Black Rose have not returned to the city."

Going out the service panel was out of the question. The sergeant major had it wired.

Her first place to hide was the obvious, the closet.

The intruder didn't waste any time in the foyer, but came directly into the sleeping area. Montran could hear breathing. Whoever was in the room knew exactly where he or she was going. Was this person expected and welcomed? Maybe she shouldn't have deactivated the T&Ts.

Instead of capturing the metradame, why not this person? Anyone snooping in Black Rose quarters either knew more than most or was incredibly stupid.

Montran's back was getting tired from her bent position. Shifting her weight slightly caused the clothes pole to drop, just as she had planned. She leaned forward to avoid becoming entangled in the mess and inadvertently pushed the closet door open. There was no way to dignify her surprise entry, but she did manage to drop to one knee as a white-haired male figure pointed something at her. She was already changing direction when the first shot went wide. Rolling forward, she knocked the weapon from his hand and kicked his midsection. He bent forward with a whoosh, and she jumped on him, trying to render him unconscious. They rolled to the floor, trying to get a grip on each other.

Breaking, they were quickly on their feet. Her white-haired adversary pretended to toss something and then feinted into her guard, nearly getting his hands around her neck. Easily, she deflected the grab and kneed him in the midsection, bringing him to his knees. She stepped back to kick him in the shoulder, but he had pulled a stunner. She pushed past his extended arm, reached for his wrist, and snapped the spring that held the weapon in place. He bumped her off balance.

From his knees, he pushed against her and used his shoulder to slam her against the wall. Both of them fell, with her adversary wrapping one arm across his chest as though his arm were injured. The Second Skin and suit absorbed the blows she sustained, but she had to end the wrestling match before they attracted spectators.

The man wrapped his arms around his chest and butted her, knocking them both back, but Montran used the momentum to flip them. She landed on top of him, knees first, and knocked the wind out of him. Rolling free, she grabbed a short ceremonial saber that had come loose from the sheath on his utility belt. He grabbed his fallen sidearm and was awkwardly bringing it up when she tossed the saber toward him. He gave a terrified shriek, tumbled sideways, and brought up his arm in a swinging movement, as if to ward off a swarm of bees.

The blade hit him between the eyes as though she had thrown it with intent. Her mouth open in astonishment, Montran watched him fall against the bureau. She had not taken aim at all. The tossed saber was merely intended as a distraction, so she could draw her weapon.

"What happened? I wanted a prisoner!" She breathed out explosively. For a moment, she thought she was going to throw up. Firmly, she reminded herself she was a veteran of bloody battles that made this one look mild.

She heard Guardian's voice. "The blade is new on the market. It can be programmed to target a vital point on the person it is pointed at. Apparently he had it programmed for between the eyes. It appears to be a recently purchased weapon, since I have not seen it on him before." Guardian sounded surprised. "You have just eliminated a key player. That was Lord Chaney."

"Oh, Helga's bloody moon." One of the people she had concentrated hard on not seeking retaliation against, and here she had nailed him. “I’ve never seen a weapon like that. I hope they’re banned. That’s all we need to have added to an assassin’s arsenal.”

“I have activated the mortician’s robot. It will pick him up and prepare him for delivery to his next of kin. He will be kept in a freezer until then.”

Montran turned to the body and went through Chaney’s pockets. While she patted him down, she wondered if killing him meant she’d failed her first test to prove she had risen above her Spartan programming.

In his utility belt, she found small, but deadly toys—stars, tenjas, and some buzzers. She found his identity card and a small device attached to it. She put them in her utility belt to study later.

The mortician bot entered, followed by small utility bots.

“I see you’ve reactivated the small cleaning bots, too.”

“To help you get rid of the evidence. From my information on the sword, the owner shouldn’t fear it being used on him. It appears Lord Chaney didn’t set the safeties that would have eliminated the possibility of his being the target.”

The utility bots seemed to know that the clothes pole was not supposed to be balancing precariously in its slot. They set it up correctly, with the clothes separated by color and spaced as they were earlier, exactly as it had been before Montran tampered with it.

The mortician bot looked like a gurney with arms. It searched the corpse, removing the body jewelry and leaving it in a pile on the floor. Lord Chaney was hoisted up onto the gurney, the knife still protruding from between his open eyes.

Montran turned her focus to his jewelry. His GCFC ring of authority was familiar. Hadrie had one. She found another ring, a horse with a horn between its dull black eyes. *Odd.* This was added to her pouch. She then rose and turned her attention to the dresser drawer that he had left open.

Underclothing? He was interested in a Spartan’s underwear? Correction… in a woman’s underwear? This was not his style. It didn’t fit his profile. So, what was here that would be of interest to him? A leather thong? *Ooh, I like these.*

She brought up the subliminal on the image of Sergeant Major Jina Gari. The Spartan’s features were hard, but other mug shots showed a plain face that would be easy to forget.

Her boot kicked something. Leaning down, she picked up a small spray vial, with no identifying label on it. She knew better than to smell it, and it was added to her plunder. No closer to figuring out what might have interested Chaney, she resumed looking in the drawer.

This Spartan obviously had another life, one that required little fabric. Montran held up another garment, letting it dangle between her fingers as she studied it. Turning it, the fabric brushed against her skin, eliciting a sensuous feeling.

It has a skin sensitizer on it.

Montran sensed a presence behind her. She turned toward the doorway and looked into the pale green eyes of a tall, athletic-looking woman, probably a Jlish mixed with human variants, who was leaning languidly against the doorjamb watching her. She had dark brown hair, fashionably interwoven with colorful cloth ribbons, which reached past her shoulders. Her stylish suit spoke volumes of the credits needed to purchase it. This must be Chaney's bodyguard.

"Harriet Montran," the woman's voice cooed seductively. "You have the whole outpost looking for you… and here… you are."

She approached Montran, her walk slow and sensuous. In all her wildest imaginings, this was exactly what Montran had pictured a metradame would be like. Her heart beat faster, and a hot flush infused her face.

"Are you the one responsible for those little…" she leaned close and whispered in Montran's ear, "tricks in Lord Chaney's room?"

A pleasant shiver skittered down Montran's spine as puffs of warm air tickled her ear.

Sheila stepped back and casually let her eyes roam Montran's body.

Montran tried to control her erratic breathing and move her unresponsive limbs. She couldn't turn her eyes away.

"I had thought Lord Chaney was here, but I see he's not." Sheila moved unhurriedly around the room, disappearing from Montran's sight. Then she came back, and her alluring smile sent another tremor down to Montran's very wet and swollen center. She tried to tell herself to ignore the sensations, but it wasn't working.

"Perhaps we can enjoy some pleasant moments before Lord Chaney is done with you." Sheila ran a finger down Montran's motionless arm, moving her limb just enough to study her sidearm. She circled her captive, lightly tracing patterns over her body, and came to a stop in front of her. Her hand cupped one of Montran's breasts. Tweaking an erect nipple, she smiled at the effect she was clearly having on Montran.

Montran's chest was heaving. She strained to come into contact with Sheila's hand as it was removed.

"Yes. I can see you want to, too." She touched Montran's cheek with the back of her hand, again sending chills of pleasure through her victim's body. "Why don't you wait right here while I go see where Lord Chaney could have gone. When I return, maybe you'll be inspired as to what we can do. I won't be long."

Lips brushed her ear as the words were whispered, nearly causing Montran's knees to buckle. Another touch was all she needed to send her into an orgasm. If only her voice would respond, she could beg Sheila not to go yet. The knowledge that Sheila was a bodyguard and might kill her had no effect on Montran's emotions.

Montran couldn't get her eyes to inspect the area to see if any evidence of their fight remained, or if the bots had cleaned it up before Sheila arrived. That was the last sensible thought she had before the sexual fantasies took over.

Maud found Montran lying on the floor, shaking from repeated orgasms.

"I see you've met Sheila, the former Lord Chaney's goddess of lust." She laughed softly and placed a small instrument against Montran's neck. Moments later, Montran was breathing normally. Maud helped her sit on the bed.

"Goddesses and angels, what a nightmare!"

"Nightmare?" Maud raised her eyebrows, just as Montran herself would have done.

"I think I've just had enough wet dreams to last me the year."

Maud looked like she was trying not to smile. "What I've just given you will prevent the paralyzing gas from affecting you again. As for the rest, I've heard that once bitten…" She left the remainder unsaid, but her grin did not look encouraging.

"I'm surprised someone hasn't killed all the metradames if this is their effect."

"No," Guardian's voice said softly in her ear. "Only Sheila was equipped with what they call a lust gas. If it makes you feel any better, she released enough pheromones in the air to set off an entire roomful of species sensitive to the chemical, of whatever gender. Lord Chaney spared no expense in her training."

Guardian's voice hardened. "You two will need to get out of there. Once Sheila finds her former master's body and scans its retina for the killer, she will shut down momentarily and come back up in assassin mode."

Maud sorted quickly through the pile of Lord Chaney's belongings that the cleaning bot had dumped on the bed. "You'll need his ID card. Pinching both sides simultaneously, on these marks, will render Sheila inactive for a few stan minutes. When she's in assassin mode, there will be only a moment in which to act."

"Isn't there a way to shut her down completely?"

"During that pause, if you can press these two colors on the ID in front of her eyes, the pulse it emits will nullify all of Lord Chaney's commands. You will then be her new mistress."

Montran studied the card. "That sounds just a little too easy."

"The directions say it is supposed to work," Guardian said. "After all, you are talking about a select group within GCFC territories who can afford such creatures. They certainly did not want to make deactivating them too difficult. The owners and their families were afraid that the slaves might revolt, so the dealers made sure they could be easily put to sleep by nullifying their programming. The metraperson would then have to be brought back to the lab and, for a fee, reprogrammed."

"So, you don't know if this is going to work?"

"It is not like I have a laboratory full of willing test subjects donated by their owners. You must leave. Sheila has found the body."

"Do we continue messing with the troops, or find someone of importance to kidnap?" Montran asked.

Maud looked at her with a familiar expression of disbelief.

"This time, I'll use my stunner first," Montran said, embarrassed. "I was surprised. If we kidnap people, we'll eliminate them from returning. Surely you have a prison on this planet."

"You were going to kidnap Lord Chaney when his bodyguard was on the same planet?" Maud asked. "You don't believe in stirring a pot the easy way, do you?"

"I didn't know it was him. He wasn't the image Guardian gave me."

"Lord Chaney likes to have a different persona, including facial and hair changes, when he's with his smugglers. The man thought he was clever with his disguises," Maud said. "Are you feeling ready to move?"

"Right." Montran tested her legs, but they were still wobbly.

"We have to move on with Guardian's plan and head to the broadcast area. Kidnapping will have to be put off for a bit. If we run them off, maybe we won't need to imprison anyone. We have fifteen stan minutes before the storm moves out and then a two-hour window before the next one. The Second Skin will assist your recovery."

They went down a flight of stairs to the other side of the small area occupied by the troops and smugglers. Montran's weakness quickly left her. She dismantled T&Ts as they moved along the corridor, removing some to take with her and place elsewhere. That should disturb both sides further, though she thought Chaney's death would be hard to surpass. The majority of traps were attached to concussion bombs. When they went off, they would not harm the life support lines, but they would knock anyone near them to the ground. Some traps contained poisonous gas canisters, which Montran, in keeping with Guardian's beliefs, removed and dumped into trash bins for him to neutralize.

Eventually, they reached the room where prisoners were being held until they could be auctioned off by the smugglers. Montran deactivated the T&Ts there, but left them in place so that Maud's escape route wouldn't be noticed by a guard making spot inspections.

The women moved back up the corridor, out of sight of the target room.

"Any sign of Sheila, Guardian?" Montran asked worriedly.

"No. She's avoiding the monitors."

Montran and Maud stepped into a corridor on the other side of the Command Center, just around the corner from the room where the screening of the auctioned goods was being held.

"The auction broadcast has been going well so far," Guardian said softly. "However, soon they are going to get a message that their broadcast has been sent to a public station. It has been ten stan minutes since the feed has been moving to the various satellites. Public calls to the broadcast stations should be starting."

The swish of a door opening and the sound of boots running told them that the relaying for the video was being delivered topside, to be transmitted to the ship above, which would then beam it to those dialed into the auction, and, thanks to Guardian, to other citizens of the multiverse.

"It's time for me to move the captives, so your job is to create a diversion here," Maud whispered.

"Right."

Maud laid the few captured traps she was carrying on the floor near Montran's feet and returned to the service tunnel.

Montran began setting her own T&Ts. When the first went off, it would detonate the others, and the concussion would knock everyone out. After a quick glance to see that the placements were right, she moved behind a corner to wait. The hair on the back of her arms stood up, and her pulse became more rapid. Had something gone wrong? "Are we ready?" she asked, speaking softly into her mic.

"We certainly are." Sheila's throaty voice came from behind her.

Montran rolled out of the way just as something shiny slashed down where she had been standing. It pinged as it hit the wall. She lifted her foot to knock Sheila off balance, but Sheila threw a kick that knocked Montran's leg aside. Montran whirled to the ground and entangled Sheila's legs with her own. They rolled apart and bounced to their feet. Each looked for a weak point in the other's stance.

Sheila jumped forward and expertly pinned Montran against the wall. She shifted her weight to whip Montran's feet from under her. Montran expected it and pushed her back. Sheila's foot entangled with Montran's, and Sheila went down.

Back on her feet, she tried to pull Montran off hers. Montran broke her grip and knocked Sheila to the ground.

A band of smugglers came around the corner. One pulled out his weapon and took aim. Montran spotted him and gave Sheila an advantage in their grip so that she would be between her and his aim.

"Blasters! Get the metradame out of the way," he bellowed, dropping his arm to gesture to one of the smugglers behind him.

The others would have done something, but Sheila paused in her struggle to take stock of the situation, which gave Montran a chance to break free and activate two of the concussion bombs. It would only be a matter of time before the whole hall was shaking.

The first bomb went off and knocked everyone to their knees. Sheila, standing in front of Montran, took most of the shock. Both of them bounced against the wall. The second bomb banged Montran's head against the wall, but her helmet automatically activated and absorbed most of the impact. Stumbling over to the service panel, she got into a tunnel before the other bombs went off.

"Guardian?"

"You can return to base," Guardian said. "Lord Chaney's body has been discovered by the smugglers. And now, with their auction broadcast busted by its transmission to the whole galaxy, they are in full evacuation. You have no need to risk yourself there. We will wait and see what develops. I hope to have my outpost back soon."

"Right. Umm... how do I summon my ride?" Montran asked as she jogged along the tunnel.

"Simply call for it."

Montran felt a little embarrassed. "As in, 'Here, car'?"

"It is that simple," Guardian replied.

Montran stopped jogging and turned to look over her shoulder. Was that a sound her helmet's amplified hearing picked up? Not taking any chances, she exited the service panel, sprinted along a corridor until she came to an elevator, and then accessed another service tunnel. As she dropped down a level, she was hit from behind. The impact slammed her against the wall. Sheila lifted her easily and threw Montran into an exit door, knocking her out of the service tunnel and into a corridor.

Unharmed, Montran rolled under Sheila's feet, entwined their legs and pulled her assailant to the ground. Both then bounced back to their feet. Getting a good handhold, Montran banged Sheila's head against the wall and moved away. Sheila came back on the offensive, but Montran knocked her off her feet again. Montran escaped through the ceiling panel and back up the ladder. The first chance she got, she dropped down a level to get to the travel tube.

The third time, Sheila didn't take her unawares. They battled in the small confines of the tunnel, their grunts echoing along the passageway. Sheila suddenly changed tactics and surprised Montran with a punch to the head. The force of it drove her into the wall, and the service panel door behind her opened, depositing Montran in the middle of a dark area.

Sheila pinned Montran down, and with a blade in one hand, used the other to lean her weight on Montran's helmet and deactivate it.

Montran saw the short sword and brought her knee up into Sheila's back. They rolled on the ground, each trying to gain control. Sheila struck Montran in the head with the hilt of the sword. Stunned, Montran's grip on Sheila's wrist loosened. She panicked as the knifepoint flashed at her. Then the Second Skin kicked in, flooding her system with adrenaline, and her eyes cleared. She had a larger than life view of Sheila raising the sword.

Suddenly, Sheila's weight was knocked off her.

Struggling to her feet, Montran swayed for a moment. Maud and Sheila were locked in rolling combat. Montran yanked out the deactivator card and held the button down. All motion from Sheila stopped.

Maud gently pushed Sheila to the side. "Please, Commander Montran. Shut that off." Maud covered her ears.

"Oh." Montran's fingertips were white from her tight pinch on the card. She sank to her knees, taking the opportunity to catch her breath. "The cavalry arrived just in time."

"You can now reset her permanently," Maud said.

"How sure are we this is going to do anything?"

"It won't if you waste time asking questions, Commander."

Reluctantly, Montran moved over to the metradame's prostrate form and held the device near her forehead. A shiver ran up her arms as Sheila's darkened eyes locked onto hers. With shaking hands, Montran pressed the reset. A flash of pain crossed Sheila's face before her eyes closed. Montran looked guiltily at Maud.

"Do you have the unicorn ring?" Maud asked.

"The what ring?"

"The horse with the horn in its head."

"Yes." Montran fished it out of her utility belt pocket.

"This is her homing device to you."

"Wait a minute here. Are you telling me that she was able to find me because of this ring?"

"Yes."

"She's been locating me because of this?"

"Yes." Maud took the ring from her palm, turned Montran's hand over, and slid it on her finger. "You must wear it so she remains near you. It's for her safety, until she knows how to manage on her own."

Montran flexed her fingers at the unaccustomed feeling of wearing a ring. "Why didn't you tell me?"

"Guardian made the observation during her pursuit of you. She was finding you too easily. He narrowed it down to the ring. When she awakens, she is yours to program, rename, and command."

"I don't want a robot. I..." Images from the sexual haze that Sheila had left her in flooded all her senses, as though she were back in the moment.

Maud grabbed Montran's arms and shook her. "Commander Montran, that was a joke. Seriously, you both need to get out of this part of the city. Guardian wants to flood the area with sleeping gas and clean up some of the debris the intruders left, and I have

Guardian's guests to tend to. These feelings will wear off," she added in a softer voice.

Montran nodded. "How long is she going to be like this?"

"We don't know. Call your car and I'll help you put her in it."

"Car," Montran called hesitantly.

The car rolled to a stop by their waiting figures. Montran stepped in first and turned to Maud, who passed her Sheila's unconscious form. They settled the metradame's limp body in the seat and secured her with the harness. Glad of the chance to rest, Montran sat across from Sheila, secured by her own harness.

"Until we meet again, Commander Montran," Maud whispered into her communicator. "Best activate your helmet. One of you needs to be protected should the car be attacked."

"Right. Until we meet again, Maud. Seeing as we have so much in common, I think we should be on a first name basis, don't you? And, thank you."

"You're welcome, Harriet."

The car moved quickly out of the area, and the increase in speed pushed Montran into her seat. She hoped there would be food, drink, and rest at the other end. Suddenly a small screen appeared in the left corner of her visor.

"I hope you do not mind," Guardian said, "but I would like to monitor Sheila's bios."

"No, not at all. I should have done that myself. Guardian, can the blend feature work when I'm off this planet?"

"No. The suit mimics matter that can be found on this planet. It affects many species' visual sight, and all monitoring mechanisms I've tested so far, by altering the vibration of the object I wish to hide. What gives me pause is its potential for misuse. That is something about which I wish to confer with others."

"Sharon once told me that even if we think we are the sole creators of something, in reality, others were thinking of it at the same time. So maybe your idea could already be hitting the galactic patent office, wrapped up in another company's logo."

"It is already registered. Or, the beginnings of what is now completed are. And as a scientist, I also believe that others might have the same concept. With the search abilities my computers offer, I can follow any ideas that are recorded by anyone in known space. There are about forty-four companies in GCFC space alone that are working on such a suit, but none of them has a finished product."

Montran leaned back in the restraints. “Well, you’re right about the corrupt getting a grab on it. If the GCFC hears of it and decides it’s worth something to its security, your patent will be classified security-sensitive and you won’t be able to sell it on the open market.”

“That is why my laboratory is in neutral space. They will learn about the helmet only when I release it. Scientists may attempt to mimic it, but they will not be able to have a fully functioning version without my full cooperation.”

“You sound like you have your interests covered. Good for you.”

Sitting in the darkened car, Montran continued to watch Sheila and read her energy level through the visor. Gradually, her eyes slid shut.

Before long, an abrupt change in speed and a sharp intake of breath from Sheila brought Montran out of her nap.

“Welcome home, Commander Montran, and a welcome to your companion.” Guardian’s voice came over the speakers in the car. “Commander, I have a friend of yours in the infirmary who needs to be taken to her quarters. Would you mind escorting her and seeing that she is settled? Charles is busy with something else, and I think when she awakens she would feel more comfortable in her quarters than alone in an infirmary.”

“A friend of mine? What’s wrong with her?”

“Jina Gari, but you remember her as Cadet Zohra. She is surfacing.”

The car came to a sudden halt, much like her thoughts.

Cadet Zohra? Images of a young athlete came to mind, overlapping images of a dancer.

“The car was not meant for riding in without a Second Skin,” Guardian said quietly in Montran’s ear. “Your companion will need a few moments to recover. She will need your close support and supervision until we know more about her.”

Montran brought herself back to the present. She studied the readings on Sheila’s bios then retracted her helmet. “No, I don’t think leaving her alone would be a good idea. You’re sure she’s no threat to me?”

“It depends on what you call a threat. Whatever chemical effect she had on you is not so pronounced now. Just a bit of the afterglow, so to speak.”

“If ever I see someone in heat, I’ll know exactly how they feel and how helpless they are to control it.”

“Well then, something good did come out of your encounter.”

“I can think of other things I would rather encounter in order to learn empathy.”

The lights in the tube station were on when the car door swung open. After the restraints lifted, Montran took a minute to remove her gloves. Sheila stirred slowly, eyelids fluttering and breath shallow. Montran tried to remember how she felt on her first shuttle drop. Collecting herself, she exited the car and turned to see if Sheila had followed. She had not.

Montran leaned in and held out her hand to Sheila. “Need some help?” she asked quietly. Sheila took it without hesitating and climbed out of the car. A slight tremor passed through their hands as they made contact. Montran gripped the hand harder, feeling a firm squeeze returned. Her heart beat faster and her thoughts moved to heated bedroom scenes. She was startled by the intense feelings and embarrassed by her distraction.

The visible change from dangerous seductress to demure stranger confused Montran. How was she going to handle the effect Sheila’s presence was having on her senses and mental processes? She struggled to think of something that would change her mood.

Sheila stepped away from Montran and waited quietly.

Of course—focus on picking up Zohra. “Map to infirmary,” Montran said. She studied the diagram then headed toward the marked exit, acutely aware that Sheila was following. Their footsteps echoed softly in the corridor.

“Infirmary,” Montran said. Standing in the close confines of the elevator, Montran felt her skin pebble as though Sheila’s fingers were dragging along her arm.

The elevator opened into a well-lit corridor that lacked any art or other signs to indicate where they were. As she stepped into the hall, Montran could smell the difference from the level where she was quartered. A distinct lemon scent filled the air.

The walls were transparent, but without any interior lights, they couldn’t see beyond their own reflections. Montran’s focus heightened. She had someone to meet. Cadet Zohra… Sergeant Major Jina Gari. Memories of the intimate clothing in the sergeant major’s drawer didn’t help her maintain a professional attitude. Of late, it seemed that nothing was helping.

The infirmary was at the end of the corridor, and the double doors opened silently. Once Montran’s eyes had adjusted to the low lighting, she easily located the gurney.

The unconscious woman's face looked grim. There was a bruise on her forehead and an old scar along her chin.

Cadet Zohra. She didn't look anything like Montran remembered her. Aside from her battle scars, the discoloring on her eyelids and lips indicated she had recently experienced bad air. A dip in the hot tub with Ald's remedies would take care of that.

Suddenly, she remembered the vial in her utility belt pocket.

"Guardian, I need this analyzed."

A robot standing in a dim corner became active. Montran placed the small vial in its outstretched hand, and the bot sped away.

She studied Zohra's unconscious figure, not sure what bothered her most about this moment. Was it the changed appearance of someone whose image had carried her through dark times? Maybe it was the circumstance they were now in. Or was it just that the metradame was driving her body crazy with desire and she kept picturing the intimate clothing in Zohra's drawer?

No. It was something else. Something about the energy around Zohra.

The off balance feeling disconcerted her. She was a soldier, with many combat missions behind her, so she should be able to shrug it off. But she couldn't, not right now. Maybe if she had a name for it.

"Are you all right, Commander Montran?" Guardian asked.

"I'm just surprised. She's changed. From a cadet to a sergeant major in the Black Rose… is there a story here?"

"She is an operative for Naboth's Vine. She has been undercover for about nine years. That part of her duty is complete. Her orders are that she can now resurface as herself," Guardian said.

"I see. Nine years is a long time." She pursed her lips. "When she regains consciousness, will she remember whose side she's on?" *Will she remember me?*

"She has been debriefed. She will remain unconscious for another eight stan hours, however, to let her process her debriefing subliminals."

"Where will she be quartered?" Montran asked lightly, her tone belying her anxiety.

"She will be staying in the room adjacent to yours. Since I have not yet received word on when reinforcements will arrive, I will be relying on the two of you for your military expertise. It will also give the two of you a chance to get reacquainted. Major General Aglauros will be happy to hear that she is safe and is not alone."

"*The* General Aglauros? I've heard of her. Have you met her?"

"We are on a passing-packets-of-information basis," Guardian said, sounding pleased that his status in his guest's eyes had apparently risen.

"In Collective space, her reputation as a warrior adept is frequently mentioned. As with all rumors, I've wondered how much is true. But Guardian, about Zohra and her membership in the Black Rose. Few soldiers survive long enough to retire from that squad, and those that do, limp though the rest of their lives. I don't mean just physically."

"That is true of all soldiers who have experienced combat situations. It was not intended for her to be undercover for so long. She elected to stay, to see her assignment through to the end."

From what I know of you, Cadet Zohra, it would be in your nature to stick it out to the end of a game. I just worry what kind of mental scars you'll be carrying. Will the psych techs arrive in time to spot potential problems? And what then, my Dancer? After so long, will I lose you to something neither of us can fix?

Montran looked along the sides of the gurney for some kind of a control.

"Mistress, may I help?"

Montran jumped at the unexpected voice above her. Turning to face its origin, she found her face so close to Sheila's that she could feel her warm breath. Blood pounded in her ears, and her hands were shaking from the sexual rush.

Nervously she moved to the other side of the gurney, and the intensity of the feelings lessened. Her heart began to slow down, and the hot flush that had surely reddened her face diminished.

"I'm looking for the controls for the gurney," she mumbled awkwardly as she went back to her search, not yet focused on anything other than the receding heat in her face.

"It is already programmed for her quarters. You only need to follow it," Guardian said.

"Okay."

The two women accompanied the hovering gurney as it exited the infirmary and headed in the direction of the elevator. Montran found the elevator ride bearable, since the energy field with which the gurney surrounded its passenger also separated her from Sheila.

"Guardian, is there anything I need to worry about?"

"No. The appropriate people have been notified in Collective and GCFC space, and the smugglers have vacated the premises. We have a dozen unwanted visitors with two ships still above. I am curious why the delay for the last group."

"I hope they're not mining your city."

"They are not bringing anything down. I will keep you apprised."

"Any word from my CO?"

"No, I have not received any further messages from Admiral JoCastao."

The gurney passed Montran's quarters, and the door to the next room slid open. The artwork, noticeably different, had sports as its theme.

"Okay, we need to transfer her to the bed," Montran said. Sheila moved in front of Montran and lifted Zohra from the gurney to the bed without any assistance. The gurney left, and the room butler was there to take the discarded clothing from the two women as they undressed her. In the low lighting, Montran studied the scars scattered on the lean, tattooed body. Zohra was lucky to be alive. One scar was recent, and still pink.

"Let's get her into the shower."

Effortlessly, Sheila lifted Zohra again and placed her on the shower seat. Both women stepped back as Ald moved forward to take over the business of cleaning.

The Spartan reminded Montran of a veteran gladiator, not a triathlete whose galaxy record for most consistent high scorer still stood and whose cadet ranking was outstanding.

No one would recognize her now. I wonder if her career path was chosen with that in mind.

Who was that femme fatale that was hanging on her at the academy? Will she return to her? Nine years is a long time to wait for someone.

Right, Harriet. So why have you?

She took a deep breath at the realization that although she had fallen in love with Sharon, she would have had serious doubts about the relationship if Zohra had reappeared in her life before now.

"Are these scars tribal or culturally desired?" Ald asked.

"They are not desired." Battle scars were part of the Black Rose persona, certainly something the surfacing agent needed to leave behind her.

After Zohra was cleaned, Ald applied a purple gel that soaked quickly into the scarred areas. The scars began to fade as the gel disappeared. Ald moved back, and a soft light glowed around Zohra's body, accelerating the healing of the scars.

Sheila returned Zohra to her bed, and Montran pulled the covers over her and leaned close to her ear. "Sweet dreams, Dancer."

Deep inside her, a need awakened—a profound ache to connect—then its intensity lessened, settling to a dull throb.

"My… our quarters are this way." Montran motioned to Sheila. She felt exhausted. Sheila would have to be dealt with tomorrow. The door to her sleeping area opened at their approach.

She led the way to the kitchenette. "Do you... are you hungry?"

"Yes, Mistress."

Montran felt her face turning bright red. Heat rushed through her body. Maud's "once bitten" comment ran through her mind. Swallowing a few times with a dry mouth made her long for a nice cold drink that would knock her out, but she really couldn't afford that right now. She took time to collect herself. "Do you have a food preference?" she finally asked.

"No, Mistress."

Montran turned to Bach. *Mistress.* She took a few breaths and found the heat lessening. "Two light meals, Bach," she said. Since the bot had chosen her morning meal with such accuracy, she expected it would be as proficient now.

"Would either of you care for a beverage?" Bach asked.

Sheila was silent.

"I would like something that's good for sleep. How about you, Sheila?"

Sheila surprised her by asking Bach for a list of beverages. Her choice ended up being the same one Bach selected for Montran. There was a brief silence while Bach busied itself.

"I'm going to take a shower. Have a look around," Montran said. She plopped down in the chair in the bedroom and attempted to pull off her boots, giving up when the butler offered assistance. Her clothes were taken from her, pockets emptied, and her Second Skin went into its own drawer. A soft blue light came on as the drawer closed. In the shower, her tired thoughts circled around the subject of Sheila. Though Montran's lust wasn't as intense as it had been during their first encounter, she still wondered how she was going to be able to look at Sheila and not feel like an animal in rutting season. It was embarrassing. She nearly banged her head on the tiled wall in exasperation.

Ald had a towel and robe ready for her as she stepped out. "Can you run the tub and add something for bruises, Ald? I'll take a soak after I eat."

"My very recommendation for you both, Commander Montran," he said, breaking her train of thought.

Both of them in the tub at the same time? *Oh, great.*

Back in the bedroom, she sat with her robe tucked around her, trying to concentrate what to do for sleeping arrangements. Keeping an eye on Sheila meant they had to sleep in the same area.

She awoke to a touch on her shoulder.

"Your meal is ready, Mistress. Though your bios say you are tired, you do need nourishment."

Montran blinked a few times, letting the image of the metradame become clearer. Still weary, she stumbled to her feet. There was only one plate of food on the table. "Did you eat already?"

"No, Mistress. I will eat when you have finished."

"Unless you prefer not to, I don't mind you joining me for meals." Sheila's appearance showed she had been in a fight. Embarrassed at not having noticed it before, Montran dropped tiredly into her seat.

Bach brought a plate for Sheila, placed a steaming cup of lemon tea before each woman, and then stepped back. Montran chewed her food thoughtfully, glancing across the table now and then. "Do you have a name you would like to be addressed with?"

"Whatever pleases you, Mistress."

"You aren't my slave or servant. You're my equal, under my protection." Montran picked her words with care. "You may choose a name for yourself. I advise you not to use Sheila until you're fully your own person, because there might be some who would like to see you as theirs and try to take advantage of your…" She paused, trying to find a word that didn't refer to the metradame as mindless.

Staring into her eyes, Montran was frightened for her. Sheila showed no sign of interest or thought.

"…take advantage of your present situation," she said, finally.

"I don't know of any name."

"Give it some thought. You're free to speak and to share ideas and to go where you wish, although Guardian does have rules, since this is his outpost."

Green eyes that gave away nothing blinked at her, and Sheila nodded politely. Montran felt she had made progress when Sheila didn't reply with "Yes, Mistress."

Montran finished her meal quickly. As she rose, she waved Sheila back into her seat. "Please, eat your meal at your own pace.

I'm going to soak a bit and then go to bed. All the facilities are at your disposal, so if you need a shower or soak before you go to bed, you know where the bathing facilities are. We can share the bed until... until we work out something else. That is, if you don't mind."

"Thank you, Mistress."

A flush rose to Montran's cheeks and then quickly heated other areas. Sheila might have simply been eating her dinner and looking up at her for a brief moment, but to Montran, there was a seductive tilt to her head, an inviting smile curving the sensuous mouth, and eyes… green as the ocean on Emery.

"Until the butler gets you some clothing of your own, we can share what's in the closet." Montran forced herself to breathe normally. "Maybe we can get over to Century City later and pick up your belongings." She couldn't think of anything else to say.

The smell of the herb bath lured her to it, and she continued into the bathing room. Grateful for the distraction, she slid into the hot water.

She leaned her head back comfortably on the tub's padded rim and listened to the soothing music while bubbling waters massaged her bruised body. A few minutes later, she groaned as she heard the shower running. Images of how the water must look pouring over Sheila's body were vivid and thrilling. She wished her mind would shut off.

The shower ended. Moments later, a throaty voice asked, "May I join you, Mistress?"

"Yes," she whispered, her voice husky with desire.

The water shifted as Sheila slid in.

Montran took a shaky breath and then continued, not recognizing her own voice. "Do you remember…?"

"Yes, Mistress. Everything."

"Ah, umm..."

"Does your shoulder hurt, Mistress?"

Montran nodded.

Sheila's hands rested firmly on Montran's shoulders, guiding her to turn around, facing away from her. Skilled hands kneaded her sore shoulders, working out one sort of tension and replacing it with another. A groan nearly escaped Montran's lips as the fingers worked their unhurried way down to the small of her back, sending small electrical charges up and down her spine.

She was definitely aroused. Did she have the energy to rise to the occasion? Sheila said she remembered everything. What if she strangled her in the middle of…?

Sheila's hands slid in a slow arc from her back around to her breasts, cupping the soft, white mounds. Montran moaned loudly, surrendering to the throbbing need.

After a long time had passed, which the two women spent discovering each other's pleasure points, Sheila picked up Montran and carried her into their shared sleeping quarters.

Sheila's husky voice whispered her desire in Montran's ear, and Montran hummed her approval as she latched her lips onto Sheila's neck. Sheila deposited the dripping woman on the bed, straddling her to sit comfortably on her stomach.

"Romantic mood. The forests of Ameick. Summer. Warm breeze," Montran whispered.

As Sheila leaned down to capture her parted lips, beams of light filtering through the giant redwoods gave her a breathtaking backdrop. Birds chirped, squirrels chattered, and leaves rustled in the slight summer breeze that swept over them. Two pairs of lips met hungrily.

The last thing Montran remembered was Sheila massaging her foot, which had cramped in the midst of their passion.

Sometime during the night, Montran awoke and stumbled, half asleep, to the toilet. A small light lit the way. When she made her way back to bed, Sheila was holding the covers open for her. Gratefully, Montran snuggled up against Sheila, her skin tingling at the contact.

"I would like the name Carol, Mistress," Sheila whispered in her ear.

"Carol," Montran repeated sleepily. "That's a nice name."

Chapter 8

Heavy cumulus clouds gathered overhead. As she strained to see into the darkness that rushed in their direction, the atmosphere changed. Small sparks flew as her younger brother stepped forward.

"Don't move!" their father warned.

Their guide had told them that it could happen, but probably wouldn't today; the sun was too bright. But it was happening. Electromagnetic pulses set off by their body movements, together with changes in the atmosphere, would set off small flashes that could incinerate them. Would the dark funnel also appear and pull them up into its whirling center?

"There, to the left!" Nanny called out.

The funnel moved quickly toward them, pushing dark clouds before it. But the clouds were a mixed blessing, for suddenly large drops of water showered on their unprotected heads. The water washed away the potential for the reaction their off-world bodies had formed with this electromagnetic storm.

By the time the sky was clear and the warm sun was upon them once more, they were soaked to the skin, cold, and experiencing mixed emotions about their new home. Their species naturally became partners with a planet's spirit. Could they find a peaceful coexistence with the spirit of this wild planet?

In her sleep, Carol shuddered at the memory. She felt the comforting arm around her body tighten reflexively at her cringing movement.

* * *

Cadet Montran was tired, yet too twitchy to sleep. A glance at her roommates told her they were deeply asleep. Not wanting to wake them with her restless pacing, she gave in to the pressing need to take a walk in the moonless night. She kept to the well-worn path, so as not to come upon anyone by surprise. As she neared the edge of the forest, she could sense another's presence. It felt as though she were expected. Curious, she moved farther into the trees that surrounded the glen.

She spied the form of a woman nearly hidden in the shadows of the trees. Montran knew intuitively that she had sensed this woman's presence. Instinctively, she reached for her, reveling in the warmth of the connection and excited by the unfamiliar, sensuous passion that lay just below the surface of their contact.

She was waiting for her. Why?

The woman started to dance. It was familiar... something from Montran's childhood, its meaning forgotten. She took a deep, slow breath, realizing that although it was pitch dark everywhere, she could see the Dancer clearly.

Gracefully, the Dancer moved from one step to the next, her hands tapering to fingers that gently curved into recognized mudras. As the dance progressed, the intensity of the energy within Montran heightened, taking her by surprise. An ethereal part of her separated from her physical form and merged with the Dancer, breathing the same air, and feeling muscles strain as though they were her own. The image of a dragon appeared in her mind.

The sacred Dragon Dance. The ritual that binds lovers through sexual energy. But... they weren't lovers.

Cadet Montran could feel the weight of the braided hair behind her head and the cold air that filled her lungs. She heard the leaves high above them rustling in the breeze. Time and awareness blurred as the Dancers moved in the energy of the Dance.

The Dancers called upon their energy reserves for the most difficult move, the flying stag. They rose to an impossible height, suspended under the twinkling stars, arms raised like antlers, fingers fanned out, touching a pair of stars, and then finally, as the Dancers dropped back to the ground, the powerful surge of sexual energy that shot through Montran loosened her concentration. She was not able to sustain it, and not knowing what to do, she felt their connection break. Her body vibrated with such force, it shook her composure. Her yoni strummed to the silent scream of release. She weakly gripped the tree against which she had collapsed, looking for the support and strength her legs lacked.

Montran's body continued to vibrate strongly as the blood pounded in her veins and ears in the aftermath, leaving her too weak to respond to the pull to go out to her Dancer. While she waited for her legs to stop trembling, she tried to sort through the barrage of emotions. She was feeling a mixture of shame and excitement, wonder at what it all meant, and fear of its implications.

After that night, each time the twin moons hid their faces on the other side of the planet, she could feel the pounding energy in her yoni, demanding sweet release at the hands of her Dancer. Uncertain, she resisted the pull. She wanted to know more of whom she had shared this sexual connection with, and what it meant.

Just before summer break, she put a name to her Dancer. As she was relaxing with a group of friends at an off-campus tavern, Montran glanced up at the new crowd of cadets that had entered the hall. One of her friends explained that the other popular alehouse had closed for two days. The bantering and noise in the room were louder than usual, and she began feeling twitchy. Her face flushed, for no apparent reason. Her gaze was drawn to the other side of the room. Noises around her became muted as dark, intriguing eyes captured hers. Shivers cascaded down her spine. Time stopped in the moment of mutual recognition.

Someone leaned over and whispered the name of the woman who had captured her attention.

Merely saying the name to herself inflamed her desires. Images of the woman as an athlete in televised Galactic competitions, which were her life before she enrolled in the academy, replayed in Montran's dreams. They had met as young women in a shrine of Aphrodite on a distant planet. She had just started her menses, and was placing the traditional offering at the altar. The only memorable thing about the occasion was the erotic dream she had that night, of the young athlete. At the time, she had attributed it to a rush of hormones. Now, she knew it was because she had witnessed the Dragon's Dance the night before, in her dreams. Who had called whom for the first dance of A Shunja, the Dance of Invitation?

Turning restlessly in her sleep, Montran felt someone next to her shift to accommodate her movement.

The next dream started in an entirely different vein.

A recently promoted captain stood in front of her new squad and wondered what she had gotten herself into.

The Degas squad was composed of the military's rejects, and they all knew it. She had been given only two stan weeks to become familiar with them. That should have told her something was amiss, either about the squad, or her assignment to them. She had no previous combat experience, and they were to be dropped right behind the enemy lines.

* * *

In the morning, Montran woke to find herself pressed against Carol, holding onto her as though for comfort. She had one hand draped across Carol's hip, her fingers dangling near the soft pubic hair. She sensed that Carol was already awake, and with her own senses awakened, also came the sexual haze that encouraged her to push closer into the warm body.

"Good morning," she whispered, sliding her hand down Carol's thigh. Her fingers trembled in yearning as the soft skin pebbled under her fingertips.

Carol turned in Montran's arms, their faces close, her eyes dark in the dim light. A smile brought up the corners of her lips. She picked up Montran's warm fingers and began kissing them, one at a time. By the time she got to the third one, Montran's body was quivering with anticipation. She could recall feeling no desire this strong or urgent as she threw back the covers and straddled the equally aroused Carol. Once more, they willingly gave in to the sexual heat of their passions. An hour later, exhausted, Montran rolled to her side and pulled Carol into her arms.

"Carol?"

"Yes, Mistress?"

The sultry voice was driving her crazy. "How much of… this… is from the effects of… of our first meeting?"

"All of it."

"But you're reacting as if it means something to you."

"It does, Mistress. I'm affected by you as much as you are by me."

"Does it wear off?"

"Yes, Mistress."

Montran was quiet for a while. "Do you mind me being with you like this?" She studied Carol's face, fearful of her answer.

"You have been kind enough to return the pleasure. In the past, it was for the amusement of others, with my own satisfaction of no consequence to me or them."

Montran felt a mixture of emotions. "So, we just…" She couldn't finish the sentence.

"We just continue until it wears off," Carol said. "Is it bothering you, Mistress?"

Montran laughed, embarrassed. “No. I just hope I can survive. How long does it last?”

“I’m not sure about the duration, Mistress. For some it’s longer than for others.”

There were so many personal questions Montran wanted to ask her, now that the intensity of passion had abated somewhat. Instead, she silently enjoyed the warm body that pressed against her and the fingers that made gentle circles on her back.

A soft ding sounded.

“Good morning,” Guardian said. “I hope I am not disturbing you, but Major Zohra has been up for over three stan hours and is restless to get to work. I thought it would be good for all of us to get together first.”

“Good morning, Guardian,” Montran said. “Major, is it?”

“Within her Shield House and Naboth’s Vine, that is her rank.”

“What is happening that Major Zohra would like to get to work on?”

“There is no GCFC, to speak of. The Council of Rings has suspended the authority of all members until an official investigation of the slave trade, and which members were involved in it, has been concluded. The biggest worry is Alan Fermin. The new GCFC, once formed, will banish Alan to the Hinterwield Prison Colony without hesitation. He knows this and will do something to strike back. What that is and where it will occur is not certain. Knowing Alan Fermin, there will be multiple situations and there will be violence.”

Montran shook her head in consternation. “It’s curious that his father, with all his fortune, couldn’t control Alan. Gustaf had to know that his son’s heinous behavior would act against his own petition for a seat on the GCFC.”

“Mistress, it is while he is in this madness that he contributes to his father’s fortunes.”

“How?” Montran asked, surprised.

“Alan has the ability to read patterns in little sticks he throws. He can only see the patterns when he is not taking his medication. By reading these patterns, he is able to predict with great accuracy winning and losing business deals, and who is friend or foe. He has done this for Lord Chaney, too,” Carol explained.

“That is something to consider,” Guardian said. “It could be one reason why he has always been a step ahead of the authorities in their investigations.”

Montran glanced at Carol. “Let’s get dressed. We don’t want to keep the major waiting too long. Give us about a stan hour, Guardian. I intend to eat a hearty morning meal, since it may be my last for a while.”

* * *

Carol looked dubious as she studied the Second Skin the butler held up for her inspection. The bot patiently explained why she needed to wear it when she moved around on the planet. Montran muffled her laugh, wondering if that was the same expression she had worn when first introduced to the suit. Carol finally agreed to wear it when Montran told her to do so.

She left Carol to her dressing and went into the front room to order their breakfast. Carol joined her in a short time. Just as Montran was handing her emptied plate to Bach, they received their first visitor.

“It is Charles,” the familiar voice said.

“Enter.” Montran was curious at this unexpected visit.

“Good day, Lady Harriet and Ti Carol,” he greeted them pleasantly.

Regarding Charles’s brightly colored shape and all its appendages with obvious uncertainty, Carol moved quickly to her mistress’s side.

“Lady Harriet, Guardian has received a coded message for you from Lord Hadrian DeMonte. You will have to go to the Command Center to access it.” Charles turned to Carol. “I will need to take some bioreadings from you now that you have your Second Skin on. Metrapeople have their own bioregulators, and we need to make sure the blend is harmonious.” He adjusted his various appendages to different heights. Montran was almost as alarmed as Carol, until he started explaining what each appendage would measure.

“Well, that sounds okay to me. What about you, Carol?” Montran asked, adding, “It’s really great that you get your own AEG. There’s no telling if we’ll end up in hostile territory.” She had also been wondering how she was going to ask Guardian questions about Carol if she was always with her. “The bioreading shouldn’t take too long, with all those arms working on it. You can join me in Com-C when Charles is finished.”

Carol’s eyes revealed her displeasure at her mistress’s decision.

Montran walked quickly to Com-C, eager to see what message was waiting for her. The door swished open as she neared it. The dais was lit up with an interesting holographic image of Guardian's version of himself as a middle-aged Copoc.

"Nice outfit, Guardian. You're certainly coming out in style. You said Hadrie sent me a message?"

"Yes. It is but one word."

"One word?" she said.

"Mem."

"It has no meaning to me either. If it's in code, he's going to have to send me a deciphering ring."

Montran's senses picked up someone else's presence. She glanced around, settling on a shadow seated in the darkened conference room.

"Permit me to introduce you to Major Delorita Jina Gari Zohra, from the Shield Maidens of Athena's House on Velta V. Major Zohra, this is—"

"Lieutenant Commander Montran," Montran quickly said, not wishing to hear her long clan name and title sandwiched in with her military rank. She nodded warily at the shadowed form.

The lights came up slowly, revealing an alert version of the figure she had tucked into bed the previous night. The major's long legs appeared to be stretched out before her, but Montran noted that they were not totally extended, giving her leverage if she should have to leap up suddenly. The scars and bruises were gone from her face. There was no indication of recognition or warmth.

"Good morning, Major Zohra."

The major nodded without changing her expression. Montran looked at Guardian in order to break the hold the dark eyes had on her. She knew the major was evaluating her and wondered what she used for measurement. Probably Black Rose standards. Montran wondered what Zohra remembered.

Major Zohra had been studying Lady Harriet Montran from the moment she entered Com-C. She took pleasure in Lady Harriet's natural self-assurance. Zohra was accustomed to brutish military swaggering or wary posturing, and she took a few moments to enjoy the difference. Lady Harriet looked strong, indicating she kept up with her field training, but Zohra already knew that from reviewing Guardian's recordings of her. For a moment, she thought of what it would be like to grapple with her, each testing the other's strengths and weaknesses.

One of the many lessons she had learned as a Black Rose was not to underestimate an individual's capabilities. She was looking forward to testing Lady Harriet's limits… and strengths.

Zohra felt a quickening as dark green eyes flashed with humor at the holograph of Guardian and full lips smiled, showing even white teeth.

Warmth. She was exuding warmth. Zohra suddenly frowned. Lady Harriet was showing too much trust that the room was secured. But Zohra's attention quickly returned to the change Lady Harriet's presence brought to the room.

Where was the energy coming from? Guardian was right. She had some kind of power, more than what Zohra remembered from when they were cadets. Was Lady Harriet aware of it? No. Otherwise she wouldn't let it shine everywhere. Shine? What kind of a description was that?

Zohra suspected that Lady Harriet's hesitation as she thought about the message Guardian had delivered was more than a pause for thought.

What was Lord Hadrian, one of the most important people in Naboth's Vine, informing Lady Harriet of? Was it something Zohra needed to inform the sisterhood about? She didn't think so. Lord Hadrian was not one to play his own game.

"I am sure you both remember each other from earlier days," Guardian said.

"Lady Harriet Montran." Zohra's voice was low and curt. "How are you doing?" she asked after a slight hesitation.

Now Montran had a voice for her Dancer. She nodded and then answered, "Well. And yourself?" She wondered if Zohra would answer.

She received a slight nod. Zohra had moved her hands to her lap, holding them in a classic mudra pose for centering. A blush tinged Montran's cheeks when she realized her eyes had rested too long on her hands.

"We have some issues to clear up before moving on," Guardian said. "The first one concerns you, Major Zohra. The JG personality you have lived for over nine stan years may be difficult to erase fully with only fifty-six stan hours of debriefing. Though JG has an impeccable war record, off-base she was abrasive, confrontational, and a nonconformist."

"I knew who I was during my undercover work. There will be no conflict involving personality adjustment. However, I wouldn't recommend any sudden surprises."

Was that a joke, or was she serious? Montran wondered, sitting down. "What about any operations we may have to undertake against the Spartans in the city, Major? Most notably against the Black Rose."

After a long, aloof stare at Montran, Zohra replied, "I think I can manage not to get you, or anyone else under my command, killed, provided you don't do anything rash. And you won't have to worry about the Black Rose, Lady Harriet," she said, her tone slightly mocking. "Guardian has them locked up tight until a neutral party arrives to pick them up for questioning."

Montran felt her face color noticeably. Guardian hadn't told her that. That was the second indication that this operation was under Zohra's leadership. The "Lady" bit was a damned good clue, too.

"That clears up quite a bit. The other thing is Carol," Guardian said. "You have some questions, Commander Montran?"

Montran hesitated as her thoughts shifted. How did he know she wanted to ask questions? For some reason, she felt uncomfortable talking about Carol in front of Zohra, but she was going to have to get it out now, before Carol walked in.

"Who was she before she became involved in all this, and what can be done to give her back her life?"

"I have been researching it with others," Guardian said. "We have agreed that we must know what type of personality we are about to let loose, especially with all the training she has received."

"Are you saying that Sheila, I mean Carol, was something—"

"Sheila? Lord Chaney's Sheila?" Zohra sat forward in her chair.

"Yes. Is there something you wish to contribute?" Guardian sounded surprised.

"Where is she now?"

"She's in my quarters," Montran said. "She'll be here shortly. She now goes by the name Carol."

Zohra glanced at the holograph and then at Lady Harriet, but refrained from asking for details. "I'll have to clear any information on her with my superiors."

"Unless you can give me a good reason not to, I'll proceed with my plans to encourage her to become self-determined," Montran informed them firmly. The challenging look she received from

Zohra made her add, “I won’t let anyone use her as a pawn in a political game—”

“You have no say in this matter, Lady Harriet,” Zohra interrupted curtly. “There’s too much at stake for uninformed meddling, no matter how well-intentioned.”

“Don’t give me the political yak crap or military dung about how one person or two or even a village is perfectly okay to sacrifice for the ‘greater good,’” Montran said. “I’ve been there, done that, and will not be a part of it again. And neither will Carol. This is neutral territory, and I won’t let you and your backers strong-arm her into your schemes.”

“Self-determined, you say? What if she agrees to be sacrificed?” Zohra said.

“No one is going to be sacrificed on my planet.” Guardian’s indignant voice interrupted Montran’s hard glare in Zohra’s direction. “That is *not* an option, Major. And since you know that, my guess is that you are testing Commander Montran.”

For a long moment, Zohra and Montran exchanged stares, neither gaze wavering.

Montran didn’t believe she was being tested. She could see that Zohra believed that, in the heat of the conversation, she had shared too much.

“Commander Montran, I noticed you like to work out,” Guardian said.

Montran glanced at the hologram. She wondered where he was going with this. Maybe he was offering Zohra a chance to beat the stuffing out of her.

“I have downloaded all known fighting techniques to date, with combatants from beginner to master levels, so that you will not be bored waiting for our reinforcements. Until the briefing in five stan hours, there is nothing planned. I am sure Major Zohra would like to keep up her skills, as well. Perhaps after she has been debriefed by her own command, she will join you.”

The door slid open. Charles and Carol entered.

Montran could sense Zohra’s interest shift to Carol. This was much to her relief, for she could feel her stomach tightening and her sex swelling at Carol’s proximity. Firmly collecting herself, she gave Carol a smile. “Carol, this is Guardian, who oversees Merker’s Outpost, and Major Zohra. Guardian, Carol. Major, Carol.” She hesitated, wondering if further introductions were needed, but then decided they weren’t. “Guardian says he has a dojo set up, with trainers at whatever level we can manage.”

She turned to Guardian. “Since you have no need of us for the moment, we’ll change into workout clothes and be in dojo.” Even to her own ears, her voice sounded distracted. She and Carol left.

Zohra had noted Lady Harriet’s flushed cheeks and sudden uncertainty when Carol entered the room. How the metradame had come to be known as Carol was something she intended to find out soon. Her eyes narrowed as she recalled the silent interplay between the two women, including the unfriendly stare she had received from Carol. Did Carol remember her as a member of the Black Rose? Just what did “neutralize” cover in Guardian’s vocabulary?

Obviously, they were intimately involved. Was that how Lady Harriet was going to give Sheila back her life? Part of her found it difficult to believe that Lady Harriet would stoop to something as low as that, and she concluded sourly that she should wait and see what was going on before making judgments.

Guardian chuckled.

“What’s so funny? And what happened to Lady Harriet?”

“Have you heard about the lust gas with which Sheila was equipped?”

Zohra’s eyes widened a little and she nodded, her lips forming an O. That did put the picture into a different light.

“Major, we need to discuss your prickly disposition,” Guardian said, interrupting her thoughts.

“Care to elaborate, Guardian?” She leaned back in her chair, wondering how this computer thought it was going to “handle” her.

* * *

Carol and Montran changed into proper workout clothing and had no problem finding the dojo. When the elevator doors opened, there was no mistaking where they were. The artwork was magnificent, including life-sized statues of sports celebrities in action. Montran paused at one mural that covered a door. A young girl waited pensively for her turn on the equestrian field. One hand held the looped reins of her tall horse while the other rested on the mare’s neck. Horse and rider appeared to be gauging the competition on the field as they waited. The girl was Zohra of Prime V, her Dancer, the year she became Galaxy Champion in the steeplechase—the first year she had competed with the adults.

“Either Guardian or the previous tenants must have been sporting types, though I’ve never known a scientist who was interested in athletics." The image of Sharon and the other scientists she had come to know rose to mind. Gambling on sports was the closest they came to participating.

Montran pushed through the double doors into the workout room.

"Okay," she said, glancing around, "I'm going to warm up with the holograph." She looked at Carol. "And then we'll spar and see who tosses in the towel first."

"Tosses in the towel?" Carol asked.

"Ask for mercy, call it quits, get beaten," she explained, grinning.

"I find it commendable that you warn me that you'll be 'throwing in the towel.'"

"We shall see about that."

It amused Montran that Carol could initiate a joke. It reminded her that she needed to do some research on metrapeople. Was humor an indication that she was becoming more self-aware? So far, Carol's behavior seemed far from mechanical, even when she had been Sheila and trying to kill her.

Montran settled into her warm-up. After thirty minutes, her holographic partner signaled the time she had set was reached. A dojo bot appeared with liquids and towels for both women.

"Are you ready to spar, Carol?" She felt ready to take on a few Black Rose troopers herself, at the moment. She bounced on the balls of her feet and shook out her arms.

"Yes, Mistress."

"I would like you to find all my weak spots and keep after them." Unbidden, the image of Carol biting her neck came to her. Maybe taking on a Black Rose would be better. Another image rose of Zohra, wearing one of the leather stringed outfits she'd found in her drawer. She quickly squelched it.

Montran moved into a ready position at the center of the room. For the next thirty minutes, Carol trounced her mistress, laying her out on the mat time and again.

Montran rubbed her sore hip, warily looking at her opponent as they slowly circled each other. At first, the distraction of touching Carol's body kept her off balance. Her skin still tingled from the last toss, when they had landed on the mat with limbs entangled, fighting for the top position. Muffled giggles and startled squawks at the intimate grabs had both of them breathing heavily.

Montran had rolled free and laughed a challenge at Carol.

Thump, bam.

"Oof."

Now Montran was back on her feet and in a defensive position, circling. Carol charged her, and Montran responded intuitively with a fake to the right. Finally having the advantage, she prepared an offensive. Just as she was ready to attack, she realized they had an audience, someone who had been in the room for a while. That momentary lapse of concentration allowed Carol to land a well-placed kick to her midsection. Montran flew a good distance and landed flat on her back. She lay still, recovering from having the wind knocked out of her. She looked up and saw two pairs of eyes staring down at her, both unconcerned.

* * *

"When will the effects wear off?" Zohra asked Guardian, as they observed the two women from monitors in Com-C.

"It has already started with Commander Montran, and by the end of the week, it should be completely out of her system."

"Rumors were that it never wears off."

"For those who do not have the antidote, that is true."

"How is Carol doing?"

"She is an unknown equation. Due to the chip that is still implanted, it is difficult to tell. Her bios are running along the same lines as Commander Montran's, given the species variation. From what I have observed during Lord Chaney's previous visits, he wanted his metrapeople to be more advanced than bots, so he allowed them more freedom of behavior than most owners do. Carol's humor and tastes in clothing are her own. That says a lot about the sophistication of the chip implants.

"I believe Commander Montran knows that you are in charge of protecting the outpost and its special assets," he added, "though I do not believe she knows all that is here. But it is only a matter of time. She is sensitive to the energy."

Zohra didn't smile, but amusement reached her eyes. "I don't think that's a problem, Guardian. I rule the land, and she gets the sky. So, you think she's sensitive, huh?"

Looking back at the screen, she nodded toward it. "Is there a safe distance at which they can work without being so distracted?"

"Skin contact has the strongest effect on them."

"I thought you said your Second Skin will protect the wearer against most physical harm?"

"Yes. The Second Skin protects against an attack to the wearer's system, but I hadn't anticipated anyone using a love potion. Pheromones are a natural part of the chemical reaction of lust and part of the natural prelude to sexual enjoyment. Also, they release other natural body chemicals that help heal and maintain the health of the host body. So, I left them alone." A deep chuckle followed that remark. "If satisfaction was not received, that would be another story."

A beep sounded. "A transmission. It is your major general," Guardian announced. "It appears she is in flight."

Zohra's face took on a softer look, changing her persona completely. She sat up as the official seal of the Sisters of the Shield quickly changed to display the image of her much-loved and missed general.

"Daughter!" General Aglauros greeted her lovingly.

"General Aglauros," she said formally and then smiled affectionately. "Mother." Zohra paused to treasure the moment. "It's been a long time since I've had the chance to say that." For the first time in years, she let the weariness of the job catch up with her.

Aglauros studied her daughter closely. "Are you well?"

Zohra nodded. "Just tired," she said.

"You have changed much," Aglauros said. "I was hoping that once we had Lady Harriet Montran safe, we'd be rid of this trouble and you could come home for a well-earned rest." Her expression hardened.

"Alan Fermin is our chief worry. From what our informants have told us, he plans to either take over Merker's Outpost or destroy it. Neither he nor his agents have been able to use the portal located on Merker's. Since the portal can reach Arnica, which is where he has sent over half of his army to set up his next home, we can only assume he wants to prevent anyone else from using it to go there."

She took a deep breath, looking worried. "His violent behavior is escalating. According to the psych techs, it will continue to do so. He's still obsessed with Lady Harriet, and unfortunately, as his acts of violence increase, so does his madness for her. Your assignment has two unfinished tasks: defend Merker's, and return Lady Harriet safely to her home base."

Zohra's stomach tightened.

"I'm sending four battalions," Aglauros continued. "Two are on *Moon's Reflection*, and the others on *Respite*. Healers will be coming through the portal within days, depending on whether the guardians feel it is safe to travel through it at this time. The ships are a little more than two days' jump from you, assuming they experience no delays. With GCFC reforming, thieves and smugglers think they can get away with attacking any ship without an escort, and every military vessel is working double time. Send daily updates to *Respite* so they know what they're heading into. You'll get updates from the Four Corners as soon as we have something for you. I shall be there as soon as I can. Be aware that Naboth's Vine has joined with the Collective's Centurion forces to keep order where necessary, until the new representatives of the GCFC are elected."

She gave a disgusted snort. "The members that aren't being replaced are already arguing that since a new group is being formed, the committee's name should be changed.

"Rear Admiral JoCastao is the Collective's delegate," Aglauros said. "I'm sure she'll be sending a representative of her own to the outpost, besides Lady Harriet. I will head the military forces to protect the portal side of the planet. The admiral and I are still getting acquainted and ironing out a plan."

Zohra smiled, but refrained from teasing her mother. What her mother meant was that she and Admiral JoCastao were in charge of setting up the planet's protection, and they were evenly matched in stubbornness as to how that protection was going to be arranged.

"As soon as the medic arrives, get cleared quickly so you can assume leadership of the troops when they land. Be safe, Major Zohra, beloved daughter. Guardian, thank you for your continuing updates. Out."

Zohra leaned back in the chair. For a few moments she savored the reconnection with someone she loved deeply. Her mother had found ways to send her messages while she was undercover—a picture, a song, a scent, or sometimes a person seen from afar. Sighing, she brought her attention back to the present. Clearing up the situation on Merker's was still up to her, but there was an end in sight, and that really did help her morale. She hadn't realized how tired she was until she saw her mother.

She turned to the holographic image of Guardian. "What did she mean by *continuing* updates?"

"I am a member of Naboth's Vine," Guardian said, as if that told her everything.

She studied the hologram for a few moments and then asked, "You've been my contact for the past—"

"Yes."

She hated it when people answered before she finished her question, and by the grin on his face, she suspected he knew that.

"You had some most interesting test questions to see if I was to be trusted. Your mother was entertained."

"You had to ask her?"

"Who else was I to trust with your life?" Guardian said.

"So, we still have to worry about the portal."

"Portals. We believe if one is disrupted, it will cause a chain reaction in the others, endangering each host planet. The other guardians are employing a great deal of caution in securing their portals."

Zohra's attention returned to the screen showing the dojo. Carol was throwing Lady Harriet more often than not, and they were spending a lot of time wrestling on the ground.

"I think I'll go rescue the women from their hormonal urges." She pushed herself out of the chair. "They're having far too much fun." Guardian's chuckles followed her out of the command center.

Zohra entered unobserved by Lady Harriet, but Carol noticed her presence. Until the chip was removed from her, Zohra suspected Carol would protect Lady Harriet with her life, unasked, because that compulsion was part of the chip implant's programming.

Zohra wondered if they would allow each other out of sight when she took them on recon missions. She intended on scoping out Century City and topside before reinforcements arrived. Between Guardian's assessment of the Spartans and her own knowledge, she would have a comprehensive report ready for her mother when she arrived to take command.

Zohra laughed silently as she contemplated continuing the tricks that Guardian did so well, driving the remaining Spartans crazy. She didn't feel sorry for them. They couldn't be trusted, even when they were in front of you. She was looking forward to being on the other side of the rude surprises Guardian had made them suffer through for the last two years.

She turned her attention back to the two women, a decidedly less stressful topic of study. From a technical standpoint, they put on a good demonstration, even with the laughs, teasing, and passionate kisses that preceded the bone-shaking takedowns.

Her glance moved to Lady Harriet. She had noticed Harriet's hesitation in accepting Guardian's word that she had been deprogrammed. Montran was right to worry. Though Zohra felt that she had no conscious problem recognizing whose side she was on, something was buried deep within that she hadn't yet been able to bring to consciousness. Three years ago, her dreams had taken on a different tone. The more she attempted to find the cause, the more elusive it became. Many times she had intended to discuss it with her contact, but for one reason or another, she never brought it up. She shrugged off the worry. When the healers arrived, she would mention it to them.

Thump, bam. Lady Harriet's reflexes were not what a Black Rose would call impressive, but she didn't have to be a one-woman killing machine. Her balance was good and she had the right moves. She didn't let thinking get in her way as she responded to some of Carol's moves. Zohra guessed Lady Harriet was controlling more of this game than she appeared to be.

Zohra didn't need to study Carol, for she had seen her in practice when Chaney visited. Besides, he didn't want Sheila to train with anyone who could later use their knowledge against her, so he'd had a special computer program designed for her training, and the Black Rose squad on Merker's had a copy of that program.

Her thoughts returned to the problem they were facing. Since Alan Fermin was on his way, his personal army of metrasoldiers would be arriving before him, to secure the outpost. From what she had read, he had over a hundred soldiers who had been programmed to kill. She doubted he would send them all to Merker's, but two squads would be more than a handful for the three of them, or four, if she counted Guardian.

Alan would take advantage of this time when the outpost was vulnerable, but maybe Chaney's death had caught him off guard and his troops were scattered. Where would he have had them stationed?

She had seen and competed against various members of Alan's elite group. They wore black clothing, almost like that of the *yobashi*, the elite assassin organization, though she knew they weren't part of that group. Fermin probably chose to dress them that way in an effort to instill fear on sight. The fear was justified.

Compliments of Chaney, Fermin's soldiers had trained in the compound the Black Rose squad used for their advanced tactical training. At first, the Black Rose members were angry that Chaney invited others to "their" training compound, but when Alan's metrasoldiers were offered as training tools, most changed their attitude. Zohra wondered who else Chaney rented it out to when they weren't around. She was sure Naboth's Vine knew.

Her breath caught as Lady Harriet spun in the air, pulling a surprise move on Carol. She imagined what it would look like if

Lady Harriet had long hair, loose and flying in slow motion like an orange wave about her head… without any clothes on.

She sat up higher, startled at where her imagination kept going. She really needed to keep her thoughts on a professional level. She was an officer now.

Zohra's movement caught Harriet's attention, giving Carol the advantage. Carol kicked her in the stomach and sent her sailing. She ended up flat on her back.

Somewhat guiltily, Zohra rose to join the two. Staring down into dark green, glassy eyes as Lady Harriet struggled to fill her lungs with air, she felt her heart warm. This was the woman she had joined with so long ago. Did she see something more behind the unfocused eyes? Did Lady Harriet remember watching her? Of course she did. The masters emphasized to all their students the power behind the dragon energy that the Dance called into play.

As Lady Harriet's eyes cleared, Zohra could see an emotion behind her stare, but it disappeared as she took her first deep, shaky breath.

"Good shot," Montran wheezed. She rolled to her hands and knees and pulled in a few more breaths before rising to her feet.

"It was a sucker shot," Zohra said, unsympathetic.

Montran looked irritated, but didn't speak.

"Have you ever studied ChomTai?" Zohra asked the women.

"No," they answered in unison.

"I'll teach you some basics. Alan's soldiers use this particular form of combat, which is based on the *yobashi* style." Her eyes moved to Carol. "When I'm done teaching you, if a lethal blow is delivered, you'll know the reversal. I'll also show you how to recognize when it's delivered."

Zohra knew Carol was learned in the ways of the *yobashi*, but probably not in ChomTai's few killing strikes. Sparring with Carol was tempting, though not for the same reason she'd felt about Montran.

Zohra demonstrated each strike and explained its intention. Then she demonstrated the countermove. Her voice was soft and she used few words, letting the movements themselves do the teaching.

As Lady Harriet countered her moves, Zohra discerned a slight tremor at their contact. Pretending not to notice, she grabbed Lady Harriet's wrist to demonstrate another move. She reminded them how to breathe and what to visualize.

Zohra smirked to herself as her victim struggled to stay focused on the lesson. Every time they touched, Lady Harriet's pulse quickened or her limbs trembled, and it occurred to Zohra that between the lust gas and her touches, her opponent might be distracted. Wickedly, she continued anyway. But when Harriet made two simple errors in a row, she decided to end her game.

"That's it for now. We have a briefing with Guardian in a stan hour, so I suggest we clean up and get something to eat before then."

"I could go for some solid food." Montran kneaded her sore thigh.

Lady Harriet accepted the towel from the bot with evident fatigue. Her hair was sticking to her wet scalp, and the damp outer clothing clung to her body. She looked lighter than the soldiers Zohra was used to being around. It left her more vulnerable to hits. Zohra pulled her eyes away and looked at Carol. Carol was watching, expressionless, as Montran took a sip of water.

As they exited the room, Zohra fell into step beside Carol and struck up a conversation. She wanted to get to know Carol and to see whether their brief meeting when Carol was Chaney's bodyguard would cast shadows on their present relationship.

Montran, deep in thought, fell in behind Zohra and Carol.

She watched Carol interact politely with Zohra. The questions were military in nature, and Montran knew Zohra was assessing the skills of another player she would use to defend the outpost. Carol probably knew as much about the outpost as Zohra did. For a brief moment, Montran wondered if the two women had been lovers, but she quickly squashed that thought. Jealousy was an emotion with which she had little experience.

Zohra paused a moment, bringing them to a halt. "Lady Harriet, would you mind if Carol and I have a private chat?"

"No, of course not." Montran curled her fingers into a ball to refrain from touching Carol. She glared at Zohra, to remind her that she would not let Carol be duped into being anyone's pawn.

Zohra raised her eyebrows in seeming innocence and continued up the corridor toward her quarters. Carol glanced at her then at Montran.

"I'll see you at dinner," Montran said to her.

Carol nodded and proceeded to catch up with Zohra.

Montran's Second Skin had absorbed the sweat from the workout but didn't help with her hormonal rushes.

"I need a cold shower," she muttered, as her door shut behind her.

The shower refreshed her and gave her a new burst of energy, and towel-drying her hair, she watched the bot lay out a change of clothing. That reminded her that they needed to visit Century City to pick up Carol's belongings.

The bot laid out more selections than she'd previously been given. Someone was keeping up with their wardrobe needs. Shaking her head, she walked into the kitchenette.

"Bach, I'd like an Alterian Club sandwich."

"Three layered or two?" Bach asked.

"Two, and lemon tea with a small dollop of honey."

She took a seat at the computer. "Since metradames are a major factor in my life, it would be prudent to see what they're all about." She studied her reflection in the monitor then changed her focus.

"Computer, find information on Cadet Zohra, graduate class of..."

For the next hour, she read. Second Lieutenant Zohra had been assigned to a science vessel and had received the usual timely promotions, making her currently a major. Her ship was reported to be exploring a new sector of space.

She moved on to study the files on Jina Gari, the Black Rose Spartan. She was an orphan, recruited from Melarz into the city guard. When rebels decimated the city, Jina Gari was the only soldier to survive. She escaped in the underground waterways, herding the mayor's family, along with a few others, to safety, while the capital fell to the enemy. After one year of being a Spartan on the battlefield, she started moving up in the ranks as her talents became evident, until she was transferred to the Black Rose. There, she worked up to sergeant major. Her personal hobbies were listed as BDSM, and her favorite vacation spot was the Caves. Montran snorted. That bit of information was what the individual added to her profile.

She skimmed over Jina Gari's advanced training and knew why the Black Rose had accepted her: she had kicked their butts in all the barroom brawls they'd shared. The specialty training meant that a lot of subliminal work had been done on her. That was something Guardian should worry about, if he insisted that deadly force was not to be used as a first alternative in defending his outpost.

And the Centurions had worried about *her*? They should get a look at Zohra's record.

She chided herself. She should be studying something they could use. With Alan Fermin's soldiers in mind, she typed "metrapeople" into the computer.

The screen quickly started to fill up, scrolling down as the list grew. "I'll need to put a few more qualifiers in the search. This is more than I can scan in a day."

Chapter 9

For most of their respective seasons, the five Wieldworlds were inhospitable planets, except to the very hardy and stubborn. Also called the Five Wild Outlands, at one time they had separated the GCFC and Collective spheres of influence from each other, acting as a neutral zone.

The military, interested in bringing order to the cosmos, divided space into sectors. The Wild Outlands ended up touching four sectors: Juan, Getty, Zed, and Ectron, thus giving the Outlands a new nickname, the Four Corners. They were oddly situated, but still held to their neutrality.

Of the five Wieldworlds, Hinterwield, by some slick amendments to the charter of neutrality, was used by the GCFC for imprisoning their social failures, the psychopaths they couldn't control but wouldn't put to death.

Dwellers on Magewield liked to think of themselves as a spiritual community. Their abilities to overcome the harshness of life, as well as their community spirit, were the basis of their survival and pride. Though the inhabitants were spread across the planet, they were tied to each other through telepathic bonds, as well as more common means. Magewield found that by setting up vacation residences for all factions of the galaxies, they kept up on events that even broadcast news groups didn't know about.

Rene came into physical existence on Magewield, in a family that was well prepared for s'her birth. The village of Mount Rayhan welcomed the two-spirit baby with celebrations. Two-spirit or dual-gendered souls were eagerly looked for. They often became shamans or healers, and sometimes the leaders of their communities. Like Rene, these dual souls were sometimes born into the gendered body of one sex while feeling inside as another, or they matured with the genitalia of both genders. An 's' was added before the pronoun of the gender with which they identified to reflect their two-spiritedness.

At puberty, some decided on a physical sex change to fit their inner view of themselves, while others kept their split identities, comfortable as they were. Due to their natures, their perspectives were considered both unique and enlightened, and they were eagerly welcomed throughout the planet.

At Rene's presentation to the community at six moons of age, the oracle directed s'her parents to send s'her for apprenticeship to Pilar under the mentorship of SH'a Grou, once s'she had reached the appropriate age. S'she was also to attend the monastery school there. Rene would learn the ways of the off-worlders, to prepare s'her for s'her purpose in this life.

As Rene grew, s'she saw many dimensions of the web of life, with its interconnectivity to all things. Both the seen and unseen were tangible, living entities for s'her. By the age of five, s'she knew s'her life path and had been working with the local shaman for two years, preparing to move to Pilar, where s'her formal training would begin.

* * *

SH'a Grou's head turned to s'his apprentice, interrupting a lesson in breathing. A telepathic call from a villager held s'his attention.

"*A member of the Fermin family is ill and needs assistance quickly.*"

Young Rene recognized the shift in consciousness within their link. Quickly, s'she placed a cushion for SH'a Grou's body to rest on as s'his spirit left for a consultation.

S'she moved into the herb room and gathered the herbs s'her mentor mentally requested. With that done, s'she proceeded to prepare their traveling ponies. SH'a Grou had soon let her know that one of the off-worlders that rented a guest house along the cliffs of Magewield had requested the shaman's physical services and s'she would accompany s'him there.

"Halt! Who dares to invade this residence without invitation?" a heavily accented voice called out.

"I invited them." A dark shadow moved, as a woman who had been waiting out of the wind stepped into view and raised her hand in greeting to the shaman and s'his apprentice.

The guard sullenly stepped aside, apparently unhappy that his intimidation of the locals was so quickly terminated.

"I am Lady Artha, one of the guests in this lovely residence," she politely informed the two, speaking in their own language.

SH'a Grou honored her by raising s'his hand in blessing. "I hope the House of Illusions is to your liking," s'he said.

The residence was cut into the side of Mount Eloise. If the visiting Fermin family thought they were secure from any intruders because of the location, the Magewieldians didn't tell them otherwise. Guests didn't need to know that there were many exits and entrances to their residences.

"Very much so." Lady Artha led them to a room inside the mountain.

"Strange place for a sickroom," Rene thought to SH'a Grou. *"No fresh air or view of the outside."*

The sick child was fourteen-year-old Tess, the third daughter born to Thordis and Gustaf Fermin. SH'a Grou laid s'his bag of herbs beside the bed and placed s'his fingertips lightly on the limp wrist of the barely breathing form. Rene pulled the small pouches of herbs out of the larger bag and laid them out.

"We will need boiling water, a bowl this size, and cloth to bathe her." Rene indicated the size with her hands.

Lady Artha nodded to the servant who was waiting by the door.

SH'a Grou moved to the young girl's feet and pressed s'his thumbs against her soles. The girl's chest expanded in a deep inhalation, which was a good sign.

Rene pinched herbs into the bowl the servant had brought and ground them until they were a fine powder. The servant from the village added hot water, and the steam from the bowl was passed several times under the sick girl's nostrils. When the mixture cooled, SH'a Grou poured it between Tess's stiff lips. For an hour, SH'a Grou and Rene ministered to her, alternating between massage and the use of thin needles inserted in careful patterns across her bare body. As the blue color in her lips and eyelids faded, SH'a Grou placed moxa cones at other points on her body. Smoke from the burning moxa filled the room.

"Rene, you must distract the young man who did this."

Rene rose and nodded respectfully to Lady Artha. S'she found Alan Fermin easily. He was leaning against the wall outside the sickroom, watching through the doorway.

"I would like you to show me where the food is prepared," s'she said to Alan.

Normally Alan would have dispatched a servant to take care of the visitors' needs, but Lady Artha, with one look, commanded her young cousin to take the stranger to the kitchen without argument.

When SH'a Grou saw Alan was no longer outside the door, s'he turned to Lady Artha.

"This child does not suffer only from poison. Her will to live is not there, and without it, she will not throw off the effects of either the poison or that which has touched her heart."

Lady Artha nodded. A twice-removed cousin of the girl's parents, she had been asked to run the Fermin household and school the Fermin children in the ways of the upper class. From the day of her arrival, she had tried to put a stop to Alan's harassment of his siblings. Life for the children had become more stable and safer, or so Lady Artha had thought.

Thordis, the children's mother, was busy either producing the children her marriage contract required, or recovering from their delivery. Sweet Tess was the only child during whose pregnancy her mother was happy.

Gustaf, the legal owner of the children, busied himself with bartering off his numerous daughters and sons and doing whatever else it would take to get himself the coveted vacant chair of the BenHanna on the GCFC's lower floor.

Alan was prone to rages, which were attributed to his mother's bouts of depression during her pregnancy with him. However, he also possessed a talent for picking businesses that bore fruit, which his father found sufficiently beneficial to keep him and to ignore his shortcomings.

"Tess has just been pledged to a distant cousin," Lady Artha told SH'a Grou. She looked down at her young cousin's face. "She's only fourteen. Tess would rather become a singer. She has a lovely voice."

"The person who poisoned her will do it again until she is dead," SH'a Grou said. "He feels an unforgivable transgression has been committed against him personally."

Lady Artha knew the shaman was referring to Alan. Tess's transgression against Alan was that he had seen her mingling with the villagers. "Like a common slut," he had said, angrily accusing the surprised Tess. It didn't matter that the youth he had seen holding her hand was a palm reader.

"Her brother Alan poisoned her. If I banish him to a reformatory school, he'll learn to manipulate the situation to his own advantage, and when he's released as an adult, he'll be worse than he is now," Lady Artha said. "I can assign bodyguards to make sure he won't harm others, but Alan is resourceful. If he wants to get rid of his sister, he will, whether he is locked away or not."

As SH'a Grou picked up s'his herb pouches and returned them to s'his medicine bag, s'he gave instructions for Tess's care for the next ten hours.

At the gate, s'he turned to Lady Artha. "Dream well and dream deep. An answer shall come to you tonight."

"What about your attendant?"

"S'she can take care of s'herself."

Chapter 10

Alan led the SH'a's young apprentice through a maze of corridors. The girl seemed unconcerned as she moved the multihued scarf back onto her shoulder. She was the type Alan enjoyed tormenting.

Nervously, he glanced behind him to make sure Lady Artha wasn't around. Aside from his sister's sickness, there was nothing to interest him. Now he had someone else to toy with. He intentionally kept up a fast pace, leading her through corridors they had already passed through. If she noticed, she didn't mention it.

He gave her his curled upper lip look, slitting his eyes so he looked mean. *I am mean*, he assured himself. The young girl paid him no heed.

"What's your name?" he asked.

"Rene."

"You're with that dallier," Alan said in a disdainful tone. He looked at her slyly to see how his insult registered.

The expression on her face reflected humor.

He was immediately incensed. "What's so funny?"

"I am amused," Rene said. "A dallier, by your culture's definition, is one who spends time with those much younger than him or herself. That's true. SH'a Grou is with those younger. I don't understand why you consider it an insult."

"He has sex with them. Forces them to do things they don't want to do."

"Whomever SH'a Grou has sex with is not my business. As for forcing s'his students to do things they don't want to do, what is that exactly?"

Alan turned on her. "Are you taunting me?"

"No. I'm asking you for clarification. Has no one instructed you in the art of discussion?"

He changed tactics. "Are you his servant?"

"I do serve s'him as a student, to learn the shaman arts," Rene answered.

Alan snorted. "A girl can't do anything better than a man."

Rene smiled. "Men do have more serious issues to contend with, while girls are still enjoying their childhood. Age sometimes has advantages."

"Men do it better."

"And what is that exactly?"

"You stupid witch. All women can do is have babies."

"Well, since SH'a Grou is both genders, s'he has the advantages of both."

"Both genders? Is that why you keep saying s'he and s'him?"

"Yes."

Alan was appalled. "A freak. He's a damn freak."

"Freak means something different from the majority. Yes. Are you not also a freak in your society?"

Alan glared at her. Frustrated, he turned and left her in the hall.

Undaunted, Rene made s'her way to the kitchen. S'she found the place where Alan hid his poisons, and s'she replaced them with harmless substances. Alan wouldn't know the difference. S'she left the room and turned down the hall Alan was hiding in.

"Hello, Alan. Have you decided to continue our discussion?"

Alan was pressed up against the wall in the darkened hallway.

"Walk with me to my pony, and we can talk," Rene said.

Alan suddenly seemed shy.

Rene had made the choice to intersect s'her own lifeline onto his web. SH'a Grou and s'she had talked about the implications, and what would happen if they chose not to try to help this lost soul. The events were written before the Fermins had rented the House of Illusions.

"What are you?" Alan asked.

"Me?" Rene picked up his confused thoughts and laughed lightly. "Under this clothing, I have a body like yours, but I feel as a girl. We are called twin-spirits."

"You're a freak, too," Alan said triumphantly.

"We have something in common, then. Do you want to learn to control your anger, that which takes you into the darkness?"

He snorted as though it were of no concern to him.

"If you don't, you'll be sent to Hinterwield," Rene said.

"That won't happen. My father will see it doesn't."

It was no secret that when Alan was younger, his father had paid compensation to the families whose children he had harmed.

Instead of leading Rene to s'her pony, Alan showed s'her to a fountain in the inner garden. "This is my favorite spot," he said, almost grudgingly.

The place was stark and lacking in color, an abrupt contrast to the rest of what s'she had seen of the colorful residence.

Rene sent a mental greeting to Trotter, s'her pony, who informed s'her he was finding meager grass to chew on. Rene assured him that when they reached the sweet grass of home that he was so fond of, he would get an extra handful of the corn that he also loved.

S'she touched Alan's mind.

The red-faced infant boy wailed and thrashed his tiny bare feet and small fists until he was exhausted. A sudden shake awakened him, and the wails started up again. A face appeared over the tall sides of the crib, and the wails stopped as nourishment was supplied by a bottle thrust roughly into his open mouth.

At two, the toddler raged against the adults who ignored his tugging on clothing to be noticed. Beating his fists on his father resulted in his world suddenly turning upside down, as the tall figure grabbed him and held him away in disgust. He was dangled by one leg and thrust toward his nanny, who grabbed at him furiously.

Older now, perhaps by five stan years, the dark-haired lad watched with equally dark eyes as new victims headed toward his hidden trap. As expected, the toy monster popped out, scaring the nanny and her charge, his older sister. Their screams were not polite screams; they were terrified screeches that hurt the ears.

Alan leaned back against the wall and let the feeling of satisfaction find a way to his almost nonexistent pleasure center. However, it was short lived. He was yanked up roughly and shaken like a rug, rattling his teeth in his head.

"You worthless lump of flesh!" his father shouted, his voice seething with rage. He dropped Alan back onto his feet, where he landed off balance and fell on his back, shivering in fear.

"Get his nanny," his father said to one of his men. "Get out of my sight. You disgust me," he told Alan, who had not moved.

Alan rolled to his side to get up. His older brother, his father's favorite, stared at him in contempt.

"You're no Fermin," Joey said in a low voice. "You have no sense of honor, or loyalty to your own family. You'll be locked away before you even reach legal age." With that, he marched after his departing father.

Alan's nanny grabbed him painfully by his ear and dragged him toward the children's residence.

"You are a sick child. You'll be locked up before long. The cook found a dead rodent in the flour and said it was you that did it. Do you know what a dead rodent will do to food? Your father has ordered that you be taken to QeLapand."

She pushed him ahead of her and stomped behind him. "I'm not going to that place. He's going to have to get someone else to watch over you. I knew there was something wrong with you from the day they stuck me with you. Never a moment of peace."

She pushed him into his bedroom and tried to close the door, but he stopped her by pressing his hands flat against it.

"I'm not going!" he yelled.

The woman pushed him away, slammed the door, and slid the lock into place.

"Get packing!" she shouted through the door.

For a year, Alan lived on QeLapand, where he was observed by a medical staff. He was released back to his family's care under medication, but by then he had learned how to conceal his harassment of others.

"Can I see you again?" Alan asked awkwardly. This was the first time he had ever reached out to another person.

"I shall be back tomorrow. Good dreams," Rene said. They parted at the gate where s'her pony was waiting to take her home.

Since Alan felt no threat from Rene, he allowed himself to become fascinated by the novelty she presented. His life was not so boring, after all.

Before Alan's mother left late that night with her staff, Alan announced to her and to Lady Artha that he was staying with Lady Artha and the reduced staff, who would be assisting the ailing Tess. She was too ill to be moved. Alan had no plans other than to watch his sister die.

The shaman's herbs did their work, leaving Tess exhausted from purging through the night. Alan believed Tess's pallor was an indication that she was sure to die. Village servants were entrusted with her care while Lady Artha slept on the cot in the same room. In her dream that night, Lady Artha saw a plan to keep Tess safe from her brother and also from her father's plans.

The shaman and his apprentice visited the next morning to look in on Tess.

Lady Artha watched the apprentice and Alan in the garden for a while. She had never seen Alan interested in anyone before.

The shaman nodded at the still form on the cot. Whispered directions were given to the young woman who was tending the girl, and then Shaman Grou rose from his crouched position and picked up the herb bag as if to leave.

Lady Artha looked down at Tess. She could see that the yellowish tinge to hers skin was gone, replaced by an almost translucent look.

"Honorable One." Lady Artha bowed her head to the shaman. "I have indeed dreamed."

Shaman Grou held up two fingers, and she nodded. The villagers would take Tess in two days, to be raised by them. By acknowledging the dream, Lady Artha knew that she had agreed to the plan.

Two days later, Tess was pronounced dead, and a sham funeral was held without the presence of her family. Her life as a Fermin ended and her new life began. Still weak and delirious, she was moved through underground tunnels to another village—a three-day journey. If she survived the harsh life on the Wieldworld, she would become a singer. The Village of Lee had an opening for the training of a storyteller and singer. Music and art were greatly honored during the hard winters, when no one dared venture beyond the perimeter of their own village.

Gustaf, his father, was furious when he learned of Alan's role in his sister's death. He banished him to the family estate in the desert of Kasam. During that time, Alan focused his energy on preparing for his rite of passage into manhood, as well as on studying the family business. He was unrepentant regarding his sister's death, and saw his exile as no more than an inconvenience. When he returned to Magewield a year later, he resumed his friendship with Rene.

"Greetings, Alan," she signed and then spoke.

Awkwardly, Alan returned both the sign and a polite greeting he had learned from her. He paused in confusion as he noted her apparel. He tried to understand what this more feminized version of Rene meant. "Why are you dressed like that?"

"It's what women wear on Magewield," Rene said.

"But you're not really one of them." He waved that aside, quickly losing interest in something that wasn't about him.

"I've undergone a change, and I'm one of them now. What life change have you experienced?"

Alan missed the irony, picking up on the question about him, which was easier for him to deal with than Rene's revelation that she had gone through a sex change.

"Lord Chaney has recommended that I attend a military academy."

He felt important. It meant he would be wearing a uniform and people would be saluting him. People that worked for the family business already did what he commanded, but the uniform and salutes were privileges of power he could only legitimately get from military service, or if he formed his own army.

"I thought you were going to run your father's businesses?"

"Huh?" He looked distracted. "I am. I already do a lot of the business now," he lied. "It's not hard to go to one of those schools. Except maybe the physical workouts, but I'll get out of those."

"Alan, if you're not going to do the whole program, why go?"

"Lord Chaney thinks I need the discipline," he told her sulkily. "Father listens to him only because he's helping us get a seat on the GCFC. It will look good if I graduate from a galactic space academy."

That was Lord Chaney's argument, but now, saying it aloud, it did sound like a good plan. "I'm going to a school on Janu to start preparatory classes."

He didn't bother mentioning that his grades wouldn't even come close to qualifying him for an academy waiting list. In addition, even he recognized that he needed more than academic help, for his social graces were severely lacking. If his father hadn't convinced him that this was his family duty, he would have found a way to mess it up, so that one of his younger brothers would have to go through this four-year drag.

"When do your classes start?"

"Tomorrow. Father called early this morning to tell me that Lord Chaney finalized the deal."

He nearly winced at what he'd just revealed. His father was going to give Lord Chaney a metragirl, a new type of biobot, for pulling strings to get his name on the enrollment list. Lord Chaney's predilection for young girls was becoming an issue with his fellow GCFC members, so the metragirl would be a politically expedient substitute.

* * *

Rene saw Alan every year during his preparatory program, sometimes for only a few days. Alan had become serious about attending the space academy, and that was why s'she was surprised to get a communication from him in his first year at the academy, saying that he had been booted out for behavior unbecoming an officer. Alan had struck a female cadet, though he insisted it was by accident. Instead of leaving, he simply transferred over to the Diplomatic Corps Academy, which shared off-campus facilities with the military space academy.

Three stan years later, Alan arrived on Magewield early one morning. "Take a message to SH'a Rene. Tell her I need to see her now!" his voice was hoarse as he shouted at the young man who was barely awake. "She always knows when I'm going to be here. Why isn't she here waiting?"

As the hours dragged by without word from Rene, he ranted. His bodyguards wouldn't let him leave the premises in such a rage. They had already failed to prevent him from hurting any more women. He had recently tried to kill a DeMonte, but hadn't succeeded.

Furious as he recalled his failure to kill Lady Harriet, he picked up a stick and beat a statue in the winter-dry garden. "She lives! Damn the DeMontes! Damn the Montrans! Stinking clans! I'll get you yet!" He continued to beat the statue until the stick had shattered into pieces.

He wouldn't leave the garden. For two days, there was no Rene, and his screams escalated to violent threats. Finally, his bodyguards wrestled him down to administer a drug he had refused to take. He slept for a few hours, and when he woke, Rene was there. He picked up a club from the ground and slammed it against a tree.

"Where were you? I needed you!" Alan wailed.

"I was in another village. Why do you need me?"

"I'm accused of assaulting Lady Harriet Montran. Work your magic and fix it for me."

Rene could see the wildness in his eyes. The news of his monstrous attack on a member of the respected DeMonte house had been broadcast everywhere. He implored s'her for a solution only death could give him, and that wasn't something with which s'she could interfere. It wasn't his time, unfortunately.

Now was s'her moment. S'she looked up into his eyes. They were those of a madman.

"I won't do that," s'she said. S'she held his eyes as he brought the club down, and then there was darkness.

"Oh, gods! What have I done?" Alan dropped the club near Rene's body. He felt numb, and his brain struggled to function. He was aware of the bodyguards cursing and saying that, of everyone, they thought the shaman would be safe with him.

Alan heard what he thought was the small transport shuttle. He sank to his knees and stared tearlessly at the crumpled heap that was his only friend, Rene.

"Alan."

His head shot up. Bewildered, he looked around. His father stood there, along with a Spartan captain.

"Father," he said hoarsely. "Father, I… I didn't mean to hurt her. I don't want her to die. Please, Father, you can make her a metradame. Please."

Gustaf felt Rene's neck for a pulse, but he couldn't detect one. "Alan, this is too much. You nearly killed a Montran in front of witnesses, and now this."

Alan ignored the contorted expression on his father's face. Keeping Rene alive was all he was interested in. "Father. I want her. Please!"

"Only if you get on the shuttle with me and agree to enroll in the ADDM program. If you don't… Listen to me. If you don't do as I say, it will be the end of my plans to build this family into an empire. They will send you to Hinterwield. Do you hear me?"

"Will you take Rene's body to the metralabs, Father?"

"Will you do what I say?"

"Anything. Just make her my metradame."

"All right." He turned to one of the bodyguards. "Have the servants secure the body for the metralab. We only have a four hour window to save her. Do you have Alan's meds? Give him a shot. I don't want him going crazy on the flight." He added in a low voice, "Captain, contact my lawyer to take care of her disappearance."

Chapter 11

Rene's eyes opened and showed uncommon liveliness when the first charge was sent delicately into her brainstem. Dr. J'us leaned over her to check the marks for the insertion of the chip that was the heart of the metraperson's new personality. The implant allowed the scientists to suppress old memories stored in the brain. It also enabled the master or mistress to send waves of pain into the pleasure centers if the metraperson refused to obey a command. Eventually, the pleasure centers failed to function. If the owners cared, they sent their metraperson back to have the center for laughter recharged, for some were more comfortable with a pleasant servant than with one who couldn't enjoy a joke.

Rene was bound to the operating table with straps from forehead to ankle. For a few moments, her eyes held the eyes of the doctor. Was the chip inserted? The doctor knew it was, for she had checked off all the important points of the operation as they were completed, just as she did for all the metrapeople that passed through her hands. She was a metraperson herself, programmed under the threat of pain to be precise.

Rene understood that she had been changed into a metradame. Her dual spiritedness had been suppressed, but her inner strength as a shaman had prevented much of the chip's control over her mind. Now she was sitting in the display room, where owners came to check out their new toy. Alan appeared, alongside his father. Both men walked quickly across the entranceway and up the long staircase to the showroom, and Rene noted how changed Alan was. Parts of her abilities as a shaman had been damaged by Alan's blow, but she had confidence she could undo that. Certainly, she could sense Gustaf's fury as he saw how Alan had her dressed. Her face had been changed, too. Now she had the face that had haunted Alan when he was a child, that of his first nanny.

Of course, Gustaf recognized the face. "What is this, Alan?" His father's voice was rough with controlled fury.

Alan cowered. "Well… she's mine, Father. I can do what I want with her."

"You had no business—"

"I'm not yours, Alan. No one owns anyone," Rene calmly interrupted them. She tried not to laugh at the two very shocked faces before her.

"You… you're supposed to wait until I program you." Alan's stutter sounded like a child who had found the freshly baked cookies turned to stone.

"Alan, shut up," Gustaf said. "Sit there with her. I'll find out what's wrong."

"Alan, you have to stop trying to control people. Isn't that what keeps getting you in trouble?"

"Rene, my sweet Rene. What happened to you?"

"What happened to you?" Alan's changed behavior astonished her.

"It's the programming. I'm on meds and… I'm all right, Rene. I promised Father I would go to this reeducation school if he saved you."

"So, I owe you thanks for this face?"

Alan's cheeks reddened. "You should be thanking me for saving your life."

"You're the reason I ended up having to have my life saved."

He looked contrite. "I'm so sorry. I was off my meds for a couple of months and I just… I just lose it when I'm not on them."

Rene shook her head at this version of Alan. She guessed the scientists who worked on the metrapeople shared information with the scientists who worked on the behavior modification program that had been used on Alan. He was changed, but even with her sensitivity blunted, she could still feel the malignant dark force that was at his core.

"I can't take you with me, and I'm not going to let Father take you."

"Alan, why are you chewing on your thumb?" Rene asked.

"I don't know. Nerves, I guess. Probably another one of the side effects of this stuff they're giving me." He jammed his hands in his pockets. "Listen, Rene, I have an apartment along the river at ElDor. You can stay there until I get out of this place." He lifted his eyes to stare at her. She could see his fingers twitching in his coat pockets.

"I don't want to stay at your place. I want a life of my own. I can't go back to Magewield."

At that moment, Gustaf returned, red-faced and looking irritated.

"Okay. Okay." Alan began to rise from his seat and then quickly sat back down. "Father, I want—"

"I don't care what you want. Shut up and let me get this mess straightened out."

"No, Father. Leave her. Leave her!" Alan grabbed his head with one hand as if it hurt, and with the other he continued to grab at his father when the lab techs came to take Rene away.

Rene realized what was happening and reached out to everyone's minds, with the exception of Alan's, which was too messy to get near.

Two hours later, the three were in Gustaf's personal vehicle, stopping at the tenth clothing store so that Rene could have a decent wardrobe rather than the brief attire in which Alan had her dressed for her coming-out event.

"We've been at this for two stan hours. I've had enough," Gustaf said gruffly.

"Me, too," Rene said. "I wish to be enrolled in a science university. The woman in the store said the most prestigious is the one on Sintafie Prime."

"And you want to go there?" Alan asked, sounding impressed.

"Yes."

"Father can get you in there," he said, with a boy's confidence.

"Why do I want to enroll you in a school? You're a metradame. You do our bidding. Damn Magewieldians. Last time we'll take anyone from that planet," he said darkly. He was feeling all the more uncomfortable, being in the car with two demanding people who were supposed to be malleable to his control.

"If you let me have my freedom," Rene said, "I will send some impressive, credentialed people your way, via the insurance scam you're running."

"I've got agents for that, I don't need you." Gustaf paused for a moment, realizing that she had knowledge that was not given to even the stockholders. "How did you know… Alan!" He turned to his son, who was squeezed into the smaller seat behind the autodriver. "I told you to keep your mouth shut. I don't blab my business to my whores."

A slight twitch of pain registered in Alan's eyes, informing Gustaf that his remark had hit a nerve.

"But, Father, she's right. Even Lord Chaney says the only people the agents are getting are low class. You can use already educated metrapeople instead of spending all that time educating them in the labs. You can even arrange to have your own army."

Gustaf was about to say something when Alan added, "She's mine, Father. And the deal she's offering is a good one."

Gustaf looked at the son who had caused him so many headaches and lost him so many credits. However, he had to admit that since Alan had begun participating in the company business, he had contributed to the buildup of his empire by over fifty percent, which more than paid for what he'd lost. Gustaf just wanted to drop off the metradame, who was not acting like one, somewhere, and get back to the business he knew.

"Fine. I'll set it up," he said. "Are you going to keep that face?"

"For now."

Rene spent her first evening in a very expensive hotel, watching the watchers and eating strange foods. Later, at Alan's insistence, Gustaf had her set up in a nice apartment complex within walking distance of the university she would be attending. The clothing Gustaf had paid for would be sent ahead of her, along with a maid. Alan felt she needed one to help her learn the customs of the wealthy. He seemed to be thoughtful when he was on his medication, but Rene knew the truth behind his help.

She pressed her face against the window, looking out at one of the few natural rivers on the planet. Her thoughts went back to the span of time she had spent unconscious. She had visited the Grandmother of the Web. Grandmother Spider was the most important initiation a shaman passed through. If she had become tangled in her web due to the illusions she created for herself as she looked for Grandmother, she would not have returned. But she did return… to find herself with this strange face. Rene stared at her reflection.

"New face, new life, and new name—Sharon Teal," she said. "Well, Sharon, let's see what this university is like. I suspect it's filled with scientists who can't see past their theoretical noses, and who admit only what their bosses want the masses to hear."

* * *

Sharon attended the university for only a year. She knew more than many of the professors, and she was causing too much of a stir with the questions she asked. Challenged by one of her professors, she took the tests for accreditation and passed with high scores. From there, she started her research project and completed and published it within three stan months.

Academic credentials on file, Dr. Sharon Teal took a job aboard the science vessel *Nettle*, studying the re-seeding progress on a planet. The planet was out of GCFC space, so Sharon didn't need to worry about Gustaf's agents or Alan's sudden appearances. It had taken six stan months of travel to reach her new quarters. *Nettle* was home to a hundred scientists, a light military security force, and a maintenance crew, along with their family members.

Sharon's new life was busy. She worked on case studies as well as her own projects. One project was to mitigate the damages the metralaboratories were doing to souls who should have been allowed to depart the physical world. Ways were being studied to return the current metrapeople to their own lives, with as few bad effects as possible.

Sharon also worked with a clandestine group that opposed the use of metrapeople and other abuses of those who were outside the reach—and protection—of common law. The most influential members of this secretive group belonged to the Council of Rings, Naboth's Vine, Brothers of the Shadow, and Hekate's Inner Circle. From among them came volunteers, who became double agents. In her dealings with this group, Sharon remained anonymous.

* * *

Sharon had been working on *Nettle* just short of a year and was more than comfortable with her routine, when her life took a surprising turn.

Her dinners were usually light affairs, eaten late at night when most people were in bed. She liked the empty dining hall that was dimly lit, quiet, and offered a panoramic view of space.

Alone in the dining hall, she had finished her salad and was idly watching the small patrol ships changing guard. They kept the area free of sightseers and mischief-makers. She nearly dropped her teacup when her senses registered a new energy aboard the ship.

Curious, she set down her cup and tried to perceive the source of this new energy. She sensed that a cloud of despair had settled in one part of the ship. A new recruit, perhaps.

The next day, she checked the log for new arrivals. Her finger paused on the name of Lieutenant Harriet Montran.

"Hmm. How many Harriet Montrans can there be in that clan?" she said softly. "Probably more than one, considering how large it is. How many would travel to another galaxy to get away from family politics?"

She pulled up the picture. "If it's the same Harriet, what a cosmic joke this will be."

Framed by orange hair that curled attractively around ears that looked almost elfin, dark green eyes stared back at her from underneath a military cap. The expression was serious, and tilting her head a little, Sharon decided the officer had felt uncomfortable posing for the image. "So, Alan's Harriet Montran is here." She shut off her screen and paced. She needed to consult her runes.

* * *

Two stan months passed before Sharon saw Harriet Montran in person. Dressed in a flight suit that showed off her slim figure, Montran was talking to Ensign Jimmy J'aimine in a low tone. When they finished, Montran left and Jimmy spotted Sharon.

"Hi, Dr. Teal. Seen any interesting flares while I was off?" Sharon enjoyed Jimmy's youthful charm and the light banter they shared without worrying about him misreading her friendliness. He was enamored with a mechanic in the hydroponics bay on deck two and was very loyal.

"No, Jimmy. Nothing unusual. Where did you go this leave?"

"Fort Bragg, on Prime IV."

"I thought you said you weren't going to go there again, because they robbed you in the casinos."

"You got that right. Actually, the new lieut, Montran, asked me to take her there. She wanted to see if they really did rig the tables. A couple of noncoms in her squad complained about losing their entire pay there. Helga's Moon, but she paid them serious attention." He lifted his hands and shrugged.

"She visited seven of the big casinos and took them for a lot of chips before they cornered her and walked her to the big guy's office. I don't know what arrangements she made with him," he said, "but she didn't leave the place until she was satisfied there were more winners than when we arrived. I have a feeling she won't have to go back there for a while."

His eyes lit up. "You know what she did with the money she won? She dropped it in the alms box at the shuttle station. 'Those charities are rip-offs,' I said to her. You know what she told me?" Sharon shook her head. "She said, 'This one isn't.' Now, I wasn't going to argue with her, since she just busted seven of the big casinos, but I still have my doubts."

"She looks pretty grim."

"She's all right, Doc. Rumor says she used to be a captain in the Spartans. She doesn't talk about it, and she'll give you a real cold stare if you ask. My uncle was like that after he came back from the wars in the Pedia Cluster, so my guess is she's seen more death than most. Sanous has quarters next to hers. She says the lieut has nightmares." He grinned. "Sanous has been asking for a different shift for some time, so this worked out well for her. Now her downtime is when the lieut's on duty."

Sharon patted his arm. "I hope for her sake that the lieutenant does recover. Moving people around won't always work, and drugs aren't the answer." She said that more to herself than to Jimmy, who nodded in agreement.

That night, Sharon set out her candle. Sitting comfortably on a small cushion, she lit the incense and established a protective circle around her physical form.

Sharon's spirit was outside *Nettle*, observing it, when she noted the wisp of energy that was Harriet and followed it.

Her spirit entered the cramped military quarters, where she found a naked Harriet Montran sitting on her small cot, legs crossed and a flute case open in her lap. For some time, the lieutenant just stared at the silver flute inside. Sharon's spirit remained until Harriet shut the case without touching the instrument.

For four stan months, Sharon witnessed the same action, or lack thereof.

She continued to visit Harriet's quarters whenever she pulled out her flute. Six months passed before she played and then only a note or two before she would cry herself to sleep. A year after her assignment to *Nettle*, Harriet finally completed a full song. She played for an hour, and the release it gave her opened her spirit and dispelled the dark cloud that surrounded her. That night, Sharon saw Harriet's spirit rise to meet with another, a woman Harriet addressed as Gedaliaha. In spirit, Harriet was a young child, her long orange hair decorated with beads and ribbons. She sat at Gedaliaha's feet as if she were her student. Gedaliaha sang her a teaching song while she stroked her hair. When the song ended, Harriet's spirit drifted back into her sleeping physical form.

Now that Harriet was able to play her flute, Sharon noticed more liveliness in her eyes when she saw her in the cafeteria during meal breaks.

Sharon read the runes, searching for a pattern in the web and finding Harriet at the center. Many lives were being pulled toward her, for she was like a hub of a wheel, and they the spokes.

But why?

Sharon would have searched further for answers, but she was tired. Bone tired. She had so much to do yet, and adding Harriet to her tasks might turn out to be more than she could handle. How could she protect her and work on her own projects? She would have to sleep on it. But first, dinner.

The dining hall was nearly empty, as it usually was at that time. Sharon picked up a tray and selected real food from the menu, rather than synthesized. She was deep in thought when she tripped over the leg of a chair, and her salad, heavy with dressing, landed on the chair's occupant… Lieutenant Harriet Montran, as the Ladies of Fate would have it.

"I am so sorry," Dr. Teal said.

Salad dressing slithered down Harriet's uniform tunic.

"I... it's okay," she said. "I can change." How bare her unfamiliar uniform looked, without the ribbons she was accustomed to wearing. She pushed the thought away. After a week spent training aboard *Ziggy*, she was emotionally and physically exhausted.

"I hope you aren't going on duty," Dr. Teal said.

"No, I just got back. I have a few days to recover." Harriet managed a smile, and Dr. Teal returned it.

"Please sit down and let me get you another salad. I can see you're tired." Harriet jumped up. At the food counter, she consulted what was on her uniform to duplicate the choice of salad dressing.

Harriet set the salad in front of Dr. Teal and accepted her thanks. She had finished her own meal, so there was no rational reason to stay while Dr. Teal ate. Nodding a polite good night, she cleared the table of her empty dishes and returned to her quarters.

Once Sharon and Harriet found that they typically ate at the same time, they began to share a table. On impulse, Sharon asked Harriet a few weeks later if she would like to see one of the planet's flare-ups from the science observatory. Her lab had all sorts of instruments visually recording the events and adding to the drama, or so most scientists felt. Harriet accepted, not mentioning to Sharon that in her small patrol ship she observed them quite often.

* * *

Sharon glanced at Harriet, who had barely been able to sit still through the flute recital.

"Harriet, did she play that badly?" Sharon asked as they walked back to her quarters.

"No." Harriet laughed softly, blushing. "I think it was the choice of music."

The flute had whispered of love and yearning, and Sharon had become acutely aware of Harriet's nearness. Harriet, with her strong connection to the flute, must have felt even more moved by it. Sharon's heart beat a little faster.

They stopped outside Sharon's quarters, and Sharon peered into dark green eyes that wouldn't meet hers. "Why are you embarrassed?" she asked softly, watching the unusual energy swirls around Harriet.

Harriet shook her head. "Can we talk about it another time? It's late. Thank you for inviting me." The blush increased in intensity and then receded.

Sharon wondered what she was thinking about, or should the question be "whom"?

Harriet leaned over to give Sharon a kiss on the cheek, but Sharon turned her face, teasing her. Their lips touched, and they kissed.

Sharon slid her hands around Harriet's waist, drawing her closer as the kiss deepened. The heat of their bodies commingled.

Harriet cupped Sharon's soft cheeks in her warm hands. Her tongue explored the outside of Sharon's lips. She grew bolder as Sharon parted her lips and drew in her tongue for further exploration. She slid her arms around Sharon's waist, lifting her a few inches. Without breaking their kiss, she fumbled to open the door, carried Sharon into her quarters, and set her down gently.

Sharon's hands ran over Harriet's athletic body, and she reveled in the feel of the heated skin under her sensitive palms. She tugged Harriet's shirt out of her slacks, and Harriet shivered at her touch. Sharon groaned and began to unbutton Harriet's shirt, wanting more. Harriet broke their kiss, her lips and tongue leaving a wet trail along Sharon's jaw to her neck. Sharon's breath caught and she pushed her body closer to Harriet's, needing to feel her more intimately.

Harriet's shirt fell to the deck, and the rest of their clothing quickly followed.

* * *

Sharon woke the next morning, when she felt Harriet's movements. As memories of the previous night came back to her, Harriet wrapped her arms around her and nibbled on her neck. Sharon groaned softly, shivers coursing through her body.

"I need to get back to my quarters and check for messages," Harriet whispered in her ear.

"Just like a doctor, always on call." Sharon turned in her arms and drew her close for a soft kiss.

"You're right, Doc. You can always call me." Untangling herself from Sharon, Harriet slid out of bed and began to dress, plucking her clothing from the commingled pile.

Sharon rose, drew on her robe, and sat on the edge of the bed to watch. As she admired Harriet's body, memories of caressing her brought a fresh surge of desire.

Harriet finished dressing and moved to Sharon, who stood up. They embraced.

"This is going to lead us back to bed," Harriet said.

"Yes, and neither of us will be on time for our watches."

They slowly stepped apart.

After Harriet left, Sharon decided a cold shower might help her overheated condition. She enjoyed the companionship, and after an intimate introduction to Harriet's body, she most definitely liked the feel of it against hers, and all the other things it did to her, but was it wise to get involved? Harriet was mixed up with Alan's madness.

Sharon laughed at herself. She was part of Alan's madness, too.

When Sharon returned to her quarters at the end of that day, she found a beautiful flower resting at the bottom of her mailbox, along with a note from Harriet. Until then, Sharon had only received deliveries for her laboratory. A gift from the heart was a pleasant surprise.

Both women were busy for the next few nights, but they made plans to see a movie on the fourth evening. Harriet appeared at Sharon's door dressed casually, in a loose-fitting green blouse and dark brown pants. Sharon's gaze traveled over Harriet's body, and she appreciated what she saw.

"Sorry," Sharon said, "but I'm running late. I had an experiment that took longer than expected."

"No problem. We have time… if you hurry."

They laughed and then embraced. Harriet kissed Sharon gently on the cheek.

"I'll be just a minute more," Sharon said, smiling into eyes that were dark with desire. Her own body throbbed from the brief touch.

She returned to her bedroom and picked out a necklace that would hang just above the V-neck of her top. She couldn't get the clasp fastened right. "Harriet, can you help me with this?" she called out, exasperated.

Harriet stepped into the bedroom, took both ends of the necklace, and waited for Sharon to turn her back. Harriet's fingers trembled slightly, and she kept missing the clasp, as well.

"There, I got it."

Sharon turned around to face Harriet, and the clasp came undone. The weight of the necklace pulled it down into her cleavage. Harriet made a reflex grab for it, and her fingers brushed Sharon's breast.

Without hesitation, Sharon pressed the hand firmly against her breast and leaned in to kiss a surprised Harriet.

Sharon heard a groan, which could well have come from her own throat, as Harriet's fingertips pinched her taut nipple. She slid her arms around Harriet's waist, pulled her closer, and hungrily devoured her lips. The kissing turned into passionate grappling and clothes were shed. The movie was completely forgotten.

Harriet had the next two days off, and Sharon had nothing scheduled at work, so they remained in Sharon's room, exploring their sexuality and sharing accounts from earlier in their lives.

As a shaman, Sharon attempted to heal some of the darkness in Harriet's soul while they were making love. However, some places were shut tight, even when Harriet was experiencing the heights of passion. Sharon had already seen that the only time Harriet opened up fully was when she was alone in her quarters, playing her flute, so she made sure she gave her that time. She knew Harriet might shut down if she invaded that space.

Harriet needed to experience the darkness so she could understand despair and its levels. As an empath, Harriet's connection with others was intense, no matter how much she might deny that the emotional tie was there. Experiencing despair for herself broadened her awareness. Not all empaths took that difficult learning path to develop themselves, but those who did had, on some level, set this course for themselves.

Sharon used prayers and chants to push back the dark cloud that had engulfed Harriet until she would be able to rebuild her own energy. She asked the healers on Magewield to add their support.

After a year of living separately, Harriet moved in with Sharon.

* * *

Four years passed, along with the usual problems two compulsive workers in the same relationship encountered. Sometimes they were ships passing in the night.

Harriet was promoted, and her new duties had her spending more time on *Ziggy* than *Nettle*. If she returned late at night, Sharon would wake for a moment and then snuggle into her arms before falling back to sleep. Such had been the case the previous night. Sharon felt Harriet get up for a moment to use the toilet then lie back down. She opened one eye and stared at Harriet, who was studying her.

"What's creasing your brow, Commander?" She ran a fingertip over Harriet's brow in a caressing gesture.

"Your body," Harriet said in a husky voice.

"What about my body?"

"You always keep it covered."

Sharon's pulse quickened. "Ah. You want to see more?" She rolled Harriet onto her back and straddled her.

As though lying in wait to pounce on their play, Harriet's alarm clock went off.

* * *

Sharon paused from her work at noon, and while waiting for her lunch to heat, picked up her messages.

One was from Harriet, reporting that she had been called back to *Ziggy*, and she would be away for a while. Sharon sighed.

"Harriet, you're spending more time there then here. You should post *Ziggy* as your permanent station, instead of *Nettle*."

She caught her breath as the meaning of her seemingly casual comment deepened.

"Fata Morgana!" she said in exasperation. "Of course, the change is near. I've been ignoring it, as if putting off what needs to be done will make any difference."

She closed her eyes for a moment and took a deep, pain-filled breath. "So, the time is upon us, love. I'll have to shoo you out of our nest." She paused to wipe tears from her eyes. "I'm sure you'll forgive me sometime in the future, but I'll miss you and worry that you'll go into this dragging your stubborn heels all the way."

Sharon let the empty feeling of Harriet's absence fill her, so she could get a handle on the emotions she would experience when she asked her lover to move out. She had to come up with a good reason. She would use her abilities as a shaman to ease Harriet's hurt, if she could.

She slumped back in her chair and let the tears fall. Sobs tore from her throat as her heart ached for what she had to do. After a while, she took a deep breath and tossed her collection of tissues into the waste bin. She sniffled and grabbed another tissue to blot her wet face. Glumly, she went on to the next communication.

"Oh, fey. It's from Alan. Just what I need." As she read it, she realized his words were more vehement than usual. Not bothering to respond, she moved on to the next message.

Three days later, as she was again going through her mail, Sharon found a coded message from one of her covert agents.

She jumped up from her chair. "Yes! The time is now."

The small changes that had taken place throughout the galaxy had been a prelude to a larger change. A shift in one galaxy's power structure was affecting others. Addressing her reflection in the shiny surface of her work area, Sharon spoke aloud. "It really has begun."

She had played a dangerous game, avoiding Alan Fermin's insistent and increasingly irrational demands to deliver Harriet into the hands of one of his agents. Afraid that he was demented enough to try to kidnap her from *Nettle*, Sharon and the spirit, Gedaliaha, had devised a plan to protect her if he should be successful. Sharon's operatives, in fact, were already in place. But for the moment, she had to separate herself from Harriet and somehow get her farther away from Alan's reach.

A week later, Harriet returned from duty and Sharon asked her to move out, citing their increasing involvement with their own work and claiming that she wanted her space back. Hurt, but also relieved, Harriet agreed. Her nightmares had increased in frequency and severity, and she'd been afraid Sharon would start questioning her about them.

Harriet's duties with the Centurion Corps on *Ziggy* had been expanded to working with the group that planned raids on smuggler dens, resulting in an uneven division of her time between *Ziggy* and *Nettle*. Shortly after Harriet moved into her own quarters, *Nettle* suffered hull damage and had to be hauled into a yard for repair.

Sharon's fears for Harriet eased when Harriet received transfer papers making her a permanent crewmember on *Ziggy*. Meanwhile, she and the rest of the science crew from the damaged *Nettle* resettled on their new vessel, *Curious Cat*, to continue monitoring the planet.

Any renewal of the intimate relationship between Harriet Montran and Sharon Teal seemed unlikely.

Chapter 12

Montran labored her way through the medical jargon in the articles on metrapeople. Guardian's library had an extensive collection of information on the subject. The four most prolific contributing authors wrote under pseudonyms: Acronym, Iwilla, Maa, and Heartstone. A biography search on the names turned up nothing useful, so she returned to the menu. With her limited time, she needed to concentrate on the meat of the information.

A buzzing sound disturbed her mental processes as she was trying to absorb the data on chip implantation.

"Yes?" She rubbed her tired eyes.

"Are you too busy to visit Guardian?" Charles's polite voice inquired.

Montran glanced at the time on the bottom of her screen. Two stan hours had passed.

"Oh, blasters!" Jumping up, she knocked her partially eaten meal to the floor. As she ran out of the room, the cleaning bot was picking up the plate and the remains of her sandwich.

From her limited research, she suspected that the scientists in the metralabs knew the bodies they revived were living people, with fully functioning brains and self-will. It explained why chip implantation was necessary in order to enforce compliance.

In Com-C, she found Charles and Guardian. Guardian's dais was lit up, presenting him as a holographic image of a smug Copoc spinning puzzle pieces. Charles held a cup of steaming tea. "I'm late," Montran said.

"No. As a matter of fact, you started early on your project," Guardian said. The puzzle cube disappeared, and the holographic Copoc leaned forward in its seat. "Major Zohra is pleased by your initiative."

Guardian's words conjured up the image of a dog getting a pat on the head. Irritated, she said, "Could you be clearer?"

"We need to learn as much as we can about metrapeople. I have the relevant information and my own opinions, as do others, but another's view would be invaluable. So, what have you synthesized thus far?"

"Well, umm…" Conflicting thoughts on Zohra's opinion of her initiative and the weak excuse Guardian had given made her hesitate. Her own prickliness also had her off balance. Taking a deep breath to collect her thoughts, she sat on the edge of a chair Charles provided. He handed her the warm cup of tea he had been holding, which she acknowledged with a nod, vaguely aware of taking it.

She felt like she was being manipulated, but for the moment there was little she could do but see where it would lead. Pursing her lips, she mulled over what she had read.

"Like you said, the victims all signed a document that gave one of two insurance companies total ownership of their remains after death, provided the body was taken within four hours of being legally declared dead. The survivors, wanting to collect, notified the company quickly and teams arrived within the allotted time.

"The metrapeople show no evidence of brain damage. They don't exercise self-will, however, even when their lives are in danger, unless an override is part of the program. They are people, in effect, who have been programmed to be mindless slaves."

Montran took a moment to sip her tea. "However, even with all the programming, some awareness of self remains within metrapeople, otherwise the pain inducers, which also suppress certain memory functions, wouldn't have to be implanted. It sounds similar to the lobotomies that some planets used to perform on their problem citizens. But metrapeople can be educated and taught new skills, should their owners' needs change, whereas a lobotomized individual is permanently brain damaged.

"According to Iwilla, one of the authorities on metrapeople, there's a universal tone that can nullify all the previous programming, but she didn't say what it was. She did discuss the danger of using it, preferring the single deprogramming tone to which each metraperson is set. In the case of Alan's metrasoldiers, I can see her point. Zohra mentioned they were all procured from planets that practiced genocide warfare.

"One problem they pose is that they're trained to kill themselves and as many of their captors as possible. Snagging them one at a time will be a daunting task."

Montran grimaced at the thought of trying to arrest a fighter that was rigged as a time bomb. She had seen that happen, and had been part of the clean-up crew.

"Some of the research I reviewed was on recovering erased personalities and the possible dangers inherent in that." She paused and took another sip of tea, this time noticing the tangy taste. "If there's that much information on the subject, why hasn't it raised red flags with the scientific community? And not just in GCFC space, but the Collective's also?"

She glared up at Guardian's holographic figure. Since he was once a scientist, she was calling on him to justify the moral depravity she had found in a group she'd once thought had higher values than those apparent from her research.

"The documents in my system," Guardian replied, "are not available to just anyone. Most of what you read was intended for private study by a select group of scientists, who were interested in participating in the experiment when it first started up."

Like willing your brain to science, Montran thought, *so they can hook it up to a computer and make part of you immortal.*

"The more recent work," Guardian said, "was done by a group of scientists gathering data to present before the Council of Rings on the immorality of this practice. This subject has more impact than the indiscretions of the GCFC members that the recent broadcast revealed. One group fears that the Scientists for Ethical Practice will challenge the practice of chip implantation that allows psychotic citizens to live in normal society."

He held up two of his hands to forestall her angry retort. "At least one in four wealthy and powerful families has a member that has such an implant. Among the less wealthy, over the last several years it has become standard practice to insert chips in citizens judged so violent that some sort of behavior modification is necessary. It is that or move them to Hinterwield, which is getting crowded."

"What awakened the sensibilities of the judicial system?"

Guardian cleared his nonexistent throat. "You."

"Me?"

"Alan's attack on you made every galactic news agency. When his history was exposed, and he still was not sent to the Wield prison colony, there were mass demonstrations in front of every government judicial office.

"To quiet the masses, the governments felt they had no choice but to grant all citizens in GCFC space that were convicted of violent crimes the same chance Alan was given: to receive a chip implant and live with their families, instead of being shipped off to prison for the rest of their lives. It was bound to happen, anyway. The companies involved with producing the implants have been petitioning to expand their business into the public market."

Guardian continued speaking, clearly anticipating her objection. "As you pointed out, it is not tamper proof. Therefore, in six stan months, three groups of scientists will attend a hearing to present their arguments for and against the practice of implanting chips to control violent behavior. The gathering has not been made public because those who stand to lose the most are claiming that announcing the possible discontinuation of using the chips will cause riots among the populace. Silence about the hearing is being enforced with stiff penalties."

"What a mess," Montran said. "Thank the goddess I don't live in this part of the galaxy." She looked at Guardian, perplexed. "Was there something specific Major Zohra wanted me to study?"

"Nothing specific."

Her thoughts moved to the types of people the metralabs were enslaving. If Alan was using violent personalities from closed planets for his soldiers, what was to prevent others from purchasing that type of personality for use as their own bodyguards? Or to use as assassins, or worse yet, to form private armies that no one knew about until it was too late? And what was the difference between behavior chips for violent personalities and those for metrapeople?

"I need to read more of Iwilla's work on her subjects' dream states. She believes the suppressed personality resides in dreams." Montran paused, trying to put aside the pain she felt for those who had been turned into metraslaves. Her gaze wandered to the monitors. "Where is everyone?"

"Maud is resting. Major Zohra and Carol are on a recon mission. Freight from *Spinner's Tale* was dropped nearly a day's march from its intended mark. I have scrambled the soldiers' locators, so it will be a while until they can find it.

"We are grateful that you have given Carol permission to be away from you," he added.

Montran cocked her head to one side. "A test of my morals, huh?" she said, joking. "My intention remains firm, Guardian. I mean to help her reclaim her ability to choose her own future. It's one of the reasons I'm studying memory retrieval. I don't want to hinder her recovery, and I don't want someone else to be able to grab a key card and turn her back into a helpless slave."

She changed the subject. "Why am I not surprised about the misplaced freight, or is that your doing?"

"Someone forgot to recalibrate the harmonics after the last wind storm. Major Zohra wanted to see what is in the package, render it useless if it is harmful, and then harass whoever picks it up."

"Let's hope the major hasn't bitten off more than she can chew and doesn't end up surrounded by a squad arriving to reclaim their toy." Montran shrugged. "But then, once a Black Rose, always a Black Rose."

She thought of the swagger she had seen in Zohra's stride as they walked from the dojo back to their quarters. Memories of the dark figure performing the Dance, which required a lot of athletic ability and endurance, made her smile. Zohra had good reason to be self-confident.

A thought suddenly occurred to her. If she had considered the possibility of planting programmed people in sensitive places, then others had, too. Perhaps even Alan. Maybe he was planning to use Merker's Outpost to test such a weapon.

"Guardian, can you make it so we don't appear on your screens?" Montran turned to look at Guardian's hologram. If she weren't so serious about the question, she would have laughed at the expression on the Copoc's face.

"If Alan, or an agent of his, got in here," she said, holding up a hand to stop Guardian's reply, "we would all be easy targets. You said that a few squads will be landing soon. Alan will have spies among them. If not *his* spies, then people who, when they see your gadgets, will see a rich future for themselves by selling your ideas. I know you've thought of that."

"If you remember, I told you I have everything patented."

"I'm not referring to patents. I'm referring to the illegal side, like theft, smuggling, selling information about what you have here. You'll have an onslaught of thieves, buyers, and adventurers."

"It is the reason why I have kept the planet closed."

"You need a backup plan, should a disaster happen. We need a way to keep our suits from being monitored, in case we need to rescue Com-C or some other strategic place without anyone's knowledge."

"She asked the same questions, for the same reasons," Guardian said.

"Major Zohra?"

"Yes."

"Did you tell her?" Montran was a little disappointed he had talked to Zohra first.

"No. She told me I needed to make up my mind before the reinforcements arrived, so everyone involved would know their role."

"Uh huh. So unlike a computer to be uncertain. Is it that you don't trust us? You have my life history on a dot in your memory banks. I've never—" She stopped, remembering her imprisonment by the enemy over seven years ago. The last time they had not been looking for secrets. Would she give up information if she were caught again?

"It is not just a matter of trust, Commander Montran," he said softly.

Her head lifted and she stared at the hologram, not seeing it for a moment. Blinking a few times, she turned her attention back to the matter at hand and let out a short laugh. "I get it. Power. You told me that when we first met."

"Yes."

"Maud knows, so apparently you trust someone outside of your computer environment."

"She is my fail-safe."

"I wouldn't intentionally put you, or her, in danger, nor would I give up any information if it put someone here in harm's way." A shaft of pain shot through Montran as she remembered the dead Spartans, who had trusted her.

"The demise of that squad was already decided," Guardian said. "What you gave them was more than they could ever have hoped for."

"They died. Many of them painfully."

"They died with their dignity and with pride in what they had accomplished. Everyone is aware that the Degas were once a proud squad. Their downfall was sealed on the day Lord Chaney humiliated himself in front of them, and they laughed. After that, every deadbeat, deserter, and otherwise lost sheep in the Spartan corps ended up in that squad. He made them bait with no teeth. You turned them into a proud, shining example of Spartan guts and adaptation. They had nothing to be ashamed of. Neither have you."

Suddenly, Montran was incensed. "No one has the right to use others for fodder."

"True, but they were used that way. Because of Lord Chaney's position, he got away with it. In the short time they served under your command, you gave them a reason to believe in themselves as a unit. You and I both know they would have been losers if they had walked away from the military and tried to make it in civilian life. The squad gave them community and dignity, and you showed them pride."

"I turned them into killers," she said bitterly.

"They were soldiers and killers already. And in the record, it says they became raiders, stealing supplies from the enemy, not killing citizens who were caught between warring factions and the military police hired to put down riots."

Montran gave a short laugh, and the tense lines of her face relaxed. "Well, the majority of them were thieves, so stealing supplies came naturally. Guardian, can we talk about something more important than my past?"

"The loyalty you showed them leads me to trust you with Merker's life and all those in its sphere."

Covering her embarrassment, Montran smirked. "So, are you going to let me become completely invisible at my own discretion?"

"Yes."

"Okay." Montran settled into command mode. "Let's get down to how, and under what circumstances."

She was silent for a few moments, thinking up various scenarios. "I want to be able to give false readings, but if someone should stumble on where I'm supposed to be, I'll need a fallback plan. The worst possible scenario would be if someone got into your system, so this program has to operate separately from yours."

The holographic Guardian nodded.

"I'll also need to be able to contact Maud without others knowing, which includes you, so we can work together."

"You intend to leave Major Zohra out of this, I take it."

"Like you, I think the best kept secret is one that the fewest people know. I'm not sure where her loyalties lie, whether with Naboth's Vine or her Shield House." *Or somewhere else.*

"And what about your loyalty to your admiral?"

"Until she reassigns me, I'm yours. Since she didn't pick me up on one of the passing ships, my guess is that she means to leave me here, perhaps as an observer." Montran grinned. "But this observer has a tendency to do 'hands on' observing."

Guardian agreed, and they went over their plans, conferencing in Maud, who offered her own suggestions.

"You're going to have to erase this conversation," Maud said to Guardian once they had agreed on a plan, which Guardian immediately implemented. "You must also forget, my friend, so anyone reviewing your memory won't find this. Now, I must go."

Montran moved over to the screens. "Guardian, you might want to have the record show that I was studying charts or just watching these screens. Zohra isn't one to be fooled easily, so you'd better make it good."

"I have done this before, Commander Montran," he said.

"Not in an attempt to fool me, I hope."

"No."

She was curious, but then she decided it could wait for another time, should the matter even come up again. She walked to one of the screens that showed a group of soldiers in Century City moving a weapon into position on an elevator. She noted there were fewer people in the other screens.

"Looks like an almost deserted city."

"Except for a scattering of Spartans. Lord Chaney's ship has returned, and a squad of Alan's soldiers arrived a few stan hours ago."

"So, Alan is interested in this place." Montran leaned forward and stared at one of the screens. "That's a Chatlin cannon." Suited figures struggled to set it on a mobile robot. The cannon used sound waves to destroy specific targets. A deadly weapon on the open battlefield, it would be devastating to the life support systems of an underground city.

"They need a specialist to maintain it, or the operator ends up being on the receiving end."

"That may be Ensign Everett, from *Spinner's Tale*," Guardian said. "Unless I know what sound wave will be emitted, I will not be able to shut it down before it does harm."

"Right."

"What do you suggest?" Guardian asked.

"First off, lock up Everett somewhere, and then grab whoever else looks like they know how to handle it."

"Getting to him is going to be a problem. He never leaves the ship."

"If he doesn't come down to the planet, there must be another tech. I mean, what does he plan to do, call down the instructions? It's not that easy to sync them. It would be suicidal to have only one tech. And that elevator they're using, where does it lead? I don't recall seeing one with that emblem on it."

"It is the primary morgue elevator."

She moved to the screen that showed the storage room next to the morgue. "Strange that they would choose one place to keep all their supplies, including weapons. On the other hand, with so few guards left, maybe that's a good idea."

"The morgue area has its own life support system, like the laboratories in this section. It was designed that way to prevent anything stored there from contaminating living spaces."

"I think a reconnaissance is needed to do some inventorying."

The lights in the adjacent conference room came on, and a map appeared on the wall. Montran stepped into the meeting room and studied the large map. "Nice detail. Do you have cameras covering this location? And can you give me a one-month history of the T&T rotation?"

Enlarged shots of the area came up and showed a pattern of traps and trip wires laid and moved by various Black Rose soldiers. Absentmindedly, Montran slid her empty cup onto the table behind her and crossed her arms.

"It looks like they left a back door open for their return. Odd that they would do that on a smugglers' base. Most smugglers are always ready for a raid and focus on evacuation, not on defensive setups to recapture their den. Isn't this where you sealed off their incursions into the rest of the city?"

"That is correct. Is this good for us?" Guardian asked.

"I don't know yet."

Montran continued to study the pictures. "Are there maintenance or transportation tunnels near?"

"Yes. But on levels they have not been able to access."

Timed clips came up, and she frowned as she watched the patterns change. "They've been rotating the T&Ts on a regular basis, at least until this clip here. Wait. Go back—yeah, yeah. Stop. Now, slowly go forward. I want to see who changed the last one."

"I did."

Montran jumped at the sound of Zohra's voice next to her. Exasperation that anyone had been able to get that close to her without her being aware of it overlapped with an all-too-pleasant shiver from Zohra's nearness.

Zohra flopped into a seat. Fine powder from the planet surface dusted the top of the table as she crossed her booted feet above its shiny surface.

Montran moved her gaze to Carol, who stood quietly beside her. The same powder coated Carol's outer suit, as though she had been crawling or lying in the stuff.

"Major Zohra, how did your job go?" Guardian asked amiably.

"You monitor this place, check it out for yourself."

"Is there something we need to know, Major Zohra?" Montran asked.

There was a brief silence, and Montran watched as Zohra's hands tensed and then relaxed. "Recon went fine," she said.

"Is there something we need to worry about?" Montran asked again. Zohra's dismissive manner seemed forced.

"I said we had no problems."

Montran wondered what had caused her to return with such an attitude. She gestured toward the screen and changed the subject to reduce the tension. "Can you tell us what to expect when we try to get into the storage room from here?"

"Forget it."

"Why?"

"On my last visit, I set a T&T Web as a permanent fixture." For a few moments she looked like she wasn't going to add anything more, and then she continued. "We have another worry."

"What?" Montran and Guardian asked in unison.

Montran studied Zohra closely, wondering again what it was about her that felt off. Zohra had spent years being a sergeant, giving reports and going on recon expeditions. This was within her everyday experience. Was she having problems changing her allegiance?

"Alan's army is here with explosives, enough to blow up an underground city," she said. "That means whatever he intends to do with this place is starting now. We need to make plans. His group must not get a permanent foothold on this outpost or be allowed to plant explosives."

Zohra's tone was vehement enough to convince Montran that in spite of whatever inner turmoil she was experiencing, she did recognize the danger to Merker's and sought to warn them. Of course, Montran could have figured out the danger on her own, just by watching Guardian's screens.

"They moved a Chatlin cannon down to the storage room next to the morgue," Montran said.

"Is that why you're looking at that entrance? You can't get in that way. Too time consuming."

Zohra rose from her seat, went into Com-C, and studied the screens. "I count twelve of his soldiers in the city. No telling where they're going to be posted. Alan keeps track of his minions via a transmitter, and I have that code. It's in my quarters in the city."

Montran blinked at her suddenly cooperative mood.

"Carol would be a good backup to take along, since she knows the city as well as you," Guardian said. "Meanwhile, Commander Montran and I will monitor troop arrivals and their positions and give them to you as we get them."

Carol looked at her mistress hesitantly. Montran nodded and smiled. Major Zohra had already started for the door, and Carol fell in behind her.

"I take it you are not buying the major's story about not being able to enter from that side?" Guardian asked, after the door swished closed behind them.

"I believe nothing is as it seems. Is there a reason why I'm not being asked to go along?"

"You are the reserve, so to speak. Are you anxious to do something?"

Montran turned from the screen and smiled at the holographic image of Guardian. "I guess just getting my toes wet during the first foray has me interested in jumping in with both feet now." She looked back at the one trap that bothered her. "Zohra's right about the time factor, but I've never run across a T&T Web that I couldn't dismantle. And that way in has the huge advantage of surprise."

"I monitor that area. I do not believe she is hiding information about it," Guardian said. "Are you two going to be able to work together?"

"I don't expect her to suddenly drop the façade she's used all these years for survival. It's annoying, but I've spent enough time with prickly personality types to be able to adjust to it. It just caught me off guard."

She was disappointed in her Dancer. That realization brought a pang.

"Two new ships have arrived above my planet," Guardian said. "They are A class. Small haulers that can handle up to forty personnel, along with a month's provisions. I have notified the others."

Shortly, more of Alan's soldiers entered the underground city. Four of them were carrying a clearly marked crate of explosives.

"I can't believe this," Montran said. "If they set that off, you'll have firestorms inside the city. Is he planning to exact revenge for Chaney's death, or is he storing these weapons here to use somewhere else?" She ran her fingers through her hair. "Guardian, how many cities are there, here?"

"There were fifteen at one time, only three of which are habitable now. Why?"

"If Alan plans to destroy Merker's Outpost, it would make sense for him to leave explosives in each city. So, if we see more of those crates being unloaded, it would be prudent for us to consider that as his aim."

"Major Zohra and Carol are still on their way to the city."

Montran straightened up, determined to visit the city, believing that somehow she could find out why Alan's soldiers were unloading heavy explosives. "Tell them I'll be joining them." Guardian didn't argue.

Montran left the room to suit up. "Brief them and send a note to anyone else you've been working with," she called over her shoulder. "They need to know about the firepower being stored here."

Montran's rail car was twenty minutes away from her stop when Guardian contacted her.

"Commander, the major will continue toward her goal to get the device to monitor Alan's soldiers, and she will meet you on the second level for a conference."

"Guardian, did you get a reading on that vial I left with you?"

"A partial one. It is a derivative of a highly toxic and addictive drug. I did not find anything in Zohra's bioreadings that would indicate that it is in her system."

"So, you think I got there just in time?" Montran gave a short laugh. "Call me overly suspicious, but Lord Chaney in her room with a highly addictive drug, and her suddenly snappish behavior... Don't you think they're related?"

"I did a complete scan on her bios," Guardian said, but he sounded doubtful. "There was nothing that looked like a trigger for that drug."

"Was there anything in her system that you couldn't identify?"

"I have not been able to discover the exact difference, only that there is a change in her chemistry from what it was when she was in the academy. If the major is addicted to something, what do you suggest we do with her?"

"I don't think she could have been on anything for long. She would have needed a fix sooner. Let her work off the effects, if that's what's causing her sudden change in behavior. What about the rest of the Black Rose squad? Do you know their status?"

"I've rendered them unconscious to prevent any attempts at escape. When *Respite*'s sister ship arrives, they will be turned over to the Yellow Rose Guard of Triton. I'll monitor their bioreadings closely until then."

"Well, I won't be waiting for Major Zohra and Carol. I want to look at that side of the supply corridor without Major Zohra's interference."

"Maud is headed to the station. She has finished administering to my guests."

"Is there a way to stop this car in the closed part of the city?"

"The closed section of Century City has no support system or lights. A side rail will take you to a repair depot, and I will disengage my barrier in the tube. You will have to open a door between the two parts of the city, using an override to prevent a breach."

Montran traced the image of the city's schematics that appeared on the car's wall. "There's a passage to the corridor that I want to get to. C4 is your code for that area."

"Yes. That is the buffer zone between the occupied part of Century City and where I have been keeping the rescued survivors. Stopping just past the station will require a sudden deceleration, but I believe the suit can handle it. So far I see no one in the area, but that does not mean they will not be there when you arrive. The fast-moving vehicles make an unmistakable sound. Fifteen stan minutes more. Once you are past the terminal, the speed will decrease. The car will return to its normal place after you have disembarked."

"Good."

Chapter 13

Montran used her suit light to scan the walls and ceiling of the pitch black service tunnel. Within fifteen minutes, she reached the Web that Zohra had set to prevent anyone from entering the inhabited part of the city unannounced. It took another five minutes to find out why Zohra believed Montran wouldn't get by.

Grinning, Montran flexed her fingers and then began to dismantle the Web. She had learned the skill as CO of the Degas squad and honed it further working with Commander Nelson, who liked to set Webs in odd places during her training sessions. It was a valuable skill, since while the Collective's forces didn't use them, the outlaws they hunted did.

After another twenty minutes, she wiped her tired fingers on her pants and then carefully pulled down the last Web filament. Nothing snagged, but she was still cautious. She didn't want to find out, too late, that she had missed a trip wire. Finished, she laid a new trap, setting some of Guardian's stingers and sonic sounders in place. That would leave them paranoid. Feeling quite proud of herself, Montran shook out her tired arms and hands. Up the corridor, just short of the bend in the hall, was the wall panel for the surveillance switches. It took her two minutes to reactivate the equipment the Black Rose had shut down.

"Guardian, can you see me?"

"Yes. I can see you and down the corridor as well. The connection you established is engaging the other surveillance cameras as we speak."

"What can you see on the other side of where I am?"

"I see one guard from *Spinner's Tale* standing outside the storage room. He has a timer device in his hand. Six Spartans are inside the room with the explosives. They are engaged in heavy betting on the card game they seem to always be playing. Alan's team, the one that delivered the explosives, is on the second floor, conferring with others of their group."

"Then this is a good time," Major Zohra said, "for us to neutralize the explosives."

Startled by the voice coming through her communicator, Montran looked behind her.

"We're in the opposite wall from you, Lady Harriet."

Montran could hear the smirk in Zohra's voice. After a moment, a small picture appeared in one corner of her visor.

"You can control which camera you want to view by tapping the blue dot on your left forearm," Guardian said. "You can move between current and previous camera views with the raised symbols on the button."

Montran tested it out, getting a view of Carol and then one of Zohra. She zoomed in on her, noticing the lines of strain around her eyes, and then tapped again to see views of the corridor.

"Guardian," Zohra said, "you have a gas that can neutralize one of the compounds in the explosives, making the rest harmless. The gas I'm thinking of is pinkish, unless you have more than one pink shade."

"I know which one, and it would, but I do not have access to the morgue area with any gas. You will have to move the explosives to another floor."

"That can be arranged," Zohra said.

Montran studied the image of the Spartan who was guarding this part of the hall.

Turning her head slightly, she watched Zohra and Carol moving toward her.

"Nice work on the Web. I underestimated your skills," Zohra said softly. "It won't happen again."

Montran tried not to smirk.

"It's standard practice," Zohra continued, "to have one guard for this side of the corridor." She looked into Montran's eyes and then quickly away. "But something's not right."

Montran pulled a piranha star out of her utility pocket.

"Nice toy," Zohra murmured. "How fast can you sprint?"

Montran held up the star. "Fast enough."

"When you're ready, Lady Harriet."

When they came around the corner, the guard was walking in a small circle, probably trying to stay alert. He looked in their direction and froze. Then the star grazed his cheek, immediately numbing him. Zohra caught the surprised soldier before he hit the ground, and Montran made a successful grab for the timer. She deactivated the device and tossed it into a waste receptacle for Guardian's bots to dismantle.

While Montran watched for company, Zohra dropped the soldier and sprinted farther down the corridor and around the corner. Carol did her part by placing a sleep patch on the soldier's neck then they both waited for Zohra's return.

"Guardian, do you have someplace to lock him up?" Montran asked.

"Yes, I can reactivate the holding cells. They are only one floor below the recreation area."

"Do it," Zohra ordered softly, and then she reappeared next to Montran and Carol. "And while you're at it, why don't you add the others Carol and I captured and left in closets."

"It means moving them into parts of the city I have closed off."

"Can your bots do it now, or not?" Zohra asked.

"Not just now. I am bringing the environmental system online as we speak, which brings the bots online, too. In thirty stan minutes, I will have them gathered up."

"We need a place to dump this one until your holding cells and bots are ready. Do you have any suggestions?" Zohra's tone was distinctly mocking, and Montran frowned.

"There is a place nearby. Not a closet, just a cubbyhole," Guardian said, just as a long panel near the floor slid open and a bot rolled out, "that he can be stored in."

Zohra retracted her helmet. "Lady Harriet, please do the honors and drag him to his temporary quarters. Don't spend too much time making him comfortable." She gestured Carol toward the storage area's entrance.

Montran dragged the unconscious guard to the opened space. "What does this guy eat?" She grunted as she shoved him into the space. Once the door closed, she sprinted to the corner and hugged the wall. Peering carefully around the bend, she spotted the rest of her team waiting near the entrance to the morgue's storage area.

"Ready?" whispered Zohra.

Montran stood on one side of the door and Carol on the other, prepared to step into the first containment space that led into the area.

"Go."

No one was in it, nor were there any T&Ts. When the second door unsealed, the three fanned out and immediately fired their stunners, catching almost all the card players unawares. One short cry was all that escaped as the men slumped over, unconscious.

Montran and Carol found something to bind them, pasted sleep patches on their necks, and left them hidden behind storage equipment until the bots could collect them.

"I'd rather take my enemies out permanently," Zohra muttered, searching for the explosives. "Then I wouldn't have to worry about dealing with them a second time."

Montran and Carol joined in the search.

Guardian spoke again. "Five Spartans just arrived with what appears to be another Chatlin cannon."

"That makes three. That crazy Alan," Zohra said in exasperation. "Let's find the explosives, dump them in a room where Guardian can neutralize them, and then we'll see if we can steal us a Chatlin cannon and rattle some cages with it."

With a grunt, she slid a crate back in place and went to another. "I could use a grav lifter. The smugglers probably took them all." She let out a string of curses when the crate lid she was balancing dropped near her foot. She pulled a canister and then two more from within the crate.

"Eureka," she said under her breath as she peered at the canister's label.

"We need something to haul them with," Montran said. "Carrying them by hand is going to take too much time."

"I have a few bots online now," Guardian said. A bot rolled out of a storage bay and lifted the three canisters onto its flatbed then wheeled over to the sealed door and waited for one of them to open it.

"That will do it." Zohra looked pleased.

"If you let the bot out, it will find its way to the elevator and to a room on the upper level where I can neutralize the contents," Guardian said.

That done, the three turned to their next task. Zohra took the lead, setting a fast pace through the halls and up a stairway where there were no traps set. Maud would meet them on the second level, where Guardian had told them a group of Alan's soldiers was moving along with the cannon, cautiously and slowly. This didn't make sense to Montran. Why slowly? Were the soldiers expecting trouble? Then Maud came into sight, and Zohra stopped abruptly.

"My twin, Maud, Guardian's assistant." Montran introduced them briefly. "This is Major Zohra, and this is Carol. At your last meeting, you two didn't get a chance to exchange names."

Zohra gave Montran a strange look before nodding a greeting to Maud.

“All right,” Zohra said, “listen up. We have two goals. To capture and neutralize weapons and to immobilize as many of the soldiers as we can. Let’s go.”

They dogged the group for thirty minutes, making their progress to the morgue area even slower, and giving them plenty of surprises both before and behind them. Alan’s soldiers were soon whittled down to five in number. Guardian’s bots dragged off the unconscious soldiers once the others were out of sight.

Suddenly, the soldiers split up. Three guarded the cannon while two attempted to escape through one of the panels. One was successful.

“Guardian, give us a close-up of the cannon,” Zohra ordered, crouched behind the service panel she had propped open. The other three women were sitting behind their own service doors, pinning down the three remaining soldiers.

“It has been decommissioned,” Guardian reported. “The barrel number came up in my search as scrapped from battle. It is probably from one of the late Lord Chaney’s business associates, who owns a salvage company. I do not want to alarm any of you, but there seems to be an active charge on the weapon.”

“No wonder they’re moving so slowly,” Montran said. “Why would they bring an armed weapon down below?”

“Maybe because there’s a passageway near the morgue that leads to the transportation tunnel,” Maud said.

“It’s unlikely they’re moving the cannon somewhere else,” Montran said. “If so, surely they would disarm it first. But they also wouldn’t be using it to knock out the transportation line so early in the game. Then they couldn’t use the mobots to transport the explosives to the other cities.”

Zohra looked at her. “Your idea of setting explosives in the other cities looks like a good possibility.”

“A mobot?” Carol asked.

“Mobile robot,” Montran said. “Program it to take explosives to a site, and both go up with a nice boom. The only loss of life is on the other side.” Montran shifted her weight against the wall and leaned her head back to think. “Guardian, is there anything going on around the morgue area?”

“If you activate your helmets and ask for a view of the morgue…”

They followed his suggestion.

“A change of guard has arrived,” he said. “They did not find anyone to change duty with. They are jumpy at the moment. I see some more of those soldiers dressed in black, Alan's group, heading your way. The one that got away is hurrying toward the morgue."

The images changed rapidly, showing the different levels Alan's soldiers had infiltrated.

Montran wanted to get back to the morgue. It felt too much like they were intentionally being kept busy here. "Major Zohra, I think something's happening in the morgue. Will you be short-handed—"

"I was thinking the same thing. Since you're volunteering, go ahead. But remember, you're only one person and we're pretty busy here."

"And rescuing me from my own folly will not be immediate. I hear you."

Montran slipped into one of the service tunnels. She found several T&Ts and an intricate Web along her way; it looked like Zohra's handiwork. Rather than dismantle them, Montran slid by them, murmuring her thanks to Guardian for the trace elements her helmet was able to pinpoint, which enabled her to find weak spots and slip by them. "Guardian, what's happening?"

"Alan's soldiers are bringing down a fourth cannon. They have not moved the other cannon into the morgue area yet. On the first level, another group of soldiers has just arrived."

He showed her the image of ten soldiers entering the city compound.

"One is holding a small package very carefully."

"Can you tell what's in the package?" Montran asked.

"Trace elements around it indicate that it is Tricom."

"More explosives?"

"Yes."

"I don't see Alan as an arms dealer. With all that's being delivered here, you would think he was getting ready for a war. Who's he fighting with?"

"The only active cannon is the one Major Zohra is now dismantling."

"I think that cannon was used to draw us there, so we would miss something going on elsewhere. With the mobots moving the explosives, it could take a few days to reach cities like the Lair. You can't move explosives fast, or the momentum and heat will detonate them. I sure would like to know if they have enough mobots to do that. Do these metrasoldiers only follow orders?"

"I will reactivate my sentries and search for anything that does not belong. This is the first time Alan's soldiers have visited my outpost, so I have not had much opportunity for direct observation.

As with all metrabeings, how much of their own ingenuity comes into play depends on how much the owner allows the program to be independent of commands. As of yet, there has been no action that would require these soldiers to use independent thinking."

"So, depending on how psychotic and cryptic Alan was when he gave them their marching orders, they may or may not have a set agenda."

"Yes. But you have to take into consideration the culture of these metrasoldiers. They are from a planet where war is a way of life. Most nations that acculturate their inhabitants to war believe the end justifies the means, that civilian casualties are part of war, and that torture is part of life."

"Okay, so we need to find out how much initiative each soldier has. Does that also apply to commanding officers, and do they have commanding officers? If so, we'll need to take out a few of them and cut their communication with Alan."

"I will bring up that plan with Major Zohra. She is preoccupied right now, and conversation might distract her."

"I didn't leave her in a bad situation, did I?"

"Her bioreadings show she is enjoying herself," Guardian said.

Montran arrived at the robot's service entrance without opposition. Given her past good luck in using the smaller entrances, she continued her pattern of crawling through them. She had her stunner in hand, extended before her.

She pulled herself forward on her elbows, listening after each movement to be sure that whatever noise she made was not amplified through the vents. Dragging herself to the bot exit, she stopped when she saw a shadow move across the slatted door.

"I see five in the room," Guardian's voice whispered in her ear.

"What's the total live body count of enemy soldiers on Merker's?" Montran asked softly. Pictures of rooms with soldiers, both Spartan and Alan's, flickered in the edge of her visor.

"I count about forty."

Montran heard an entrance seal release.

"Gunny, they're here," a voice said. "It looks like they need help."

"You two go help out. Maxwell, go outside and stand guard. And stay alert. We don't need any more names on the MIA list."

Judging from the sounds of grunting and muttering, heavy crates were being brought in and shifted about.

"That'll do it," a deep voice said, followed by the shuffle of feet leaving and the door closing.

"How many still here, Guardian?" she whispered.

"Four."

The shadow moved away from her hiding place, and Montran decided to risk using her small spy camera. The fisheye view quickly changed to a focused view of two guards leaning against a stack of boxes. One moved out of sight, and the other went with him. By their sighs, she assumed they were sitting down. She could see no one in the area in front of the vent.

Montran unlatched the door and slid out onto the floor. She eased the door closed and crawled behind a stack of crates, looking around for any monitoring equipment. Finding none, she studied the labels she could see. Food. Why have a lock and seal on food?

Glancing around quickly, she returned her focus to the seal. She had learned how to get by them without anyone being the wiser, a handy trick when you're tracking down smugglers. You find their cache, empty it, and then wait for them to discover that they have nothing to trade. Working for the Centurions was much more fun than her job with the Spartans.

The lock was easy to pick, and the lid slid back quietly. Montran caught her breath at the infantry rifles and spare ammunition clips that were revealed. What were they doing here?

"Trouble heading your way," Guardian's voice whispered.

A voice rang out. "Everyone on your feet. Those deadheads are on their way here."

"At least this time they called ahead," one of the guards near her muttered.

"Most likely wanted to make sure we were still here, not like the other bunch that disappeared," one of the others said.

"Blend on," Montran whispered, activating her suit's camouflage function. She quickly slid the lid back into place, circled around one of the crates, and retreated behind another when a guard moved and blocked her exit. She didn't want to risk depending on the blend. Too much space yawned between her and the wall, unless she slithered along on the floor. That wasn't something she wanted to chance.

She opted for hiding in the box she'd just inspected, repositioning the lid to her hiding place and making sure the seal was over the lip by reaching through the tiny opening, pulling it into place, and then letting the lid drop the rest of the way.

Lying on rifles and ammunition clips was uncomfortable. It seemed like a long time had passed, but the helmet clock indicated that only ten stan minutes had gone by when the talking outside of her box got louder and turned into an argument between the Spartans and the new arrivals. The loud voices dropped to mutterings, and soon came sounds of scraping and grunting. It sounded as though boxes were being shifted.

Montran's box was lifted. From the smoothness of the movement, she guessed a mobot was being used.

She could hear no voices to give her a hint as to where she was being taken. The forward motion was slow at first, but then it picked up. About fifteen minutes passed before the box stopped, and then the direction was changed. She bumped along for a few short minutes, and then the box came to rest and something was dropped on top of it.

"Guardian," she whispered, "where am I?"

"In the transportation bay, up the line. They disrupted my barrier, but I have reestablished it. Whatever they used has compromised your suits, and some functions have shut down in order to keep your life support going. It will take a while for it to balance, but some of the ancillary features are already coming back, such as the bioreadings on your visor. That means your blend function is down for now. I am working on a way to prevent recurrence of this problem."

"I knew I was a test subject."

"Even a well-tested weapon, once placed in the hands of a professional, will demonstrate room for improvement. Nothing is fail-safe."

"Right, right. I'm just being grumpy. Have they posted a guard?"

"They have sensors spaced to set off alarms, should anyone approach their belongings."

"Who are they expecting, phantom soldiers?"

"From the conversations I have overheard, their apprehension is due to the disappearance of soldiers, including some of their own, compliments of Major Zohra and Carol. They think they are facing a large army."

"Tch, tch. Like the Black Rose?" Moving carefully in the small space, she felt for her sidearm. "Right now a bot would be a great help to get me out of here, but there may be traps around the box, too."

"Conflag filaments," Guardian said, confirming her guess. "Major Zohra and Carol are still engaged with their business, and Maud is attending to a disturbance among the rescued prisoners."

Montran was really disgusted with the current consequences of her independent venture. She should have known better. A lone wolf operation was always discouraged, unless it was well planned and well thought out.

Her fingers wrapped comfortably around her sidearm, ready to lift it should she need it. She closed her eyes and did what soldiers in combat situations usually do, which is grab some sleep whenever an opportunity presents itself.

* * *

Scratching sounds on the box alerted Montran. She heard the hum of a grav lifter. Whatever was on top of her box was removed, and after a few moments, the lid slowly opened. She raised the tip of her weapon, but a light blinded her. Before she could recover and aim, a stunner paralyzed her. The lid slid farther back. Against a dark background, she could see a young, helmeted face peering in.

"It's her!" a voice squeaked, muted by the helmet. "Wait till they see what I found." The stunner's charge had blurred Montran's vision and frozen her fingers in their grip around her sidearm. Her nerveless arms hung limply against the walls of her prison. Again, she cursed her choice of hiding places. The lid slammed back down, and she heard clumsy booted footsteps running away.

Needling pain stabbed through her limbs. Time passed in slow agony as she sweated out the effects, and she cursed the imbecile who had switched his stunner to such a painful setting.

Someone pushed aside the lid. Through her visor, she could make out the outline of a helmet like hers. Arms reached in, pulled her out, and dropped her over a shoulder. She felt like a bag of potatoes, but she was grateful she was being rescued. At least she hoped she was.

She grunted involuntarily as she was jostled and bounced on the runner's shoulder. She could see nothing but a back. Her useless arms flopped about, annoying her and probably the person carrying her. Finally, her journey ended. She slid off the shoulder that she could now feel was bony, and gentle hands leaned her against a wall. Her arms and legs tingled as feeling gradually returned.

"Harriet, you get into as much trouble as you dish out." Maud retracted Montran's helmet and injected something into her neck. "You need a bodyguard to make sure you don't put something important in the proverbial lion's mouth." She pushed some sore spots on Montran's head, neck, and face. "It's painful, right?"

"Yeah." Montran's voice sounded raspy. "Whatever it was must be potent if Guardian's suit didn't block it. I guess he hasn't got it fully functional yet."

"You were protected. Normally the recipient would be screaming when sensation returned to the limbs. How are you feeling?"

"Better." She managed to put her stunner back in its holster, and then bent her arms, fingers, and legs, shaking them out.

"Good," Maud said. "Guardian will have his bots confiscate the supplies in that tunnel."

"Alan is either an arms dealer or he plans on having a war down here. I thought he wanted to blow up the planet's core, but since those weapons are being stored, it means they plan on coming back for them. I've got to return to the storage room."

Maud gave her a look. "Haven't you had enough trouble for one day?"

Montran held up her hand. "I promise not to put anything in the lion's mouth this time."

They trotted through the tunnel and stopped at the maintenance entrance to the morgue's storage room.

"Can you wait here and keep watch? By now the group in there should be sleeping."

"Every seven stan minutes, give me a check that you're okay."

"All right. And thanks, Maud."

"I hope this run of good luck continues for you."

"Is that what you call good luck? Ouch."

At the maintenance grate, Montran sent her small peeping-eye camera through the vent. No one came into its view, but she could hear more than one person making noises typical of sleep. She unlatched the panel and silently slid it open, crawled out, closed the panel, and snaked over to a nearby crate. A soldier slept on top of it, snoring in gusts and whistles. She affixed a sleeping patch to his palm.

Montran heard movement. She spun around, dropped to her knee, and yanked her stunner from its holster. Zohra stood there, her hands open, showing she had no weapon. Carol was pulling herself out of the service tunnel.

Sighing in relief, Montran holstered her stunner and finished her mission, making sure the guards stayed asleep, while Zohra and Carol started opening the suspect crates. She caught up with Zohra, who was carefully inspecting the contents of a crate that contained a regular cannon. Zohra cursed.

"What's wrong?"

"It's armed with a timer, set for 0400 tomorrow. We'll need to move it topside so I can set it off." She sniffed the inside of the crate. "Smells like they've got the big bang in here, too. Tricom." She pointed to where small packages of powder were stuffed in the cannon's barrel, along with material to absorb dampness.

"Since it won't explode without Herculeon acting as a catalyst, maybe they're just storing it," Montran said.

"No liquid ampoules here, but they'd undoubtedly be hiding it. But why all this mix of weapons?" Zohra asked. "The lack of catalyst indicates they're not intending for it to go off with anything more than a small pop, although they could use it to set off something else." They looked around, but couldn't find anything in the crates that would explode.

"I'd guess they mean to move it soon," Montran said.

"There's too much overall activity going on."

"Maybe the intention is to keep us putting out fires."

"That occurred to me, too. I feel like there's more than one war plan in operation here. Let's move this stuff, so they're missing additional pieces from whatever they're scheming to do."

As the three of them struggled to lift the cannon out of the crate, the service panel slid open and Maud appeared on the other side. "The tunnel is still clear," she said, "but there's activity on fifth level, south elevator. The cameras have been disengaged again."

Zohra looked surprised. "That's the elevator to the crew's quarters. They could be setting charges, looting, or taking it over for themselves until Alan gets here. A recon in the area would give us an idea."

"While you're moving the cannon, I want to disable as many mobots as I can," Montran said.

Carol stepped forward. "I will assist my mistress."

"Good idea," Zohra said. "Maud, you and I will dispose of the cannon, check out the crew's quarters, and take a look topside. Guardian, we need some of your bots to carry this thing."

"There is one waiting here in the tunnel," Maud said. A bot scooted past her and into the storage room.

Zohra glanced at Montran. "When you're finished here, return to base."

"Aye, aye, Major," Montran replied automatically. She was grateful Zohra hadn't mentioned her recent misadventure. Maybe she didn't know about it yet.

Zohra gave her an odd look then hurried after Maud and the bot.

Montran popped the cover off of the control panel of the mobot and removed an essential part. She showed Carol how to damage the pad so the bot would be useless without major service and part replacement. She was gambling that Alan didn't have a fully serviced repair shop on any of his ships, or many spare parts.

In one stan hour, they sabotaged a dozen mobots, as well as other equipment. They moved quickly and efficiently, resealing the crates so a quick glance wouldn't reveal which ones had been tampered with. The trash receptacles were kept humming as they vaporized parts.

"Commander Montran," Zohra's voice said. "You have some metrasoldiers heading your way. You have seven minutes to get out of there. We can't back you up right now."

"Carol, get the sleep patches off those soldiers." Montran waved to one side of the room while she headed for the other. She was withdrawing her hand from the neck of a sleeping guard when the seal opening on the door to the hall startled both her and the guard. Fortunately, the guard fell off the crate on the opposite side, before he could see her. Carol crouched behind a crate within Montran's view. Montran gestured at the service panel Zohra had left open and moved in that direction. The two guards remained out of sight as the visitors entered, the sound of their heavy boots indicating that they were wearing AEGs. Both women exited safely.

"I got four, Carol. Did you do the others?"

"Yes, Mistress."

Montran carefully reset the T&Ts outside the panel and followed Carol down the service tunnel. Carol took an unexpected turn at the second branch and got ahead.

Just then, a service panel door opened in front of Montran and a concussion bomb dropped in. She made a diving catch and tossed it back through the closing panel. Hurrying on, she picked up the sound of small arms fire around a bend.

Carol!

Montran paused just behind the corner. It was a perfect place for an ambush, and the attack from behind was quick and unexpected. A net captured and immobilized her and then a quickly administered drug dropped a black curtain over her senses.

Chapter 14

Zohra and Maud lay on their stomachs in the topside dust, undetectable by any scanners. Alan's soldiers trudged slowly in the heavy atmosphere, lining up in nice, tight little formations. If Zohra could have had even one of those cannons they'd seen, she would have happily mown them down.

A general marched off the shuttle, and the squad started moving into the city. Zohra chuckled to herself. As tough as they might believe themselves to be, the soldiers were feeling the effects of the planet's atmosphere and were not moving as snappily as she had seen them doing at Chaney's training compound. Even their general was lagging. She hoped one of them would fall. The other soldiers' reactions would give her an idea of the temper of the group.

"If they were my squad, I'd have had them out in this atmosphere working on maneuvers until they moved like they meant business," she whispered to Maud. "Guardian, are you monitoring their communications?"

"Yes. They are using code. I am breaking it now."

Zohra signaled Maud that they follow the soldiers. With Guardian's "wonder wear," as she called it, Zohra was fast learning how Maud had avoided detection and capture by the Black Rose patrols.

"They have ordered a detachment to the morgue," Guardian said.

"Commander Montran, you have some metrasoldiers heading your way. You have seven minutes to get out of there," Zohra whispered. "We can't back you up right now."

Maud and Zohra crawled to an emergency maintenance entrance and reentered the city.

"Which floor?" Zohra asked, stamping her feet to remove any dust that might give away her presence. Small tubes appeared from the walls of the elevator and sucked the dust off their suits.

"Seventh. Stop," Maud ordered the small elevator.

Maud's physical likeness to Montran had mixed advantages, most of which Zohra appreciated. She had a chance to accustom herself to working alongside a woman she had long fantasized about, without worrying about making a fool of herself by staring at her too long or saying something she shouldn't. However, only Maud's outward appearance was the same as Montran's. As they crawled through the opening in the elevator ceiling and squeezed into the maintenance space between the two levels, Zohra swore she could physically feel the difference between the two women.

Maud retrieved a net from a storage space in a larger maintenance area. "I've been saving this. Guardian built a neurostunner into the strands, but it may not work on the metrasoldiers. We haven't had a chance to test it."

"Then come on, let's go spring a trap."

Maud and Zohra waited above the seventh floor for the arrival of the general and his entourage of subordinate officers. The rest of the soldiers weren't that far behind them, so they'd have to be fast. The elevator activated.

"This is it," Zohra whispered.

They watched in their helmet viewers as the elevator passed the floor at which the group intended to disembark. Since there was no panel to register floors, the occupants had to rely on their voice commands being obeyed. Apparently, they did, because when the doors opened, the general and his four officers stepped out. They didn't seem to notice anything wrong, probably because all the areas around elevators looked the same.

Then the ceiling opened and the metrasoldiers reacted to the sounds overhead. But they were too slow, and the weighted net dropped and spread out over them, putting them to sleep. Bots rolled out from their storage areas and helped Zohra and Maud drag the bodies back into the elevator, and the women took them to their special holding cells.

Zohra studied the stasis chamber area to make sure it was as secure as Guardian and Maud had assured her it was.

"Major Zohra."

Guardian's distressed tone startled her.

"Carol and Commander Montran have been captured."

"Show me," Zohra said.

Maud and Zohra leaned over a desk monitor in the small security room of the stasis chambers, watching Chaney's soldiers drag Montran in one direction and Alan's soldiers drag Carol in the opposite.

"We can't let them leave this outpost," Zohra said.

"What do you propose to do?" Maud asked.

Zohra gave a heavy sigh, but it didn't loosen the tight fist clenched around her heart. "Wait and see what each group is going to do with its prisoner. Carol is worth more to Varina Chaney than Harriet is. To Alan, Harriet is worth more than this whole planet. My guess is that there's going to be a swap."

For the next few minutes, they watched Chaney's soldiers carry the unconscious Montran to their part of the city and Alan's soldiers take Carol to the command center.

"We removed their leaders, so they will have to contact Alan directly for instructions," Maud said.

"That will work in our favor. We can track the signal to Alan's location." It then occurred to Zohra that the two groups could be setting them up, but there was little she could do at this point other than watch and wait.

The soldiers tied Montran to a chair used for immobilizing prisoners. A civilian appeared, followed by a few others.

"That's Tolec," Zohra said through gritted teeth. "He used to work for Lord Chaney. He'll torture her. The others are probably there to make sure he doesn't kill her."

An injection wakened Montran, and the questioning began. Usually interrogation was a slow process, first undermining the victim's belief that she would be rescued and then her belief that there was a purpose to her existence. Tolec simply broke Montran's hand and then proceeded with more physical torture. Both Zohra and Maud could only suffer through watching the interrogation, since they were unable to interrupt it.

"Where's Carol?" Zohra asked, her voice tight with emotion.

"Topside." Guardian showed them a picture on the monitor of Alan's soldiers and Carol outside. One of the soldiers was talking into his communicator.

"She's got a neurolock around her throat." Zohra touched her own neck.

"She's wearing Guardian's suit," Maud said.

"Normally the spoils of the victor include removing the hostage's valuables and keeping them. Maybe it's because they're metrasoldiers that they don't take anything without Alan's order."

"They are speaking directly with Alan," Guardian said.

"Let's hear what they're saying."

"…General Lare or his staff."

"Who has Montran?"

"Lady Varina Chaney's security. Lord Chaney is dead, and we have captured his metradame, Sheila. They wish to trade Lady Montran for our prisoner."

"Montran is to be turned over to you with no marks on her. Only in that condition, unmarked and alive. She must be fully awake, moving on her own, and coherent when you make the exchange. If she is ruined in any way, fry the metrabitch and Chaney's soldiers. You hear me?"

"Yes, sir."

"Well, do it! Out."

The soldier nodded to the others, and they reentered the city. Guardian's monitors followed them as they met with another detachment in the Com-C of the city. The soldier wore no officer bars, but he handled himself like a leader. He contacted Chaney's guards, and the negotiations began.

"Chaney's side is stalling for time," Zohra muttered.

"His guards want information from Harriet," Guardian said, "but by the looks of it, they are not going to get it. For her sake, I hope they realize it is a waste of time."

"Tolec's nickname is Painmaker," Zohra said. "He'll keep her until the last minute. With the medbot, they can break every bone in her body and still be able to repair her in time to turn her over to Alan's deadheads. No telling what mental state she'll be in, but that's of no consequence to him."

"They haven't removed Guardian's suits from either of them," Maud said as Montran slumped forward, unconscious. A nerve gun had been pressed against her neck.

In her years as an operative, Zohra had learned the necessity of distancing herself from her emotions. The surest way was to focus on analyzing the situation and making plans.

"They're in a hurry to extract information. Guardian, were you able to locate Alan?"

"He is a week away, if he encounters no obstacles or delays."

"They'll make the exchange in neutral territory, topside, where they're both handicapped. The weapons they currently have aren't going to work well in this atmosphere. Concussion bombs will create a good distraction, so we'll take a couple of those." Zohra glanced at Maud and winced internally at her startling likeness to Harriet.

"The exchange has been agreed upon. Topside, as you surmised," Guardian said. "I am sending you the coordinates."

"Got it," Maud answered. "It's one stan hour's travel from their position, or ten minutes if you know the shortcut. It will take them that long to heal the damage they've done to Harriet."

"We need to pick up a universal neurokey," Zohra said. "I have one in my kit, and I can pack my gear at the same time."

"Maud can pack Carol's belongings," Guardian said. "Bots will carry the bags to the car."

"All right. But we must hurry."

* * *

Montran woke to pain. A slap bounced her head against the back of the chair. Her whole body hurt, and she couldn't see out of one eye. Confused, she wondered if she was still a prisoner of war. Maybe a nightmare of her past was stalking her. Her head was jerked back, and she stared into the eyes of a Harnivan.

No, this wasn't something from her past. She had never met a Harnivan, but she had heard about their interrogation techniques. Why didn't he use his other limbs to pound on her? Then she remembered that he had. They'd been asking her about Lord Chaney and her business with the metradame.

She spared a moment to thank her mentor, Commander Nelson, for encouraging his staff to take interrogation classes from Hum, the Ve'tumac. Hum also taught the reverse, how to survive an interrogation. She wished she had known those techniques when the Degas squad ran into trouble on Zed4Z44.

"Why were you chasing the metradame?" the voice demanded again. He had moved from breaking bones to using nerve stings. But he waited a little longer this time before applying another one. Prolonged use caused irreparable damage.

Her scream froze in her throat. All sensation stopped, and she dropped into a dark, self-imposed unconsciousness. Another skill learned in Hum's class.

Sometime later, a dull thudding against the base of Montran's skull traveled behind her eye sockets, giving rise to yet another spasm of nausea. Male voices droned nearby, as she focused on not retching. With great difficulty, she inventoried her condition. She opened her eyes. They worked. Pursed her lips. They were no longer swollen. She cleared her throat. It wasn't dry.

They'd put a medbot to good use, taking care of surface injuries, but leaving her ribs and legs bruised and sore. She tried to stand, to stop the painful drag on her shoulders. Her handlers shook her. Painful jabs of light shot to her brain. Her head fell back, and she nearly returned to unconsciousness. Fighting off the darkness, she struggled to pay attention to her surroundings. They were surfaceside.

"You give us the metradame, and we give you Commander Montran. We trade evenly, or there's no trade," the familiar deep voice of her inquisitor said, from somewhere near her.

"You will give us the Montran woman, and you will disembark from this planet with your lives. That's the trade," the other voice stated.

Montran's hands were bound behind her. Her legs were shackled, too, which would make it difficult to run. If running in this atmosphere had been an option, which it wasn't.

She saw Carol, who had a neurolock around her neck. She stood motionless between two burly guards. Montran's heart missed a beat. Even beneath her visor, Carol's face looked bruised, possibly bleeding, and her eyes had a vacant look. She, too, still wore Guardian's outer suit. Montran tried to figure out what this was about, and how to get out of it.

"We both know Alan will be very upset if you don't bring her back in usable condition. Now, I'm going to shoot off one part of her body at a time. This female only has five limbs, so we shouldn't be here too long. Let's start with the head first."

Montran heard the *thunk* of a weapon against her visor.

"Commander Montran," Guardian's voice whispered to her. "Your suit is back to one hundred percent. You will be rescued. Be prepared to follow Major Zohra's orders."

Carol was pushed toward the leader of Alan's group, who yanked her to stand in front of him.

Montran wished her head would stop pounding, so she could concentrate.

"Remove the neurolock," the being holding Montran said.

The neurokey was tossed his way, and whether by intention or not, hit him on the shoulder and dropped into the dirt.

Alan's soldiers rushed Chaney's soldiers, as well as they could in the heavy gravity. Their weapons were useless at long range. That may have been part of the agreement for the meet. Montran's handler pushed her back, and she fell heavily onto her side. It hurt.

Carol was grabbed by one of the metrasoldiers and thrown behind him. She went down and lay motionless.

Montran forced herself to inch toward the key mechanism, which was being kicked deeper into the shiny dirt particles by scrambling feet. She couldn't reach it. It occurred to her that neither group seemed to be calling for reinforcements. It was also odd that she hadn't been stepped on in the melee.

Panting, Montran rolled to the edge of the scuffle and looked around for potential escape avenues. Flatland was everywhere. She couldn't see any sign of an elevator plate or any rescuers.

A series of taps on her leg surprised her, and the leg cuff was released. Zohra must be present, using her suit's blend function, and would tell Montran when to activate her own suit and vanish. Zohra obviously didn't trust their suits' communication links. Montran wanted to laugh, but her side hurt too much. She distrusted the blend mechanism, and Zohra distrusted the communication.

Suddenly, one of Lord Chaney's soldiers dropped to his knees near Montran and pointed his weapon in her face. At that short distance, the weapon would do damage.

"Now would be a good time," Montran said under her breath.

One of Alan's soldiers knocked Chaney's soldier away from her, and both men landed on the ground, hard. Montran knew it would be difficult for them to get back on their feet.

"Blend now!" Maud's voice came over her comm, and the ground moved under her as if an explosion had been set off.

"Blend on." Montran would have started to roll away from the fracas if a tug on her bound arms hadn't pulled her in another direction. Dirt and dust dropped around everyone, masking who was who. A moment later, her arms were freed from their bindings. She glanced in the direction of the continuing pull, and from a small window in her visor, saw Zohra crawling ahead, leading her. She glanced back and saw that the man who had shoved a weapon in her face was now grappling with one of Alan's soldiers.

"We can make our escape in this dust cloud," Zohra said. "Rest a moment. We have another concussion bomb coming."

Montran panted from exertion and pain. Oblivious to what went on around her, but taking comfort in the presence of Zohra near her, she sat down in the dirt.

"Clear, Maud. Ignite the second charge when ready," Zohra said.

"Carol is safe with me," Maud said, and counted down to the explosion. "Five, four, three, two, one…"

The ground moved under them again, and thicker red dust and small rocks pelted them.

"Let's get out of here." Zohra rose, pulling Montran up with her. When Montran was unable to get her legs moving, Zohra picked her up and started walking. Sometime during the bumpy ride, Montran blacked out.

* * *

Montran's consciousness returned, along with flashes of light behind her eyelids. When they ceased, a soft conversation between Zohra and Guardian encouraged her to open her eyes.

We're in a car. Probably heading back to the Lair. Montran squinted and then blinked to clear the shadows from her vision. Carol, her eyes closed, slumped against her restraints in the adjacent seat. She no longer had the neurolock on her neck.

Zohra sat across from Montran, not looking any the worse for wear. The seat next to her held a duffle bag and an equipment bag. Another bag, which looked more like a civilian's, rested on the floor.

Montran took a deep breath and felt a twinge in her side. Secured in the harness, she didn't have much room to move her limbs and see how well she functioned. For a moment, she fought the fear of being restrained.

"How are you doing, Alexandra?" Guardian's voice sounded far away.

"How are you feeling?" Zohra asked at almost the same time.

Montran tried not to think about the interrogation. "How long was I out?"

"From topside to the car, about thirty stan minutes." Zohra's gaze moved to Carol. "You both look like you need a medbot and a good soak in something to make you sleep well."

"Dreamless, please." Images from another time and place played in Montran's mind, and she struggled to change her focus. "Where's Maud?"

"She stayed topside," Zohra said. "She had some reconnaissance to do."

"What went on topside?"

"Guardian kept us constantly aware of the situation. Chaney's guards grabbed you, and Alan's soldiers captured Carol. Each side had what the other wanted. Your interrogators administered a drug to loosen your tongue, but you spoke in a language the translators didn't recognize. You'll have to tell me how you did that."

She looked toward Carol, who appeared to be sleeping. "They didn't bother questioning Carol. They probably thought her owner would have made it impossible to get any answers from her."

"What happened to the neurolock?"

"I had a key." Zohra frowned. "Varina Chaney wants her father's metradame back, unmarked and undamaged. Alan's group made a mess of the bargaining, because they were instructed to capture you if you were alive and unharmed, or destroy Carol and Chaney's soldiers if you weren't."

"So, can we assume that if Alan gives his soldiers a direct order, they don't deviate? Lucky us, if that's true."

"He's only had this group of soldiers for a stan year, and he's been assessing how much initiative to give them. He's afraid to give them too much freedom of thought, because they might kill him for what he did to them. He tested their fighting prowess at Chaney's training compound against veteran Black Rose fighters. Chaney was contemptuous of them, considering we beat them in the majority of our skirmishes. Carol must have trained against Alan's soldiers, too."

Carol's eyes opened at that, and she nodded. "Once. Lord Chaney wanted to know just how good I was."

"He didn't want to test you—as Sheila—against the Black Rose." Zohra said, and laughed. "We would have learned your weaknesses and used what we knew against you if we got the chance."

Montran studied Carol for a few moments and then said, "Carol, are you well?"

Carol glanced at her. "Yes, thank you for asking." She moved her hand up to her bruised cheek. "Guardian's Second Skin protected me from any infection I might otherwise have picked up."

Montran nodded. "My stomach is a lot better, but the rest of me feels like I've been used as a punching bag."

"They don't know about the Second Skin or the outersuit, or they would have stolen them," Zohra said. "Since the suits are lightweight, the soldiers may have decided they weren't worth taking as trophies." She leaned her head back and chuckled.

Montran shifted in her seat and gulped down rising nausea. *Trophies.* Images of a previous interrogation room stormed into her brain.

"Flashbacks?" Zohra asked quietly.

Montran shrugged and looked toward the bags. "I see you've picked up your belongings."

"These two are mine." She tapped the other bag with her boot. "This glitzy bag is Carol's."

Montran stared at the duffel bag. Images of Zohra in her thong underwear had her clearing her throat.

Chapter 15

"Welcome back, warriors." Charles handed out steaming cups of tea and energy bars.

Montran had been fixated on the idea of soaking in a hot bath that would numb her aching muscles until she got a whiff of the tea.

"Arora." She hummed with pleasure as she recognized the herb. It was great for dulling pain, which was just what they needed.

The three women sank into the chairs Charles provided.

"Well, we have certainly shaken up their operation," Guardian said.

"What are the two groups up to?" Zohra asked, looking at the screens.

Four screens were active. On one, Alan's group was assembling outside of Com-C, as if they'd been given orders. Another showed Spartans in a game room, gathered around someone Montran didn't recognize. He was gesturing as if he were giving an impassioned speech. A third displayed a group of Chaney's and Alan's soldiers, who appeared to be arguing. The fourth gave a view of the morgue. No one seemed to be on duty there.

"Why didn't they carry heavier weapons for the swap?" Montran asked.

"They don't have any that work efficiently in the outside atmosphere," Zohra said. She rose from her chair. "You'll let me know if anything develops, huh? I'm going to take a shower, soak out some of these bruises, and then hit the sack. I'll see you two at 0600 hours in the workout room." The door swished closed behind her while Carol and Montran were still rising to leave.

"How much time do you think we'll have before there's trouble?" Montran said.

"Alan has disappeared again. We believe he's delaying his arrival here because of the patrols that are looking for him," Guardian replied.

Montran nodded, leaving it unsaid that his arrival was inevitable. She went to the door then stopped and turned to Guardian. “Why is he trying to turn this outpost into an armed camp, or to destroy it if he can’t do that?”

“This planet is very valuable. Its cities can support various species, it contains several up-to-date, fully operational laboratories, luxurious—”

Montran lifted a hand. “Can we resume this conversation tomorrow? I’m sure by then you can decide whether you want to tell me what’s really so important about this planet that Alan wants to either occupy or destroy it.”

“We can resume this conversation after you have had some sleep,” Guardian agreed pleasantly.

“Thank you for the tea, Charles.”

“Sweet dreams, warriors.”

As they walked away, Montran said to Carol, “I want to do a meltdown in an herbal tub of hot, bubbling water, saving just enough strength to crawl to an undisturbed recovery in bed.”

“Oh, yes.”

When they entered their quarters, Carol heard the bath water running and breathed in the fragrance of the oil-imbued water. She was relieved they would not have to wait long for the tub to fill. She was tired and hurting. More sensations her previous program had not allowed her to feel. She touched the injuries Alan’s metrasoldiers had inflicted on her face. Her capture had kicked in the survival instincts that were a part of her bodyguard training.

Varina Chaney had a lot to worry about. Carol knew why she wanted to possess her, and it wasn’t just for personal pleasures. Much of the information Lord Chaney had imparted to Sheila was to protect him from the threat of assassination by his ambitious daughter, or by some other political figure on whom Lord Chaney currently had a vise grip.

If he were to be assassinated, she had another program that would become active. Lord Chaney called it *Stealth Mode*. Once all those responsible for his death were completely ruined, Sheila’s program would self-destruct.

As far as she could see, he had anticipated all the ways she might be prevented from completing her mission. Her training in assassination was part of that. But apparently, it had never occurred to him that he might die at the hands of someone who wasn’t motivated by politics, or who intended to kill him, thus only giving her the default revenge-killing program.

Montran let the butler remove her clothing. She hurt too much to do it herself. She looked at her side, worried because even with the Second Skin she felt injured. For a moment, she closed her eyes against the images of her recent interrogation. It unleashed memories of the helplessness she'd experienced when she was captain of the Degas squad. She struggled to stay in the present, not wanting to face the remorse she tried to keep just below the surface of her mind.

From the shower, she moved into the warm bubbling waters of the tub. Carol slid in next to her and held Montran's hand, comforting her. "Thank you, Carol," she whispered, staring at the fern. Her eyes were unfocused, but she was afraid to close them. Carol gave her hand a squeeze.

Montran's thoughts moved to her injuries, another safe subject. She'd thought she had cracked some ribs, but Ald hadn't found any.

"Do you mind if I join you?" Zohra asked.

Montran started and would have slipped off her perch if Carol hadn't grabbed her elbow. "No, not at all." Montran didn't watch Zohra's athletic body as she stepped into the tub, but the slight rise of the water level was noticeable. She tried to distract herself, but the pulsing jets and the recorded waterfall sounds playing in the background turned her thoughts to vivid images of that body. Her hands twitched to study it in detail. Guiltily, she looked at her companions and was relieved to find each one wrapped up in her own thoughts. After five more minutes of struggling with distracting thoughts that went from Carol to Zohra, she decided she had enough.

"Well, I'm done here," she said.

* * *

Montran shifted in bed and put distance between herself and Carol, afraid of keeping Carol awake. Closing her eyes brought overlapping images of her capture on Zed4Z44 and her recent torture at the hands of Chaney's soldiers. Montran concentrated on her companion's breathing, and realized that Carol wasn't sleeping either. She rolled on her side and faced her. "Are you all right?" She heard a little sigh.

"No. I seem to be having problems getting to sleep," Carol said softly.

"Me, too."

"Why, Mistress?"

Montran was going to give a short reply when she remembered Carol probably had a lot of nightmarish memories of her own to process. "I keep reliving the unpleasant parts of being captured."

"I am also seeing things I find unpleasant," Carol said. "What do you do with these memories?"

"Live with them."

"What if they're too terrible?"

"I think about Skiht, a veteran soldier who lost his sight and all of his limbs in a freak accident. I met him in a hospice garden where he was singing a beautiful song, extolling the beauties of nature with a lovely smile on his face. I asked him how he could be so happy after the terrible thing that had happened to him. He told me that there's a reason for everything, and that the recent events had given him a new purpose to his life, one that didn't require him taking another's life or doing violence to anyone. That made him very happy. Seeing someone who was truly at peace was quite extraordinary, though at the time I wasn't able to appreciate it.

"The army offered to fit him with limbs and sensors for sight. He told them to save it for someone who would need it. He believed the only way to find meaning in his circumstances was without the modern conveniences that would help him escape his situation.

"I ran across him again, about two years later. He was known by another name, but he remembered me. He's one of the greatest healers in GCFC and Collective space, working exclusively with war veterans and their loved ones."

"Why didn't you let him help you?"

Montran laughed, embarrassed that Carol knew her secret. She still felt wounded by her failure to protect those who had put their trust in her. She took a deep breath to loosen the tightness in her chest. "He told me I was afraid to look for meaning in my own issues."

"What I have done is not something that I can forgive myself for by finding meaning in it," Carol said.

Montran understood. Covert operatives were expected to do horrible things to fit in, to survive. They didn't think then of the burden they would carry or how much it would change them, perhaps making them into the very thing they were opposing. How many agents stayed in the field too long, so that their employers had to send out special teams to capture and neutralize the wayward member? Maybe she and Carol could help each other.

"What have you done that you feel you can't return to a normal life?" Montran said.

"I accompanied Lord Chaney to many of his torture sessions. I felt pleasure in the pain of some of those people."

"Did you administer the pain?"

"No. Tolec did."

Montran shivered, remembering her introduction to him. She was surprised, though. She had thought Chaney a coward who wouldn't like to witness the messy results of torture. "Did you watch?"

"No. Lord Chaney merely liked to see the fear inspired by Tolec's appearance. Then we would leave."

"I can only tell you my own approach. When I find myself in situations I'm powerless to change, I ask for guidance and the strength to do what's right. A person who believes strongly in his or her cause may believe that hurting another is justified, but I'm not responsible for that person's choices. I'm responsible for myself. I know that intentionally torturing people, or purposively taking life, isn't a path I want to walk, so that's how I live my life." She watched Carol's face, hoping she was able to process the words.

"We aren't perfect, Carol. Even Lord Chaney did the best he could, according to his beliefs. My belief system is what sustains me. If it fails me, I will face that dark night of my soul then and search for a meaning. That search, I believe, is my initiation into something more profound." She laughed abruptly. "Of course, as you can see, I don't do too well with facing all my demons."

Montran brushed a lock of hair from Carol's forehead and peered closely at her darkened eyes. "I can give you a back rub, if you like. It might help you relax."

Carol rolled onto her stomach. It wasn't long before her breathing evened out and she was asleep.

Chapter 16

Montran woke, and sat up quickly. Tentatively, she flexed her hands. No pain. Lucky her.

Carol's breathing changed.

"Go back to sleep," Montran whispered. "I'm just going to make some tea." When Carol's breathing deepened again, Montran slipped out of bed, picked up her robe, and walked into the front room. She tossed her robe onto the couch, moved to a cleared space, and began her exercises. Closing her eyes, she concentrated on each limb as she stretched into different poses. She wanted to know how well she had healed, and this was a good way to find out.

Her focus shifted to her inner quiet place and then expanded. She touched lightly on her connection with the planet's consciousness and found it aware of her. She paused and concentrated. There was something different in this touch, a disturbance in the ebb and flow of the energy. It felt as though something were interfering with the usual chaos.

She finished her exercises with a silent mantra. Even in silence, the mantra vibrated her body—cells and spirit. She could feel the tingle in her toes, fingertips, and right up through her head. She had not felt such a strong effect since… well, not for a long time. Maybe because she wasn't on a ship, suspended in space, where molecules and living cells vibrated at different speeds than they did when land-based.

Montran donned her robe and turned to the politely waiting Bach. "Leaha tea, medium hot." She took the tea when it arrived, sat in front of the computer screen, and thought about metrapeople.

Her brow furrowed.

A dream remnant came to her. She tried to tease it out but it faded, like all dreams that weren't ready to be examined.

Montran called up the work of Iwilla, looking specifically at her exploration on dreams, and began to study.

Carol wakened again a little over an hour after her mistress left the bed. If Montran had been only been getting a cup of tea, she should have returned already. Carol got up, slipped her robe on, and left the bedroom. She could see her mistress's hands moving quickly over the keyboard, the teacup sitting to the side. Carol guessed its contents were cold.

Yawning, she went into the kitchenette and asked Bach for a repeat of the previous order. She had had another dream. Though she didn't remember the details, she remembered that she'd dreamed.

Standing behind her mistress, she held the cup of steaming tea and read over Montran's shoulder.

Dreams are important because they are bridges to what once was... Carol looked at the title of the article her mistress was studying, "Metrapeople as Dreaming Beings," by Iwilla.

"Of course we dream," she said.

Montran turned to face her. "What did you say?"

"I just read the title of the article you're studying. Here's a fresh cup of tea."

Montran accepted it. "Sit here." She called for another chair next to the computer. "No, Bach can put the cup away. I want you to read this article, and then I want to ask you some questions about what this author is saying."

Carol settled into her chair and read the article. When they'd finished the article, Montran got up and moved to the couch, taking her tea with her. Carol joined her.

"Let me start with this question: do you remember what you dream?"

Montran watched myriad emotions animate Carol's face. When she smiled, Montran's heart brightened. Carol was probably thinking a lot more than she ever had in her metradame existence. Montran wondered whether she knew that Iwilla was a metraperson, or realized that her work showed that freedom from the chip's programming was possible.

"When I was Sheila, I wasn't aware of dreaming," Carol said slowly. She let out a loud sigh, which took both women by surprise. She gave a short laugh and looked down at her folded hands, as if to recover her composure. "Now, without the control, I remember that I have dreams. What they're about, I don't remember on waking."

"Do you remember dreaming last night?"

"Yes. And some from the previous night seemed familiar, as if I'd dreamt them before."

Carol looked toward the bedroom.

"Is Zohra up?" Montran said. Carol nodded. "Well, I guess we should be ordering something to eat for three. Do you have a special request?"

"Did I hear the word 'eat'?" Zohra called through the bedroom.

"Yes, you did. Would you like to join us?"

Zohra came into the living room through the bedroom, wearing her robe and with her hair pulled forward over her shoulders. She was blotting the long strands with a towel.

"Eat light," she said. "It ruins the workout when someone gets sick."

Montran was having a difficult time moving her eyes and thoughts from the sight of Zohra in a robe, drying her hair. Such a simple thing, yet it raised an incredibly powerful yearning in her.

"I think I'll take a shower before breakfast," she said, and headed that way, passing by Zohra.

While she washed, her thoughts worked overtime on what to do with Carol, Zohra, and how to protect Merker's from Alan's onslaught. Groaning, she slapped the wet wall. She was thinking way too much.

Montran stepped out of the shower and the bot dried her hair. She picked up her tea and looked into the mirror. When she let her vision lose focus, the background became black. She felt her spirit move outside of her body and take the cup of tea from her hand. The cup was then held out for her to gaze into.

An image appeared, of a child running alongside a colt. They were playing tag. Montran smiled as the child laughed when the colt took a bite of her tunic and shook it like a dog. Herself? No, it looked like a boy. Then the child aged, changing from a boy to a girl. She remembered the Holy Ones, and an early teacher who had been born into the world as both male and female.

She saw the child again, this time as a young woman. Her seated figure was haloed by a sunset that reminded Montran of the Wieldworlds. The sun there appeared purple, with bright yellow streaks that crossed its face at sunrise and sunset. The seated woman was near a dark shadow… no… it was a person.

Alan!

He looked furious, gesturing and threatening. He held a stick in his hand and brought it down across the face of the smiling woman. Montran felt the blow across her own face. Stabbing pain shot through the center of her head, burning its way through her brain and down to her toes. The cup of tea dropped to the ground, and she crumpled to her knees, feeling mortally wounded. She was unaware of Ald catching her before she fell over.

Moments passed in a haze, seeming more like hours. Slowly, the pain lessened and her vision came back. She had experienced another's dying process before, at Kela's death, but she didn't remember it being as intense as this. Even her insides were shaking.

She gulped down a breath of air as her stomach heaved. Her tunnel vision gradually expanded to normal sight, and she saw Zohra and Carol kneeling next to her. Carol was using a damp cloth to wipe Montran's tears away.

"Are you having a vision?" Zohra asked.

Montran blinked a few times and then took a deeper breath to see if her stomach would settle. "No. Why do you ask?"

"You were saying something when we got here. What's going on?"

Breathing in again, Montran moved her jaw, realizing she had been clenching it. "I'm an empath. I had to close my channels when I went into combat, and now…" At that moment, she had a flash of insight. She had never lost her empathic ability, as she had believed; she had deliberately muted her senses.

Ald had administered an herb, and it was taking effect. Her pounding heart slowed and her stomach settled.

"An empath? If you closed your channels when you were a Spartan," Zohra said, "and are now reopening them, aren't there consequences?"

"What consequences?"

Zohra crouched in front of her, only a few inches separating them. "Reliving events that are highly emotional. Painful ones, and not only from your life, but from the lives of the people you are sensitive to. People you knew and know. Are you ready for that?"

"Why does it matter to you?" Montran asked.

"It matters to us. To protecting Merker's. Healers will be arriving soon. I think you should stay here at the Lair and not go out on any more excursions."

"I can handle it." Montran rose to her feet with Carol's assistance.

"You don't know what it's like!" Zohra shouted. "This is just the beginning. My mother lived in agony because she couldn't endure the intensity."

The others stared at Zohra, startled into silence. Zohra herself looked shocked at her outburst. Her lips tightened into a thin line, and her hands clenched.

"You are one of Lord Chaney's daughters," Carol said.

Zohra shifted to a defensive stance. "What made you say that?"

Montran was caught off guard by Carol's accusation and the sudden change in Zohra's demeanor.

"You have the family mark," Carol said, "which appears when one of you is highly emotional. Though you have a skin patch hiding it, I can see it now that you're upset."

Montran's eyebrows rose at the revelation. She couldn't see any mark on Zohra.

Was that why Chaney had been in Zohra's quarters? Why would he be drugging his own daughter? And why did she hold such high positions in two organizations that were bent on removing him from power?

"I'm one of the few that survived Varina and her mother's reach," Zohra said in a reluctant tone. "You're going to ask me if my father knew who I was." Zohra stared defiantly into Montran's eyes. "Yes, he knew. His one conversation with me on that topic was to say, 'Stay out of Varina's reach.'"

"He selected you for the Black Rose?" Montran asked.

"No!"

"Guardian," Montran said, "have you found out any more about that chemical Lord Chaney left in Zohra's quarters?"

"What chemical?" Zohra said.

"Yes," Guardian answered. "Specifically, it is from the Berrian territory. Berrian food gives a protective effect, and for them it is a narcotic, used for healing. Non-Berrians, who do not ingest those same foods, will eventually be killed."

"I saw the replay of that fool rifling through my belongings. Whatever he was looking for, he didn't find. There was no poison."

"Why don't we go into the sitting room where it is more comfortable?" Charles said.

Everyone turned to stare at the brightly colored bot, which had entered the bathing room unnoticed.

"Good idea." Montran hoped the change of space would give Zohra time to gather herself. "I'm fine now, Carol. Thank you." Montran patted the hand that had a firm grip on her elbow.

As the women made themselves comfortable, Charles moved among them, handing out refreshments. Montran looked up, startled, as Carol folded a blanket around her. "I'm not an invalid, Carol. I'm fine."

She returned her attention to Zohra, who remained standing, and had refused Charles's offer of a beverage. Her aura was unsteady, as if she were at odds with herself. Montran's heart felt heavy at the prospect that Zohra might be a spy. She didn't believe it, but she had to know for sure. "So, Guardian," Montran said, "for a non-native, it would be like the substance arsenic?"

"To some species."

"Like I said before, what's the point?" Zohra asked.

"My point," Montran said as she dared to stare into the dark eyes, "is that you haven't come clean with us on a few items, such as knowing about Lord Chaney visiting your quarters when you were out. His room was just two doors away from yours." She paused as Zohra advanced toward her, looking angry.

"What are you implying? Do you think I'm in some sort of plot against you? Is that what you're driving at?"

Carol moved to Montran's side as Zohra came closer.

"You need to be reexamined," Montran said softly.

"What?" Zohra said. "You're crazy."

Charles was behind Zohra. He lifted an appendage slightly and she fell. Charles, Carol, and Montran caught her as she toppled forward.

"I thought I was thorough." The disappointment in Guardian's voice was echoed in Montran's heart.

She held the nearly unconscious Zohra and looked into her face. Zohra's heart was beating rapidly, and judging by her partially closed eyelids, Montran was pretty sure she could still hear. "It's possible that she's under another's influence, maybe through a deeply planted chip. They do it to metrapeople and psychotics, why pass up the opportunity to implant key people you can move around as you like? That's very scary, isn't it? A private army or legion of spies where the participants don't even know they're someone's puppet."

Was she wrong to think there was something not right about Zohra? No. She had suspected as much before her senses had been opened, but now she could see darkness over part of Zohra's head.

"As a scientist," Guardian said, "I would go with the chip, but why do you say so?"

Montran squeezed Zohra's arm reassuringly, though she wondered if it was any consolation. "Isn't that the idea behind the whole metrapeople program? Control with little outside effort?

What if Chaney or Varina had a chip implanted in Zohra that would prevent her from taking any action against them, and the drug was merely to hide its side effects?"

"Yes. One of the researchers explained why the implants for the reeducation of social undesirables caused side effects, requiring drugs to suppress them. It has something to do with their dreams."

The door slid open and a gurney bot moved in.

"Iwilla described the chip implant for conscious thought monitoring in metrapeople, and compared it to dreams." Montran paused as Charles and Carol lifted Zohra's body and settled it on the gurney. She moved to stand next to Zohra and drew her fingers across the furrowed brow, as if to smooth the lines. She rested her fingers on Zohra's cheek for a moment. Leaning forward, she whispered into her ear, "Be well, my Dancer." Then before she did something irrational, she stepped back and the gurney left the room.

"She'll be fine, Commander Montran. Charles will accompany her. My restraint techniques cause no trauma."

"To some, any form of restraint will result in a trauma." Montran paced, gathering her thoughts. "There are two types of nanochips on the open market that I was able to identify. The one used for metrapeople interferes with behavior and memory. The second kind monitors thoughts, speech, and behavior. You're right about the drugs. The idea is to keep the subject from having nightmares about having something implanted in their brain. In the beginning, many of the subjects killed themselves trying to dig it out.

"Think about the political advantage of implanting chips that can control and track people's personal information, location, and conversations. You could have assassins planted anywhere, without their own knowledge. It's happened in the past, and it's obviously happening again.

"Just about every GCFC or Collective planet's recorded history has stories of corporations and governments engaging in mind control. It was outlawed, because it was the only way they would be allowed to travel in space. But from the use of the chip technology these days, I would say it's still a flourishing business. Anyone can be a spy. And that means that the allied troops heading here might include soldiers who have been implanted by Alan or anyone else who bought the technology and has an interest here. Gods, but I feel like I'm ranting."

"You are frightened," Guardian said, "and have just cause to be. With the GCFC reappointing members, the influence or the removal of key players could change not only its face but also its intentions. Some authorities have expressed an interest in changing the charter to put aside the requirements for peaceful coexistence on a planet before it can petition for space travel and membership in either of the organizations."

"And we know how easy it was to join the GCFC and still disregard many of the rules in its charter."

"I will convey your thoughts to Naboth's Vine and its friends," Guardian said.

Montran looked at Carol. "I could use some nourishment that's not so hard on the stomach."

"Fresh fruit," Carol said, "and something to settle an unhappy stomach."

"Sounds good to me."

As she and Carol sat at breakfast, Montran silently tried to adjust to the changes within her. When she was a child, her life had been full of colors, sights, and sounds that whirled around everything. Distracting for some, to her it was part of her energetic world. Within the protective walls of school, she had no reason to mute what was around her, and the few times she had gone outside the school, she'd had guardians who protected her with their spells and energy. After she'd witnessed the death of her mentor and had fled the protective walls and her guardians, she had muted her senses, mistakenly believing she had closed off her empathic side permanently.

Montran took a deep breath as enlightenment came to her, and realized that her lessons had continued on other levels, without her conscious awareness. She now understood that she'd continued being an empath, but in a subdued state that sensitives used so they could move around when not protected by their homes or spiritual ground. Her empathic ability had helped her face the demoralized spirit of the Degas squad and bring them back from a dark place before they met their ends.

"I think I'll go back to being called Alexandra," she said aloud.

"Who is Alexandra, Mistress?"

"I am. It was my name when I was a young student." She picked up a piece of fruit and studied it. When she relaxed her vision, she could not only see interesting colors and textures, but also hear and feel their energy. She compared the fruit to the plate. The differences were remarkable; each vibrated on a different level.

"Just as I changed my name and destiny," Carol said.

"Yes, exactly." Alexandra observed the colors pulsing around Carol. "I believe that your control chip can be removed without damage to your brain. Dr. Sharon Teal, who writes under the name of Iwilla, knows how to do this. Wouldn't you say so, Guardian?"

"Iwilla. You know of this writer?" Guardian asked.

Alexandra smiled. "Just as I know you to be Maa."

"And how do you know all this?"

"Because you write like you speak, and Iwilla writes like Sharon sounded when she described her work to me."

"I will have to tell her that you have found us out."

"You had me fooled for a while. I thought perhaps you were implying that she was trying to hand me over to Alan."

"You are a difficult person to enlighten when you are not inclined to listen."

"So I've been told," she acknowledged ruefully.

Do you happen to know who Heartstone is?" Guardian asked.

"An off-worlder on one of the Wieldworlds. He uses descriptions of the sunsets as examples too often to be a tourist, and has too much information to be a casual dabbler in the business."

"All residents of the Wieldworlds are off-worlders," Guardian said. "But now I know more of which direction to look."

"Now that you mention it, I would try the prison colony first. It's an ideal place to study implants without the interference of regulators." *Politics and abuse of power everywhere. I sure wish I had a flute to escape thinking for a while.* "Guardian, you don't happen to have musical instruments here, do you?"

"Yes, in the recreation room. It is on the same floor as the dojo, but to the left as you exit the elevator," Guardian said. "So, you have resumed the name Alexandra. I am happy to hear that. It is a strong and noble name."

"Strong and noble?" Alexandra laughed with embarrassment. "If that's the case, I have plenty of work to do to grow into it. But first things first. I could do with some exercise. Carol, would you like to work out with some hand-to-hand training?"

"Yes, Mistress. I would love to test your reflexes."

Alexandra was relieved that the customary erotic thoughts were not followed by an intense need to drag Carol off somewhere to act on them. "My reflexes are just fine, thank you."

For the next two hours, they worked on the moves Zohra had shown them earlier. Guardian provided holographic training figures that showed them more advanced ones, which they added to their workout.

"You know, Carol, this particular style is for killing only. Look at the *Sham'hara* move. One thrust to the heart or another vital organ, and days later the target organ fails. No one even suspects the true cause. There's no physical impact, and thus no bruises remain."

Carol wiped her brow with one hand and drank deeply from the water bottle a bot handed her. "You look troubled, Mistress."

"This could certainly explain why so many influential people have been suffering from heart conditions in the past few years, hmm? Everyone assumed they had been poisoned by rivals."

"I hadn't heard about that," Carol said.

"I remember reading it... no, Sharon was reading an article about it and discussing it with me. They didn't die, but were rushed to a medical facility to get heart replacements." Alexandra stood still for a few moments, drinking her water and thinking. "It would certainly present a perfect opportunity to implant chips in them without their knowledge."

She handed her empty water bottle to the bot and rubbed her face with both hands. "I'm always looking for an enemy, never knowing who it's going to be. It's a weary life, Carol. Ready for a cool-down? Tai chi."

Even the cool-down was tiring. After they finished, Alexandra watched Carol carefully as they drank more water and wiped sweat from their faces. She wondered what type of relationship they would have once Carol was past the "Mistress" stage.

"Let's go find some musical instruments. Do you play any?" She tossed her towel toward the bot and took a last gulp of her water.

"Yes, Mistress."

Alexandra was as surprised as Carol looked. "What's your preference?"

"I don't know, Lord Chaney wasn't interested in music." Carol blushed. "I think I'm experiencing a buried memory."

Pleased, Alexandra grinned. "Then this is an important experience."

They walked down the hall, looking through windows into the rooms that lined it, more out of curiosity than anything else. Halfway down the hall, Alexandra stopped and glanced toward the end. An energy pulse emanated from there. She relaxed her gaze and could see a soft glow, composed of purple, blue, and green with a white center, pulsing in a soothing rhythm. A dark blue shape formed in the center of the glow and grew larger. It appeared to be moving toward them. Alexandra was aware that Carol had stepped to her side.

"Mistress? Are you all right?" Carol's voice seemed to come from far away.

"Can't you see it?" Alexandra spoke softly, as though a normal voice would scare off what she was witnessing.

"I see an empty hall. What else is there?"

Alexandra continued to stare at the image. Her eyes watered from the intense light shining around it. She put her hand out to stop Carol from moving forward.

The form seemed to turn around and go back into the energy field. When the dark blue shape was no longer visible, the field folded into itself and disappeared.

"Mistress?" Carol asked softly.

"I think I know now why Alan wants this planet. There's a portal here." Alexandra's heart was pounding in excitement.

"A portal?"

"Do you remember the childhood tales of Blenda and Mal, and their trips across the galaxy?" Carol shook her head. "Childhood tales often speak of truths that adults no longer believe, wrapped in protective symbolism so that children's minds can assimilate and understand, and remember them into adulthood. You see, it's understood on a sense level…"

Carol looked at her blankly, glanced down the hall, then back at Alexandra.

"Okay, skip that part. In these tales, Blenda and Mal traveled across the galaxy through portals instead of in space ships. These portals were entrances to corridors that take travelers to specific planets. Like, planet A's portal goes to planet B, and B to C, and so on. Not everyone could pass through the portals, only those who vibrated to a harmonic compatible with the portal. Anyone else would go up in flames the moment they stepped across the threshold.

"The stories were about two young girls, idealistic and upstanding, who did heroic and kind things wherever they visited. They had two animals that traveled with them.

"I grew up on the tales. Even in the monastery, they spoke of the two travelers as if they were real." Alexandra paused. "I'm digressing here. Anyway, what I just saw was like the stories: the colors, the form coming out of the light… It's incredible."

Carol looked skeptical. "Incredible for you, but I saw nothing."

"It's an energy gate of some sort." Alexandra tried again, not understanding why Carol wasn't getting the idea—or was she just not interested? "The life-forms that enter it must be on a vibration level that's attuned with the gate or they'll die."

"Well, Alexandra," Guardian said over the speaker system, "I see you have found us out. Please step back, so as not to endanger Carol. The chip implant may cause her great harm should she get any closer. The music room is the one nearest to the elevator, but I suppose you want to talk about this discovery."

"Yes, I do." Alexandra's insides quivered. Her childhood fantasy was true, after all.

"Can you wait until tomorrow? The guests arriving through the portal will have settled in by then, and we can schedule a meeting that will be comfortable for everyone."

"All right." *The healers must be using the portal.*

The two women were quiet as they headed back to the elevator, and Alexandra's thoughts were busily dredging up all the tales she could remember about the two children who traveled the galaxy, stumbling into one adventure after another. Kela had mentioned that all planets had openings that allowed properly prepared travelers to reach different worlds. Alexandra had thought Kela was referring to astral projection. Now she understood.

Once she was in the recreation room, her mind focused on her immediate need—music. She found a flute, and Carol picked out a small instrument that fit into the palm of her hand. Carol blew into it tentatively.

"I don't recall playing this," Carol said as they rode up the elevator, "but it makes a pleasant sound, doesn't it? Har-mon-i-ca," she read from the side of the casing. "Even the name sounds melodious."

Alexandra nodded as she tapped the keys on her flute. The pads were made the old-fashioned way, and the feel of the cool metal, warming quickly against her palms, was comforting. "The harmonica can sound sad or happy. I remember hearing one played by a soldier. It was small, and easy for him to carry around."

When they got back to their quarters, each encircled herself in a soundproof bubble until she had mastered her choices well enough to play for the other.

"I really believe you once played that instrument," Alexandra told Carol as she dismantled and cleaned her flute.

Carol, eyes luminous with joy, took a deep breath and let it out. "I can't describe how wonderful it makes me feel. It reminds me of something I can't quite remember."

Contented and soul-satisfied, Alexandra prepared for bed. It was heartening to see Carol's aura look so vibrant. Maybe music was the key to healing a metraperson. Sound released the program and could wipe it out, so maybe sound in musical combinations… Her brain stopped. She was too tired to pursue the idea.

Chapter 17

"Hey, Montran! Wait up."

It was evening, and Cadet Montran was walking alone back to her barracks. She was hoping for another chance encounter with her Dancer.

Alan Fermin, from the neighboring Diplomat Academy, hurriedly approached her. A few of his friends were trailing behind, and alarms went off in her head. She could sense danger, like a black cloud heading her way. Smiling at Alan, she mentally forgave him for what he was about to do.

Time sped forward, and memories of her last drop with the Degas squad played out. In this space, it seemed her incarceration was for a short time. Along with the physical torture, she suffered emotionally for the lost lives of her squad. Finally, they had been proud of themselves and of wearing the Degas squad patch, but they were no more. Only she remained.

Her dream body was jerked away from the morbid replays and compelled to continue to another place, where souls gathered for their lessons while their physical selves slept. A soul she recognized as her grandfather was explaining something to a student by way of—

Her struggle to comprehend his method nearly yanked her back into her physical body, and would have if Gedaliaha, one of her mentors, had not tapped her on her forehead as if reminding her to pay attention. Obediently, she took her place. Once she focused on her grandfather, all the other souls disappeared. When it was time for her to leave, she was reluctant, as always. Grandfather gave her a nod as she withdrew, and this time she felt she would remember the content of the lesson.

* * *

Carol woke up with a start, her heart pounding. The small nightlight came on as her bios changed. Her mistress's deep breathing indicated she hadn't disturbed her. Carol attempted to go back to sleep, but couldn't. She recalled that Alexandra had said she played her flute when she felt like this.

Carol eased out of the bed and picked up her robe on the way to the front room. She engaged the soundproof bubble again. When she'd played the harmonica earlier, something familiar had tugged at the edge of her consciousness. She wanted to stop wrestling with her thoughts and try to connect to her feelings. Perhaps the harmonica could help her do that.

She hesitated, not knowing what piece to play. She closed her eyes and began a composition she didn't consciously remember knowing. Images came to her of a man she felt was her father. While he played his harmonica, a woman Carol identified as her mother made music on a fiddle, as she and her two siblings danced around them. They were happy in their new home.

Carol stopped playing. Previously, what bits of her childhood she had been able to remember were at the monastery. A buzzing sound had her shaking her head, wanting to be rid of it. What was it? Outside the bubble, an unfamiliar figure sat on the couch, watching her. Carol released the bubble.

"I am from your past. You do not remember me, nor do you need to. I have come with a message. For you, from you." She held out her hand; a case rested in her open palm.

Carol reached eagerly for the case. Her hand passed through the apparition, but the case was solid. "I'm not sure I understand what you're saying."

"You volunteered for this job. Now it is finished. You set up the parameters of recovery. Memories and flashbacks of who you once were are coming back to you, but should you choose not to remember, they will stop. It's your decision." With that, the apparition disappeared.

Carol looked at the case in her hand. When she heard movement coming from the bedroom, she put it in her robe's pocket. Now was not the time. She knew she had been a woman among many in a religious community, and that she had come to them young, but she didn't know how she got there. After the vision she'd just had of a happy family, she was sure it was not voluntary.

Alexandra stepped into the front room, fighting a yawn. "Good morning, Carol. Did you sleep well?"

"Yes. And you, Mistress?"

"Yes, I did. Have you eaten yet?"

"No, I was waiting for you."

"Thank you. I'm going to do some stretches, work out a bit, and take a bath before I eat. If that's too long for you, don't wait for me. When Guardian's guests start arriving, our days will be filled with introductions, shared dinners, socializing, and planning. Just the thought is tiring me." Alexandra disappeared back into the bedroom.

Carol settled in front of the computer and read about metrapeople until she heard grunts and other small noises, indicating Alexandra was practicing a kata. She peered into the bedroom, where the bed was gone and the dialed environment had produced a bare padded room with plenty of space.

Alexandra felt Carol enter the room and turned to see what she wanted. Carol bowed, removed her robe, and moved into a horse stance. Alexandra took her place directly in front of her. Both were without clothing, giving them an even footing for vulnerability and distractions.

"This is going to be interesting." Alexandra smirked.

"You are at a disadvantage," Carol said.

They worked out for over an hour until Alexandra stepped back and bowed, calling a halt to the workout. "Good workout. Thanks."

Carol returned the bow, and they headed to the shower to rinse off before soaking in the tub.

They were floating in the tub when Alexandra let out a sigh of bliss that set both women laughing.

"I love this life. Nothing to do but relax."

"Are you bored, Mistress?"

"After this soak, I intend to find something to keep me occupied that does not deal in war or violence." She paused before going on. "Carol, when this is all over, I'll be shipped back to *Ziggy* and you… your life can be wherever you decide is best for you." Alexandra looked into Carol's eyes while she entwined their fingers underwater. "I wouldn't mind if you wanted to come with me. But I want you to think about what you want to do with your life and not feel obligated to be with me."

"I understand. We'll enjoy the time we have together. Tomorrow is for tomorrow."

Alexandra wanted Carol to come with her so she could protect her, but not unless that was what Carol wanted. And then there was Zohra. Could the chip be removed without harming her? Alexandra closed her eyes, mentally saying a prayer for all of them. She felt so out of touch with the military culture that until now had been her entire adult life.

The music softly playing in the background lulled Alexandra into a relaxed frame of mind. With great reluctance, she eventually rose from the water, peering at her wrinkled hands.

Carol followed and took the towel handed to her. She pulled Alexandra close. "I know for sure that I was a lover of women before this change," she whispered in Alexandra's ear. "And even had circumstances been different, I would have enjoyed a sexual liaison with you."

* * *

"Greetings, Alexandra and Carol," Guardian said. "I have good news. Our second relief group has arrived."

Well, I guess my vacation is over. Alexandra was disappointed.

"Admiral JoCastao has seven Stealth Class A ships above us, spreading a protective net over the planet to prevent any of Alan's group from reentering orbit or slipping off-planet. They brought soldiers from the Vine and dropped them in Century City. They will set up a command post there and then start sweeps to root out the Spartans and what is left of Alan's soldiers. The four ships they found above us, including Chaney's, have been seized and impounded for investigation."

"No one's complained about all the military presence you have here?" Alexandra asked.

"Since this is neutral territory, who I invite to protect my facilities is my business."

"What about Alan?"

"No one has had word of Alan's whereabouts since yesterday. Only one death to report—Gustaf Fermin."

"Was that Alan's doing?"

"Naboth's Vine doesn't believe so. He had a love-hate relationship with his father, but not to the degree that he would have sent out an assassin. The Vine suggests that his death is a suicide."

"I guess when all his plans folded, he had nothing else to live for."

"We found a nanochip implant in Major Zohra. The consensus is that it was not Lord Chaney's doing, or the entire Black Rose squad would have them. Implantation is not an involved process, but only two of the team were gone for the length of time it would take for it to be done. Maybe Lady Varina knows something and would be willing to talk about it. Do you agree, Carol?"

"She will not talk about anything that deals with family business," Carol said. "She, like her father, keeps her own counsel."

"She can be questioned in front of the Tribunal about anything pertaining to her father's known illegal business ventures and her attempts on the lives of the other legal heirs to his estate."

"She has Thebain genes," Carol said.

"Her birth records do not identify either parent as Thebain."

"Lord Chaney's grandfather was Thebain. The characteristics skipped Lord Chaney, though he had his persuasive means, but both Major Zohra and Lady Varina inherited that ability. I imagine all his female offspring have the trait."

"What about the males?" Alexandra asked.

"He produced only girls."

"So we wouldn't know if they're lying to us."

"That is true," Guardian said.

"Why didn't Zohra use it?" Alexandra was puzzled, for she knew about Thebain abilities. They would have believed Zohra if she had chosen to lie about her family.

"Perhaps she does not know she has it," Guardian suggested.

"From what Lord Chaney said, they do," Carol said.

"Lord Chaney knew both Zohra and Varina had this ability?" Alexandra asked in surprise.

"The conversation I overheard was between Lord Chaney and one of his money managers. He always cross-checked his daughters' verbal reports. It has to do with the voice."

"Maybe that's why Zohra was able to stay alive for so long in the Black Rose," Alexandra said. "I wonder if that was one of the reasons for the implant, aside from making her a cleverly planted assassin."

"It would be like Lady Varina to compel Major Zohra to kill her father," Carol said. "Lord Chaney decided to train a metradame bodyguard when an assassin slipped past his guards and mistakenly killed his metragirl. She was in the wrong place at the wrong time, he said. But it scared him enough to invest in better protection."

Alexandra frowned. "What did he do with his metrachildren when they matured, or did the chip prevent maturation? If Lord Chaney was able to enslave children for his pleasures, what about others doing the same? And what's going to happen to them when they're released?"

"A reeducation plan is in the works," Guardian said. "Part of the healing is that their memories of being metrachildren will be blotted out and their faces changed. The Healers' Houses in both sectors has been working on where to place them and how to train them for productive lives. There are many concerned and compassionate beings working on how to reestablish all the metrapeople we can find. We will try to consider what is best for each individual."

"Isn't that being presumptuous?" Alexandra asked.

"Yes. That is why the Monks of Hela will help decide what is in line with their soul's path."

"But you don't agree."

"It is not that I agree or disagree. Many would say that I am not in the position to decide what state a person is better suited to live in." He sighed. "I do not have the same emotional feelings that living in a body would give me. Right and wrong are not in the colorful hues I remember."

"I hadn't thought of justice-making quite like that," Alexandra said softly. "I guess for Zohra's part, we'll just have to wait until she tells us her story, though I don't see her as a chatty person."

"Lady Zohra, technically." Guardian's tone held a hint of humor. "She has been left a title and an island to go with it on El, a wilderness landmass on Anim. However, I am told she does not care for the title or the land. It will no doubt go into her Sisters' Shield House holdings."

"Lady Zohra? That's going to take some getting used to. How's she doing?"

"The chip has been successfully removed, and she is being debriefed."

"What was the chip supposed to control?"

"We are not certain of its purpose, only that her mind is now free of its influence."

Alexandra breathed a sigh of relief. "When can they start on Carol?"

"The process has already begun. She has been ingesting caciu in her tea. It increases the acid level of her blood just enough to dissolve the chip. If you read more about the chips, you will see that they are biodegradable in some species and the brain can eventually absorb the nanochip without the seizures produced by prolonged use of the implant."

Alexandra pulled off the unicorn ring and handed it to Carol. "A memento, if you want it. I think that's great, Carol."

Carol took a sobbing breath and nodded. Her fingers curled around the ring in Alexandra's outstretched palm. "Thank you, Mistress."

"I don't think that title applies anymore." Alexandra felt her eyes tearing. "I'm Alexandra to my friends." Carol smiled, but her eyes held a hint of mischief. Before she could say anything to embarrass her, Alexandra addressed Guardian again.

"It's a relief to know the safety of your cities is in capable hands. Who's going to oversee the permanent guarding of your planet?"

"The War Forum is not yet complete. So far, space protection has been assigned to Rear Admiral JoCastao. One of the civilian positions has been filled with De LiTien, also from Collective Space. The other two positions for ground defense and the other civilian chair are still being discussed. Many are interested in the positions, but I have reservations about most of them. I am waiting for my representative to shorten the list to a half dozen."

"A War Forum? I guess I shouldn't be surprised. It's a big operation, since your planet is so close to a major jump gate. Who's your representative?" Alexandra hadn't thought that Guardian would need a representative.

"Charles. He has always handled that end of the business." Guardian paused a moment. "We have another problem. In my discussions with the other guardians of portals, we have identified what we think is an Alowan here on Merker's. We suspect Alowans have found a way to force portals to allow them to pass through."

"Alowan?" Alexandra hadn't heard of the species.

"They are from a star system in Eckron sector. They are designated 0eck003."

Alexandra's eyebrows rose. "A closed planet."

"Sudden appearances of one and sometimes two Alowans have been reported on different planets around the galaxy. If the area is remote from any settlements, the two will grow to a dozen, and soon their numbers will populate a village, town, city, and so on. If they are challenged during this process, they will mount a violent attack. They make no attempt to communicate with or placate the previous owners of the lands on which they have settled. Even the Monks of Hela have had no luck opening a channel of communication with them."

"That's unusual," Alexandra said. "The monks communicate on a multitude of levels, including dreamtime."

"The Alowans have brutally killed every representative that has been sent."

"That's a concern, then, especially with all the weapons that have been brought here. The mixture of infantry weapons and heavy explosives that can damage the core of a planet doesn't make sense, unless… Gods, I hope that Alowan doesn't find the explosives, and use them somewhere else."

"That idea has crossed a lot of minds, military and nonmilitary both. Until we capture him, we will not know for sure. I have convened a meeting of other guardians to discuss what we are going to do about the Alowan incursions in general. We also need to address the Alan Fermin problem. His plan to disrupt the gates has us all worried. Forced opening of the portals by the Alowans, together with destruction of portals by Alan, would cause a devastating reaction on all planets within the explored and unexplored galaxies."

There was quiet for a few moments, and Alexandra imagined the damage that could be inflicted through an energy portal that crossed vast regions of space, and what it could do to the multiverses. The possibilities were too terrible to contemplate.

Guardian spoke. "The Lair will be filled with activity. I have many guests arriving through Merker's portal, as well as by spacecraft. Those that are residing in the Lair are staying on the tenth and eleventh levels, close to the laboratories and the gate. The soldiers that will be arriving to protect the Lair will fill the first, second, and third levels."

"Have I received any further orders?"

"No. Your admiral said you are owed a vacation, so until otherwise notified, consider yourself on shore leave. There is really nothing for either of you to do until the others arrive."

"Guardian, would you mind if I asked you a personal question?" Alexandra said.

"You may ask."

"Why haven't you developed a clone from your body cells instead of putting yourself into a computer? And for Charles, too, for that matter. You have the laboratories and the scientific knowledge."

"We have developed clones. The answer is timing, and I will admit, the power I have is difficult to give up. Charles's species is rather difficult to clone, but we have been nurturing one for him into adulthood for longer than I have been here." He sighed heavily. "But now it is time for that move. My cloned body is ready. With all the scientists arriving, I would be foolish not to take advantage of their presence to complete the melding process."

"I guess it would be like dumbing down. Seeing Charles with less color would be different." Carol and Alexandra exchanged grins.

Guardian laughed. "Wait until you see how he dresses when he has a living body."

"What about the other cities on your outpost?" Alexandra said. "Would you mind if we looked them over while we're waiting for everyone to arrive?"

"Not at all. The small group the Vine has deployed is still securing Century City and not able to extend beyond that. I have not been able to reestablish communication in the other cities, so you will be on your own until you bring up their communications systems. I am sure your sightseeing would be fine with your admiral," he said, a hint of mischief in his tone.

"I gather she told you that until I'm debriefed, I'm to be left out of all combat situations."

"That was the gist of the conversation concerning you."

"I'll be sure to stick to sightseeing, and I'll just bring up your monitoring equipment in those cities while I'm at it. Does that sound compliant enough?"

"It sounds safe and unexciting."

"Are there citizens left in any of those cities?" Carol asked.

"No. I believe everyone has left. I was not in any condition to monitor the evacuation, but when my system came back online, Maud visited them and she found no one. But that was years ago, and for the last two, we have been rather busy."

"Well," Alexandra said, "I'm all for exploration to prevent boredom." Suddenly she turned to Carol. "That is, unless you have something else in mind."

"I would not mind exploring, Mistress." She grinned when Alexandra made a face at her form of address.

"Good. I am looking forward to seeing what is there," Guardian said. "I will prepare subliminal tapes on the cities. Which one do you want to visit first?"

Alexandra rubbed her chin. "I keep picturing a vast amount of water with single room dwellings on the various docks that circle the water."

"Avanster," Guardian said, "or WaterLand. I do not advise swimming in the water, as it is like entering another's home. Uninvited guests are not welcome."

"I thought you said no one was there," Carol said.

"The water is a living thing, though its inhabitants may have left."

"Do you have any information on their culture?" Alexandra asked.

"I'll add it to your subliminal. Unless you would like an audiovisual study?"

She glanced at Carol, who nodded. "Subliminal and a nap are fine."

* * *

Alexandra woke, aware of having dreamed about her Dancer, but it was vague knowledge only. No nightmares. Stretching, she mused that not only was she in a good mood, but her body felt completely healed from its earlier abuse.

Carol wasn't around, so Alexandra began her Chi Gung workout to wake up her body, then showered and dressed. While she ate, she reviewed the information from the subliminal. She noticed that the information was making its way to her consciousness faster than the first time. A sound from the bedroom made her look up as Carol walked in.

"Alexandra, are you getting ready to leave?"

"Yes. Is Zohra in her room?"

"She is sleeping now. She was having a bad dream, so I stayed with her until she fell back to sleep. Bach, a sandwich and qava juice, with pulp, please."

They finished their lunch in silence.

* * *

The journey to Avanster was shorter than the one to Century City had been, but then Avanster wasn't on the opposite side of the planet. When the car door opened, reflections from the water flickered on the car's ceiling. Carol stepped out first and glanced around. They were on a shoreline below the planet's surface, deeper in the planet than the other cities.

Alexandra stepped out more slowly as she tried to identify what she was sensing around them. Maybe it was the spirit of the water.

She turned to a sound on her right—water lapping against the shore. The sand was white, not what she was expecting, since the surface of the planet was shades of reds and browns. It was solid footing, with her weight displacing only a bit of the sand.

The dock they had arrived at was the only one that didn't have a small building standing on it. Numerous other docks were linked by thin walkways suspended over the water. Alexandra looked into the water and could see only darkness. Since the water was a living being, it should register something on her helmet.

Puzzled, she set the thought aside for the moment.

According to her subliminal, daylight was several standard hours away. Although some light was visible, and the helmets allowed them to see shadows and shapes, it was still dark enough for accidents to happen. A dim, yellow light shone from the top of the dome-shaped ceiling of WaterLand. Alexandra assumed it was a replica of a moon.

"Let's take a look at the building over there." Alexandra pointed to the smallest building, the one nearest to them.

Carol nodded, but her body language revealed that she was uneasy about something. Did she feel the presence, too?

They crossed the bridge slowly, carefully testing where they stepped. Neither wanted to find a broken spot and fall into the water below.

The first dome-shaped building had a circular doorway, so low that they were going to have to crawl on all fours in order to enter. Above the entrance was a shadowy carving that Alexandra couldn't make out. It had no recognizable form, only shadows hinting at curves. Carol seemed reluctant to enter.

Alexandra started to go first, but Carol pulled her back, shaking her head.

"Carol, it's better if I go first. I can sense things you may not."

"That's why you should follow me. You can watch what is happening when I enter. I feel something is here, and I would rather you observe than fall prey to it."

Preferring not to argue, Alexandra let Carol go in first.

When Alexandra's head cleared the entrance, she was able to stand. A winding stairway led downward. Small lights lit the steps.

Carol waited midway down the stairs. Neither spoke as they studied the walls, which had a glass-like appearance. On the other side of the glass, underwater plants swayed as if moved by a tide.

When the stairs ended, the room they entered appeared to be meant for storage, with empty shelves lining the circular walls. According to their suit gauges, the area was extremely cold.

Alexandra signaled that she had seen enough, and Carol didn't waste any time as she led the way back up and out.

The next building was larger, and this time Alexandra didn't give Carol a chance to enter first. The moment Alexandra cleared the entrance, a soft light came on. This room was circular as the other, but larger, and a circular pond nearly filled the center. A totem pole stood in the middle of it. Alexandra could see the water ripple in the dim light. She motioned to Carol to follow her, and stayed close to the wall rather than venturing near the pond.

In this culture, each ketch had a household spirit that protected the residences. Her subliminal informed her that this was where the spirit was housed.

They moved slowly around the room, their destination the opposite side, which held a dark, circular doorway. As she stooped to enter the shadowed room beyond, Alexandra silently sent a prayer to whatever being occupied the house she was invading.

Carol joined her and pressed her arm as Alexandra was about to bump into a couch. Alexandra nodded and then signaled her to search one side of the room while she searched the other. She located one of Guardian's cameras, while Carol found a small control panel in the shelves to the right of the second doorway.

"Alexandra," Carol called softly.

Alexandra moved to her side. A translucent substance that the visor didn't identify filled the shelves.

"What is this?" Carol asked.

"I don't know. I think we should contact Guardian. One of the mainframe's cameras is above the door. Shall we see if the on/off switch works?"

Carol offered her cupped hands so Alexandra could inspect the camera that was just a foot out of her standing reach.

The switch was in the off position. She pushed it on and looked to see if the power indicator had appeared. Nothing. She tried once more, with no success then dropped back to the ground.

"Perhaps it also has a switch behind here." Carol pointed to the blob on the shelf.

Alexandra pulled a screwdriver from her utility belt and attempted to push aside the translucent objects, but they wouldn't move.

"No room to push. You need to remove a few." Carol reached over, pulled out some of them, and laid them on a table nearby. "Simple," she said with a smile. Alexandra wasn't sure how Carol had done that.

The door to the control unit came open easily. Carol found the switch and pushed it. Lights flashed on the panel, and then an indicator screen showed that the system was coming online.

"The camera light is on," Carol said after a few minutes.

"Ah. It is good to see that you are both doing well," Guardian said over their helmet speakers.

"Hello, Guardian." Alexandra waved. "Anything happen while we've been out of touch?"

"Not too much. There are the usual reports from the troops searching for Alan's group. And Lady Varina filed a protest with the Council of Rings in the absence of the GCFC's Grand Council, regarding the Collective's refusal to return her men and her ship, due to their attack on and mistreatment of one of their officers, namely you." Guardian paused. "I am not sure she understands that one government official condoning the kidnapping, imprisonment, and mistreatment of an officer from another government is a serious crime even in peacetime."

"She understands perfectly. So, I'm going to be asked to attend the hearing?" Alexandra dreaded the idea of an inquiry.

"Your presence is not required. Since you were my guest, I have launched the protest. My recording of your capture and treatment has been presented to the Council of Rings. It is better to let people who are skilled in these matters handle the case."

"We'll discuss it further when I return." She gestured toward the room they were in. "Do you know where we are?"

"Yes. You are in the chancellor's library. Actually, it became his son's. I see that he left his readers behind. That is curious. I would never have thought MaaSa would leave without his collection."

"Then these are books," Carol said as she picked up one of the shapes she had laid on the table.

"Yes, you could call them that. They are data cards. You place one on that table, and the system plays it on the screen, either audio or visual. It would not work for you, however, because you do not know their language or see with the same vision as they do. They could be out of the water for a while, but did most of their living underwater. The library was set above the water to see if the data cards would last longer."

Alexandra turned to the doorway and listened for a moment. Did she hear a sigh? "Let's move on to the next structure. We have a lot to do, and I'm sure not all of it will be this easy."

Carol passed first through the doorway. As Alexandra entered, a force lifted her and held her against the wall. The energy in the room was neither friendly nor familiar. She could see what looked like a lifeline coming from the water and attached to a gray cloud that was leaning over Carol, crowding her to the wall on the other side of the pond. Alexandra broke away from the energy restraining her and patted the lifeline with her gloved hand. The gray cloud instantly surrounded her with all its malevolent energy. No wonder Carol was pressed against the wall. The energy force was staggering. Alexandra remembered some protective incantations from her childhood, which she mumbled as she tried to back away from the pond. She couldn't see Carol.

She resigned herself to the entrapment and sat down. Quieting her fears, she centered herself, as she had done long ago when frightened. Startled out of her meditation when someone tapped her shoulder, she looked up to see Carol smiling down at her. She was not wearing her helmet. In fact, she was not dressed at all. Alexandra laughed. "So, you are the guardian spirit of this home. Perhaps you know of MaaSa?"

The presence suddenly vanished. Carol was beside her quickly, helping her up.

"Are you okay, Carol?"

"Yes. Are you?"

"Yes."

They heard a splash on the outside, and the building rocked gently. The entity that appeared before them was a colorless glow, but the center was grayish.

"Well, MaaSa. Welcome!" Guardian said, surprise in his voice.

"MashiMaa, it has been a long time since I have heard you speak, and a long time since I have used this language."

"We could speak in your language, but my emissaries would not understand," Guardian said.

"I had heard you were no longer," MaaSa said.

"And I had heard everyone had left Avanster."

"It is good that neither of us believed."

"I cannot take credit for that. Lieutenant Commander Lady Alexandra Harriet Montran felt the deserted cities needed a long-overdue inspection."

"Yes. The one who sent a message to me. How do you know of our ways, Lieutenant Commander Lady Alexandra Harriet Montran?" MaaSa's form moved toward the two women. Alexandra felt pressure against her forehead.

"Don't be hostile so hastily," Guardian said. "She asked for a subliminal of the Enuit culture, MaaSa."

"You have information on my Enuits? I thought I had destroyed all records of us."

"Not all. So, what have you been doing with yourself all this time?" Guardian asked.

"I have been doing what I have desired to do since I was a youth."

"Writing?"

"Yes. I have finished eleven stands, which represent books to you. I am now outlining the final. We write in twelves," MaaSa said.

"What will you do when you have finished?"

"You shall send them home for me. I don't have any desire to return. I like it here. I am free to write or wander without anyone telling me I can't do it."

"I shall do as you ask, MaaSa," Guardian said.

"So, now that you have found someone, what more do you want?" MaaSa rumbled his question to Alexandra.

"Are you the only one here?"

"Perhaps. Is this something MashiMaa is asking, or is it your own question?"

Alexandra's subliminal was telling her she was presenting questions not asked in this culture. Enuits were a secretive group compared to humans and most of the other clans in the Zed sector, but Alexandra felt an urgency to push past the cultural barriers and to advance a plan that had come to her in a dream and now made sense.

"There is one named Alan Fermin who wishes to destroy this planet if he can't take possession of it, and he has already found he can't possess it."

The pressure from MaaSa lessened for a moment. "So, what are you wishing to impart regarding my city?"

"We are concerned for your city's safety."

"You wish to stay here and protect it?" he asked slowly.

"No. You will need more than that. You have a ritual called *sesshi*."

"She did not get that from my subliminal," Guardian hastened to say.

"How do you know something that is not even written about?"

MaaSa asked it softly but Alexandra felt an increase in the pressure on her forehead. She used her hand to flick away the energy as if it were a fly. "I heard a story of a far off land and the disaster that had befallen it, and what saved its inhabitants. It occurred to me that the story might well have been about the Enuits, or relatives of yours. I also have my own spirit guides, who whisper suggestions in my ear." She added that last to suggest more authority than she really had. However, sometimes expedience required a little trickery.

Guardian spoke in her defense. "MaaSa, you must admit, she is very resourceful."

"Who did you hear the story from?" MaaSa was not relenting.

"From an ancient storyteller on San Standard. She would not use the correct names for anyone in the tale, fearing that it would open the door to the evil that once resided in this long-lost planet."

"The storyteller is correct," MaaSa said. "A terrible evil turned the water people against the land people. Both peoples listened to the whispers of this evil." There was silence for a moment. "But it was a long time ago. Do you wish to become part of a *sesshi*?"

"Not I." Alexandra turned to Carol.

Carol's eyes became wide. "Me? I don't know what this is."

"I think somewhere in your lost memories, you do know, only you called it something else. It's a psychic link to another. It has different names in different cultures, and there are different ways of practicing it, but basically it's sharing another's consciousness. A joining of minds."

"Why?" three voices asked.

"Because if Alan invades this part of the city, he will either wipe out everyone who is still here or do something that will cause irreparable damage to your spirit. If he's casting his sticks, there's no telling what he's seeing. His soldiers were delivering explosives to Century City, remember. With the mobots, he could send them down the travel tubes to the other cities."

"What does *sesshi* have to do with this?" MaaSa sounded skeptical.

"Alan would have studied your group through the use of his sticks, or a channeler, and would know who to use to infiltrate. If Carol were here, MaaSa would not be overwhelmed to the point of not being able to resist. Alan is violent. Carol can absorb the violence, but MaaSa can't."

"Why do you think that?" MaaSa asked.

"You're not a violent race. That's why the evil one of long ago won. Suspicion was the mortal wound to your races."

"Yes."

"I don't think that's a good idea," Carol said.

Alexandra noted her objection wasn't presented with vigor, only hesitation. She wondered if her empathic interpretation of this water city was correct. Now, however, was not a time to doubt. Alan presented a real threat to these people, and this plan could help them and help Carol.

"You'll need to think about it," Alexandra said. "Normally it's a three-stan-day ritual, but it has been done in one. It'll mean that I'll have to remember that when I talk to you, I'm also talking to MaaSa and his tribe."

"His tribe?" Carol said.

"Yes. I feel others here. Not everyone has left, Guardian."

"That's true," MaaSa said. "We had grown accustomed to the life force here, and it graciously merged with our own energy. We have become part of this planet."

Guardian was undoubtedly happy to reconnect with MaaSa, but Alexandra was tired. She began looking for an opportunity to excuse herself so they could leave.

"So," MaaSa said, "is the cloning project to recreate Charles's adult biological body nearly completed?"

"Yes," Guardian said, "quite soon. His body needs just a little more aging. He is in another container, rolling about the Lair in his usual colorful way."

MaaSa and Guardian laughed, apparently sharing a private joke.

"And you, then? Surely you don't need 200 stan years to produce a new biobody."

"No. We have had some problems and delays. But soon."

"How did you know that I remained here?" MaaSa asked Alexandra.

"Actually, it was Carol. I wasn't sure of what I felt, but if Carol was sensitive about something around here and not in other parts of the Lair and Century City, then she had to be species-sensitive to the energy your species generates. Perhaps she has Enuit relatives."

"What makes you think Carol is related to the Enuit?" Guardian asked.

"I don't know any Enuits," Carol stated flatly, then added, "What is an Enuit?"

"Enuit is a name given to the little-known inhabitants of Halemas, a colony located on a planet just three months from Gela," said Alexandra. "There are more tales about them than actual knowledge. It is said that, due to the influence of the Evil One, they closed their planet to visitors and no longer wished to interact with outsiders. It is on the lost planet we spoke of earlier. The Evil One was an off-worlder. I can't see the data cards, but you not only saw them, you were able to discern where to lay them. You laid them on the recorder, and that turned the recorder on. That must have been what woke the sleeping guardian. I also noticed that the family protector didn't engulf you as it did me. It simply crowded you into a corner."

"Halemas was our sister colony," MaaSa said. "Many young Land and Water Enuits traveled there to learn whether it was habitable for all of us. We never heard from them again."

"Carol, does any of this sound familiar to you?" Guardian asked.

"No. I, I don't feel like any of this is familiar. It's true I can see the cards, and I knew to lay them on a recorder table."

"Someone in your genetic line may have been Enuit," Guardian said. "Your DNA scan shows some of the same markers, but many have similar DNA. It just expresses itself differently. You don't look like a Land Enuit and certainly not a Water Enuit."

"We need to determine what possible weaknesses Alan may find here to exploit," Alexandra reminded the others.

"The Enuit oversaw the construction of WaterLand themselves," Guardian said. "I do not know what they did to protect their city from unwanted visitors."

"Nothing. We thought only Enuits and friends would visit, and those that were here had arrived by portal.

"You did not keep watch, MaaSa?" Guardian asked, worry coloring his tone.

"We were aware that Century City had been occupied, but we were accustomed to our solitude and had no intention of ending it."

"How did you know that the city was occupied?" Alexandra asked.

"We are connected with the planet. She told us. She is not happy with the harmful energy that has settled within her, and the disruptions she is experiencing at various vortices are causing her discomfort."

"She didn't tell you Guardian was alive?"

"She has no thought of Guardian."

"Since all that we can do here has been done," Alexandra said, "perhaps you will excuse us, MaaSa. We need to prepare to visit Ilo, the next city."

"You will visit Ilo uninvited?" MaaSa asked. "Guardian?"

"There is no one there," Guardian said.

"You are sure?"

"The life support has been shut off."

MaaSa was quiet.

"You don't feel that's true, MaaSa?" Alexandra said.

"The Spirit of the planet reports that there is life there."

Alexandra felt MaaSa's energy diminish.

"It's time we left here," Alexandra said to Carol, who nodded.

"You are not waiting for MaaSa to return?" Guardian asked.

"The communication link is back up, and we still have other cities to prepare for."

"You sound as though you are in a rush to get the cities online." There was a pause, and then Guardian said, "It is not because you are worried that once the War Forum has the planet under their protection, you will have nothing to do until your admiral calls for you, is it?"

"You got me." She forced a laugh, not sure whether that was truly the reason, or it was because she had a feeling that something was amiss in the other cities.

* * *

When they arrived back at the Lair, the atmosphere had changed noticeably. As they walked down the hall, Alexandra saw green occupancy lights lit up on the outside of quarters that had previously been vacant. She glanced at Carol, who had a distracted look on her face. Alexandra let her vision blur and could see the swirling energy around Carol. Suspecting she was thinking about the merging in the *sesshi* ritual, she decided that was a decision Carol would have to wrestle with on her own.

She sighed. Life was getting complicated again. The energy of *knowing* that she had tapped into when she was with the Spartans had been toned down empathic knowledge. However, now it was going full blast, and closing her eyes was not enough to quiet it.

The door to their quarters slid open, and Alexandra stopped in the kitchenette, where Bach was waiting to serve her.

"Cha, warm," she said. Carrying her drink, she trailed Carol into the bedroom. She could hear the shower shut off and water running in the tub. Removing her clothes, she prepared for a shower. Perhaps she should explain her empathy about the *sesshi* to Carol and tell her why she had suggested such a radical thing, except that when she said it aloud, it didn't sound rational even to her.

Alexandra showered quickly and then headed to the tub area. A pop inside of her head caused her to involuntarily take a deep breath. It wasn't a painful sensation, just surprising. She blinked her way past the distraction and stood by the tub. Carol floated in the herb-scented water with her eyes closed. Colors, strong and pulsing, rose from her and spiraled above the tub, creating an energy vortex.

"I have decided to merge with the Enuit, Alexandra," Carol said in a quiet voice.

"So the herb bath is the beginning of the preparation."

"Yes. It wakens the *Qi* and opens the senses."

Alexandra rubbed her forehead. "I noticed. Would you like to be alone?"

"No. I would like your assistance. I don't know much about the preparation."

Alexandra settled into the water. "How were you able to choose this herb?"

"I asked Ald."

"A bot with a wealth of herbal information. The more people involved, the higher the vibration we can create to meld and to protect you and whoever is going to be a part of this melding. We also need to find out if MaaSa has agreed or found someone on his side to participate. Guardian?"

"Yes?"

"Has MaaSa mentioned anything about the meld?"

"Yes. His people have selected him."

"Okay. Carol has also agreed to go through with it. I trust he knows what to do on his side. On our side, we'll need more people."

"How many participants are needed?"

"The normal sitting is seven. Six for the directions and the seventh to observe the ritual and watch the outer perimeter. We noticed you had a lot of rooms activated. Perhaps some of your guests are familiar with ritual preparations."

A familiar voice called, "Indeed, Alexandra," and Gedaliaha stepped through the clouds of steam.

"Gedaliaha!" Alexandra jumped out of the tub and wrapped her dripping arms around her old mentor. She was dressed in her usual long robe of soft pastel colors.

Gedaliaha gave her a strong hug, then gently pushed her back and took a better look at her. "My dear Alexandra, it is nice to see you are doing so well. Hmm. I see you have finally shed that awful energy you had about you and have become involved with others again."

Alexandra flushed at Gedaliaha's implication.

"The shamans have foreseen the need for this gathering, and those who are to participate are preparing," Gedaliaha said. "We have more who will maintain the protective ring."

"Gedaliaha, this is Carol. Carol, this is Gedaliaha."

Gedaliaha's reply was in a singsong voice, the language foreign to Alexandra.

Carol raised a hand in greeting. "I don't know what you said, but I greet you, Wise Mother."

Gedaliaha nodded. "Greetings and blessings on you, and on your family's hearth." Gedaliaha seemed to study Carol for a moment. "We have three with yang energy who have been across the bridge of *osho* many times." She turned back to Alexandra, gesturing that she should step back into the water. "The three with yin energy are you to the West, Sharon Teal to the heavens, and Maga Le to the planet."

Standing on the third step, Alexandra went still, unsure whether the warmth infusing her was from the waist-deep water or hearing Sharon's name resurrected from her past.

"You shall both prepare for the next two hours. I shall assist, as you are novices and may languish at some point in the ritual," Gedaliaha said.

The room quickly changed from a tropical setting to simulate the interior of a ritual bathing area at the temple at Helop in the province of Ra.

The energy in the room intensified. Taking a deep breath, Alexandra held the herb's essence in her lungs and felt it penetrate her cells. Gedaliaha demonstrated the mudra position of the hands and fingers, elbows even with the shoulders, and then the breathing rhythm.

Alexandra closed her eyes and let the energy in the room transform her senses and move her to another state as the power of the pose and the environment propelled them into another dimension. Inside the energy of a ritual, time did not exist.

She experienced sudden awareness of others, gathered in a semicircle in the sitting room of her quarters. A loose saffron cloth draped her in ritual folds, vibrating the color green. Gedaliaha's form was white and sitting out of the consciousness of the circle, but Alexandra spotted her and *knew* her. Just like she *knew* Sharon was present, though she was not familiar with the energy. From a distance, hovering above the circle, she studied everyone. Then her attention was drawn back to her own part, and she focused her energy toward the center of the semicircle, where the others were directing theirs. Carol sat there, draped in a sheer white cloth. The light in the center became so bright that it blotted out Carol's physical form.

The process of the meld began as a vibration. Their combined thoughts and mantra set up a tone that shot through Carol's form in colorless energy, radiated for a moment above her, then spread outward, touching them all. The touch was both gentle and foreign. Alexandra became faintly aware of another energy that was outside the circle. Gedaliaha. Like a bright hurricane funnel, her energy moved toward the new energy, spinning around it and sucking anything not wanted up into the central core where it disappeared. When her energy withdrew, yet another energy entered into their circle, bearing a tingling, cool sensation. It merged into their combined vibration, and the tone of the circle changed.

Alexandra felt the splitting of the energy fields. There was no feeling of anguish, but rather curiosity and intense intelligence radiated from both spirits as they shared space. A sudden surge of her own energy returned, and Carol's physical form became more solid.

Those in the circle remained seated as they began a slow chant, and her own voice joined in with the sounds resonating in her breastbone. Alexandra changed the mudra of her hands and then—either instinctively, or influenced by the group—extended her legs into another pose, changing the energy of the room. Thus, gradually, the sacred ritual came to an end.

Sighing, she stretched her body, just as the others were doing, and let her gaze travel around the group. Everyone seemed very pleased. One of the men directly across from Alexandra looked too young to be a shaman, but when he opened his eyes, they were like those of an old man, faded and nearly sightless. He smiled at her and rose gracefully, patting Gedaliaha on the shoulder as she remained sitting. Alexandra's glance fell on Sharon. Her heart raced as she watched her and the others move the furniture back in place and then assist Carol to the couch. Sharon turned slightly and gave Alexandra a warm smile.

Gedaliaha spoke softly. "You're leaking your thoughts, Alexandra."

Alexandra turned to her mentor. She saw her in a new light. Without changing her vision, she could see the white glow about Gedaliaha and feel the radiation of her power.

"I…" Alexandra let out her breath audibly. "I had no idea of any of this."

"You have been a good student during dreamtime, but terrible in the waking state. Your waking side is slow to catch up," Gedaliaha said.

Alexandra felt Sharon approach, and turned to face her.

"Hello, Harriet." Sharon gave her a kiss on the cheek, as if it were only yesterday they had last seen each other. "I'm happy to see you've stayed out of Alan's reach, so far."

"You know about Alan?"

"I told you I did, in a dream many months ago. You should start remembering our conversations from dreamtime now that your channels are fully open. You've experienced the higher energy of the *Qi* channeler."

"You're a shaman?"

"Yes. Before I took the identity of Sharon, I was a shaman on Magewield, one of the planets visited by Alan's family. When Alan's father arranged to have me processed as a metradame, I chose to become Sharon Teal."

Sharon's demeanor was different from what Alexandra remembered. A sense of loss hovered on the periphery of Alexandra's awareness, and she held it there firmly. "Did you know we were going to be in a relationship before…?" She couldn't finish.

"The Web of Life has strange and interesting crossovers in its patterns, but no, I had not foreseen that we would become lovers. It was a natural and pleasant progression of our friendship. But remaining with me would have put your life in serious jeopardy. Alan feels he has a debt to collect, and you needed to be farther from him, in a safer area. However," Sharon said, and laughed softly, "you seem to do a very good job taking care of yourself, no matter how hot a fire you jump into. You also have a fine mentor, who looks after you very well."

"And a bunch of guardian angels," Gedaliaha said, laughing heartily.

"I must go back now, before I'm missed." Sharon looked directly into Alexandra's eyes.

Alexandra saw only deep, dark pools, without any reflection. She nodded, trying not to show her disappointment. There were so many questions she wanted to ask.

Sharon hugged her and whispered in her ear, "We shall meet again, and very soon. We'll talk then."

The energy emanating from Sharon made Alexandra tingle. She had forgotten how nice it was to hold her. Then she released Sharon and dropped her hands to her sides. The others, also leaving, nodded at Sharon and Alexandra. They all looked tired.

Gedaliaha remained. When the door closed behind Sharon, Gedaliaha touched Alexandra gently on the elbow and motioned for her to sit in the chair across from Carol.

Alexandra pulled the loose-fitting cloth around herself and sat down, studying Carol's vibrant form. There was nothing subtle about the change. She was now Carol-Maa.

"The energy you feel will lessen as your physical body absorbs the new spirit," Gedaliaha explained to Carol. "Now your awareness is split between the two dimensions, and will be that way until both spirits get used to the new energy. Then both consciousnesses will be able to experience the two worlds simultaneously without confusion." Gedaliaha nodded at Carol and Alexandra. "You two will be having interesting dreams from here on out. Carol-Maa will be sleeping between two realities, and you, Alexandra, have moved to another level in your lessons. You're coming along rather quickly, but I see no danger in that at the moment."

Head tilted slightly, she regarded Alexandra. "Don't forget your night rituals. Protect yourself before you sleep. I would rather you two sleep separately for a while. You're working on different issues and shouldn't be disturbed by the other's energy. Guardian has notified us that Carol-Maa will be taking the room Colonel Zohra has been using. The Colonel has moved to temporary quarters with her Sisters. It is their way." Gedaliaha waved her hand. "The Sisters of the Athenian Shield, along with their Brothers, will take over responsibility for the military protection of the outpost, and the Centurions will protect the space over the planet. Your admiral has put you on temporary leave, Alexandra. Moving away from this warrior energy is advisable for now."

"As if." Alexandra shook her head. "Somehow, I don't think the admiral will take my change too well."

"Why do you feel that way?" Gedaliaha asked.

"Military types don't put much value on anything they can't touch or see."

"But they do believe intuition is a valuable asset," Gedaliaha said. "Alexandra, right now a different type of awareness is commingling with your perspective of the world, and it will take time for you to adjust to the multitude of new sensations. I've explained that to Admiral JoCastao, and she agreed that you should have it." Alexandra shrugged her shoulders, tired.

"*Colonel* Zohra?" The promotion from major suddenly registered with Alexandra.

"Yes. She's the most qualified to oversee the ground protection of the outpost until Major General Aglauros and the other high-ranking officials arrive. Now, you both need to sleep. It's been a long day, and I can see your energy level is about to drop sharply. I shall be staying awhile on this outpost and will see you when you wake. I'm in the room across the hall from yours, Alexandra. To bed, both of you." She ushered the two to the bedroom.

Carol-Maa was looking around, occasionally waving her hands before her face as if to clear something away.

"What are you doing?" Alexandra asked.

Carol-Maa turned to her and smiled. "This dimension is very interesting, Lieutenant Commander, Lady Alexandra Harriet, Alexandra, Harriet, Mistress. So many names. How do you wish me to address you?"

Alexandra cleared her throat. "I… Montran is my clan or family name, Lady is the title from my home planet, Lieutenant Commander is my military rank, but Harriet or Alexandra would be fine, too."

"You look different through these eyes, and the space you live in is most peculiar."

"It will give you a whole new subject to write about."

"That is something I will work on with Carol."

Alexandra hadn't thought about how their relationship would change with the melding of the two spirits, but now she was grateful Carol would not be sharing her bed. "Good night and dream well, Carol-Maa."

"And you, too, Alexandra."

Chapter 18

JG dreamt of her childhood friend Katrina. They had shared the honor of being among the forty Sisters in the athletic finals competing to represent their Sisters at the Youth Galactic games, held once every four stan years. The pretrial consisted of a weeklong endurance challenge that required them to compete in seven separate areas of skill, which had been predetermined by the games committee. Both were chosen for the team.

She sighed deeply.

The memories were from so long ago, she wasn't sure if they were even from this life. She frowned. She hadn't been called JG then, but… Delorita? No. She couldn't remember ever having felt comfortable with that name. At her Coming of Age ceremony, she had added Zohra, but that was when she was still a young woman.

She resisted the pull to go farther back into memories of her youth. Instead, she focused on the faces and names of those she had been ordered to protect. She snickered to herself contemptuously. There was no way she was going to protect that pack of lawbreakers. One of them was her half sister. She nearly burst out laughing at the audacity of assigning her to protect Lady Varina Chaney. As if! *Lady* Varina was perfectly capable of protecting herself from all the half sisters their father had sired, and had survived several assassination attempts already.

Finally, her unfamiliar surroundings trickled into her awareness. A voice was calling her, and a very bright light was shining above her. She had a headache. She also had a distinct feeling that a long time had passed. But from when to when? What yesterday was she measuring this time with? She wanted to shake her head to stop the buzzing in her inner ear, but it was being held immobile. She fought a sudden feeling of panic.

"It's all right to feel threatened. You don't know where you are. Just wait until you're completely awake before you move, or you'll land flat on your face," a soft voice said.

JG held herself still. She analyzed sounds, smells, and the pattern on the ceiling in order to keep from screaming. Where was she? And who was she? Sergeant Major JG, a member of the Black Rose…? No… she was a Major… Major Zohra of the Sisters of Hekate clan, a Shield Maiden to Athena's Warriors, and bonded to…

Her mind's eye filled with the image of Cadet Lady Harriet Montran. She had bright orange hair that flowed down her back in long tresses. Glittering beads were threaded through the long strands at the sides of her face, setting off bright green eyes that lit up when she laughed.

Zohra's vision cleared and the buzzing stopped, then the restraining mechanisms released. Slowly, she sat up, assisted by a woman dressed in the mantle of the Sister House on Media, which was a healers' clan.

"How many fingers am I holding up?" the woman asked.

"One," she replied.

"Very good." The woman stepped away and another figure moved into her view.

"I am Lady Crystal of Triton, Lady Zohra."

"Lady? Not a title that fits me," she said in a hoarse voice. She couldn't stop the corners of her lips from curling up at the image of another lady who did fit the title. "I'm a soldier, not a socialite or politician."

"Your late father's will has been read, and he recognized his offspring, making them official holders of titles, lands, and funds. He had quite an empire to leave behind. Apparently, he took his estate-planning responsibilities seriously. Your adopted mother, Aglauros, will more than likely talk to you about it, but as your physician, I thought you should know the basics now. I understand you warrior types can be rather defensive on issues you don't like to face, and I didn't want you to be blind-sided."

Lady Crystal spoke with dry humor, and Zohra had to admit that her observation was accurate.

"We removed a small chip from your brain that your sister, Lady Varina, had ordered implanted. It's believed to have controlled your emotional response to her, and to your father."

"Where am I?"

"On Merker's Outpost, as the guest of the Guardian of Mer's Portal. The nausea you're feeling will pass soon. It's one of the aftereffects of the subliminal programming."

Zohra rubbed her forehead again. “Mer? I wasn’t aware the portals had names.”

“For very good reason. Names give power. Alan Fermin wishes to damage the portals to keep them out of use for a while. If he damages one, it will set up a vibration in all the others. No one knows how long a disrupted portal takes to repair itself, because no one has damaged a portal since guardianships were established to watch over them.”

“I remember this place.”

“Not this place, but the nanochip was introduced into your system in a room similar to this one. Lord Chaney was displeased with Lady Varina’s interference with you, and with her other siblings as well, and was attempting to diminish the chip’s influence with a drug. The intention was for the two factors to neutralize each other. It worked, to a degree, but we’re not sure of the chip’s entire function, or why he tried to disable it rather than having it removed.” Lady Crystal paused, but Zohra remained silent.

“It’s being studied now, and we’ll notify you when the information is available. Now, would you like to eat? Your Sisters should be arriving soon, and I’m sure you will have little time for such things after their arrival.”

Zohra realized that she was hungry. “Yes.”

Lady Crystal summoned another woman, and after somewhat awkward farewells, Zohra followed her out the door.

“Where are we on Merker’s Outpost?” she asked her new guide.

“Near the portal, Major Zohra.” Zohra shuddered, and her companion said, “The energy from the portal is what kept you strong for the process of extraction. The scientists didn’t want to dissolve the nanochip because they hoped to study it and find out just what it was programmed to do.”

Zohra’s jaw tightened in repugnance at the thought of something foreign in her body controlling her actions. “The energy from the portal?”

“Yes. What do you know about the portals?”

“They are doorways to other planets through which only a few may pass.”

Her companion pointed to a table, on which were placed dishes and plates of food. Zohra’s stomach growled in appreciation.

“Actually, many can pass through the portals, just as you did when you were younger. It doesn’t take much to prepare yourself for the passage. But those below the sixth harmonic level can't enter without harming themselves."

Zohra took a plate and filled it with food as she listened. "Sixth level and below are people who do harm to others intentionally, right?" She received a nod of agreement. "Is it possible for a person near the sixth level to control a portal and become its guardian?"

"You mean like Captain Miller of the Black Rose proposed to do?"

"Yes."

"When he was captured, we found a harmonics synthesizer in his clothing. Attempting to enter a portal would have killed him, because the energy in the portal vibrates in many octaves simultaneously. The changes between octaves are too quick for a synthetic harmonizer to follow. The portal is a living and self-organizing structure and the harmonizer is not."

"What would have happened to those standing outside the portal?"

"They would have perished as well."

Zohra finished eating in silence. Inside a ship, the bulkheads between her and the outside continuum blunted the experience of traveling within living space. But her one trip through a portal was an unforgettable experience. She had been cocooned in an energy field of living matter, feeling her surroundings in a kaleidoscope of emotions that changed as planets and stars moved by. She had found it an intensely disorienting experience, especially once she had arrived at her destination. Captain Miller's had been naïve to think he could take possession of something that beautiful. As a living entity, a portal chose its own guardian.

Zohra pushed her plate away. Before her Sisters came, she needed to prepare for the arrival of the forces that would see to the protection of this planet. She had charts and up-to-date information on the cities to gather.

"You have eaten very well, Major Zohra," her companion said, nodding with approval. "Some people can't eat after the operation. But you must not overexert yourself for a day. The incision isn't the only thing that needs to heal. If the chip had been lodged any deeper, the surgeon wouldn't have been able to retrieve it. Now, your neural pathways need to reassert their old ways."

"I want a detailed report on just what they find."

"You'll have it. You should avoid physical exercise and worry for the next few days, if at all possible."

"That leaves me with nothing to do."

"Dream."

"What?"

"Your mind and your body will both heal while you dream. A subliminal will be played for you while you sleep, which should counteract any deep programming we may have missed."

"How will I know if there is any deep programming remaining?"

"You'll have nightmares."

"Good thing I sleep alone." She sighed. It was going to be hard to rid herself of some habits she'd practiced as a Black Rose, like looking for a bed companion to unwind with.

"We will have someone nearby to monitor you, Major."

She was escorted to the elevator. "This is where I leave you. I believe you know your way from here. Sleep and heal."

Lady Harriet and Carol didn't appear to be in the area when Zohra arrived at her room, so she rinsed herself and went into the tub to soak and think, letting the bot massage her sore shoulders and back. Relaxed but restless, she decided to see if her Sisters had arrived. "Guardian."

"Yes, Lieutenant Colonel Zohra."

Zohra's eyebrows rose toward her hairline. "Lieutenant Colonel?"

"General Aglauros has promoted you. Your new orders are to head the security forces here in the Lair and offer as much assistance as you can to Commander Hyes in Century City, until the general's arrival."

"Very well." Zohra tried to absorb all that had happened to her in less than a week, and gave an amused snort.

I have major brain surgery, and look what I wake up to. I haven't even gotten used to being called major. It's not every day a soldier starts out a sergeant major, becomes a major, and then a lieutenant colonel. Not to mention a Lady.

She was Lady Harriet's superior, sort of… until she was reassigned to a ship, and that wouldn't be for a while. She wondered if Lady Harriet would make a good staff officer. Perhaps she could order her to remove her boots… naked …

Zohra shook her head to rid herself of the image. It wasn't a new one. Since the Dance, Zohra had had many erotic thoughts of Lady Harriet, usually having to work off the energy generated with others. She had to get her mind off Lady Harriet.

"Guardian, have my Sisters from the House of Athena arrived yet?" she asked thickly, trying to dispel the sensual feelings.

"Three of them arrived in a Phantom Sprint ship, the *Spearhead*. They left messages for you to call after you rested. They and some members of Naboth's Vine were sent to assist the Brothers and Sisters that are arriving through the portal."

"I believe I know who they are. Tell them to present themselves to my quarters, Guardian." She laughed. She was sure they had been calling every ten minutes to see what was keeping her.

Her door dinged in a matter of minutes, as guests requested entry. "Enter," she said, standing in the center of the room with her hands on her hips, trying to keep her face serious.

"You're a lazy moufin of a Sister and a poor representative of good manners!" Clea shouted as she rushed in and grabbed Zohra, lifting her off her feet, spinning her around and holding on to her fiercely.

Zohra's pretence of sternness dropped into a smile as her isolation from the community of Sisters came to an end. The other two women wrapped their arms around her and Clea. Tears of relief were shed as the three held her, and she hid her face in Clea's shoulder until she could regain some semblance of dignity. Finally, she stepped back and grinned at them through her tears.

"Galdin, they let you out of the House of Pleasure?" she asked the woman who had been her contact during her covert years. "Business at Aphrodite's must have dropped off. Though judging by that glow on Clea, I'd say you're being kept even busier." Zohra pushed playfully at the woman she had often met under the guise of visiting her for sexual pleasure.

"Mistress JG." Galdin gave her a long hug. "It's so good to see you again." She released Zohra with a laugh. "Your presence is missed by those in the Cave." She turned to the others. "Her whipping and spanking techniques were much in demand among the Cave dwellers. When she was in town, the Cave filled up, with males and females alike, mind you." Galdin winked at Zohra. "I wonder how much of that was an act, dear Sister. You took to the role so well, and now you're a Lieutenant Colonel."

"It's been a whirlwind of changes for me. Rest assured, my days as Mistress of the Cave are behind me," Zohra said and then jumped when Clea elbowed her.

"Go on, now. We're here to see that you keep your morals intact, now that you have a more stodgy face to wear."

They all laughed.

"TeaSdak, look at you." Zohra marveled at the changes in her childhood friend. "You've put on weight since I last saw you."

"And it's all muscle, Colonel." TeaSdak laid a hand on Zohra's shoulder. "And look at you. You've lost weight since I last saw *you,* and what is this I see? You're taller too. What strange food have you been eating?"

"It wasn't from anyone in the Cave," Galdin said. "They were sucking her dry. You'd think she was saving herself for someone special. All she wanted to do was sleep, soak in the tub, get a massage, then go back to sleep, but her slaves were lining up outside the dungeon door, waiting for her to take up her role. Duty calls, you know. I'm happy to see the scars that you wore like badges of honor have been removed, Mistress Jina Gari." She brushed the skin of Zohra's forehead, where a scar had been. "You don't want your old face back?"

Zohra flinched at the touch, but allowed the hand to linger. "Not yet."

"We have some news for you, and it's rather disturbing. Shortly after you made contact with your mother, information was leaked on your role among the Black Rose."

"There's a spy on Mother's staff?"

"Or perhaps someone that doesn't know it wasn't for public dissemination," Clea said. "I sensed no malice in the revelation. I was only surprised that it was picked up so quickly and turned into what it has."

"Everyone in the Sisterhood knows of your reputation in the Cave," Galdin said, "and with the dial-a-mood in the suites provided here, you'll be the target of every submissive and wanna-be dom. They'll be baiting you at every turn."

"I'll be careful who I'm alone with."

"That's why we're here. We'll keep an eye on them so you can concentrate on commanding. We have our list."

"So, is it JG or Delorita, Colonel?" Galdin asked in a teasing tone.

"Definitely not Delorita. Between friends, JG or Jina Gari will do. I've heard those for so many years, I'll probably answer to them more readily. I'm getting used to Zohra again. The Colonel part," she said, and gave a short laugh, "is going to take some adapting to. Sit down." She spoke to the bot. "Otto, bring refreshments. Srongmor tea, and make it spicy. That okay with everyone?"

"Just like old times," Galdin said as the others nodded.

"So, who do I have on my staff? I'm sure Mother has appointed them already."

"That she has, but only because she'll be leading the forces when she arrives," TeaSdak said

"Is the spy among them?"

The three women looked at each other, then at Zohra. "We don't know who the spy is."

"But you have your suspicions?"

TeaSdak shook her head. "It's not for us to say."

"Surely it's not Mother?"

The three hooted with laugher. "No."

"All right. Don't tell me. Tell me something I can be told."

They became more serious as they leaned over the center coffee table, where TeaSdak set her planner for them all to view.

"I'll be the coordinator between you and your team leads. Clea and Galdin are part of my support staff, and we'll have our fingers on the pulse of things. Right now, we're to see that everything is set up for the troops when they arrive."

"Good." Zohra grinned at TeaSdak. "So the general found a way to make use of your talents. Didn't I warn you that if you didn't stop with the admin classes, you'd be stuck behind a desk?"

"After four years of slogging through the mud on make-believe skirmishes, you think I was going to be foolish enough to get a command in infantry where I'd get more of the same? You need your head examined. Nor was I interested in traveling the galaxy and worrying about lovers in every port. I rather like being dropped into chaos and leaving it orderly."

"So fill me in on news of the Shield. What's been going on since I last visited?"

They caught up on news for the next few hours. When Zohra's yawns became frequent, her visitors took their leave.

Sleep came quickly to Zohra. Her dreams were many, and they held an underlying tone of urgency. In one dream, she was frantically trying to find Lady Harriet Montran. She needed to explain the meaning of the Dragon Dance. She sought assurance that Lady Harriet had willingly joined with her.

Images from her youth overlapped those of the present day as she moved from one dreamscape to another. The most terrifying one was of being under another's control and not being able to warn anyone.

She was dimly aware of Carol holding her and stroking her forehead. Carol's voice encouraged her to work through each dream, and carried her through the dark shadows. Finally, Zohra relaxed in Carol's arms.

Sometime after Carol's departure, Zohra's dreams shifted altogether. In the sacred grove, the sun was rising above the treetops, setting their tips on fire. The Spirit of the Dance blessed her and her lifemate by drawing them both together for the Dance of Attraction, the second dance in the Dragon series. But unlike the other dreams, this time when she lit the candles and made the offerings, she had Lady Harriet's image in clear focus. Standing before her dressed in the ritual clothing, Lady Harriet waited her turn, green eyes fixed on Zohra's dancing form. When Zohra completed her dance, Lady Harriet began hers. Zohra watched in rapt attention as the image of Lady Harriet danced the steps that called to her, asking Zohra to join her in this life as a lifemate.

The Dance ended with both accepting the joining, and then the dream dissolved.

Zohra felt tired when she awoke, but her mind felt clearer than it had for a long time. Perhaps being so focused on staying alive had its side effects. Someone was buzzing for entrance. She slipped on a robe and went into the sitting room. "Enter."

"Sister, Colonel, you lazy soul. You're still in bed when your Sisters are waiting to celebrate your promotion!"

Lieutenant Malchi and a group of Zohra's Sisters swarmed through the door and grabbed their long-absent member. They hauled her out of her quarters to another section of the Lair, where they had a party going on. Zohra was dumped into a hot tub along with Megan Vanstar. A banner draped across one of the walls both welcomed her back and congratulated her on her promotion.

Music played, songs were sung, and there was plenty of fun and frolicking as everyone became drenched from sudden dunkings. No one was left dry for long. Chants and outrageous songs filled the air, while Zohra's name was tossed back and forth with teasing and joyous affirmation of her presence among them, which had been missed during her nine years of covert work. Decibel meters, which were standard in most public structures in both Collective and GCFC space, kept the noise at a tolerable level. Finally, Zohra was permitted to withdraw from the pranksters and revelers, with Clea and her team forming a protective barrier to give her space.

While Zohra dried off, she looked over the group. Some were in various stages of dressing, while others were getting massages or tending to bruises.

Open stares from some of the women, too bold to be respectful of her rank, were ignored for the moment.

Zohra glanced at herself in the nearby mirror and studied her reflection critically. *Too thin*, she thought. *But it's all muscle.* The scars and tats she'd needed to give her status in the Black Rose were gone. Now, her only tattoo was the owl of Athena's Shield on her back. It had been covered with other designs during her covert work. Her eyes caught Clea's worried look in the mirror.

"I hadn't seen this side of the Lair," Zohra said as she finished dressing. The Sisterhood uniform was forest green. The usual cluster of ribbons was there, and she was bemused to see all her awards for the past nine years, pinned together. While she was undercover, she'd never really paid attention to what was noted or awarded to her on paper. There was also a gold cornhusk on her collar, marking her new rank.

"Quite a large city, this Lair," Clea said. "The troops are billeted in luxurious quarters, no matter what level they're on. I don't remember staying in any barracks this comfortable. I think I'll put in a request to the Sister House." She smirked. "I can imagine the reaction Mother M'dwa would have to that request. We've set up—"

Vanstar flopped onto a bench near the two women, interrupting whatever Clea was about to say.

"Next door is the dojo with the latest and greatest in warrior training," Vanstar said without preamble. "You want to go a few rounds? I've got the high score right now." Without waiting for an answer, she looked around the group and flexed her muscles beneath her workout suit. "This set-up sure beats our quarters in the other city, no?" She glanced at Zohra, then away.

Her brisk manner and the way she was ignoring the others was rude, especially among Sisters. Zohra wondered if Vanstar was going to have a difficult time shedding her Black Rose persona.

"What's Commander Montran up to?" Zohra asked Clea.

"Lady Harriet," Vanstar said in a disdainful tone, "is being taken care of by the shamans. They've suggested that she be removed from all combat plans." Her contempt was palpable.

Zohra wondered how Vanstar would feel toward her if she found out that her father had left her a title and land.

"It's standard practice, Megan," Zohra said. Her voice was uncharacteristically gentle as her thoughts went to Lady Harriet. "She was taken prisoner by Chaney's guard the other day. They gave her to Painmaker to get information out of her. You know that after that kind of treatment, any soldier is taken off active duty until they gets a psych eval."

"I heard she's an empath." Malchi positioned herself between Vanstar and Zohra, as if sensing trouble. "You know they can't do violence to another without harming themselves."

"And," Clea said, "she served as a Spartan captain in the very respected, if be-damned, Degas squad. Don't forget that. And they weren't respectable until she shaped them up. She earned her rank. If she asked to join our Sister House of Athena, I would welcome her."

Zohra hid her smile. Clea had never been silent in the face of Vanstar's outspoken prejudices.

"How can she be an empath," Vanstar said, with ill-concealed disgust, "and still legitimately rise to the rank of captain in the Spartans within two stan years? It's just hyped up class propaganda. She didn't even finish her four-year contract." Her voice had risen as if she wanted others to hear.

By then, a dozen soldiers were listening to the conversation. Zohra realized she had to establish who was in command and what type of leadership she would be instituting.

"Lieutenant Vanstar, I will not have any of my officers practicing character assassination or passing on subversive garbage about another officer. If it continues, I will bust you down a rank and assign you to another unit. The same goes for anyone else I hear slinging mud. Do I make myself clear?" Zohra's voice carried, so all who had heard Vanstar's accusation would also hear her response.

"You all know," she continued, "that Lord Chaney tried specifically to kill Lady Harriet for over two years while she was CO of the Degas squad. She had every right to seek early release from her contract. And everyone knows he set up the Degas squad to fail. We will all show her due respect." Her eyes narrowed and she looked hard at Vanstar, who didn't appear to be taking heed.

"So," Vanstar said, "I take my reprimand with a grain of salt. Not to change the subject too abruptly, but what happened to Captain Miller and the others?"

"Guardian told me he arrested him and the Black Rose soldiers and is confining them until he can turn them over to the Yellow Rose Guard of Triton for questioning." Zohra lowered her voice so that only those standing near could hear her. "Captain Miller was a fool looking for a pot of gold. He would have killed us all had he succeeded." So many hidden agendas, she thought, sighing.

Chapter 19

"Alexandra. Alexandra!"

Alexandra woke with a start. The lights in the room came up slowly, revealing her quarters on Merker's Outpost. Something felt different. She threw back the covers and slid out of the warm bed, then stiffened. This was not Merker's Outpost. She looked for something that would give her a solid clue as to where she was. No butler was waiting for her. Then a door that she had not noticed before opened, and a butler came out.

"No, not that model," she said in exasperation.

She was dreaming!

Noises were coming from behind what should be the door to the bathing area. She cautiously approached the door and touched the open button. It should have opened automatically.

The scene on the other side of the door was a tropical forest and a swirling mist thicker than a bowl of *ozoa*. She heard an unfamiliar creature's call and then another, but they sounded as if they came from deep within the forest.

She walked slowly, hoping she wouldn't stumble over someone or something. Then she tripped over a log that appeared out of the mist, but managed to hang on to her stunner and HR as she grabbed the damp log to prevent herself from toppling over it. For a moment, she looked at the two objects in her hand and then at the log. How could she have missed a waist-high log until the last minute, and what kind of junk equipment was this? She had never seen a stunner or a locator like this. What gave her the idea that these were what they were? Instinctively, she spun around to look behind her and her heart leaped into her throat. A pair of bright yellow eyes peered at her out of the mist.

She held her stunner pointing down, not willing to shoot at something that had only scared her. The thought occurred to her that when she was a Spartan, she would have shot first and then investigated.

The mist cleared as though pulled into a vacuum, and standing before her with a very pleased expression on his face was a four-foot dwarf holding a pole with two yellow lights at the top… the scary eyes.

"Okay, let's move on," he said, giving a brisk wave.

The scene changed and Alexandra found herself standing on the edge of a crater with a very restless volcano shaking beneath her. A figure in a silver suit leaned over the lip of the cone holding a measuring device, apparently trying to get readings. Alexandra looked around for the scientist's transportation. To her dismay, she saw a small hovercraft being engulfed in hot gas escaping from a new fissure.

She cried out and the figure jumped up, startled. A string of profanity came from inside the scientist's helmet as she watched her transportation slowly sink into the opening. Alexandra stepped quickly to the woman's side as she felt the volcano prepare itself for another eruption. The roar in the core increased, and fiery lava bombs spewed forth in a dark column that poured out of the cone.

Alexandra knew it was impossible for her and the scientist to be alive during this gas and heat release, so she knew she was dreaming. And in a dream, she could create a rescue.

A craft came swooping down between the clouds of black vapor, smoothly glided to a halt beside the scientist, and hovered a few feet above the trembling ground. The door opened, and Alexandra's heart thudded when she spotted a smiling Alan in the pilot's seat.

"No!" she yelled.

With Alexandra following, the scientist leaped away from the vehicle and ran toward a path untouched by the lava flow. When the scientist reached the beginning of the trail, she nearly fell down. A flash of light hit the trail just behind her. Alexandra willed herself to run faster, and pulled up beside the fleeing woman. They were both running flat out, dodging around boulders and patches of lava.

If this is a dream, why not just dream of a safe escape? Alexandra thought.

The running figure stopped and spun around to face her, and angrily pulled off her mask. "What do you think I've been trying to do? But I keep having this same stupid dream. And who in Hades are you?"

Alexandra reached out and touched the orange-haired woman's shoulder, trying to calm her. Her hand picked up the foreign energy emanating from around the woman. "A sonic hydra. Someone has set one around your sleeping area," she said. The woman's eyes opened wide. Alexandra was about to say something more when she was jerked out of that dreamscape.

Before her was a spectacular view of a sundown on a Wieldworld. Her breath caught, for the scene was all too familiar. Sharon was sitting on the wall in front of her.

"It's my home planet, Magewield." Sharon patted the space near her, and Alexandra joined her.

"You're from Magewield?"

"Yes, Alexandra. You already knew that. You just don't remember our previous visits yet." Sharon smiled warmly. "We were good for each other. Now we must move on and share our lives with others."

Alexandra blushed at how easily Sharon was reading her.

Sharon laid a comforting hand on her arm. "We opened up parts of each other that only love could unlock, just as your relationship with Carol did something else for both of you."

Alexandra felt unhappy. "I took advantage of her. I could have requested a separate room, or two beds."

"Have you asked Carol if she felt you were taking advantage of her?"

"Yes, but how can I be sure her compliance isn't part of her program?"

"You gave her permission to speak her mind. The behavior chips cause metrapeople to see things as yes and no, do and don't. Their life isn't in color or shades of gray, even if it seems they're acting normally. And technically, I was never a metraperson. The chip implant was unable to affect me."

Alexandra lifted her gaze to look into amused, slate gray eyes that were filled with love. A sense of peace settled over her.

"I hold you very close to my heart, Alexandra. You showed me what I was missing with my single-minded purpose. Sharing that kind of unconditional love gives me unfathomable strength in my journey to help others."

Alexandra nodded, tears stinging her eyes.

"You've been seeking a meaning to the Dance," Sharon said, and smiled. Alexandra's pulse raced, and the colors around her changed.

"As a cadet, you witnessed a Dance of Attraction. It's a calling to join destinies on a higher level, and it's the second dance of four. In the first dance, the Dance of Invitation, the spirits or guardians are called upon to find one's lifemate. The two souls meet in dreamtime and decide whether or not they want to join in this life. You accepted the Dance of Invitation when you were a young girl, just before your first menses. In your dreams, you requested to see who this was, and when you were visiting a temple to honor your moon time, you met her. Do you remember that?"

"Yes." Alexandra looked at her in surprise. "I… I had dreams of her that night. They embarrassed me."

Sharon nodded. "When you saw Cadet Zohra dancing, she was hoping to use the steps to bleed off the energy your proximity was creating in both of you, but the two of you went like moths to a flame, and willingly danced in the sacred energy. If on any level you hadn't wished for this to take place, you wouldn't have gone there that night. The guardians of the ritual wouldn't have permitted it."

"When she's near me, I'm not sure if what I'm feeling is because of the pheromone gas, like with Sheila."

Sharon's eyes sparkled with humor. "That certainly does create confusion. It's time for you two to do the Dance of Commitment. You know the Dance already. Your master at AltaLa taught it to you, but under a different name in order to keep its higher purpose hidden from the uninitiated. Remember the four dances of the seasons?"

Alexandra nodded.

"Connect all four in one dance, and that will be the dance you will dance after Zohra dances hers." Sharon leaned toward her. "Remember." Her breath tickled Alexandra's ear. "We will not contact each other for a while."

A knot formed in Alexandra's stomach.

"Alan must not see any connection between us," Sharon said. "He has hired someone to work the ethers, and this person would recognize and be able to locate us. Any visible connection between us would bring more souls into harm's way." Sharon touched behind Alexandra's left ear with her thumb. "This is my gift to you, my love. May your journey on the path of enlightenment bring you profound joy. You will now continue your way, engaged both consciously and in dreamtime."

Alexandra's eyes fluttered open as her other senses stretched out to identify her environment and gauge its security. The lights in the room brightened slightly from their soft glow. She took a deep breath, released it, and felt the ache in her heart lessen.

She knew about my Dancer. So, Zohra and I are still bonded. She felt giddy. *I knew that.*

Then a thought struck her, and she became anxious. Perhaps Zohra wasn't aware of this, at least on a conscious level. She'd been in covert operations for so long, and something like this would be far from her everyday concerns, even now. Sooner or later, Alexandra would have to ask her about the Dance and their connection, to see if they were on the same… path?

But now it was time to start her day. "Good morning, Guardian."

"Good morning, Lady Alexandra."

"What's the news of the day?"

"Naboth's Vine is looking for the Alowan and any others that may appear. The captured Black Rose, Spartans, and a squad of Alan's soldiers have been moved off planet for questioning and safekeeping, just in case something happens and the city has to be evacuated quickly. The War Forum has been seated. Your Colonel Zohra has been given the temporary assignment of overseeing security in the Lair and Century City."

"*My* colonel?" Her eyebrows rose. "I'll try to stay out of the way. Will you keep me in the loop? I realize I have no official standing in all this, but I'd like to know whether I need to hide or dress in full regalia," she said, joking half-heartedly.

"I understand. You are still my guest and assistant, and as long as helping me does not compromise your orders from Admiral JoCastao, I see no reason to keep you isolated from what is happening on the outpost. It would be foolish. I am sure Colonel Zohra sees your value, too. She will have her hands full and will undoubtedly welcome your suggestions.

It was probably best to refrain from comment on that last, Alexandra decided. She retracted the bed and began her exercises. From there, she worked on the moves Zohra had taught her and Carol. The holographic fighter she was practicing with was nimble and short, giving her a challenge. Finally she closed the session, feeling pleased with her workout. The next time she encountered short adversaries, she would leave them flat on the mat. She chuckled at the thought and walked toward the bathing room.

The door slid open and steam rolled toward her. She sniffed the herbal scent that perfumed the moist clouds, which were so thick that she couldn't see more than an arm's length before her.

A whoop, followed by women's laughter, reminded her that she shared bathing facilities with Carol-Maa. Not wanting to intrude on anyone, she headed for the shower and made quick work of cleaning herself. When she turned off the water and stepped out to take a towel from Ald, she heard a familiar voice.

"Lady Alexandra, come and join us," Carol-Maa called from behind the clouds of steam.

Alexandra paused, torn between wanting solitude and curious to see who was with Carol. She followed the sounds, moving cautiously through the billowing moisture until suddenly it cleared. All conversation stopped at her appearance. Alexandra's heart quickened when she saw Zohra sitting in front of Carol-Maa, getting a massage. She looked away, confused by her own unsettled feelings. Were Carol-Maa and Zohra now lovers?

She looked at the other three women, whom she didn't know. Two Alterians were sitting intimately close, as a couple would. Both smiled their welcome. The third woman met her look with hostile, if not resentful, intent. The colors whirling around her were decidedly not friendly.

This must be Lieutenant Vanstar, Zohra's Black Rose partner.

"Welcome. Join us, please." The Alterian nearest Vanstar waved to a space on the other side of her lover.

Zohra moved to sit a comfortable distance away, but still beside Carol-Maa, putting her directly across from where Alexandra was to sit.

Alexandra stepped down onto the first step and found the water hotter than usual. While she waited for her body to adjust, she looked at Carol-Maa, who was watching her with a mischievous smile.

The Alterian nearest her spoke, also smiling. "Well, since introductions are slow in coming, I'll do them. My name is Galdin, this is my lifemate, Clea, and," indicating Vanstar, "that's Megan. Thank you for sharing your tub. Ours is filled with too many wild women to carry on any type of conversation below a yell."

"And then there are the countless interruptions our CO suffers through," Clea said. "But if JG didn't have such a reputation as a disciplinarian, we wouldn't have been bothered by so many pests." She grinned at Zohra, who gave no indication of how the comment affected her.

In keeping with the informal atmosphere, Alexandra quickly decided to introduce herself by first name and clan name. Since Montran was titled and from an old clan in their sector of space, for her to introduce herself with only her first name would be a social insult. "I'm Alexandra Montran. Thank you for inviting me to share your companionship." Alexandra returned the smile and nodded to the other two women before lowering herself onto the second step.

She turned to Zohra, and her eyes were captured by the dark orbs fixed on her. She resisted the impulse to lose herself in their gaze.

"Congratulations on your promotion, Lieutenant Colonel Zohra," she said casually.

"Lady Alexandra." The corners of Zohra's lips curled up into a smile, and Alexandra smiled back.

Feeling lighter, she turned her attention to Carol-Maa. "Good day, Carol-Maa. Is this atmosphere yours?"

"It's warmer than what I'm used to, but our guests were reminiscing about their visits to hot springs on a planet far from here. I was homesick for my water, and this seemed like a nice way to take care of what we all missed."

The conversation resumed, with Carol-Maa asking questions and Clea entertaining them with outrageous stories of her encounters with other cultures.

Pop!

Alexandra blinked. The pop inside her head was followed by heightened sensitivity to everyone in the water. She breathed in slowly, trying to settle the fluttering in her stomach. Somehow, she had established a link with the group. Since her senses had already been opened, it surprised her that something else was opening, as well.

Gedaliaha reminded me just yesterday that water intensifies connections with those in its environment.

Waves of sensuous energy between Galdin and Clea infused the waters and touched everyone in the tub. It turned Alexandra's desire for Zohra into a compelling need. Alexandra tried to concentrate on anything that would squelch the slow burn inside her, but it was building quickly. Her gaze moved to Zohra.

Zohra's emotions were obviously affected, too, and though her face was expressionless, Alexandra could feel her desire. Afraid that Zohra would think she had initiated the intrusion, she tried to move her thoughts to something that would break their link. Her eyes shifted to the dark energy, Vanstar, whose expression was openly antagonistic.

"So, you're the former Captain Montran." Vanstar's voice sounded truculent, challenging.

Alexandra's heart skipped a beat as her defenses went up, yet she was amused that the sensuous energy swirling around them had ignited a different type of reaction in Megan Vanstar. The colors swirling around Vanstar were a flat shade of red, with tinges of dirty brown and the off-green color of… envy?

“How heroic of you to be the only surviving member of Degas squad,” Vanstar said.

Alexandra locked eyes with Vanstar, her temper rising. “What gives you the right to judge? You know nothing about it beyond the rumors perpetuated by Lord Chaney, your master, and the very person who sent Degas squad to their deaths.”

Vanstar flinched and broke eye contact. “You stole the honor from dead soldiers. Your high-and-mighty title doesn’t excuse that.”

Zohra’s voice was low and menacing. “Lieutenant Vanstar, confine yourself to your quarters and wait for my return. Now.”

The emotions in the water intensified, and Alexandra could feel the discomfort of everyone except Carol-Maa, who seemed fascinated by the exchange. Vanstar glared at Zohra, but pulled herself out of the tub. She headed to the door to Carol-Maa’s quarters, ignoring the towel Ald held out to her.

Worried, Alexandra looked at Zohra.

“I apologize, Lady Alexandra. That was a breach of the Sisterhood’s standards of conduct and isn’t to be tolerated. I’ll see to it.” Zohra rose.

Alexandra looked up and frowned. A CO should never leave a function to discipline a soldier. It gave the subordinate too much power.

“Let her go, JG. This isn’t about friendship,” Galdin said. “You’re not in the Black Rose anymore. She needs to shed that horrible attitude.”

Zohra relaxed back into the water, looking a bit sheepish. “You’re right. This rank thing is going to take some getting used to.”

“Lady Alexandra,” Clea said, “would you mind if I ask why you remained in the Degas squad when you realized they were being used as cannon fodder?”

With Vanstar gone, the environment felt comforting, and Alexandra could easily sense that the question had been asked from the heart of a healer. She reflected on that time, though she didn’t want to delve too deeply into the issues of the past.

“I stopped asking myself that question, because I kept getting different answers.” She ran the palm of her hand over the bubbling waters as though soothing the energy stirred up by the memories.

"I remember my introduction to the squad. They were insolent and didn't care about anything. The condition of their barracks was awful, and they wore dirty, ill-fitting uniforms. Their equipment was something I would expect a band of poor rebels to have, not soldiers." She looked into Clea's eyes. "When I realized their purpose—bait with no means of defense—I couldn't let that happen."

"You felt sorry for them?"

"Oh, no. Judging from their personnel records, they weren't nice people. I just felt they needed to know that they could redeem themselves. I was a greenie, you see." She laughed at her inexperienced determination to do something for the doomed squad. "We all learned from the experience. We taught each other how to live with dignity and compassion in the midst of brutality and imminent death. It took me five stan years to understand the tremendous undertaking that it was, and four more to get over it."

"Compassion? When you were killing defenseless people?" Galdin's question held no rancor.

"Ha!" Alexandra laughed. "*We* were defenseless. Our weapons were more outdated than the equipment of the people we were dropped into the middle of. We became a raiding party out of necessity. We collected their weapons, kits, and whatever other supplies we found. Remember, we weren't there to do damage to those people. We were there to get them to shoot at us so snipers from other squads could pinpoint their location and shoot them. We felt compassion for these people because they were like us, bait for a political machine that didn't care about the rightness or wrongness of the skirmish."

"Degas squad surprised a lot of people when they kept coming back from one-way assignments—and with so many left alive," Zohra said.

"It surprised us, too."

"We all think you did an outstanding job. Even if it didn't work out in the end," Galdin said.

At one time, Alexandra believed she'd failed her squad, even though she knew on an intellectual level that she'd only delayed the inevitable. It was difficult being the lone survivor.

"Thank you." Her voice was tight. Her sensitivity to those in the water rose, and she decided to leave before something else came up and made her too emotionally vulnerable to keep her dignity intact. "I need to get some things done. May the water and its essences impart health to you all."

Pulling herself out of the tub before anyone could object, Alexandra felt the connection break when she left the water. Ald was at her elbow with a towel as she disappeared in the swirls of steam. She decided a cold shower was exactly what she needed. Her thoughts felt scattered, and her emotions were escalating, not unlike when she had been intoxicated by Sheila's pheromone gas.

She rested her forehead against the cold tile. Her senses were still heightened, and her thoughts moved from the arousing connection with Zohra to a vision of flashing, colored lights. Blinking for a moment, she realized she was seeing the energy of the wall in front of her. The smell of the vegetation, the dampness of the earth into which their roots sank, and the sounds of water dripping from leaves were all magnified. Her head lifted.

Struggling against the lethargy that began to affect her, Alexandra moved into her room and sealed the door. She tried not to cry out as a stabbing pain, not unlike a knifepoint to her forehead, lanced across her face. *Oh, Goddess. It's a cleansing. Lord Chaney.*

She had to endure the pain for a few moments. When it stopped, just as suddenly as it had started, she relaxed onto the rug. Sweat trickled down her face.

"Lady Alexandra? Are you all right?" Guardian asked.

"Yes. Yes, I'm fine," she said, in what she hoped sounded like a normal voice.

"The Sisterhood has been trying to get in touch with you to offer you an invitation to their dinner tonight. They asked me to try."

A giggle escaped Alexandra, and she clamped both hands over her mouth to stop any more from emerging. She had no intention of sitting through a boring night with women who would probably spend the entire evening telling war stories, getting drunk, and then making overtures best not spoken of. She giggled again, thinking of the woman she would like to make an overture to.

"Lady Alexandra, are you sure you are all right? I can contact Gedaliaha, but you will have to unlock your quarters. Normally, I honor requests for privacy, but..."

"Hmmf," she managed to get out around her hands. "I'm fine." She started speaking in a serious tone, but more giggling threatened to leak out.

"Well, then, the dinner is at 1900, in the Balang Area."

She heard him sign off and found that hysterically funny, too. For the next ten minutes, though it seemed longer to her sore sides, anything that came to mind sent her into gales of laughter. She remembered that the hormones released by laughter helped to heal pain.

Singing would do the same thing as laughing, she thought. *Oh, no. You don't want to sing, Alexandra. You can't carry a note, even in a duffel bag.* At that, she laughed even harder.

Gradually, she could feel the giddiness receding. She rose weakly to her feet, wiping her eyes with the sleeve of the robe the butler held out to her.

"Bach?" she asked softly. "Chumut tea, please." After two quick sips, pain gripped her stomach. Bach was quick enough to grab the cup before it dropped to the ground with her. Her legs were shaking as her stomach turned itself inside out, more painfully than she could ever remember happening before. Somewhere between bouts of dry heaves, she felt someone lift her and hold her close. Her body began shaking. If she remembered right, this would be the fear the victim experienced.

Abruptly she found herself standing outside of her physical body, watching Zohra cradle her while Gedaliaha wiped her face. She dispassionately observed herself staring, a wide-open vacant look on her face, while her body tried to curl up in pain. What was the pain from now?

"His anguish, the first time he was molested as a child," an unfamiliar voice softly explained. "Return to your physical shell. It will not be long. It's merely his remembrance of what it's like to be a victim."

She drifted back into her body. Zohra's presence felt strong and comforting, and the rhythm of her heart beating against Alexandra's back gave her a feeling of security.

Abruptly, she found herself standing at the edge of the volcano again. The woman from her previous vision was leaning over the lip again, taking measurements. This time, she turned around of her own accord and faced Alexandra. Off to the side, her craft was being engulfed in a flow of lava. The woman raised her hand and commanded it to stop. When it returned to her side, the woman spoke.

"Thank you, whoever you are. I owe you, and I don't forget my debts."

Alexandra was jerked back into her body. Disoriented, she clutched at the carpet for stability. When her eyes refocused, she found Gedaliaha's light brown eyes looking down at her calmly.

"Alexandra."

Sighing, Alexandra closed her eyes for a moment. She could hear the heartbeat of the person holding her and feel the person's concern. She struggled to stand up.

"Not so fast." Zohra gently pushed her to sit with her back against the bed.

"Drink this." Gedaliaha guided a cup of strong tea to her lips.

It tasted terrible, and she grimaced. But as soon as the tea hit her empty stomach, it spread soothing warmth that worked itself down to her toes. She looked into Zohra's dark eyes and found herself blushing. Alexandra took a deep breath to quiet her heart and the thrumming throughout her body.

"You missed the dinner given in your honor," Gedaliaha said as she and Zohra assisted Alexandra to her feet.

"That's okay." Alexandra tried to stand on her own, but her knees kept shaking. "I'm not up to eating right now."

Gedaliaha guided her to a chair in the front room. "Why did you go through a *jokarash*?" she asked with concern.

"For Lord Chaney," Alexandra said, embarrassed.

"I thought you would have cleared yourself of that already," Zohra said. "How are you feeling now?"

This was an odd conversation, coming from Gedaliaha and with Zohra present. The term *jokarash* was not spoken of, least of all in front of someone who was not initiated into the ways of the shaman. Alexandra gazed into Gedaliaha's eyes again. She leaped up, looking around her frantically. This wasn't Gedaliaha, and these weren't her quarters. The familiar porcelain statue was missing from its corner pedestal.

Abruptly, she was back in her bedroom, lying on her back. The sound of the door chiming came from the front room. Slowly, she rolled her body up, steadied herself on edge of the bed, and pulled her robe into place.

"Computer, release the lock. Enter," she whispered hoarsely.

Gedaliaha and some of the people Alexandra had met during Carol-Maa's gathering came in. She didn't dare move from the support of the bed, so she remained sitting.

"We felt a breach in our protective wall," one of the shamans said.

"Are you all right?" another asked, touching Alexandra's shoulders as if to test her energy. Alexandra knew it was erratic.

Gedaliaha said nothing as she studied the room, obviously looking for something.

Alexandra became aware of the pressure behind her ear. Now she understood. “A sonic hydra.”

She bent forward, holding her stomach, nauseated by another beam of energy from the hydra. One of the shamans sat next to her, supporting her and lending her his energy. The tallest found the mechanism stuck to the corner of the bathing door. He laid it in Gedaliaha’s palm.

“The one you call Vanstar,” Gedaliaha said, looking at Zohra, who had slipped in behind the others.

Alexandra’s heart quickened. Was this still part of the dream? She brushed her hand across her eyes, trying to sort out her feelings. A calming touch on her shoulders brought her bios back to normal. Gedaliaha was smiling, her eyes dark and unfathomable pools.

“I’ve come to invite you to a Sisterhood dinner,” Zohra said. “We have members that wish to meet you. But if you’re not feeling well…”

“I—”

“She will be there, Colonel Zohra.”

“1900 then, if that doesn't conflict with anything you have planned.”

Alexandra glanced at her and caught the slight upturn of her lips. The woman could be humorous.

“No. Alexandra needs something to keep her mind busy. Socializing is just the thing.” Amusement glinted in Gedaliaha’s eyes as she spoke.

“I'll inform the Sisters. And I will handle Vanstar.”

“I would appreciate it if you can find out how she managed to evade my security checks,” Guardian said. “It seems there have been a lot of breaches lately.” He didn’t sound pleased.

“I can tell you part of it now,” Zohra said. “She said she wanted to see how the other half lived, so Carol-Maa invited us to her quarters and offered the use of her bathing room. Vanstar used the toilet facilities before we all ended up in the tub.”

“My monitors did not pick up someone entering Lady Alexandra’s room,” Guardian noted with regret.

“We need to reexamine everyone who has been part of this operation,” Zohra said. “Might as well get moving on that now.”

Alexandra didn’t care who handled Vanstar, she just wanted to be left alone. Tired, she rubbed her temples. Which parts of her dreams were true? Any of them?

Zohra glanced at Alexandra. Then she left, the others following. Gedaliaha stayed and sat in a comfortable chair across from Alexandra. “Tell me about the vision.”

“I don’t know what’s real and what was corrupted.”

“The sonic hydra can’t create visions. It allows a trained person to go into someone’s else’s dreams or visions, and meddle with them.”

Alexandra frowned as she tried to remember where it began. She started slowly. Both women were silent after she’d finished.

“If I may,” Bach said politely, “I am also programmed for monitoring sleep and dreaming, and can give you some information you may find useful.”

“Go ahead,” Gedaliaha said.

“The first vision was tampered with, but not by the device. The second one was on a separate wavelength. It stimulated a different part of the brain as well as the normal centers, making it a true vision that should be clarified by a proper interpreter. However, the device became activated during the next vision sequence and allowed a foreign energy pattern to enter the room.”

“How was the first tampered with without the device?” Gedaliaha asked.

“Through some sort of energy that stimulated my command module. I didn’t want to endanger Lady Alexandra so I let it end, and then I canceled the energy by sending out its polar opposite. Very simple.”

“Guardian must not be happy about these intrusions into his security systems.”

“Due to a malfunction in my outlet, I haven’t synced with Guardian, therefore he doesn’t know of this.”

“I do now.” Guardian’s voice came over the intercom. “It seems there are many gaps in my security system. Colonel Zohra has some of her soldiers working on it.”

At the mention of Zohra, Alexandra’s ears perked up. She glanced at Gedaliaha, who was still talking to Guardian, but with her gaze on Alexandra. Blushing, Alexandra looked down at her folded hands.

“Well, Alexandra,” Gedaliaha said, “what are you waiting for?”

“What?” Alexandra looked up, puzzled. “Oh, the dinner. I don’t really see the importance of going to this.”

“Don’t tell me that you don’t know anyone. You know Colonel Zohra and the others who were in the tub you shared. Sharing a tub, naked, makes for relationships beyond acquaintance. And with your channels opened, the water amplified the sensing of your fellow bathers. That's why most empaths try not to make love in the water too often. It's very potent and heady stuff."

Alexandra turned even redder.

Chapter 20

Alexandra slipped soft boots over her calves as the bathing room door chimed. "Enter."

"You locked your door?" Carol-Maa asked, obviously surprised.

"Perhaps Guardian locked it." Alexandra smiled appreciatively at Carol-Maa. The dress she wore accented the contours of her body. A part of Alexandra wanted to reach out to touch and be touched, but this was not the Carol she knew. "I don't think anyone at the dinner will be looking better than you."

"We thought you would like some company."

Alexandra hoped Carol-Maa wasn't picking up on her feelings of attraction, but a warm sense of gratitude filled her. "I would. Thank you. And I'm sure that MaaSa would like to be surrounded with a lot of new information on life outside your small aquarium."

"It is indeed interesting. Not just the view, but experiencing the customs, as well."

"Well, don't forget you're seeing it from a woman's perspective, and you'll be surrounded by women warriors. If it gets to be too much, you can join the shamans."

Carol laughed, a deep throaty laugh. "MaaSa's friends are mostly male, and I have been getting enough of their view of life. I think it's only fair that he experience the differences."

A chime at the front door interrupted their chuckles.

Alexandra nervously tugged her Centurion uniform into place. It had been laid out for her when she had finished showering.

"Enter."

A very young woman stood blushing at the front door, a bouquet of flowers in her hand. "Lady Alexandra, I mean, Commander Montran. I've come to escort you to the dinner." She blushed again as she handed Alexandra the flowers.

"Thank you."

"Lady Alexandra, a private message has arrived from Rear Admiral JoCastao," Guardian said.

"Great timing. Now she wants to talk. Maybe I'm getting my ride out of here." She pushed down the feeling of disappointment.

"We'll wait in the corridor," Carol-Maa said.

Alexandra stood in front of the monitor. "Transmit."

Moments later, a stunned Alexandra joined Carol-Maa and the young woman in the corridor. She took a deep breath. Along with the news of her promotion, she also had been given orders to keep a low profile, from none other than Rear Admiral JoCastao herself.

"Are you all right?" Carol-Maa's voice was concerned.

"Just some interesting news. Let's get this party over with. Times like these, I wish I could get shit-faced," she muttered in a low voice meant only for Carol-Maa's ears.

When the doors swished open, Alexandra stopped to take in the scene before her. Rows of tables filled with revelers, just as a mess hall should be. However, above the center table was a banner congratulating Commander Alexandra Harriet Montran of the Centurion Corps on her promotion to full commander.

Oh, Helios. The admiral told them.

The roar that Alexandra had first thought was from the sound of blood rushing in her ears was actually a chant, rising and falling in pitch.

Carol-Maa leaned close to her ear. "Admiral JoCastao mentioned to General Aglauros, her army counterpart, that since your own command was not able to celebrate with you, perhaps the Sisterhood would extend those congratulations in their place. I heard a captain remark that they love to celebrate another's good news."

Alexandra was surrounded by well-wishers shaking her hand, some too hard and some with a more intent than congratulations. She smiled mechanically and replied when questioned, moving around the room like a well-trained politician. Without appearing to, her eyes sought Colonel Zohra. Carol-Maa's breath tickled her ear again.

"She's watching you from behind that tall blonde near the green pillar."

Those that had not been seated quickly found places at the tables, and the girl, still at her side, guided them to theirs. "Your places are over here." The table was covered with dishes of food from many different planets and cultures, and Alexandra smiled when Carol-Maa pulled out the seat of honor and held it for her.

"Do you like your party?" a familiar voice asked.

Warmth filled Alexandra at the sound of Zohra's words.

Taking a steadying breath before replying, Alexandra dared to glance at the source of her pleasant distress. "I'm surprised, but also pleased."

Commander, tell us a story!" someone shouted, after an hour of festivities.

Alexandra didn't realize they were referring to her until Zohra tapped her arm. Silence followed the request, and she realized they were waiting for her to tell them a war story. Coldness crept up her legs and into the pit of her stomach. Gripping her mug tightly, she tried to push aside the horror of the last drop her Degas squad had made.

"Telling it is where the healing comes from," Zohra said softly. "It's time you released the guilt, and what better place than with a group of soldiers who know what war is about? We wouldn't have asked if Gedaliaha hadn't told me you were ready."

Alexandra looked at her. Stories were told among comrades to share the loss. That was what she had always told her own soldiers, who had a lot of guilt to leave behind. Slowly, she rose to her feet, her throat tightening. She blinked for a moment as her mind went back to that day.

A uniformed messenger met Montran when she arrived at the terminal. The blue braid on his shoulder indicated he belonged to MCC, Military Central Command. He handed her orders for immediate deployment and escorted her to the base's main hall. There she met her squad, who were still wearing their off-duty uniforms and had their grips lying unpacked at their feet. Obviously, they had been assembled as soon as they arrived back on base, without even having a chance to stop at their barracks.

The CO arrived shortly after she did. He gave them a moving speech about how much they had improved their performance on all levels and therefore were being given an important job. It was a covert operation and they were to leave immediately. If they performed as well as they had before, the squad would be promoted.

She would never forget the CO's face. His words, chosen to evoke pride and unquestioned loyalty, sounded genuine, and her squad was hungry for recognition.

Montran was with the first group dropped on target, and she read the situation immediately. Too many shapes were moving toward them. Looking around for an avenue of retreat, she realized they were surrounded.

"Mayday, Mayday! Abort mission. We're surrounded. It's a trap. Get us out of here! I repeat, Mayday..."

Weapons fire from the attacking forces drowned out the squad's cries as the second group was dropped and the squad ship quickly disappeared back into space.

"What the hell is going on, Captain?" her sergeant major shouted. It was the last thing he said before his body and head were separated.

The Degas squad had dropped into the center of a depression, with rolling hills on all sides. There was no escape route. "Form a wider circle," Montran yelled. But before the group could spread out, cluster bombs landed in their midst. If she'd had time to look at her watch, she'd have seen that only five minutes had passed and half her squad was dead.

"Make every shot count," she cried. "You're supposed to be sharpshooters. Prove it!"

As the body count soared, masked figures descended upon the Degas squad in droves, mowing them down like the sitting targets they were. She rallied the few left to engage in hand-to-hand combat, but the masked attackers overran them with sheer numbers. A cry died in her throat as a blow from behind sent her facedown into the muck of dirt and blood.

Montran didn't distance herself from the pain as she recounted a censored version of the last stand made by the Degas squad. She recalled vividly the scenes the helmet cameras had recorded, but left out the capture and torture of the short-lived survivors. No one needed to hear that, and she didn't need to retell it. When she was finished, she sat down. Someone's warm hands wrapped her cold ones around a hot cup of tea. She stared into the cup, her insides shivering.

The chant started slowly. Murmuring voices filled the silence and joined with a single drumbeat. Then another, and another. The sound pulsed with the rhythm of Alexandra's heart. Without conscious thought, she picked up the chant. Drum vibrations and voice cadences flowed through her. When the rhythm shifted, she let her heartbeat change, too. Her body began to sway, muscles releasing their tension. The gentle swaying and soothing sound seemed to cancel each unpleasant memory. Gradually, the weight of all those deaths dissolved. Until it was gone, she'd never realized just how heavy the burden had been.

The drumming and the chants came to a stop. A woman stood and began telling a story. It had a happy theme, which a good storyteller would choose to follow a sad tale. Alexandra picked at the food she'd been given as she heard more stories and songs. She was getting restless. Her eyes tracked toward Zohra and found her gazing back. For a few moments, they held the connection.

Alexandra looked away and searched for Carol-Maa, wondering what she was up to. She found her in the midst of several women. Laughter came from the group, and Alexandra felt waves of positive energy emanating from them.

"It looks like your friend is making a good impression on the Sisters," Zohra said.

"That duo is on a search-and-gather mission for information." Alexandra smiled as the women broke into more peals of laughter.

"Do you feel better, now that Carol is protected from the ulterior motives of others?" Zohra said in a teasing tone.

Alexandra turned to her. "I feel better that Carol has found another adventure, and one in which she'll grow beyond any of our expectations."

A woman came to their table and whispered something in Zohra's ear. She stood up, looking regretful as she excused herself. No one took her place. The others were keeping a polite distance from Alexandra. It was a good time to slip out.

Walking down the corridor, lost in thought, Alexandra felt a slight buzzing of energy and looked around. The familiar connection was soft at first, but gathered strength, summoning her. The closer she got to her quarters, the stronger the signal became. She nodded at the two women standing guard outside of her rooms, and when the door closed behind her, pushed aside a chair to give her more space. Sitting on the floor, she chanted a protection song Kela had taught her. Blue energy appeared as a protective circle formed, then lengthened into a round wall with thin spikes of white fire that shot up into the ceiling. Closing her eyes, Alexandra welcomed the scientist from the volcano.

"I am here to repay a debt," the scientist said. "Alan Fermin had a virus developed that is aimed at capturing you. May the light of *Shua* follow you." She raised her hand and drew a sign in the air, then vanished.

Still inside the circle, Alexandra searched for Alan, looking for the dark cloud specific to him. He wasn't at the height of his manic phase, but it was far enough ascendant for the cloud to have formed around him. Alan had changed a lot from his cadet days. She could see him raving at someone or something on the bridge of a private space vessel. The console wasn't the typical design for a private yacht, and only one chair looked comfortable and well-worn. An alarm appeared on his console, and she pulled back to study the planet he was near. It was Pealnet, which was in the Four Corners. Five tiny ships from the Collective were laying a net around the planet. She wondered what Alan wanted there. Then she saw the energy lines that formed a shell about the planet. It had one major portal, and a few smaller ones scattered about its sphere.

Alexandra sought out Admiral JoCastao, then, and found her close to Merker's Outpost. Her bridge crew was busy executing an offensive against the smugglers. The smugglers appeared to have been surprised, because instead of running, they were reacting as if they were backed into a corner. Alexandra figured the admiral had cut off their retreat with another trap, and was driving them into it. She hovered over the admiral for a moment, watching the battle play out on the bridge screen.

She then returned her attention to Alan's ship, hoping to see what he was up to. Ideas were swirling around his head. Before she could decipher their meaning, she felt an urgent need to see what he had done to Merker's Outpost.

Above Merker's, she searched for traces of Alan's malignancy, but an unusual flurry of activity around the planet prevented her from following every thread. Whatever he had planned must be going to originate in Ilo, the city she and Carol hadn't visited. It was along the Southern Rim, where the caverns could hide a Class C drop ship, twenty soldiers, and enough equipment to invade a city.

She was tired.

Her spirit made a smooth transition back into her physical body. The energy of her protective shield pulsed with life, warning her that someone had attempted to penetrate it.

Alexandra dropped the shield and found her quarters full of visitors. Gedaliaha was sitting on the couch talking to them. Zohra stood in the corner and watched everyone. Their eyes met. For a moment, Alexandra drank in the attention Zohra was giving her.

"Alexandra." Gedaliaha called her back to the group. "We all felt the breach, but it wasn't Alan or one of his agents, so we let it through."

Alexandra uncurled from her position on the floor and was given a chair. "I had a warning from the woman I told you I saw at the volcano. She said Alan had a virus made specifically for me." She paused and took a deep breath to ground herself and eliminate the fluttering in her stomach. "I saw him. He was in a ship, near Pealnet. Probably gone now."

The others nodded.

"I think we should explore Ilo. MaaSa spoke against it, and I think we should find out why."

"You're not going," Zohra said.

Silently, Alexandra chided herself for blushing.

Zohra moved from her solitary position near the door to stand closer to her. "I have a team already assembled to scout out that area. Guardian's bots will finish their outersuits by noon." She hesitated, then added, "We discussed Ilo with MaaSa, as well as the reason he advised you against visiting it."

"And?"

Annoyance flickered in Zohra's eyes. "He didn't say anything that made sense to me."

Alexandra glanced down at her hands

"That's all you learned?" Zohra asked.

"I only had a warning and a glimpse of Alan. But something doesn't feel right about this planet."

"You're not the only one who feels that way. When you figure out what it is, let me know." Zohra moved to the door. "I need to see to the patrols that will be returning soon and those ready to move out." Her gaze lingered on Alexandra for a moment, and then she left, most of the others in the room following.

Alexandra longed to join them, if only to break the tedium. She no longer had Carol to visit with, and she could find entertainment in a holographic opponent for only so many days before she looked for a real person to pound on.

She rubbed her forehead. She did have one puzzle to figure out. "What did the woman mean by a virus?"

"You need to get some sleep," Gedaliaha said. "Which reminds me, you have been assigned bodyguards. One will be with you at all times."

"Hmm?" Not having heard, Alexandra looked up at her.

Gedaliaha patted Alexandra's shoulder. "Never mind. Dreams have always been a good place to find answers. May your dreams guide you to safety, Alexandra."

Alexandra sagged onto the couch and rested her head on its cushions. She let her mind wander, flitting from one thought to another. “Guardian.”

“Yes, Alexandra?”

“When I first shipped on board the *Spinner’s Tale*, I found her computer programs all—” Guardian had started to laugh. “Was that your work, then?”

“No. That virus was from the Black Rose. They had a vendetta against Petty Officer Decker, because he was responsible for a contract on one of their members. I tamper with information-gathering applications, not life systems.”

“It was a clever virus.” She ran her fingers through her hair, leaned forward on the couch, and peered down at the carved scene that curled around the base of the transparent tabletop. “If I were Alan and wanted to get onto this planet undetected, I would think about how to disable you without you or anyone else knowing about it, and there have been a lot of holes in your programs lately.”

“The word *virus* has bad associations for me. I have taken many precautions to prevent another one from entering my system.”

“What if the virus was introduced by one of your trusted bots, like the ones in Century City?”

“You believe Alan’s virus is in me?”

“If I thought of that, I’m sure Alan did. He’s very clever. Do you remember when I asked… well, I didn’t ask you, I asked Ald or Bach about the emergency system. Bots are programmed with their immediate functions, but for other things, they have an autolink to the main data bank. I asked an essential question, and under normal circumstances, they would have linked to you to get the answer for me, or any other guest. Instead, I was referred to you for more information. Bach said he hadn’t linked with you for a while.”

“I see your point. Now that you mention it, I have not had a download report from your section. It is odd that I should overlook such an important break in my communications system. You did not order privacy?”

“I have guards watching the front and back exits. I unlocked the doors myself. I thought you had locked them to protect me.” She sighed and rubbed her forehead again. “With this possibility in mind, I don’t think you should download any information from these bots. If Vanstar was able to get as far as she did, she may have accessed bots in this area, as well as in Century City, where she barracked for two years.”

"I shall contact Colonel Zohra. I shudder at the thought of being invaded by another virus, but I am in this for the duration. Good day to you, Alexandra, and congratulations on your promotion."

"Thank you." She laid her head back against the couch and closed her eyes, smiling as she thought of Zohra. Her jaw stretched into a yawn as she found a more comfortable position.

So many people to protect her, and yet it only took one madman to plant a deadly person in the right place. Alan would probably use his moles to keep the outpost security jumping so that everyone would be too busy watching each another to notice him moving into position.

* * *

Awareness of a presence in her room crept into her sleep, accompanied by a dull pain in her neck from the odd angle of her head. Her Dancer was nearby. The feeling changed as Zohra moved out of the front room. Alexandra breathed in slowly and deeply as her body hummed at the contact. She could feel Zohra return, heard the faint sounds of her settling into the chair across from her. "Did you find anything?" Alexandra said. She felt Zohra's surprise and then her amusement.

"Your abilities have sharpened, Lady Alexandra."

Alexandra opened her eyes, and they regarded each other in silence. For the first time in a very long while, they were alone.

"So, what brings you to my quarters?" Alexandra remembered Gedaliaha mentioning a bodyguard, and she started to laugh. The dark eyes watching her warmed.

"You're laughing because…?" Zohra asked softly.

"I just remembered something Gedaliaha said." Alexandra looked down at her hands to prevent herself from getting giddy. The pleasant thought of Zohra being her personal bodyguard made her blush.

"And that was?"

"She said I'm being assigned a bodyguard. I take it you're clearing the place before my bodyguard arrives. Don't trust her or them?"

"I'm the most qualified, given my familiarity with the outpost, and other things…" Zohra's voice trailed off.

"Ah." Alexandra hoped her guards would take their time arriving. She noticed a small muscle twitch in Zohra's jaw, and got the impression she was trying not to laugh.

"So." She started to speak again, but couldn't think of anything to say. Instead, she reached for a cup of tea that sat on the table beside her. She felt an iron grip around her wrist, and a surge of desire ran through her arm and settled in her belly. Zohra spoke, but she had a hard time focusing on the words.

"I would rather you eat and drink from the Sister's kitchen from now on. You make an easy target." Her voice had become softer and huskier as she spoke, and she let go of Alexandra's wrist slowly.

Zohra's energy was distracting, and Alexandra fought to maintain her composure. "I'll keep that in mind, Colonel."

Zohra extended a hand. "You'll be more comfortable in your bed. Less chance of getting a neck ache," she said, in a more normal voice.

Alexandra reached up for the proffered hand, and the touch only added to her heat.

Zohra pulled her up and toward herself without stepping back, intensifying the feelings with which Alexandra's body was humming. For what seemed like another long moment, she stared boldly up into Zohra's eyes, reading the desire mirrored there. At length, Zohra released her and stepped back.

Alexandra turned toward the bedroom. She needed a cold shower and some time to bring her feelings under control. She cursed herself for not having the nerve to take Zohra into her arms and drag her down onto the soft carpet. A chuckle tickled her throat at the likelihood of wrestling Zohra to the ground if she didn't want to go down. It would be fun to try, though. Muffling the giggles that threatened to escape, she focused on getting undressed.

The butler had turned down the covers at both sides of the bed, and sleeping attire had been laid out on both sides, as well. Alexandra stopped short and turned to Zohra, who was watching from the doorway.

"You're my bodyguard?" she asked, not sure if she was reading the situation correctly.

"Like I said, I'm the best qualified, and the best way to keep track of you is to be near you. You don't mind if we share the bed, do you? It's big enough," she said in a teasing voice.

"No. No, I guess you have a point there. But isn't it highly irregular for a lieutenant colonel to babysit a… well, anyone?"

"Did you have someone else in mind?"

Alexandra clamped her mouth shut tightly to keep more undignified giggles from escaping, and did her best to regain her composure. "What about handling the outpost security?"

Zohra gave a small smile. "You don't think I can handle more than one job?"

"I know there aren't enough hours in the day for one person to cover everything," Alexandra said.

"I have a good support staff."

"Really? Just what is going on, or am I not privy to that information?" Alexandra realized her tone sounded sharper than she'd intended. She was feeling left out and was taking out her feelings on someone, who like her, was merely acting on orders.

"Nothing secret. We've moved into the third phase of establishing a safe perimeter around Century City and the Lair. Guardian and Charles are being moved into their cloned bodies as we speak. It's earlier than they had planned, but it's safer to do it now. The main computer is being combed through to find where it was tampered with, and we're running the outpost on the original program rather than the backup. If the primary is contaminated, chances are the backup is, too. Guardian's name, by the way, is Merker L'uenbeng."

Alexandra was surprised at the detailed information, and that Zohra had supplied it voluntarily. The last fact made her chuckle. "I hated his textbook at the academy."

"Not many people liked his challenges of culturally biased ethics. He took a rather blunt approach."

A lengthy silence passed while the women stared unabashedly at each another. Alexandra broke the impasse. She picked up her robe and headed into the bathing room, irritated at being left out of the action.

Zohra's eyes followed Alexandra's naked form as she walked into the miniature jungle. Here they were. Together and alone. Letting out a long breath, she chided herself for not saying what she really wanted to say—the kind of words she was out of practice using.

An image came to her of Alexandra in the uniform of a Spartan captain. She stood proudly, with battle ribbons that many envied, her hair shorn close to her scalp, leaving only an orange sheen where her beret didn't cover. Her arm was around the shoulders of an equally proud sergeant major. They were at his retirement party.

The battle-scarred soldier had pulled the holographic image out of his well-worn traveling bag and showed it to Zohra. He was becoming more maudlin with each drink she provided him. He had a collection of pictures of his retirement bash, but only one picture interested Sergeant Major JG.

She'd met the old man in a bar, where he was swapping stories with other soldiers. He had become incensed when another retired soldier made a snide comment about Captain Montran surviving when her squad had perished. If Sergeant Major JG had not intervened, she was sure one of the quarreling drinkers would have ended up dead.

She had taken the retired Spartan aside and quieted him down, then got him stinking drunk. He was on his way to a relative's wedding and had done what he had promised himself he would never do again, which was visit a bar frequented by Spartans. Survivor guilt was a heavy burden to carry.

"You can't tell anyone about this. You have to promise," he had said.

She was skeptical, having heard too many drunks start tales with "for your ears only," and nearly just put him on a shuttle for his next stop. Something stopped her, though, and she had reluctantly admitted to herself that she wanted to hear about Captain Montran.

"We used to get this feeling, like we were all connected, and we'd get real focused, like… You're going to think I'm crazy, but it was like we were one person. It was just awesome." He wiped the back of his hand across his lips. "Just awesome," he repeated reverently, and then his head hit the table as he passed out.

Montran was clearly a charismatic leader. After all, she herself was also under this captain's spell. What was the old saying about being too close to a situation? She had become too close, after promising herself not to let something like that happen. Not until her assignment was over. Then she would look for Lady Harriet Montran.

She repeated "Alexandra" silently a few times, liking the way it made her want to smile.

Here we are, after all this time. She's an empath, she reminded herself humorously, *so you have to be careful what you put out.*

Zohra breathed in deeply, not sure what being an empath meant. To find out, she'd scheduled a talk with the shamans the next afternoon under the guise of working out the finer points of protecting Lady Alexandra. All they had told her so far was that someone needed to room with her and stay near her at all times.

In the military, a grunt didn't bunk with an officer, especially a flag officer from another sector. A bunkmate had to be someone of equal rank, and that was her. Rank did have its privileges. It had gotten her sharing a bed with a fellow officer.

The shower stopped running. Zohra rose from the bed and pulled a small packet out of a pocket in her trouser leg. She was mounting the item to the wall above one of the pillows when she felt Alexandra standing next to her.

"What's that?"

"An intruder alert."

Alexandra's magnetism brushed against Zohra's senses, and she wondered if Alexandra was aware of her effect on others. Warriors weren't used to that type of energy, but after Alexandra recounted the details behind the Degas squad's last mission, she had won over any warrior who still had misgivings about her. The Sisterhood, if for no other reason than to honor an officer who had tried her best to save her squad, would honor the Degas squad at the annual Remembrance Day for fallen comrades. No one deserved the type of death her father had arranged for them. *Your father*, her mind emphasized angrily. Zohra quickly squelched any more thoughts about her father, knowing that Alexandra would pick up on them.

She turned to face Alexandra. In the subdued lighting, Alexandra's irises were open wide, as if offering Zohra a view of her soul, if she cared to look. She was not yet ready for that. She could feel Alexandra's eyes on her as she stripped and handed her clothes to the butler.

Zohra didn't know what was preventing her from pulling Alexandra toward her and making love to her. She was certain they were going to be lovers, but when? What was she waiting for? She was the one who always controlled the situation. Was that why Alexandra didn't move on her, when her eyes showed that she wanted to? Or was it because she wasn't sure about *them*?

She remembered the rapid heartbeat under her fingertips when she had grabbed Alexandra's wrist earlier, the flushed face, and the unmistakable smell of a woman aroused.

In the shower, Zohra loosened her long hair from its leather thong and thought how it would have been to run her hands through Alexandra's hair when it was still long. She closed her eyes, thinking of the pleasure of holding Alexandra close and feeling her body respond to her touch.

Zohra finished her shower and waited as her hair was blown dry. Ald offered a robe, but she waved it off and returned to their room unclad. The lights were dimmed, and her bed partner was sleeping. She glanced around the room one more time before slipping between the covers.

* * *

Alexandra felt a vibration before the accompanying noise sounded. She bolted out of bed and onto her knees in the soft carpet, searching around frantically. The sound bleeped off. She didn't know whether it was real time or a dream. Another noise grounded her with frightening certainty.

Zohra jumped up, awake the instant Alexandra moved. They waited for a few moments, and the alarm ended.

"I guess that's your intruder alarm." Alexandra tugged at the nightgown that had become twisted around her body.

"Yes. You moved before it sounded."

"I heard a buzzing in my ear." Alexandra shivered. It might have been Alan's attempt to control her dreamtime again.

A concerned voice came over the speaker. "Colonel, is everyone clear?"

It wasn't Guardian, Alexandra noted then remembered he had been moved to a biological body.

"Yes, Sergeant Major. Did you get a fix on the sender?"

"Affirmative, Colonel Zohra. Admiral JoCastao has been notified."

"Good. Out."

"Out, Colonel."

Alexandra tried unsuccessfully not to study the naked body before her without being conspicuous about it.

Zohra's eyes were overtly fastened on the outline of the hardened nipples pressed up against the soft fabric of Alexandra's nightgown. With a small movement, Alexandra twitched the bunched gown back into place. She swallowed and hoped it didn't look like she was drooling.

Zohra climbed onto the bed and slowly crawled over to Alexandra's side. She extended a hand to Alexandra, who was watching her with undisguised desire. Alexandra took the offered hand and was guided into bed.

Zohra pulled the covers over her and then settled near her, lying on her side so she could study her profile. Even in the low lighting, Alexandra was visibly tense. Smiling to herself, Zohra asked, "What's wrong?"

"At the moment, everything."

"I can do something about that." Zohra's tone was provocative, and she watched as Alexandra's face darkened.

"What's that?"

"Roll over onto your stomach, and I'll demonstrate." Zohra grinned at Alexandra's hesitation, and waited for her to position herself. "Better."

She lifted a pillow out of the way and rubbed her hands together, stirring up the chi before placing them on Alexandra's shoulders. Zohra's grin widened as a soft sigh came from below her.

For a moment, she studied the pale face, and then her hands began their work. Her fingers prodded and found knots that she gently worked out. Minutes passed, and they both relaxed into the rhythm of her ministrations. Carried away in her own daydream, Zohra dug a little harder than she'd intended.

"Hey, ouch." Alexandra flinched, abruptly rolling away from Zohra, who withdrew in surprise.

The nightgown twisted, outlining a small breast. Zohra held her breath as she waited in vain for her libido to simmer down.

"Zohra" The whisper was so low, it was almost a growl.

They moved toward each other. Zohra's hands lighted on Alexandra's shoulders and slid down her arms to her hands, their fingers intertwining. Breasts barely touched.

Alexandra pressed her lips against Zohra's, her tongue seeking entrance.

Both women groaned as mouths and tongues explored new territory. When they finally broke for air, Zohra pulled Alexandra closer.

"Zohra," Alexandra's impassioned voice whispered again.

"What?" she asked in a husky voice.

"Take me… take all of me."

Zohra's lips twitched in amusement. "Maybe something given so easily isn't worth taking."

Alexandra surprised her by flipping her over and sitting on top of her. "Then I'll do the taking," she said in a low voice that quickened Zohra's pulse. "And you can tell me later if it was worth being taken.

"Computer, set mood: the forests of Fania, western side of stream, afternoon, midsummer, sun with cool breeze. Make it... a lover's nest." She leaned close to Zohra's ear. "I want to see all of you in the sunlight."

Zohra felt the soft texture of the bedding beneath her change to hard ground, and thin blades of grass tickled her skin. Looking up into Alexandra's darkened eyes, she felt her own heart beating rapidly and her center throbbing. "It's not safe to be near a stream in the wilds, you know," Zohra whispered in a strained voice.

"There's just you and me here."

Zohra laughed nervously, her excitement rising. "I hope you have the safeties engaged, because upsetting the wildlife with our lovemaking isn't something I'd advise doing."

"Maybe that's what I like... the danger in ravishing you while surrounded by wild animals."

Alexandra shifted her weight. Smiling down at Zohra, whose body trembled, she rubbed her wet center on Zohra's stomach.

"Oh, gods, that feels good," Zohra breathed.

Suddenly, her senses were flooded as Alexandra connected with her. The intensity of the erotic connection had Zohra summoning her willpower to keep from rushing to a climax. She felt like she was drowning in the sensations as Alexandra's hands buried themselves in her hair, and strong fingers stroked her scalp as lips ravished hers.

Two pairs of hands explored, taking time to savor each sensitive spot as it was discovered. Soon, both had small bits of bark and twigs in their hair.

Zohra climaxed so many times she thought she had reached her limit, but then another one rocked them simultaneously, leaving them spent on the forest floor. Zohra wrapped her arms around Alexandra, not wanting to break contact. She kissed her forehead and sighed softly.

"What?" Alexandra's voice was muffled, pressed as it was against Zohra's neck.

"Alexandra, would you be offended if I asked you something?"

"You can ask me anything."

"Was that almost as nice as... making love... to, uh..."

"You mean having sex under the influence of the pheromone gas? Two different types of sensations. With pheromone gas, you're never sated. The emotional bond is inconsequential, however. That's not what our relationship is about." Her voice dropped to a seductive whisper. "We can drive each other crazy because we want each other. Don't you think this is so much better than a drug that makes you desire a stranger?"

Zohra's body tingled at the sexy tone of voice. Her hand caressed Alexandra's body and then moved to cup her moist center. She was glad she hadn't made any moves on her as a cadet.

"What are you thinking" Alexandra stroked her furrowed brow.

Zohra shivered. "I was remembering when we were cadets, and I first saw you."

"And when was that?"

"The first time was in the tavern."

"Things would be different if we had met then," Alexandra said, "but I don't think it would have been easier. When I saw you in Guardian's infirmary, I didn't recognize you because you'd changed your face." She gently laid a palm on Zohra's cheek.

"In the cloak-and-dagger business," Zohra said, "a distinctive appearance has its disadvantages."

Alexandra pulled Zohra's face to hers and gave her a long and passionate kiss.

"So," Alexandra said, somewhat breathless after the long kiss ended, "where do we go from here?"

Zohra tenderly stroked the face that was smiling at her. "This is so different from what I'm used to."

Alexandra pursed her lips and hesitated for a moment, then decided that they should have no secrets between them that could cause harm in the future. "I was wondering how you could fit in so easily with the Black Rose group." Alexandra felt the change in her lover like a door slamming shut.

"End program." Zohra rose from the bed and accepted a robe from the butler. Alexandra followed her as she moved into the sitting room.

A good cup of strong tea would have been nice, but they had brought only water with them. They settled at either end of the couch, angling their bodies to face each other.

"I don't really know how to explain it," Zohra said.

Alexandra waited patiently, taking the opportunity to study the stranger's face before her, yet feeling the familiar deeper connection that reassured her it was the person with whom she had bonded so long ago.

"I guess it's because I have Thebain genes, which makes it easy to take on a role, and just as easy to discontinue it and take on another."

Alexandra smiled and leaned forward. "I like this role." She cupped Zohra's face between her warm hands and gently kissed her lips.

Zohra wrapped her fingers around her wrists. "Are you sure?" she asked, her voice hoarse.

"Well," Alexandra said huskily, "if you don't think you've convinced me, you're welcome to spend some more time persuading me… but maybe another time, when we're not so tired."

Zohra rested her forehead against Alexandra's. "You're right. I am tired. But I don't think I can sleep right now." She let Alexandra tug her to her feet and lead her back into the bedroom.

"Lie on your stomach, and I'll show you a trick I learned about putting someone to sleep gently." When she felt Zohra resist, Alexandra tugged her hand and pushed her back down on the bed. Before five stan minutes had passed, Zohra's breathing had slowed and she was asleep.

Thank you, Sharon, for that handy tip. Alexandra rolled off the slumbering woman and settled down to her own dreams.

Chapter 21

It seemed to Zohra that she had only been asleep for an hour when the chime sounded. “Goddess,” she muttered, blinking her eyes open to find green eyes smiling back at her.

The voice over the intercom sounded amused. “Good morning. As for the Goddess part, I’ve been called that on more than one occasion.”

“Clea. What time is it?” Zohra tried to focus on business, not the woman next to her.

“Late for you, Colonel. We let you rest longer, just in case you had problems getting back to sleep after the intruder alert.”

Alexandra slid out of bed and disappeared into the bathing room.

Zohra gave a silent sigh. “What’s the status?”

“Teams are just now reporting in. Intruder alerts occurred in Century City, too. We haven’t determined who was responsible, yet. Some of the metrasoldiers are still loose; there could have been computer glitches, or maybe the Alowan. No gate disturbances, so we know there aren’t any others joining him, nor did he leave. The general thinks he’s still here, just keeping a low profile.”

“Do we know how many of Alan’s soldiers are still loose?”

“Close to twenty.”

“Just enough to make trouble. Are Captains Chilali and Raizel available?”

“They went to bed four stan hours ago, and they’re still sleeping. But Sergeant Malta has a hand-delivered report for you.”

“Let me know when they wake. Give me a moment to shower and dress.”

Alexandra was out of the shower already, towel drying her short hair so that it stuck out in different directions.

Zohra’s heart pounded at the thought of their time in the woods, and then she laughed, remembering the twigs that got in the way.

"Something you'd like to share?" Alexandra cupped her hand against Zohra's face. How beautiful Alexandra looked when she smiled, Zohra thought.

"Yeah. Next time we do it in the woods, I want a blanket." Zohra leaned forward and kissed Alexandra's lips.

"Mmm. I'll hold off your messenger while you prepare for company, Colonel Zohra."

"Thanks," Zohra said. "But I think you need to dress first. No need to have the Sisters in a dither at seeing a flag officer in a robe." She disappeared into the bathing room.

Alexandra watched the butler wheel out with her clothing. It was her new uniform, adorned with her commander's pin and the thin gold trim that designated a flagship officer.

"Quite a tailor you've got here," she muttered. Once dressed, she took a quick glance in the closet mirror and then entered the front room to receive the messenger, just as the bell rang.

"Enter." Commander Montran stood waiting as two soldiers wearing Sisterhood uniforms entered and looked around. "Good morning. Would you like to sit down?" she asked, trying to be a good host until Zohra was ready.

The chime sounded again. "Enter."

Two more women came in, carrying food and beverages. Her stomach growled its approval.

By the time the food was set out, Zohra had emerged from the bedroom, dressed in a fresh uniform and with her hair neatly bound up. The women braced smartly, bringing open palms to their hearts.

Alexandra picked up an apple to nibble on and left the room to let the soldiers give their report. When she heard them leave, she rejoined Zohra for breakfast.

Zohra watched Alexandra's face as she made selections from the plates. She seemed different since last night. Or was it Zohra herself? She felt her face redden, recalling Sergeant Malta's quizzical expression as she delivered her report. Undoubtedly, they were all asking themselves the big question.

"So," Alexandra said, "since you're my bodyguard and you run the show in the Lair, what do you have in mind for me today?"

If she were still a sergeant major, Zohra would have given a flippant answer, but a lot had changed. That included her sensitivity to the woman before her. Alexandra's underlying tone gave warning that locking her up for safekeeping, with guards posted outside her quarters while Zohra made her rounds, wasn't going to work. "I was going to ask you what you had planned for the day."

Alexandra looked up, obviously surprised. "You were?"

"You can follow me around, if you like, but I imagine you have business with the *mantes*."

"Ah, yes. The shamans and sensitives. Wouldn't it make your job easier if I just trotted along with you?"

"Why does that offer give me bumps... and not the kind I like?"

"Just what do you plan on doing that's dangerous?" Alexandra said.

"Nothing. Colonels don't go out and about on deployments. I guess there will be two of us bored while we wait for reports. Are you sure you don't mind?"

The door chimed and then opened, and Gedaliaha strode in. "How are you both feeling?" Neither responded, but she nodded as though she had received an answer.

Zohra offered her the fruit basket. "Anything happening I need to know about?"

Gedaliaha chose an apple and rolled it between her hands. "Rear Admiral JoCastao's group found the person that Alan was using to invade dreams. She was able to persuade him to cooperate by promising immediate protection for him and his family in exchange for information on Alan. He overheard Alan talking about a program that was used to contaminate Guardian's system. Must be the virus you were talking about, Alexandra. He's sure Alan doesn't know he heard, or he and his family would already be dead."

"We've already dumped the primary system and the backup," Zohra said. "So far, the original program we pulled out of storage is doing fine. Rather primitive when our techs found it, but it's being updated with a lot more reliable information than what Guardian had running."

"How sure are you that the virus isn't in the original program?" Alexandra asked.

"MaaSa kept the program stored in his library," Zohra said. "You and Carol were the only ones who visited his city recently."

Gedaliaha nodded. "The seers cleared it, also. I will see you two at the afternoon meeting, since we do need to talk. I'm sure Alexandra would rather not be bored with our discussions, so I will leave you to find something to keep her busy. Until then, my heart to yours." The door swished closed after her.

"Shall we go and see what the troops are up to, Commander Montran?" Zohra asked, smiling. "Kidding aside, I can use your experience as a flag officer. I understand you were part of the war board for Rear Admiral JoCastao."

"I was, but I'm not sure your group would be pleased to hear from an outsider, especially since I'm partially responsible for this situation."

Zohra glanced at her sharply. "Alan already had agents on Merker's. That's why he sent you here. Not the other way around."

There was a movement from the door, and they quickly turned to face it. Vanstar stood there. Alexandra's gasped, and Zohra stepped in front of her protectively. "Lieutenant Vanstar," she said coldly.

"Good morning, Colonel," Vanstar said.

"You're here for something?"

"I have a message from the Sisters. They're ready for the meeting."

"We're on our way."

"We?"

"Yes. Commander Montran and I."

Chapter 22

They walked to Com-C in silence, the busy foot traffic stepping to their left. A group of accompanying officers formed a circle around them, with Vanstar effectively closed out.

The door to the command center swished open. The Command Chair was occupied and engaged. All monitors were peopled, and the place hummed with activity. Alexandra was escorted to a seat.

Before Vanstar could enter, Zohra pulled her aside. "Report to your quarters," she ordered softly. "You're not back on duty until I say you are." She signaled to one of the guards to accompany Vanstar to her rooms.

Military staff, shamans, outside observers, and civilians occupied seats around the table in the meeting room. The wall displayed maps of the cities that were off-line, as well as those that the new computer program continued to bring back online.

When Zohra entered, all military personnel stood to attention, with civilians following at a slower pace. For the rest of the morning and into the afternoon, Zohra heard reports and made plans, then moved to the business of the shamans and the protection of the gates. At the conclusion of the long meeting, assignments had been explained for each of the four groups: military, shamans, medical team, and civilian observers.

"Lieutenant Malchi, I would like a word with you," Zohra said as the officer prepared to leave with the others.

"Yes, Colonel?"

"Who sent Vanstar with a message to me this morning?"

Malchi's eyebrows rose. "I wasn't aware that had happened. She's supposed to be confined to her quarters. A psych tech recommended she go through a prolonged debriefing before she's given any actual duties." Lieutenant Malchi looked dismayed. "She doesn't have the same species advantage as you, Colonel. I'd feel more comfortable repatriating her, but General Aglauros wants to see her before she's shipped out." Zohra frowned, and Malchi gave a slight shrug. "Sorry, Colonel. It's in one of the dispatches you haven't gone through yet."

"Colonel Zohra," Captain Raizel said, "dinner is being served in the main mess. Are you going to join us, or would you like it served in your quarters?"

Zohra turned to Alexandra. "Would you mind eating with us grunts?"

"Not at all."

Looking pleased, Zohra nodded, and the group began walking to the mess hall. They picked up people along the way, but the same core group encircled the two of them, preventing anyone else from getting near.

The mess hall wasn't as crowded as Alexandra had expected it to be. Small groups of soldiers were huddled around various tables, eating and talking strategy. Or so she thought, until she altered her vision. The energy she was picking up on was distinctly sexual.

They were shown to a table separate from the others, with three noncoms present to serve them. As soon as Alexandra settled herself, a plate with her favorite foods appeared before her, a cup was filled with water, and a small dish containing a terriup was added to her setting. Taking a bite of the crisp vegetable, she hummed her approval at its taste, texture, and aroma. "Excellent," she said, grinning at the server. "Tell cook it's the best I've had in years."

The server bowed. "I'll tell her that, M'lady. It strokes her ego to hear that, it does."

Alexandra turned her attention to Zohra, who had not yet eaten. She had gone to speak to a young man, from Naboth's Vine by his armband. Sitting up straighter, Alexandra focused on a shadowy figure that appeared behind the man. There was a change of energy in the room as the newcomer sought to identify Alexandra. Sensing no danger to herself or the others, she watched as the figure progressed toward her table. Occasionally she got a good view, then the cloaked form would disappear behind a group of warriors.

Zohra returned and sat next to Alexandra. Though there was space between them, Zohra's elbows brushed against her energy field. Ripples of pleasant sensations touched Alexandra. As lovers, they had their own link. Zohra discreetly moved a few inches away. Alexandra understood her need to stay focused.

The touch distracted her, too, and she lost track of the visitor for a moment. Relaxing her sight, she found her again, closer. No one else seemed to take notice.

Zohra stole a look at Alexandra. Green eyes were staring ahead intently. She looked in the same direction and at first saw nothing, but then she sensed a familiar ripple in the air. She knew exactly who it was. Zohra looked at her plate for a moment to recenter.

Oh, Goddess. She's going to know about Alexandra and me, and she's going to know it's not a sudden kind of thing. Oh, Mother, are you going to be upset that I've been keeping this secret from you?

"You're not eating enough, Colonel Zohra."

The familiar voice spoke above her, and Zohra started. The cloaked figure pulled the hood from her head. A cry went up, and the room filled with the roar of warriors as they recognized their general. Obviously, they were used to her unusual entrance.

Alexandra stood with the others.

When the greetings abated, General Aglauros turned to study her adopted daughter. She hadn't seen Zohra in person since she had gone undercover. Nine years was a long time to be parted from her beloved daughter. Tentatively, she sent out a touch to her, and felt the connection between her daughter and Lady Alexandra.

Lovers... No, lifemates. My daughter has been keeping secrets, and for good reason. We wouldn't have let her undertake this long mission had we known. As for Lady Alexandra, would anyone have been able to protect her from her fate? I wonder if she's as stubborn as they say.

Zohra reddened slightly, but kept her eyes steadily on her mother's.

"I say again, Daughter," Aglauros said more softly, "you're not eating enough." She turned her attention to the others. "I would like to hear firsthand what has been going on. Colonel Zohra and Lady Alexandra will retire to their quarters and get some much needed rest, for a full day without disturbances." General Aglauros raised an eyebrow at Lady Alexandra's frown. Both women looked tired, and she could imagine why.

So, an empathic commander with the Centurions. Can't blame her for leaving GCFC space. Do they have a special corps for empaths, as we do? I shall take that up with Admiral JoCastao.

When word got out that a Spartan squad marked for death by a powerful GCFC member was returning from their missions with the majority of the soldiers alive, Aglauros sent her agents to learn more. A trained empath among the Spartans was unheard of. So much death and violence would burn out a sensitive. For an empath to also have the gift of *Galiel*, the ability to form a connection with others, was not so unusual. Military intelligence in all branches of the services kept records of such people. However, no one knew Commander Montran had either ability, and the general's agents, and others that had investigated her, had ascribed the commander's success to luck and talent. Only the shamans suspected the truth.

Aglauros glanced at her daughter and then at Lady Alexandra. *Did they form this bond in the academy when Zohra rescued her from that crazy Alan Fermin? It had to have been then. That's a long time to carry a torch for someone.* "Perhaps you wouldn't mind if I visited later?"

The general was facing Zohra when she made her request, but Zohra knew that even if she was courteous enough to make it sound like a question, generals didn't ask. "Yes. I will have some plans—"

"Daughter, please. I'm giving you the day off. Take time to relax, play, and eat. I can see that because you haven't had a mother or a lover to make you eat regularly, you've let yourself get too lean."

This exchange didn't seem to be anything new, for the others laughed as if they had heard it before.

"Mother, you always say that. I do eat."

"You pick at food," another voice said.

"Bese!" The general turned quickly and hugged the other woman. "You old war dog."

Bese gestured to two women standing a little behind her, carrying food and drink. "I'm sending plenty of food back to Lady Alexandra's quarters."

"Good." The general rubbed her hands together. "We'll get some meat on those bones of yours, my daughter."

A ripple of chuckles was heard as the general turned to Alexandra.

"Lady Alexandra, I hope you'll go easy on our Sister. She hasn't had a vacation for a long time and needs a respite from the worries of command."

Alexandra shifted slightly. Was the general implying that she was to service Zohra? She thought it wise to merely nod in reply.

"I'll stop by in a stan hour. I don't want to keep either of you up too late."

Zohra's face was unreadable, but Alexandra could feel her discomfort. Then Zohra nodded, and with a firm grip on Alexandra's elbow, left the room. The two warriors followed with the baskets of food and drink.

Zohra leaned close to Alexandra. "She was only joking. She does that to test your mettle."

Alexandra's arm tingled, and she pulled away from Zohra's grasp. "I don't appreciate being told my duty is to service you."

"I believe she was referring to your reputation for attracting trouble. I'm still your bodyguard, so she must be expecting trouble, as are we all."

"Trouble?" Alexandra looked at Zohra, but she had turned away to speak with one of the other women in the group. Alexandra tried to drop back to let them converse side by side, but Zohra put a hand on her elbow, stopping her.

"It's rather difficult to guard someone who's behind me."

Their eyes met, and Alexandra saw nothing in them to indicate anything other than duty. *Damn those unreadable eyes,* she telegraphed to Zohra. She couldn't tell if the look she got back was of amusement or annoyance.

The door opened as the group approached. The guards nodded at them, and Zohra restrained Alexandra while she waved the guards forward.

"Now wait a stan minute!" Alexandra exploded. "I'm as capable of looking for T&Ts or any other oddity as anyone here. I've also been in the room longer and would know what's out of place."

Zohra looked at her. "I don't doubt your skills, Lady Alexandra, but these warriors need the practice."

Alexandra's face heated with anger at being addressed as Lady Alexandra.

"But I can see you're going to be trouble if you don't have something to do." Zohra gave her a little grin and gestured for her to enter the room and join the security sweep of their quarters.

With four of them, it took less than ten minutes. Zohra told the two guards to note the places that Alexandra checked, and pass the information on to the other guards.

Finally, Zohra and Alexandra were alone. They sat quietly at the table while Zohra picked at her food.

"Why are they so concerned with your eating habits?" Alexandra asked, to break the increasingly heavy silence.

Zohra took a deep breath and slowly let it out. "I've always found it difficult to eat when I'm involved in projects."

"Oh. But I'm not a project." Looking into the dark eyes, Alexandra wished visitors weren't expected.

"Is that so?" Zohra said in a low, seductive voice.

Her tone sent a shiver down Alexandra's body. She wondered what they could do in so little time.

The chime sounded, and Zohra let out an audible breath.

"Enter," Alexandra said.

"Good evening, Lady Alexandra, Colonel Zohra," Gedaliaha said. General Aglauros was close behind, followed by two senior members of her staff and Carol-Maa.

General Aglauros didn't waste time with idle chitchat. "Lady Alexandra." She indicated for everyone to seat themselves. "You're in a very difficult spot. I want you to know that we are all aware of that." She regarded Alexandra with some intensity, as if trying to read her, before continuing.

"What's difficult?" Alexandra asked, honestly puzzled.

A tall colonel standing near Aglauros snorted softly. "Well, there's your social and military standing, and then the minor fact that you're a large part of the plan of a very dangerous psychopath, whom we're all here to prevent from damaging this planet."

Aglauros held a hand up to stop her aide. "We need your assistance in capturing Alan."

Alexandra knew they wanted her to be their bait, but she wanted them to ask, not tell her. "What do you want me to do?"

"We want to use you to lure him to us," the colonel said brusquely.

Alexandra looked at the woman, irritated. First Vanstar, and now this colonel. She wondered why the officers that didn't like her came out so aggressively against her.

"Colonel Alle, if you cannot keep silent, you will take your leave." Aglauros gave her aide a stern look.

"She should already know what her role is." Alle looked disgruntled.

Alexandra kept her amazement to herself. She had never heard any member of her admiral's staff speak to her that way, but then she wasn't part of the admiral's inner circle. Perhaps members of a leader's inner circle were less formal.

She glanced at Carol-Maa, who was studying the woman curiously, and then at Gedaliaha, who was sitting quietly as if listening on another level. Something was up, and Alexandra wasn't sure what it was. She looked at General Aglauros. "Are you ordering me to set myself up as bait?"

"We can't order you to do anything," Aglauros said carefully. "You're on medical leave from the Centurions, and a guest of the Guardian of Merker's Outpost."

"So you're asking me to set myself up to be captured by a psychopath who has eluded arrest for nine years in your part of space?"

"He's a psychopath, so we know that wherever you are, he will come for you personally," another aide said.

"What's your plan, Captain…?" Alexandra asked the aide who had spoken.

"Our plan?" The captain, outranked by most of the military attending the meeting, looked uncomfortable. "I'm Captain Ferald, Lady Alexandra," she said, reddening.

Aglauros came to her rescue. "We know he's interested in knocking out the portal because it gives access to a planet on which he has designs. With you here at the Lair, two of his targets are in one location. Normally we would separate you and the portal to make it more difficult for him and his troops, but the Seers have determined that shouldn't be done.

"We believe Alan will use the troops he has scattered in Century City to launch a major assault, which he hopes will give him the opening he needs to grab you. However, our intel on the city lets us keep those soldiers contained, thereby negating his attack."

Alexandra's tone was carefully neutral. "Your plan is based on the premise that only one city will have soldiers."

Colonel Alle's lip curled. "We've done reconnaissance in all the other cities. They're secured and not inhabited."

"The diagrams of the outpost aren't reliable." Alexandra made it a statement, not a conjecture.

Gedaliaha's quiet support helped her keep focused, and she sensed Zohra's surprise along with that of the others.

"What do you mean?" Colonel Alle said. "Based on Colonel Zohra's reports, the other cities were searched for any possible break-ins and weaknesses, and everything was secure."

"When I first came here," Alexandra said, "I asked the computer for a schematic of where I was in relation to the *Spinner's Tale*'s crew. The sections I saw were represented in green and gray, and one was blank. But the outline was there, indicating—"

"It had been erased," Zohra filled in.

Alexandra glanced at her otherwise silent partner, understanding that she needed to be an observer because of their connection.

"Are you saying the recon teams you sent out are not to be trusted?" Colonel Alle sneered at Zohra.

In that instant, Alexandra realized that Alle was jealous of Zohra.

"Since the team was from your Sister house," Zohra said in an even tone, "you would have a better sense of their trustworthiness than I."

"Colonel Alle." Aglauros spoke in a firm voice. "I've had enough of your sniping. You are relieved of duty. Be out of here, along with your house, in one hour. Captain, place them under guard and notify the watch commander."

If Colonel Alle had anything more to say, it was cut off when the guards standing at the door snapped to attention and moved forward to escort her out.

After the group left, Gedaliaha nodded with satisfaction. "Now, that wasn't so painful was it, General?"

"Yes, it was. A Sister house should not be playing jealous games in a time of war, and this is war," Aglauros said in an angry voice.

"Mother, it's not the whole Sister house," Zohra said. "But we need to get back to our immediate problem."

Aglauros looked as though she were going to snap at Zohra, but then took a deep breath and smiled at her affectionately. "Lady Alexandra, I'm sorry we didn't inform you that we intended to oust a group we don't trust, but it had to appear as if you were surprised."

"Does she have a chip implant?" Alexandra asked.

"No. Everyone here has been scanned for that. It's just a competitive thing," Zohra said.

"They've been competing since they were children," Aglauros added. "It doesn't help that her mother and I were competitive, as well."

"That woman has more than competition on her mind." Gedaliaha glanced in Alexandra's direction.

"I don't know her," Alexandra said quickly, as if guilty of something. The other three women laughed. "What?"

"She's been chasing Hadrian ever since you were in the academy."

"Hadrian was married then," Alexandra said. "And he's clan conscious. He wouldn't even have a girlfriend unless she was a clan member."

"We need to get back to business," Aglauros said.

Alexandra looked at Aglauros, a growing uncertainty gnawing at her. *Is that why he wanted me to visit? He's getting married again? To her?*

"Lady Alexandra, do you trust us to set a trap for Alan with you as bait?" Aglauros folded her hands in her lap and waited.

"He'll know it's a trap. You must be aware of that. What's your plan?"

"My daughter?"

Alexandra and Zohra looked at each other. Alexandra took Zohra's hand and pulled her down to sit next to her. "Do you realize what he would do to you to get to me?" she asked her softly.

"Do you realize what would happen to me if he did get to you and I wasn't there to prevent it?" Zohra said.

"Do you think he will come himself, or just send a group of his soldiers?" Aglauros asked.

"I'm certain he'll come for me himself."

Aglauros nodded. "I thought so. You've eluded him too many times. So," she said, glancing at Zohra, "we'll search for any periodic transmissions and for a place to hide a spaceship. If he has soldiers hidden in parts of the cities that aren't correctly mapped, they're probably aboard a ship in sleep pods. What better way of escaping than on your own ship, which is already on the planet? But before we take our leave, Lady Alexandra, you need a short lesson in how to tone down the energy you're putting out and how to shield yourself against mental attacks."

"Put yourself in a restful state," Gedaliaha said in a compelling voice.

Alexandra went into an immediate trance. The shaman's voice seemed to come from far away, but she heard her directions clearly. She practiced the commands in her mind, and after each time was instructed to adjust her energy and to try again. She didn't know how many attempts she had made, but she was growing weary…

She woke to feel Zohra brushing a curl off her forehead.

"You'll get a neck ache sleeping like that," Zohra whispered.

"But I have a bodyguard who can give me a massage and make the ache go away," Alexandra said in a husky voice.

"Your bodyguard is tired and will have to make arrangements for another day. Come on. We didn't get much sleep last night, and I don't want to be running on empty tomorrow." They intertwined their fingers and went into the bedroom.

Chapter 23

"Curse her. Curse that freak!" Alan's tormented mind shrieked. Rene had been turned into a metradame—however unpliable—but she had gone off to a science university anyway. He needed her, and she had deserted him.

He flung the data disk across the room, where it shattered a piece of art for which he had paid a large sum of credits just two stan weeks earlier. He had bought it on impulse when it caught his attention while he was waiting for a ride to the office, and placed it in a corner directly across from his desk. Then he had studied it, looking for its weakest spot. The pleasing sound it made as its main column collapsed didn't disappoint him.

The intent and action to destroy activated his control chip, and pain lanced across his forehead, burning deeper paths across familiar territory in his brain and sending shivers down his spine. It caused an intense feeling that he had come to interpret as pleasure.

"How dare she defy me?"

Hemmitt, Alan's private secretary, closed the office door, preventing the shrill screeching from being heard by any other building tenants. He picked up a large sliver of the shattered mirror. "You look like a rabid animal. If any of your father's associates see you like this, you will be given a one-way ticket to Hinterwield," he said.

Alan took the sliver and gripped it tightly. Blood pooled on the flat surface, then dripped down the shard. The plopping sound of each drop hitting the floor was quite evident, but Hemmitt wisely chose to ignore it.

"Do you think you can do better?" Alan asked in a dangerously low voice. Spittle matted in his beard and his eyes glinted through slitted lids like tiny beads of blackness.

Hemmitt's emotions alternated between amusement and fear. "No. I'm a secretary, not a businessman."

"Fence-sitter." Alan spat the word and his body became increasingly tense, as if he were waiting for some mistake from Hemmitt to give him another outlet for his rage.

"As long as it's a flat surface, I can manage."

Unconsciously, Alan wiped the spittle off with the back of his hand, scattering droplets of blood on himself. "Get me Slinger's number."

Hemmitt nodded and left the room. The more Alan was involved with his own projects, the more time Hemmitt had to manage the office.

If the salary hadn't been so disgustingly high, Hemmitt would never have taken the job. But he was his family's best hope for a way out of a dead-end life in a city teeming with people. Though there was a population limit and restrictions on new residential building, it was difficult to keep out the migrants who were willing to live in overcrowded rooms and work for a pittance.

Hemmitt located the card bearing Slinger's number. When he reentered the office, he found Alan drawing circles on a piece of paper. He had been doing that a lot lately. Hemmitt handed over the card and left to let Alan handle his private business, noting that he had allowed the medbot to tend to his injured hand.

* * *

A stan hour later, Slinger called back, using a disguised voice and giving a false location.

"I have a job for you." Alan's voice was harsh and demanding.

"Isn't that why you called? Get to the point."

"Find me a channeler."

"You can do that yourself. They're on every corner in your city."

"I want a channeler who has no scruples." Alan's hands shook from the control he had to exert when dealing with this person. It was Slinger's way or no business, and he was very good at what he did.

"Now that will be a problem. I'll see what I can do." The communication was broken.

Alan rubbed his temples. A giggle that had nothing to do with joy escaped his tightly drawn lips. Overindulged bigots, he thought contemptuously. The scientist who put the chip in his brain should have studied their own research on the repeated application of pain.

The body adapted, and eventually the pain was perceived as pleasure.

A laugh started at the back of his throat, and soon he was rocking back and forth, his arms wrapped around his body, chuckling mirthlessly until he had forgotten what had amused him.

Suddenly he jumped up from the chair. With a sweep of his arm, he cleared the top of his table, pushing everything onto the chair he had vacated. Spreading out his small stick pieces, he peered at them anxiously. Each piece represented a person or a place, and only he knew what each one meant. Using the pieces helped him put plans together and manipulate them as he pleased. He giggled again, likening what he was doing to the oracle-like bone throwers found throughout history.

Chapter 24

Two weeks later, Alan called for his personal shuttle. He was leaving Hemmitt behind to handle the tedious end of the family business while he took care of the web of information he had gathered on those he wished to harm. The cost had been a substantial amount of credits, so Alan's expectations were high.

He rocked back and forth in his pilot's chair and hummed a little tune. He had no idea where he was going; Slinger had set the destination. No doubt to protect the channeler. Alan gloated. The channeler respected him. People did things for his father because he had money, but Alan held the real power—fear. He continued rocking, thinking of his childhood and Rene. He had liked Rene. She listened to him and told him jokes.

"The freak!" he shouted suddenly. The pain was instant and expected. He knew precisely which thoughts caused what intensity of pain. A grim line formed on his lips in place of a smile. He would teach those scientists a lesson. He had a plan. Alan kept rocking, lost in a darkness where there were no thoughts, just numbing blackness. He'd found the dark place after the chip had been implanted. While his body endured hour after hour of pain as he fought the program, another part of himself was there, safe. He was furious he had agreed to the implantation and furious at the weakness in him that had thought he should pay for Rene's death.

Like quicksilver, his mood changed.

Rene. She was now a metradame, but she wasn't his.

"Freak," he screamed again, but without much feeling. He became worried. What if the chip stopped responding to his thoughts? He would be alone. No, it was there. He could make it work. His thoughts turned to his nemesis, Lady Harriet Montran. Thinking of her never failed to bring him pain. She thought she was better than his Rene.

"She wouldn't die," he screamed at the computer console. The pain didn't fail him. He kept raging, letting the pain take him. He would pay her back. But that freak Rene wouldn't let him have her. She kept watch over Lady Harriet Montran.

"You're probably fucking her, you freak," he shouted again. His fantasies stopped before he could start them. The chip wouldn't allow him to think of physically harming Lady Harriet. He would get around that. He had in the past.

He spent another afternoon raving and destroying anything in sight.

Back at the office, Hemmitt was preparing to leave both his job and the city. Alan was getting worse, and it was too dangerous to stay any longer. After receiving his next pay, three days from now, he would be gone. He had seen Alan playing with his sticks, and knew what they were. Hemmitt had his own soothsayer, as he jokingly called her. She had given him the information he needed and then cut ties with him. She didn't want Alan to see her in his dark cloud.

Hemmitt's desk chimed; Alan was calling for him. A dark chill climbed up his spine, feeling just like the soothsayer said it would, dark and slimy. The time had come, sooner than he had hoped. He would have to send an agent to retrieve the funds he had been saving. Alan wouldn't be able to take him to court for not fulfilling his contract because he had documented Alan's breaches of sanity and sent the information to a lawyer on a planet in Collective space.

He shivered, then rose from his desk and left the office. Quietly, he closed and locked his door and left the building through the underground corridor to avoid being seen. There was no time to use his escape plan, so he would have to use his wits. He had used them before he got a job with Alan, and he could do so again. His aim now was to join his family in Collective territories, out of Alan's reach.

"Where is he?" Alan demanded. The pale, part-time employee was shaking with fear so palpable that it excited Alan. He toyed with the frightened man until he remembered his father's warning. If he lost another employee, he was on his own. "All right, get out, you fool." Sniggering to himself, he marveled at his own power to make a grown man lose control of his bladder. He'd get Slinger to look for Hemmitt. Yes, that was what he would do.

Urot's tits! Hemmitt has the calling cards.

Since Alan periodically destroyed everything in his office, Hemmitt kept copies of important things. Alan hurried past the receptionist's desk, which was where the part-timer worked. He pushed at Hemmitt's office door. It was locked.

Where's the key? Security. Of course.

"Mr. Fermin, you have a call on your private line. It's your father."

Alan looked up guiltily. Did his father know that he had stopped taking his medication again? He quickly returned to his office, and before he picked up the line, measured out his medications and shot them into his arm one by one.

"Father?" He gulped as one gave him heartburn. "I'm sorry to keep you waiting." His head started to buzz. That was from another one. He tapped his left eye, where an annoying twitch occurred whenever he was caught unawares by his father. "I was just looking over the—"

"Alan, I want to see you now. I'm at the Hilltop. And stop babbling!" The picture of his father faded.

"Now what's happening?" Annoyed, Alan pulled out his stick pieces. "What's going on?" He pushed them about in annoyance. "Something's wrong here. Why aren't I seeing anything?" He kept pushing them around, trying to let his mind relax and see what was being shown to him. Angrily, he swept them to the floor and stomped on them.

The final and longest lasting of the assortment of drugs started taking effect. Collapsing into his chair, Alan closed his eyes and let the soothing comfort it generated move through him. He hated this feeling. Nothing interesting ever happened in this quiet state. This had been the longest he'd dared to be off his meds. How long had it been?

His mind gradually cleared as all the chemicals worked together.

Yes, he could understand a lot of things now, and what he knew was frightening. He got up and picked up his sticks. His small pieces were his little messengers. He would take them with him. It angered his father when he saw Alan play with them, but his father didn't have to know Alan had them. He didn't want to be without them for too long, and his father's meetings usually took weeks.

Where is my little Hemmitt stick? he wondered, searching around the desk. He looked at his clock and realized a stan hour had passed. His father would be wondering why he hadn't yet called in his flight plan.

His interoffice communication line buzzed. "Mr. Fermin, your father is asking when you plan on leaving."

Alan didn't believe his father had *asked.* His father never asked. His hands shook as he realized he would have to leave the absent piece behind. Had Hemmitt taken it? No, he couldn't have. The box was always near him. Except that one time when he went to see the channeler. Alan grimaced at his lapse of awareness, and glumly looked around for it one last time. It would have to wait until he got back. *Then I will move all the furniture to find it*, he reassured himself.

Tucking his box firmly under one arm, Alan gave a voice command for his office door to lock, to keep the cleaning staff he never saw from entering his room. He then left the building, forgetting to call ahead to have his ship readied for travel. Hemmitt usually took care of such details for him.

As the full effect of the drugs continued to course through his system, he was able to arrange to have his ship readied and supplied for two weeks travel without causing a scene at the docking yard. But beneath the calm exterior, he was cursing Hemmitt. He remembered to send his father a message that his ship was being prepared and that he would be there as soon as he could. Another advantage of the drugs was that he could talk directly to his father without his voice quivering.

After registering his flight plan and receiving his flight slot, Alan returned to his residence to pick up some personal belongings. Returning to his ship, he spent the rest of the time catching up on reports so that he would be prepared for whatever business his father might bring up.

Two stan hours later, a welcome chime interrupted his struggle to stay focused on a very boring account.

"This is *Ship Ahoy*, aft of you, bringing you fresh supplies and tasty treats. Prepare yourself for insertion," a jaunty sounding bot said over the com channel.

Alan leaned over to the control panel and tapped a button to shut down the alarms that would otherwise sound when the hull was breached. The report forgotten, he turned his thoughts back to the family business and the contributions he had made to his father's holdings. While he was in his psychotic state, he was able to see patterns in things. The meds blocked out that ability. Alan was sure his father was aware of that, for he didn't press him about taking his meds as much as he used to.

Chapter 25

Five months had passed since Alan's meeting with his father, when he had learned that Lord Chaney felt their petition for a seat on the Galactic Committee of Families and Communities had been refused due to *his* problems. Alan thought his father would punish him, but he should have remembered that Gustaf Fermin was a businessman who had made a fortune before his third child had arrived, and knew how to roll with his losses. And now Alan knew that his father valued his abilities over a representative's seat on the GCFC's lower floor.

Alan paced in his small craft as it made its way to the frontier, where he was having another meeting with a channeler. Once his father let go of the notion of belonging to the GCFC, he started a plan to destroy the one responsible for blocking his plans, Hadrian DeMonte. Lord Chaney told them that Lord DeMonte made the motion to dismiss them from consideration. Of course, Lord Chaney hadn't mentioned that the rest of the council had agreed without argument. Alan got that information from his spy.

His father wanted to assassinate Lady Harriet Montran, Lord Hadrian DeMonte's cousin. It would kill Hadrian's spirit, his father said. But Alan wanted Harriet Montran for himself. That was why Alan didn't tell his father that Lord Chaney's forces had control of her on *Spinner's Tale,* one of his father's merchant ships. For three months, they wore her down physically and mentally. Wandering space, without any contact with family or friends, she was effectively isolated.

It was taking Alan considerable willpower to keep from swooping down on *Spinner's Tale* and abducting her. But Lord Chaney had pointed out that someone was following Alan, and unless he was ready to disappear permanently, he would have to wait for Lord Chaney to deliver Lady Montran to him. Chaney had offered to deliver her as a metradame, submissive to Alan's commands, but Rene, Alan's first metradame, hadn't worked out the way she was supposed to. This time, he would watch the process from beginning to end to see that it was done properly. But Lady Montran's memories would be kept intact. He wanted to see the horror in her eyes when she awakened and realized she was under his command.

To take his mind off that delightful prospect, he forced himself to attend to his other business. Things were progressing as planned. He'd found a channeler who had the ability to enter dreams. Jeriad had been working for him for a month, and Alan's spies told him he was ruffling the feathers of those he had been paid to disturb. Alan picked up his notebook again and tried to decipher what he had written when he was not on his meds.

Beep!

"Yes?"

"Alan. This is Decker. Montran escaped on Merker's Outpost. I told you we should have just drugged her and shipped her to the labs. We have those Spartans looking for her, but you can't trust them."

The color drained from Alan's face, and his heart nearly stopped. That news didn't seal Decker's fate, for he was already living on borrowed time. First things first, he told himself calmly. "Where did she escape to?"

"Somewhere surfaceside, out in the sand. I fixed her suit so she didn't have good air. It's just a matter of time before I find her body. I've got my people searching the area for her now. But if the Spartans find her..."

"That's a big planet, Decker." Alan felt dangerously calm.

"The suit has a homing device, As soon as the winds die down, we'll pick her up."

Decker sounded too confident. The man was hip deep in chicken shit, and Alan hated chickens.

When Decker disconnected, Alan sat in his chair to think. Throwing his sticks would be useless, because they only made sense when he wasn't on his meds. He impatiently checked his scanners, looking for the channeler's ship. Nothing. He looked at his timer. Not due for another standard hour. He had arrived early, as the channeler requested. That was probably to make sure Alan wasn't going to set a trap around him. Why would he? He had the man's family hidden away.

"*Spinner's Tale*, this is Alan Fermin on *Rouster*, come in."

"*Spinner's*. This is Commander Martinez, Alan."

"What's going on, Martinez?"

Alan got an earful, which had him pacing his small cabin again. He also talked to Captain Miller, but was interrupted as he tried to force his will on the man. He was having problems buying Miller, and not just because he was Lord Chaney's man, but also because he was a Spartan. A Black Rose Spartan. Not even his metrasoldiers could best the members of the Black Rose squad. He couldn't kill them off, like Lord Chaney had done to the Degas squad, without losing his own life before the plan was even be put into effect. He had already received his warning.

The thought of being closed in, with nowhere in GCFC space to hide, panicked him. Collective space was out of the question. They would send him to a rehab center. That would be worse than the Wield prison-world, where the inmates were as dangerous as the planet. A rehab center would kill him with kindness, by making sure he was on his meds and taking care of himself. The thought of never again having an exciting, stimulating moment terrified him.

Frantically, Alan pulled out a book that he kept hidden for dealing with disasters, fumbling with it until his shaking hands could grasp it more firmly. Things were not looking good.

The book reminded him that he had a plan and an army to carry it out. He had procured warriors from closed planets that still practiced brutal warfare. They were his muscle, intended to carve out an empire on Arnica, a planet so far away, it took over a year to get there on the fastest ship money could buy. Unless it traveled through a portal. To Alan's dismay, his expeditionary forces had found a portal on Arnica that connected to Merker's Outpost.

He had never even heard of portals before, and was even more dismayed to learn that neither he nor any of his agents could use them. Something about their harmonic levels. But maybe his enemies could. Because of this, the portal would pose a constant threat to his plans and had to be destroyed. Thinking of his planet calmed him; it was safe and far away from the over-explored galaxies. He just had a few things to do before he could go there. Alan's lip curled. One thing had already been taken care of: Slinger had found Hemmitt. He would pay for his desertion.

Alan stared at the meaningless writing in his book then turned the page to a diagram. That he could understand. It showed how his army was divided into four groups. A fingertip touched the first circle. That was his assault group. It was preparing to kidnap a few important people on Hinterwield. He moved his finger to the second circle. That group was in stasis, hidden on Merker's Outpost. He tapped the third circle. They were testing the defenses of the

Guardian computer on the outpost, while the last and largest body of soldiers was waiting for him on Arnica, *his* planet. Perhaps it was time for a slight adjustment to his plans.

"What do you want, Fermin?" A weary voice came over his ship's intercom.

Alan jumped, and his book dropped to the deck. "I want to make sure you do as we have agreed upon."

"I don't back out on deals."

"So I've heard. However, I like to take out insurance. Am I understood?"

"You are."

Alan cut the communication. Halfway to their meeting place, he had made sure the channeler got the message that his family was missing. Alan rubbed his hands together. He smiled gleefully and then frowned. "If you are dead, Lady Harriet Montran, have no fear. I have a remedy for that, too. I own you!" He slammed his palm down on the hard surface of the console, letting the sting of the blow pass before moving on to the next step of his plan. "Computer on for coded communication."

"On," the voice said.

"To Santeeies, aboard *Shadow Fox*. Inaugurate Campaign Sigma." He thought again about the change in plan. One ship at Hinterwield would send the four prisoners he wanted freed to join him on Arnica. The other ships would be deployed to the seven planets his agents told him also had portals. He'd been told that if one portal was destabilized, the others would be also. But it was best to be sure.

"Find the portals and destroy them. Send."

Alan smiled. He was going to leave this galaxy with a very big bang. Now it was time to head for Magewield. He had hidden his plan books and detailed notes there in the family vacation house, where the GCFC had no authority to search. The thought of leaving this galaxy and his despised father's influence would have brought Alan more comfort if Lady Montran was in hand, but all in good time.

A bleep on his console had Alan looking up from where he was slouched in his favorite chair. The navigation array made no sense to him. "Ship, how far am I from Magewield?"

"Twenty-eight stan hours."

Alan pursed his lips, pleased that it had stopped giving the minutes and seconds, in which he had no interest.

Another bleep had him squinting at the comm. "Who is it?"

"This is First Sergeant Headers of the Second Battalion on Merker's Outpost, sir, calling for further orders."

Alan jolted upright, nearly falling from his chair. "What?"

"We cannot find General Lare or his staff."

"Who has Montran?"

"Lady Varina Chaney's security. Lord Chaney is dead, and we have captured his metradame, Sheila. They wish to trade Lady Montran for our prisoner."

Alan froze for a few minutes then grinned with pleasure. So Chaney was dead. Another problem eliminated, no doubt by his smuggler partner. A polite clearing of a throat reminded him someone was waiting for an order. Suddenly his anger turned to Lady Varina, whom he trusted even less than he did her father.

"Montran is to be turned over to you with no marks on her. Only in that condition, unmarked and alive. She must be fully awake, moving on her own, and coherent when you make the exchange. If she is ruined in any way, fry the metrabitch and Chaney's soldiers. You hear me?"

"Yes, sir."

"Well, do it! Out."

If he weren't so close to Magewield, he would turn around and head to Merker's Outpost. "Trust. I must show trust in these soldiers. They will do what I tell them." His mutterings stopped when he thought of Decker, to whom he had given the task of harassing Montran while she was aboard the *Spinner's Tale*. "That's all right. I have another agent who will find her."

He dropped into his seat and looked longingly at his controls. He wished he dared to push his ship to maximum speed, but blowing out an engine would only delay him further, and would attract unwelcome attention. Resigned, he took a sleep drug. The bot would wake him if necessary.

* * *

A day away from Magewield, bored, Alan scanned the news channels. "No!" He slammed his fist into the padded armrest, and watched as a rebroadcast of the major scandal that shook GCFC space played out. According to the newscaster, the events were four days old.

"What is Father going to say? Maybe with the reorganization, he'll get his seat. I'll be gone, Father, and then you'll be able to get what you want."

He eagerly scanned the other channels and found the same news, repeated *ad nauseum*, with only two exceptions. His face whitened at the second report.

"Gustaf Fermin, wealthy business mogul, died from an apparent heart attack while swimming. In a rush to litigation, his wife and children are challenging his will, which leaves nothing to any family member other than his eldest son, Alan Fermin. Alan Fermin is wanted for crimes against society. If seen, he should not be approached. Please contact your nearest law enforcement office if you have any information on his location.

"Lord Chaney, a member of another wealthy and influential family and once a member of the GCFC, died four days ago while on vacation. His surviving wife and her daughter are protesting his will, which gives all his offspring equal shares of estate he had amassed."

Alan's mind froze. Banishment was inconsequential in comparison with the death of his father. His bios rose and teetered on the edge of dangerous levels, until the medbot activated and administered a sedative to the unresisting patient.

* * *

Alan waited a few extra days to approach Magewield and secure his book. There was a great deal of unusual traffic to and from the planet, and he shouted in rage at the monitor that showed no way to land unobserved. He pulled at his beard and hair in agitation, considering his options. He would have to abandon his possessions on Magewield.

Suddenly, he smiled. "I have a backup plan. Father said a good business leader always has a backup plan." He nodded to himself as he hummed a tune his sister's nanny used to sing to her. He lifted his head for a moment and his eyes slitted in anger. "My nanny never sang to me." A warning beep on his terminal notified him of the approach of another ship, this one with military identifiers. "I'll have someone pick up the plans for me." That decision made, Alan punched in the coordinates of a small waystation where he kept supplies and his new ship, *Trojan Horse*. "Always have a backup plan," he crooned to himself.

Chapter 26

"Colonel Zohra."

Alexandra and Zohra looked up from the map they were studying with some of the unit leaders. General Aglauros was off-planet at a conference with Admiral JoCastao, Commander Ironsides, Admiral J'mai, and a monk from Hela.

"This came in from Commander Mora. We have confirmation of Naboth's Vine's suspicions regarding Alan's movements in another sector."

Zohra took the handheld message unit and laid it on the table so everyone could read it.

"He's landed five regiments of metrasoldiers on Arnica?" Lieutenant Malchi asked in disbelief. "But Arnica's off-limits. General Aglauros said a message was delivered personally to the Monks of Hela, twenty stan years ago, that Arnica wasn't interested in receiving any settlers from our part of the galaxy."

"I remember that." Clea looked worried. "That communication exposed the illegal settlement practices a few companies were trying to get away with. General Aglauros was talking about it last month."

"*Emperor's Last Chance* was dispatched a month ago. I'll bet that's where they're headed," TeaSdak said.

Zohra tapped a finger on the message unit. "Ten small assault ships have been intercepted on their way here. It says here that Admiral JoCastao has a group of fighters encircling them."

"Will there be a battle?" Alexandra asked softly.

"Metrasoldiers are programmed killers. They'll kill themselves to avoid capture and take as many of their enemy with them as they can." Zohra could feel Alexandra's uneasiness. It seemed the more they were around each other, the easier it was for them to pick up on the other's mood.

Looking around at the group, Zohra suddenly realized how tired she was. By the looks of the other women, they were, too. "Let's bring this meeting to an end." She turned to one of the serving women, who was refilling water goblets. “D’ea, can you get Commander Montran and me something light to eat that we can take back to our quarters?”

“And some Cha,” Alexandra added quickly.

She and Zohra left the hall with their dinner and a hot pot of tea. The four bodyguards that accompanied them everywhere formed the usual circle around them as they moved to their quarters.

After the door closed behind them, Alexandra laid her bundle on the table and turned to Zohra, who laid hers down, too. “Hold me, please, as if this were the last time.”

Zohra opened her arms and let Alexandra nestle close to her.

“Have faith, my love,” Zohra whispered.

They stood in the quiet embrace for a long moment, until Zohra finally stepped back. “Let’s eat, and then get some sleep.” She tenderly touched Alexandra’s face with her fingertips.

They sat in their chairs and ate, not exchanging much conversation. Zohra rose first and kissed Alexandra on the head.

“Come on. A quick shower, then bed.” Zohra pulled her up. Once in the shower, she seated the protesting Alexandra on the bench.

“When are Guardian and Charles, I mean Merker and Charles, going to be fully merged with their biological bodies?” Alexandra asked as the warm water cascaded over her. She leaned forward, and Zohra’s lathered hands spread soap in her hair, then ran around the back of her head and down her shoulders, eliciting groans of pleasure from them both.

“Another week.” Zohra said. “They need psychological sessions to deal with the trauma of the transfer. The psych techs say they’ll enter a suicidal phase after going from being omnipresent to being just like any other bioform… needing to sleep, eat, get rid of bodily waste, and sometimes having to read things more than once to understand them.” She leaned over and kissed Alexandra’s forehead. “Come on. Let’s get some sleep.”

Chapter 27

Alexandra's inner alarm went off, and she was crouched at the side of her bed before she had completely awakened.

Alan?

In a split-second reaction, Zohra jumped to the same side of the bed and used her body to shield Alexandra from the sitting room doorway.

Where?

Alexandra became acutely aware of the body against which she pressed. "I can sense Alan," she whispered. "He's not here, but something's not right. We need to dress now."

The lights in the room hadn't come up when their bio readings denoted a wakened state. Only the outlines of the doorways could be seen in the soft glow of the exit sign.

They moved to the closet and pushed it open.

"Something's wrong. The lights aren't coming up, so I know it's not my imagination." Alexandra felt for her Second Skin and pulled it out. "I hope I'm not putting this on backwards." She extended her senses, reaching out into the sitting room, then around their sleeping area. Nothing.

They hurriedly dressed.

"Let's go into the bathing room," Zohra whispered. "It has separate life support and access to some places we can escape into if necessary."

"Sounds like an ideal place to sneak in and out. I hope we won't have any visitors taking the same advantage."

"Yeah, by now everyone knows about it." Zohra moved to the bathing room door.

"Hey, we can't be going into those other places without our outersuits." Alexandra went back to grab the two suits that were hanging on the back of the closet door.

"Disengage your camera, and don't use your mic. We could be traced through either one," Zohra said. They quickly donned the suits, grateful for the helmet visors, which let them see in the darkness.

They closed the bathing door and locked it. With the aid of the helmets, they found a bot hatch.

The latch wouldn't release. Zohra grunted as she moved into another position, nearly knocking Alexandra down.

Alexandra grabbed her by the elbow and pulled her over to another cleaning bot storage. She moved the small cleaning bot out of the way and was about to crawl in when Zohra stopped her.

"I'm number one. I go first," she hand-signaled, and went in.

A muffled explosion came from the other side of the bathing door, then two more. Alexandra followed Zohra into the small space, going in feet first so she could close the door behind them. Zohra yanked Alexandra out of the bot chute by her feet and pulled her into the maintenance tunnel.

They went at a fast pace down the tunnel, their running footsteps making no sound. Alexandra accessed her internal map. They were heading toward the travel tube.

The area was dark, and their helmets registered no life-forms in the vicinity. From a collection parked by the side rail, Zohra selected a small car that could be activated with a push. While she sat behind the controls, Alexandra shoved it out onto the main track. She gave it a final thrust and hopped in as it picked up speed, moving them down the rail and farther into the heart of the planet.

At rail crossings, Alexandra would get out and switch the levers to change the direction of the tracks then move them back again to avoid leaving a trail. Alexandra suspected they were headed to the area that had been erased from the map of the planet—the city of Ilo, which Colonel Alle's Sister house had inspected. Another team should have been sent to examine that area more closely, but it hadn't happened yet.

On this adventure, Alexandra was merely along for the ride. She knew it wasn't yet time for Alan's arrival. Whatever trouble they just left behind in the Lair was probably just something he had thought up to test defenses and rattle everyone's nerves. Truth be told, she was getting bored and was looking forward to some action.

The car slowed down and stopped. After they stepped out, Zohra signaled her intent to investigate the area.

Alexandra smiled and mouthed an ironic, "No kidding?" Zohra shrugged, smiling in return.

Putting a hand on Zohra's shoulder, Alexandra followed closely behind her. She noted that the atmosphere in this area was toxic to their species. Carol-Maa had said that the planet had continued to nurture its own species in some of the cities. She wondered whether this was one of the places where the planet's natural life-forms lived.

She stopped in her tracks, and her hand dropped from Zohra's shoulder. Zohra turned to peer at her. Alexandra brought her hand up in a gesture as if to slap her forehead. Zohra signed her concern.

She pulled Zohra against the tunnel wall and signed the spelling of the Enuits of WaterLand.

Zohra shook her head and turned quickly, as though she had seen something.

"Zohra, listen to me, please!"

Zohra swung back to look at her.

"Can you hear my mental speech?"

Zohra's eyes opened wide as she nodded, then signed that she saw shadowy images passing by.

Alexandra pictured the life-forms from WaterLand and then signed that they were friends. She imagined the solid world and then something like shadows superimposed over it.

Zohra nodded and gestured over her shoulder.

Alexandra's eyebrows rose, and she moved in front of Zohra to see what she was referring to. She stilled herself and shifted her awareness, then nearly fell back into Zohra when the shadows took on the more visible form of swirling colors.

Alexandra took a deep breath and watched the energy patterns as they appeared to be going about their business. Some glanced her way, but didn't alter their direction.

Zohra tugged on her sleeve and mouthed, "What?"

Alexandra's fingers signed quickly, repeating her thoughts to be sure Zohra understood her.

Zohra immediately moved in front of her and faced forward in a defensive attitude.

Alexandra put her hands on Zohra's shoulders to help her relax, and the effect on Zohra's vision was almost immediate. She half-turned to Alexandra and signed, "I see them, too. They're coming fast, in whirling colors."

The energy patterns stopped just short of the entrance of the tunnel in which they were standing.

Alexandra slipped around Zohra, took her gloved hand, and pulled her along until they were just outside the tunnel. She tentatively connected with the spirit of the planet and sent a respectful thought, wishing blessings upon it. They waited as the various colors around them mixed closer to one shade, with occasional flashes of other colors flickering across what was now a cloud before them.

"Greetings, Off-worlders." A soft voice sounded in their heads. Images appeared, asking why they were in the city again, uninvited and unwanted.

"Zohra," Alexandra said, "can you see the image-questions they're sending?"

"Yes, inside my head. It's weird."

Another question came, asking if they had come to finally remove… The image that appeared in their minds was of a ship, with life-forms lying in sleep pods.

They had found Alan's hidden cache of soldiers.

Alexandra let out a noisy gust of air as she realized how lucky they had been. She sent out an image of herself and Zohra looking over the ship and its crew, and showing that they and others would remove the offending object. She asked that they be led to the ship, and the life-forms agreed.

She then asked if they were permitted to use their voice communication links. After an affirmative response, they turned on their mics. That might also give a location of their whereabouts to the computer, but Zohra hadn't objected.

"Let's go see what's in this ship, Zohra."

"Yeah, a legitimate recon mission." Zohra started up the path, following the life-forms. "I was getting a headache from the mental stuff."

Alexandra let Zohra take the lead. Resting her hand once more on Zohra's shoulder, she extended her senses to feel the area around them. A smile formed on her face as she touched the awareness of a small creature their eyes couldn't see as they passed; it was living in the foliage. In this other dimension, life existed all around them, each being sending little jolts of energy through Alexandra as she connected with it.

Zohra turned her head to look at Alexandra and found her eyes vacant, as though her thoughts were elsewhere. She returned her attention to the trail, careful to pick a smooth path so that her distracted partner wouldn't trip. The two were led to a vast cavern that opened to the surface. There was a windstorm in progress on the planet surface.

"I feel the ship," Alexandra whispered. "It's in there." She pointed toward a crater in the cavern floor.

Zohra nodded and returned to using gestures as she informed Alexandra that they would circle the crater in which the ship was resting and study it from opposite directions. Soon they had settled across from each other, looking down at what appeared to be a latent volcanic bole. The ship apparently used thermal energy from the volcano to keep its life support running, thus not engaging any systems that would put out an energy signature.

"Zohra?" When she looked up, Alexandra motioned toward what appeared to be a way down to the ship.

Cautiously, they made their way to an opening between two rocks. Zohra hoped the path wasn't booby-trapped, and was disappointed to see T&Ts blocking their access to the ship.

An image appeared in Alexandra's peripheral vision and she turned in surprise. One of the native life-forms was hovering near them. It seemed to be showing her another way to the ship, but it involved jumping off the edge of the crater. She stifled a laugh. Their more solid forms weren't suited to jumping. Even if they weren't injured, they'd make a loud noise when they struck the ship's hull.

Alexandra felt the light-form's confusion, but returned her attention to Zohra, who was looking around for another way down. Suddenly, Alexandra felt herself lifted on a wave of energy, carried over the rim, and set down near the outer hull of the ship. A moment later, Zohra was deposited next to her. Another laugh threatened to escape Alexandra. Apparently their newfound allies were willing to provide assistance, if it meant getting the foreign object out of their environment.

Zohra indicated they should start looking for a way into the ship. They set out in opposite directions and soon met at their starting point. All the outer doors were tightly shut and had traps set for anyone who attempted to enter.

On impulse, Alexandra put a question to the life-form following her, and was shown a picture of an opening in the ship's hull that was dumping toxic waste into the environment. No wonder the beings were angry.

Zohra and Alexandra moved up a slight incline to where they could view the top hatch. Using their helmet visors, they could see a small amount of air leaking from its seams. No traps were visible.

Zohra pressed Alexandra's arm, indicating that she should step back from their perch. She leaped into the air and, with the help of their new assistants, landed almost soundlessly on the hull. Alexandra followed, silently thanking the two shadows.

The top hatch had not been locked, and they were soon inside the airlock. Zohra was about to seal the hatch and release breathable air when Alexandra stopped her, signing a message.

Instead, Zohra carefully opened the outer hatch a mere hand's breadth, and watched as a colorful swish of something slid in and attached itself to Alexandra's shoulder. She then closed it and opened the lock to the ship's atmosphere. When the readings gave the all clear, they removed their helmets.

"Well?" Alexandra asked softly.

"We look for the pods," Zohra replied.

"Why not just send this thing off on autopilot and let our ships topside do the rest?" Alexandra didn't really want to search a ship that undoubtedly contained several traps. She saw disappointment in her partner's eyes. "There'll plenty of time for adventures, and maybe this isn't the best time."

Zohra seemed to waver. The Black Rose would have swept through, regardless of the traps, just to take possession of a ship that belonged to the enemy. It was what they did, and they did it well. "We don't want to call attention to ourselves," Alexandra continued, "especially when we just left a bad situation at the Lair."

"Right." Zohra's face broke into a grin. "Promise?"

"Promise what?" Alexandra asked, following Zohra toward the ship's bridge.

"The adventures."

Alexandra rolled her eyes. "Warriors. Always looking for a life-and-death thrill."

The bridge had seating for six, and the area looked clean, though worn. After a quick survey, Alexandra concluded it was a second-hand Que-E bus, used primarily to move groups of workers and their equipment from one star system to another. They weren't armored or armed, but the console had so many controls that she was sure it had been modified and upgraded for use as a troop carrier.

Alexandra set the ship on autopilot and enabled its beacon. The moment the craft went active, it would send out its identifier.

"Let's get out of here." Suddenly, Alexandra had a bad feeling. "Quickly." She engaged her helmet, and Zohra followed suit.

As they raced back to the outer hatch, an image of a guard bot, armed to the teeth, flashed in both their minds. Clearly, the two life-forms were still with them.

Zohra whispered a curse and altered course to run down another corridor, grabbing the handrails and sliding down to a lower level. Alexandra followed close behind. In her helmet camera, she saw guard bots being released from their wall storage slots as the ship began to power up.

She remembered that due to their vulnerability to pirates, Que-E buses always had emergency hatches for dumping cargo. “Garbage!” She leaped over a small cleaning bot.

Zohra’s stopped and turned to catch Alexandra as she bumped into her. She pushed her back a few yards, to a hatch that showed the symbol for a dumpster.

“We’re on the same wavelength.” Alexandra hit the release, and Zohra pushed her through the opening first. The life-form attached to Alexandra’s shoulder exerted an energy beam, which slowed her and Zohra and dropped them with a slight thump onto the floor of the cavern as the ship began to exit from its hiding place. The life-form now hovered just above them, as if watching the detested ship leave its space.

“Are you all right?” Zohra rolled to her feet and surveyed the area, then looked back at Alexandra, who was reclining and watching the departing ship.

“Yeah. By the time we get back, the excitement over finding this ship will have died down.”

“I think our appearance will stir them up again,” Zohra said, smirking.

“You know, I have a feeling you’ll need to be watched closely when you get bored.”

Zohra shot her a look of mock indignation, and then smiled. She gestured toward the shadows gathering around them. “We’re going to have to figure out how to remove the T&Ts in the volcano. It’s too dangerous to just leave them.”

Many exchanges later, they managed to convince the natives, who called themselves Sha’Kar, that they lacked the equipment to safely remove the traps. There were some that Alexandra didn’t recognize, though she hoped Zohra did. They agreed to go to the Lair, get what they needed, and return. Alone.

As they rode back toward the Lair, Alexandra could feel Zohra’s pensive mood. “So, did you recognize all those traps?”

Zohra glanced at her. “No.”

“Hmm.” Alexandra thought about that. “Then this is an adventure.”

“Yeah, it is at that.” Zohra grinned. “Am I being rationed?”

"No. But do try to stay away from the life-and-death ones." She wondered if she had been that challenged when she was in the Spartans.

They reentered the Lair cautiously. Alexandra sent out a mental call for Gedaliaha and received a warm welcome.

She smiled, until another being touched their mental connection. General Aglauros's reply made her blush, and Zohra saw her flushed face.

"I take it you've reached someone?"

"Your mother. She says Alan's soldiers were behind the explosions here. They were after me. I explained our escape, and what we did, but she wasn't happy that we disappeared without a trace."

"Better you than me. She's easier on you," Zohra said. She nodded to the group of warriors guarding the tube area. The corridors were blackened, and the art objects that had once adorned the area were gone. Clean up bots were already working to resurface the walls. The two women headed for Com-C.

Chapter 28

Alexandra woke from disturbing dreams. The warm body next to her stirred, then a hand moved up from her arm, tickling the back of her neck.

Zohra shifted, and Alexandra looked directly into the dark eyes that were more readable, these days. The mind link between them was becoming stronger.

"What's bothering you?" Zohra asked.

"I was trying to figure out what I fear the most about Alan's planned invasion. I've come to the conclusion that it's not the invasion, it's experiencing Alan's rage."

Alexandra brushed a stray strand of dark hair out of her lover's face. She could feel Zohra's energy settle around them like a protective shield. "His rage is on so many different levels. I can deflect his anger, but he'll simply find other ways to grow in power and continue to hurt others."

"You're saying he will have to be… killed?"

"I admit that thought often crosses my mind."

"I don't wonder. I've seen what his madness can do. But, you're hesitant?"

"Sending him into the Land of the Dead when he's maddened will only cause more havoc. He'll carry that madness into the next life, without waiting the time normally allotted for a soul to process his or her previous life."

"What do you propose?"

"I'm thinking that if he's on his meds and we can talk to him, explain to him that it's time for him to move on…" Alexandra could see Zohra wasn't buying it.

"Alexandra, I don't know of any mad person who'd appreciate being told 'Hey, before we take your life, we'd like to explain the principles of madness and the proper way of dying.' Do you?"

"Yes, I do."

Zohra sighed. “I can’t see it, not for someone as far gone as Alan. He’s been given more chances than anyone, and he hasn’t taken advantage of that borrowed time to get with the program. He has no feeling for others, so how can he have any remorse, or understand justice in the larger framework?”

“I’m not suggesting sending him to a colony like Hinterwield, because he’ll find a way to escape and be even more terrible than he is now. His condition is deteriorating, and no chip or drugs will change or slow it down. I just believe that before his life is taken, he should be pointed in the right direction instead of being left adrift.”

Zohra rolled onto her back, looking pensive.

Alexandra could guess what she was thinking about. Zohra was a warrior; she lived in the present. Thoughts of souls and other lives… that was for shamans, and the other Holy People who did that for a living. It was too far in the future for her. Her reactions were instinctive: quick moves, done without forethought or pondering over right and wrong.

Maybe that wasn’t such a bad idea. Alexandra relinquished the heavy thinking and got up. “Hey, Zohra, let’s go.” Since Zohra was teaching Alexandra self-defense exercises, they had agreed it was only fair that she learn the meditation stretches and poses Alexandra did in the morning. She moved to a cleared space and waited. Meditation first, then exercise.

Zohra sighed, then rolled out of bed and joined her.

The chime at their door came during an exercise that required speed and accuracy, at which Alexandra was significantly less skilled than Zohra. While Zohra answered the summons, Alexandra, looking worse for wear, took time to wipe her brow and gulp some water. Captains Chilali and Raizel were at the door, dressed for a workout.

Raizel chuckled. “Good morning. Looks like Lady Alexandra is warming up our colonel for us. And here I thought we’d get that pleasure.”

“Right,” Alexandra said, “I’ve warmed her up for you. Good thing you came to her rescue.” Zohra laughed with the others. “Zohra, I’ll be with the shamans most of the morning, so I probably won’t need a bodyguard.”

“Actually,” Raizel said, “a small group of Centurion soldiers was left behind. They’ll be assigned to you when Colonel Zohra is occupied elsewhere. General Aglauros talked to Admiral JoCastao, and they thought someone should give Colonel Zohra a break every now and then so she doesn't become too edgy and find some mischief to get into, taking you with her."

"We've been saved from ourselves, then." Alexandra smiled at Zohra, who grinned back at her. Another chime interrupted any retort she might have made.

A soldier dressed in Centurion uniform saluted and nodded to the group of women. "I'm Corporal Provo, here to escort Commander Montran to the shamans' meeting. Good-day to you, Commander."

"Corporal."

"Hello, Royd," Raizel said. "You're on escort service?"

A big smile formed on the soldier's face. "It's better than being topside, Captain."

"Sure is," Zohra and Alexandra chorused.

The shamans discussed Alan and ways of containing him. Representatives from Naboth's Vine were also there, arguing their position, which was that Alan had to die. There was no cure for him, no safe place to put him, and no way short of altering his brain pattern to keep him alive. Making him mindless for the rest of his life would not advance him on his life path.

They all agreed on that, at least.

Alexandra wondered how many of the group, other than Carol-Maa, were aware that a Sha'Kar from Ilo was sitting in on the meeting. Alexandra's breath caught as she received a very brief image from the Sha'Kar of danger. She looked around the group, expecting others to have noticed it, but it appeared that no one had. Carol-Maa glanced at her, and her smile turned into a puzzled look.

Alexandra smiled back at her and then glanced over her shoulder at her guard. "I'm taking a break," she whispered to him. "It's not like I'm contributing anything of great value." Corporal Provo nodded and followed her out.

Alexandra nodded to the guards outside her quarters as she entered. Two guards were posted inside, too. She already knew there were two more posted in the bathing room.

"I'm going to take a nap," she said. "Wake me when Colonel Zohra returns to the Lair."

They nodded.

Alexandra sauntered into her bedroom then quickly dressed in her outersuit. Now she would find out if a scheme she'd worked out with Guardian was still feasible, even with the changes to his programs.

"Invoke." The word fixed her bioreadings in one location. Movement of her physical presence would no longer register on the outpost's systems. It also generated a holographic image of Alexandra, sitting on her bed playing her flute. "Gamma, gamma, alpha. Maud, do you copy?" Now her voice would not register on any comm link but Maud's.

"Yes, Harriet. Or is it Alexandra?" Maud said.

"Something's wrong, Maud. I had to—"

"I know. Metrasoldiers have trapped and surrounded a Spartan patrol. They have successfully jammed all communications in the area, so we don't know what's happening. Zohra was leading a team to rescue the trapped soldiers when she disappeared."

"What about the soldiers she was with?"

"Everyone is accounted for."

"I'm going to look for her."

"I'm not surprised. You don't think this is a trick of Alan's to lure you to his soldiers?"

"No. He's not here yet, and he wouldn't let any of his soldiers capture me. The last time he left it to them, I got away."

"What do you want me to do?"

"Help me, if you can. Where was she last seen?"

"Near the rim, along the part the Black Rose hadn't surveyed yet. Guardian—I mean L'uenbeng—hadn't sent anyone there either. It's part of the Sha'Kar life space."

"Sha'Kar. Oh, great."

"What do you have in mind?"

"I'd like to get over there and have a look around."

"There's an unmonitored trolley on the ninth level. Look for the space between two figures representing the Tao. I'll meet you at the end."

* * *

Alexandra and Maud looked over the wide slice in the planet's surface. Maud turned to see another suited figure moving toward them. Neither woman was surprised that it was Carol-Maa. The Sha'Kar from the meeting was with her.

"We left the room shortly after you," Carol-Maa said. "The Sha'Kar are not happy that another group of Alan's soldiers has invaded their space."

"Can anyone see you?" Alexandra was worried about surveillance.

"We never appeared on anyone's monitors." Carol-Maa said. "Shall we go and see the Sha'Kar elders? We have an invitation this time." The others followed her.

"Do you know where Zohra is?" Alexandra asked as they moved slowly down the cliff.

"The Sha'Kar do."

"Why don't they just tell us, so we can go get her?"

"Because there are rules, and even our presence here is breaking one of them," Maud said.

The meeting was uncomfortable. The elders were displeased by the repeated invasion of their sacred space, and coming to an agreement for the information exchange took longer than Alexandra had hoped.

The three women and the Sha'Kar settled in a small crevice, which would barely conceal them if the women hadn't had their suits' blend function turned on. The metrasoldiers had set up a small secured area in one of the openings along the cliff face.

"We won't be able to sneak in there and free her," Alexandra said, looking over the site.

"Have you thought about how you'll explain having this suit?" Maud asked.

"It's crossed my mind. I promised Guardian I wouldn't give his secret away, and I won't. But Zohra's pretty resourceful. If we can stage a distraction and give her an opportunity to escape…"

"An explosion." Maud pointed at a group of metrasoldiers clothed in AEGs, practicing drills. Beside them was a stack of boxes marked as ordnance.

"Okay. Whoops." A small vehicle moved across the surface of the planet, slid down the face of the cliff, and stopped near two metrasoldiers. Alexandra ducked, then straightened up, embarrassed. "How did their ship get here undetected?"

"The Sha'Kar says they are cloaking their presence with an energy beam," Carol-Maa said.

"Let's move in and shut it down. That could be our distraction," Alexandra said, thinking of the ship's self-destruct mechanism.

"I'll take the ship," Carol-Maa said. Alexandra opened her mouth to argue, but Maa said firmly, "Carol knows how to do this."

"Okay, okay. I forgot she's a one-woman demolition team. Maud and I will watch Zohra's back."

Alexandra and Maud crawled along the edge of the cliff as quickly as they could, moving to where they could see Zohra, who appeared to be unconscious.

"She's sleeping," Alexandra said, relieved. "We can open up an escape route path for her from here. Our search parties should notice the disturbance in the area, so she won't have to go far to be rescued."

"We'll make it so." Maud looked determined.

"They have an unusual energy containment field around her." Alexandra pulled a hand reader from one of her utility pockets. "When Carol-Maa gives the signal that the ship is going to blow, I'll cut their grid power." The HR read the energy wave surrounding Zohra, and vibrated when it had a destabilizing pulse.

As soon as Alexandra felt Maud's pat on her shoulder, the signal to go, she sent a mental shout to Zohra and shorted the energy fence around her. Almost immediately, the explosion of the ship rocked the area. Debris slammed against the ground.

Zohra sprang toward her confused guards, knocking out two of them before she disappeared over the rim of the cliff. Alexandra knew she wouldn't use the suit's ability to make her invisible. It would be too obvious, and they had agreed to keep the suits' abilities concealed.

The encampment was in turmoil, but the dense atmosphere kept the soldiers from moving quickly. Alexandra was sure that was panicking them further. She and Maud waited until Carol-Maa and the Sha'Kar joined them.

"That was quick work," Alexandra said.

"The Sha'Kar led me right to the ship," Carol-Maa said. "I slipped inside and engaged the self-destruct mechanism, bypassing the clock sequence to accelerate the countdown. Simple."

"The defense forces will have seen the explosion, and should be here soon." Maud looked pleased.

"This is working out too well to be true. Let's follow the metrasoldiers on Zohra's trail. Maybe we can protect her until more rescuers get here."

The three women watched from their vantage point. Zohra was using her two years of familiarity with the outpost to her advantage. She would hide in small crevices, and when the soldiers passed her, take out her nearest pursuer and then disappear.

"She's having fun with them."

"I guess she doesn't need the blend," Alexandra said in admiration. "I'm glad she's on my side."

“She’s messing with their air,” Maud said. “You can dent the feed tube if you know where to hit it, and the victim passes out from lack of oxygen.”

“It looks like their leader has figured out Zohra’s game.” Carol-Maa pointed. “He’s sending one of his men back up here, probably to spy out her position.”

“That’s not going to be easy,” Maud said.

The atmosphere was wreaking havoc on the AEG equipment and its wearer. He slipped and disappeared into the darkness.

“We have incoming,” Alexandra said, her voice jubilant. “The cavalry is here, and we’re clear to move out.” She stayed just long enough to be sure Zohra was safe.

Alexandra slipped back into her bedroom. After a peek into the sitting room to make sure the guards were still at their posts, she quickly stored her gear and then cut the program. A shower would be a good way to finish off her successful venture. Naked, she peered into the bathing room, expecting to see the two guards. Instead, the room was filled with steam.

Thinking Carol-Maa was in the water, she started to make a joke about getting back so fast, but then yelped in surprise. Zohra was soaking in the tub.

“Hi,” Zohra said, smiling. “I heard you playing and didn’t want to disturb you, so I entered through Carol-Maa’s room. Have a good rest?”

“Er, yeah.” Alexandra laughed, trying to cover any thoughts that might leak. “I got tired of the shamans’ meeting, listening to the same arguments again and again. How was your day?”

“Same old stuff.”

“Hmm.” Alexandra murmured, then groaned as she submerged herself to the chin in the hot water. She was tired from her run back to the Lair. Carol-Maa and Maud were lucky. They didn’t have to keep up a front.

Chapter 29

The next day, Alexandra was floating in the tub with Carol-Maa, Clea, and Galdin, letting the comfortable silence between them seep into her spirit. Being wrapped in their supportive and invigorating energy was a soothing experience.

Her lifemate entered the shower area, and a different tone mixed with the pleasant hum that surrounded the four. Alexandra's eyes fluttered open.

"Will you excuse me a moment? I think Zohra's back."

The others chuckled and resumed the conversation they had dropped when the soothing atmosphere overcame their sensibilities. Questions were again asked about how Alan's men knew exactly where Alexandra was quartered.

Alexandra poked her head into the shower where Zohra was rinsing off the sweat and dirt of her day, which she had spent digging people out of a cave-in. No wonder she looked tired. Alexandra breathed in the steam as she stepped up against the body she had been picturing almost constantly.

Zohra's hands were filled with suds, and she was scrubbing herself with slow movements. Alexandra wrapped herb-scented arms around her.

"Hmm," Zohra said, "this is nice shower service. I was wondering how long I could remain standing on my own."

"I've been driving everyone crazy with this nervous energy I have around me. I'm driving myself crazy, too. You don't happen to know what's causing it, do you?" Alexandra whispered into the wet ear near her mouth.

Zohra turned around in her arms. "It's from us being so close together now. There's another dance we need to perform."

Alexandra smiled, amused at the flush that rose in her partner's face. "Uh-huh. I got the lecture from your mother today, before she left for a meeting."

"What did you do?" Zohra asked, looking alarmed.

"Nothing." She pressed a finger over Zohra's lips then replaced it with a quick kiss. "She just wanted to make sure we didn't go and exchange vows before she got back. She said if we put out any stronger vibes, she was going to have to declare the Lair off-limits for anyone not accompanied by a partner. Think that was a hint?"

"Ouch. I think I heard someone else say something similar. To some species, we apparently seem to be exuding a lot of pheromones."

Alexandra felt embarrassed. "I finally found a shaman that would talk to me about this Dance thing, so I could get the whole picture instead of parts. I still can't figure out why it's so secretive. Anyway, I escalated it."

"How?"

"I've been dreaming of the next dance."

Zohra laughed and hugged her. "Good. That means I don't have to show it to you. That would... well, let's just say that pheromone gas would pale in comparison."

"Hmm. Potent stuff, huh?"

"So I've heard."

"Are you up to soaking for a bit?" Alexandra asked, concerned by the fatigue in her partner's eyes.

"Sure."

"Come on, then. Your friends have been asking about you." Alexandra tugged her tired lover to the tub, where the conversation was still on the metrasoldier attack.

"Colonel Zohra, where have you been keeping yourself?" Clea asked as the two women slid into the tub.

"Topside. Worked at a cave-in today."

"We've been discussing the attack," Clea said. "No one can figure out how Alan's men knew which quarters were Alexandra's."

There was more talk, but no one could shed any light on the matter.

Finally, a tired-looking Zohra said, "I'm going to sleep on that mystery. Come on." She took Alexandra's arm and pulled her out of the tub, nodding to the others. "We're doing some of Lady Alexandra's exercises at 0600 in the gym tomorrow. We'll see you down there, if you'd like to join us."

Carol-Maa, who had been quiet up until then, smiled. "I would love to participate."

What's the hurry? And why move our workout to the dojo? Alexandra wondered as she toweled off.

She caught up with Zohra as she was turning down the covers on the bed. Zohra tackled her onto the bed and for a while they wrestled, with the struggle becoming weaker and weaker. Alexandra's second question was forgotten when the first one was answered.

Alexandra wasn't able to sleep after their lovemaking. Her feelings of anticipation and foreboding increased until she had to get out of bed or risk waking Zohra. She walked quietly into the sitting room and waved at the two guards that were silently moving about the room, making a routine inspection.

Alexandra decided that a cold shower would help clear her senses. As the water flowed over her, she felt the familiar touch of the Sha'Kar from the Shadow City. Images of soldiers, some of them in her room, appeared in her mind. Finally, she began to feel the presence she had been fearing. "Goddess, a breach!"

She was out of the shower and into the bedroom room in seconds, where she found Alan and Vanstar. They had weapons pointed at the fallen Zohra.

"No!"

Vanstar's aim quickly shifted to Alexandra, and she fired. Alexandra felt a burning sensation as she fell forward. *Argh! It's a stunner.*

Vanstar grabbed her, hoisted her onto one shoulder, and raced off down a dark corridor. Alexandra grunted as each step forced air from her lungs. She saw blackness for a moment, and then Vanstar dumped her onto the cold floor of a ship. She could feel the Sha'Kar hovering over her, concerned.

"Why are you here?" Alexandra asked the Sha'Kar telepathically. There was no immediate reply.

Struggling to fill her lungs with air, Alexandra closed her eyes and focused on the movement of the ship as it shifted to evade whoever might be chasing it. She heard Alan shouting and then an angry Vanstar telling him to shut up. A short time later, they were in space and jumping through the gate to another part of the galaxy.

She opened her eyes to see an older, bearded version of Alan. He wiped spittle from his chin with the back of his hand.

"Well, Lady Montran." His gaze roamed over her naked body. Then his hand went to his forehead and he grimaced. "After I get this chip removed, I have a future planned for you, a future that's going to give me great pleasure and you a new purpose in life."

His eyes clouded over as the chip apparently sent unpleasant stimulation to his brain.

Alan wanted to continue picturing the agony he would inflict on Lady Montran, but he was too hyped up to want the pain he underwent from such thoughts. The chip's punishment could easily escalate to the point where he would lose consciousness.

They had a month of travel before they reached the illicit hospital ship. There he would have his chip removed and one implanted into his victim. Meanwhile, he didn't intend to let his captured Black Rose Spartan kill herself or sabotage the ship while he was incapacitated.

He returned to his seat next to Vanstar after he instructed the medbot to give Lady Montran a shot to sedate her. He would have liked it to be something painful, but like all of its kind, the medbot had ethics built into its operating system.

Alan barely glanced at Vanstar. His agents had seized the Black Rose soldier a few years back, at the same time they captured Sergeant Major JG. Chips were implanted in both of them. The sergeant was Lady Varina Chaney's, but Vanstar was his. Alan wanted an inside agent against his supposed friend, Lord Chaney.

The chip exaggerated Vanstar's class prejudice, and just for fun, Alan had a subliminal running in her quarters that increased her dislike of Lady Harriet Montran. He smiled as he thought of getting Lady Montran to torture Vanstar, or maybe the other way around. He stroked the wild hairs on his chin in contemplation.

"Strap in," Vanstar's gruff voice ordered.

Alan hated to strap in; he ignored her.

The next maneuvers were to evade the droids that suddenly blipped onto the screen. Vanstar grabbed Alan's shirtfront and thrust him back into his chair when he tipped out on the first shift. "Strap in, you fool!"

Alan hastily complied, realizing that he had an expert at the controls as his enslaved pilot escaped not only the droids, but also the monitors for the net that disabled unauthorized craft trying to pass through the gate.

Alexandra was left to bounce around. The Sha'Kar protected her from most of the bruises by laying its body around her and acting like an energy blanket.

Chapter 30

Zohra felt the air change around her and rolled to her feet, dismayed when her ears caught the sound of a shower. Vanstar was standing in the doorframe, looking around.

"What's going—" Zohra's words froze as she was struck by the stunner's beam. She fell to the ground, paralysis burning through her limbs. As she went down, she saw Alexandra return from the shower and heard her yell. Then Vanstar picked Alexandra up and whisked her away.

Agonized, Zohra crawled to the sitting room. Both guards lay on their backs, eyes open to the ceiling, shaking from the effects of the stunner. Unconscious metrasoldiers lay nearby. She pulled herself toward the door, where she could hear pounding. Suddenly it opened and soldiers poured in, too late.

Lieutenant Malchi reached Zohra and pulled her into her lap, stroking her forehead while spasms ran through her limbs as the second stage of recovery started.

"Get her into some hot water," Gedaliaha ordered. "Move the others into the pool, also. It will reduce the pain and speed up recovery."

Gedaliaha hurried into the bathing room, pulled some herbs out of the cupboard, and tossed them into the water. She turned up the heat regulator. Carol-Maa slid into the water and Malchi handed her Zohra's shaking body.

Tears rolled down Zohra's cheeks from the cry of pain her frozen vocal cords couldn't voice. Every cell in her body burned. She closed her eyes and tried to center herself, as Alexandra had been teaching her.

"Find your peaceful center, Zohra," Alexandra said.

"I don't have a peaceful center. I have a focused center." Zohra was a little upset that the general had ordered her to light

duty. Her mother had laid out the facts: she had been working for nine years without a break and needed some rest.

She didn't need a break. She was fine. However, she was forced to admit, she was enjoying the private moments with Alexandra. So she gave her lover's request another try, paying closer attention this time.

"It's there, just a little beyond that focused center. Come on. You need to find this peaceful place just as much as that focused one you use to fight from."

She took a deep breath and let it out slowly, then opened one eye and peeked at Alexandra. Alexandra shook her head, smiling, and leaned forward until their foreheads touched. Her emerald green eyes closed, and Zohra felt stillness wash over her. It was beautiful. And peaceful.

Finally recovered, Zohra rose from the hot water, furious. "Vanstar is dead." She pushed against Carol-Maa, who was supporting her. The arms around her tightened. Frustrated, Zohra leaned back against the bare breasts, shouting her anger and fear for Alexandra. Zohra finally gave in to the hurt. She cried for the loss, and the pain of being deceived by an old friend. Her emotions spent, she was helped out of the water.

"Now we can get to work," General Aglauros called from the sitting room. "We're meeting in Com-C, in five minutes. Get dressed, Daughter."

* * *

Com-C was filled with shamans and senior officers. General Aglauros called them to order as soon as Zohra took her seat.

"This is how it stands," Aglauros said. "On the outpost, we have five sections under siege by Alowans. They're breaking through the portal with crude weapons, but we're containing them. We've also stopped the teams sent by Alan to destroy the portals on the other planets. Thank you, Brother, for your work on deciphering his black book." She nodded to the tall, orange-haired Lord Hadrian DeMonte.

Zohra studied the man, thinking he resembled Alexandra only slightly until she noted the set of his shoulders.

"Now we need to find Alan Fermin. Our spy tells us that Alan's current ship, the *Trojan Horse*, is en route to the *Shiae*, an illegal hospital ship where chips are implanted and removed. It's a month's travel from here, and that's without having to take evasive maneuvers. Thanks to Brother Regas, we also discovered the identity of Alan's plant in the Black Rose—our Sister, Megan Vanstar."

Zohra clutched the arms of her chair, and the shaman at her side gently covered her hand, calming her with his energy.

"Because of that, we were able to use Vanstar ourselves." Aglauros's expression was sad. "Brother Regas, who is Lieutenant Ninian of the Black Rose, knew that Vanstar was under Alan's thumb and was monitoring her. We couldn't tell you, Daughter, because it would have changed your relationship with her. Alan had a chip implanted in her. Her quarters here were wired to give her hypnotic suggestions to hate Lady Alexandra in particular."

Aglauros held up a hand, forestalling the comment on Zohra's lips. "Daughter, we've dissolved the chip and sent counter suggestions, but until they take effect, we have to let her continue. In two days, our counter suggestions should override Alan's hateful program. Sister Megan is resentful toward the upper classes, but not as hateful as one might think. She will rise to the occasion when she realizes how Alan has used her. I have faith in her."

General Aglauros continued summarizing, enlightening the others about the military and political activities in the galaxies.

The meeting seemed to go on for a long time, and the calming effect of the shaman's touch wore off. Zohra felt empty and lost. The farther Alexandra moved away, the deeper the depression settled.

"Daughter," General Aglauros said.

Zohra lifted her head and blinked a few times. She looked around, startled to see that the room was empty except for the two of them.

"I think you need to keep busy."

Zohra tried not to cry. She couldn't believe the intensity of the pain Alexandra's abduction had caused.

"You haven't danced the Third Dance, I take it."

Unable to speak, Zohra shook her head. "No time," she finally got out.

Aglauros pulled her close and held her as she wept. "There's a ship leaving in a stan hour to check out *Rouster*, Alan's abandoned craft. It's been monitored long enough to know he's not around, but it has to have traps on it. You're a specialist in that field."

"Thank you, Mother." Zohra kissed her on the cheek, knowing the rules were being stretched.

Chapter 31

"All right, Ensign, come about easy." Zohra was outside the hull of *Star Voucher*, dressed in a top-of-the-line AEG suit that had been provided by *Star Voucher*'s Captain Itk.

"Coming about easy, Colonel Zohra."

Zohra had already found one bomb trip sensor at one of *Rouster*'s life pod hatch openings. She pulled herself out of the way as the pilot eased the ship closer. Though Captain Itk was the commander of *Star Voucher*, Zohra was in command of this recon mission and she had directed him not to order a hull-to-hull coupling with Alan's abandoned ship. If they used the umbilical tube instead, they could break away quickly if necessary.

Zohra grabbed the edge of the extending tube and pulled herself inside of it, tumbling and twisting in free fall as the tube continued its progress to nudge gently against the hatch.

"Contact. Seals are secured. Readings say we're good to go." Breathable air rushed into the tube, and she braced herself for the heaviness that would follow environmental stabilization. According to the readings, air inside the ship was breathable, too, but one could never be sure what would happen.

Two communications personnel, an ensign and a corporal from *Star Voucher*, joined her. Orders were to leach as much data from the ship as they could, then let her go, just in case Alan returned or the ship had other purposes, such as being a booby-trapped decoy.

"Corporal, don't step there." Zohra stopped the young soldier before he placed his boot on a plate that might be rigged. She was tense, but not because of the job. This was everyday stuff for the Black Rose. She took a deep breath to bring her focus back into herself, separating personal issues from business.

Corporal Stik slowly withdrew his foot, sweat beading on his upper lip.

"Wait here. Don't move or touch anything." An alarm went off, indicating the presence of a life-form. She found a body, nearly dead, in one of the staterooms.

"Corporal, come here. We've got a live one, barely, in the third stateroom on the right. Colonel Zohra to *Star Voucher*. Send in a medbot, stat."

"I heard you, Colonel. I'm sending a *mante* over to assist with the victim."

"Captain, the fewer personnel over here, the safer."

There was a long pause. Zohra suspected the captain was struggling with her challenge to his command. "As you wish, Colonel. A medbot is coming over."

Zohra completed her meticulous inspection of the area where the two communications experts would be working. "Don't go anywhere without telling me, and that includes the can. Am I understood?"

The two nodded. "Yes, Colonel Zohra."

Standing in the cockpit, she looked at the controls. The ship could be operated by four crewmembers, or just a single pilot. It included five small but luxurious cabins, seating for eight, and a cargo bay that could probably hold a month's worth of huge trinkets bought on Centur I. Centur I's inhabitants were twice Zohra's height, and everything made there was big, and cheap for its size. Sighing, she told Ensign Haital and Corporal Stik to check the ship's logs.

A few minutes later, Haital glanced up at her, excited. "I found something. He deleted everything but the backup files. He must have been in a real hurry to have forgotten those."

"Do you think you can dump them? Looks like they go back a while."

"Colonel, based on these dates, he hasn't erased his backup files for six stan months. Previously, someone had been downloading these files and then erasing them when the download was completed. Here's the last logon."

"Where was the last place they were downloaded?"

"At his family's dock on Selen. The logon is from his family business. Do you think he downloads his own files?"

"Maybe, but why would an obsessive guy like Alan get so sloppy about doing regular dumps of his travel logs? Maybe someone does it for him… or did. A personal secretary could take care of most of his affairs, and probably all the menial tasks, so that after a while Alan doesn't even remember they need to be done."

"Like preparing his ship for flight. Look here." Haital pointed to a line on the monitor. "Log entries for cleaning this ship stopped six months ago. It should have happened whenever he docked. His last charges are dated seven months ago, signed by someone whose name I can't read."

"Keep checking, see what else you find."

"Right, Colonel."

Keeping one eye on the ensign to make sure she wouldn't run into any traps, Zohra checked the furniture in the cockpit. There were two pilots' chairs, and the most worn looking chair was also the more luxurious of the two. Something was shoved between the well-worn seat and back. Zohra knelt down and began a careful exploration, probing gently.

She drew out an elaborately carved box. She opened it cautiously and was rewarded by the sight of tiny sticks, which had been carved into crude figures, some of them recognizable. These had to be the sticks Alexandra said Alan used to read the time line. There was no mistaking one stick figure. It had painted breasts and very long orange strings pasted on its head. She didn't recognize most of the others, but she was quite sure Alan would return for them. They needed to get out of this ship *now*.

"All hands, listen up! Abandon ship."

Suddenly the control board lit up.

"What the—"

"Ma'am, I didn't touch any controls." Haital had both hands in the air.

"Too late for us to leave. Comm on. Captain Itk, get out of here. It looks like Alan's on his way. Follow at a discreet distance, and run silent."

She gestured to Haital and Stik. "He may be able to read life signs, so get in the pods."

"Ma'am, there are only two," Corporal Stik said.

"It's a luxury model, so I'm sure there's room for at least three people in each pod. Just don't breathe deeply and we'll be fine."

Zohra removed the stick that represented Alexandra and put the box back where she had found it. After one last look around, she joined Ensign Haital in the second pod. Even though it was a luxury model, it was a tight squeeze, since they were wearing AEGs.

Chapter 32

"Alan, leave her be," Vanstar growled.

He was squatting next to Lady Harriet, tracing invisible lines along her bare body, which was bruised and cut from their rough ride out of GCFC space.

"Shut up and get back to your seat," he snarled, and continued with the fascinating game of watching the unconscious woman's skin twitch when his hand came near her.

Vanstar grabbed his collar and slammed him against the bulkhead. "We're approaching your ship's coordinates. I don't like the idea of dragging *Rouster* around when we don't know if anyone's aboard or if there's a plant on it. So I'm pretty testy right now, and I'm not in the mood to watch you play when you should be up front getting ready to board your ship. Now, get dressed."

She released him and he struggled to stand up straight.

"And get her stored in the pod," Vanstar said as she turned away.

"Why?"

Vanstar turned back toward him. "Because if this is a trap, we'll want to get out of here quickly. You said you have the pod set for that planet on the other side of this galaxy, right?"

He nodded.

"Well then, you have something to bargain with—the knowledge of where she's headed. We see any trouble, I'll jettison her and there's your safe passage."

"She's important. Her cousin will want her back." Alan's head bobbed stupidly, a side effect of his meds. He hefted the body, lumbered to the life pod, and dropped her into it. He checked to make sure it was set for Arnica. One of his sisters had been sent there on a colonization ship. His lips took on a cruel twist, and his eyes slit as he thought of their eventual reunion. Slamming the lid of the pod, he contemplated whether he should put Lady Harriet in stasis now, or later.

"Alan, get into your gear and get up here."

He hit the stasis activation button. He wouldn't have had much time to play with her anyway. He trotted forward.

He watched with Vanstar as *Rouster* sailed into view on the screen. She had hidden *Trojan Horse* behind the space debris, while she considered the possible places a tail could be waiting for them.

Alan studied the security settings the Black Rose soldier had tweaked. He grudgingly admitted that her modifications yielded more information than the previous settings had. They both looked for any indication that *Rouster* was being followed. Nothing. Vanstar brought the *Trojan Horse* systems back online.

Impatient, he turned to pace in the small area, but a glare from Vanstar soon had him reseating himself. He consoled himself that though their lives were in her hands for now, he ultimately held hers in his hand. Or more accurately, in the miniature control on the back of his hand. Her life depended on him not sending a self-destruct transmission to her implanted chip, which would then cause her death. A painful death, at that.

He was quite pleased with the electronics that the metralab produced. They were manufactured at the prison colony on Hinterwield, originally to keep the violent inmates subdued, until a certain scientist took over the management of the colony and the research took on a different direction. Through this contact, he finally found a scientist who promised to remove his chip without triggering the side effects. Inmates at the prison colony were the practice subjects. There had been plenty of volunteers, as most wanted their chips removed.

"Don't touch that," Vanstar yelled, as he was about to send a life-reading probe to the ship. "If the ship's being followed, they'll sense our probes. Let me handle this."

Alan withdrew his hand. He hadn't thought of that. He was on his meds, and felt strangely adrift.

Vanstar ignored him and continued to study the ship and the surrounding space. Returning to *Rouster* was a bad idea, but she had no voice in the decision.

After the slight bump from contact with the hull of *Rouster*, the hull sensors quickly verified that the hatches were lined up properly. She released the locks and opened the two hatches, while coaxing the sluggish controls to keep their combined bulk near the center of the debris trail, so they wouldn't be easy targets in the event that a patrol ship showed up.

She was disgusted that Alan hadn't purchased an umbilical connector with his ship. Some private yacht owners shaved cost from their toys by only buying standard equipment, thinking they could get better emergency gear later.

"Get over there and back quick," Vanstar said.

Alan hit a small button that deactivated *Rouster*'s traps and prepared to board. He hadn't wanted to leave *Rouster* behind, but too many people would recognize it. Besides, *Trojan Horse* was a newer and faster model.

He had left what he had come back for on his pilot's chair. Cautiously entering the bridge, he sniffed the air. The odor of Hemmitt's fear and body excrements was gone. He didn't see the box. Ah, there it was—it had slipped between the seat and chair back. Just as he pulled his precious box out of the crease in the pilot's chair, he looked up and a fist slammed into his face. Alan's legs neatly buckled, and he dropped unconscious onto his ship's carpeted deck.

* * *

"Alan!"

A ship appeared on Vanstar's screen, broadside to *Trojan Horse*'s port quarter. She hit the disengage switch. The moment the lights showed her the hatch was sealed and the two ships no longer connected, she dropped *Trojan Horse* beneath *Rouster*'s belly, rolled her to the other side, and slid behind some debris. Alan hadn't replied, not even by activating her chip's death switch. That meant trouble. She weaved in and out of the debris field, playing a dangerous game of hide-and-seek among the moving space junk until a reasonably good spot appeared in a large asteroid. She entered it, shut off all systems that could give away her location, and waited. She knew it would take a long time for a single ship to make an effective search.

On the darkened bridge, she leaned back in her chair and considered her options. She was still alive, which meant Alan was probably powerless at the moment. The impulse to move out of range of his device was almost overpowering, but she squelched it. Instead, she walked to the back of the ship and checked on her live cargo.

"I could just release her," she muttered to herself. "No, not yet. Then I'd have to listen to Lady Montran bossing me around like I'm her servant."

After half a stan day of hiding, Vanstar decided to make a break for it. The patrol ship was still around, but she had an appointment to keep, which was made easier by Alan's failure to return. She was not so naive as to believe he would have let her go, minus the implant, after she helped him kidnap Montran, so she had made her own arrangements.

The ship's power came online quickly. *Trojan Horse* was a top-of-the-line model, and it had a lot of extra gadgets that she guessed Alan didn't even understand. If she were going to steal a civilian ship, this would be her first choice.

The asteroid was drifting closer to the jump gate. She watched her tacticals, waiting to see when the gate's deflector fields would gently push it away. Then it and the rest of the debris would be left to drift. Once close enough, Vanstar intended to hit the gate with all the g's her engines could muster. Once she was through it, her pursuers wouldn't know where she was headed.

Just as *Trojan Horse* leaped forward, its sensors picked up a ship right on her tail, and a shot hit her dead astern. It was probably meant to disable her engines, but *Trojan Horse* was better protected than the average law-abiding civilian vessel. Instead, the impact sent *Trojan Horse* too far forward and put it at the wrong angle to make it cleanly into the gate.

The ship's tactical computer immediately began the evasive maneuvers that Vanstar had preprogrammed. The sudden moves made her hand jerk, and she accidentally hit the hyperspace engage button. The ship went into hyperspace. Off balance, Vanstar was jerked sideways. She crashed into the bulkhead, the impact knocking her unconscious.

Trojan Horse shot forward through the jump gate and on toward its preset destination, without the help of its injured pilot.

Vanstar opened her eyes to a screen that showed stars streaking by. She breathed deeply a few times, trying to get her bearings, and suddenly noted that her obsession with undermining Lady Montran was no longer foremost in her mind. Tears ran down her face as she lay on the deck. Somehow, the chip had been removed.

Once her composure returned, her military training kicked in and she rose to check the ship systems.

"So, we're on our way to Alan's planet, and no overrides." She sighed. "Well, Commander Montran, it's just you and me for eight months. If all goes well, that is. At least this vessel has more power behind it than the little pod he put you in. I'd better send a message to General Aglauros. She's going to want to know what I've done with my passenger. Goddess, what a mess."

Not daring to use an open channel with smugglers around, Vanstar sent a coded message to her Sister house. Task completed, she turned to the databanks and wondered what she was going to have to entertain herself for the next eight months. Alan's programs were easy to access, and full of perversions.

"This guy is sick. I'll have to pull Commander Montran out of that pod, clear the program buffer, and put something else in there. Hope she's not going to wake up swinging. This is a hell of a time to see who has a meaner punch."

Opening the life pod's lid, and she waited as Montran's pale skin gradually began to take on color.

* * *

There was a menacing presence around Alexandra, and she couldn't move away from it. Alan's touch, as he ran his fingers over her bare body, would have made her tremble if she had been able to respond. He must have injected her with something after Vanstar brought her aboard.

She heard Vanstar's harsh voice order him to secure her in a life pod then return to his seat. That was the least Vanstar could do, considering she was responsible for Alexandra being here.

A comforting presence reassured her that she wasn't alone.

"You're here."

The Sha'Kar seemed amused by her statement of the obvious.

Alan dumped her unceremoniously into the life pod. Its program started immediately, so she didn't have any more time to speak with the Sha'Kar. The subliminal Alan had loaded began, as well. When the Sha'Kar realized the images were causing Alexandra discomfort, it interfered with the subliminal and halted its transmissions.

What seemed like only moments later, Alexandra saw a cloud of millions of tiny cells letting off sparks of energy and creating the outline of a life-form.

She received an image from the Sha'Kar of Vanstar opening the life pod and waking her.

The life pod's nurturing bed adjusted as her bios picked up, and then the lid folded out of the way. "What's…" Her voice cracked as her dry throat tightened.

Water was offered, through a long straw.

Even though her wits were still a bit scattered, Alexandra could feel a difference in Vanstar, and she was grateful for that. She wasn't in any position to defend herself.

"What's going on?" she asked in a stronger voice.

"Alan boarded *Rouster*, then I think it was seized by a patrol ship. I evaded them and jumped through a gate."

"Where are we now?"

Vanstar took a deep breath, but didn't answer.

"The short version will do."

Vanstar looked relieved. "On our way to Arnica."

"I take it we can't override?"

"That's correct, ma'am."

"You're friendly now?"

"You've nothing to fear from me, Commander. I'm feeling different now," Vanstar said, looking embarrassed.

"I can sense that you're telling the truth. Does Alan have anything on this yacht I can wear?"

"He has all sorts of uniforms."

"Good. Can you give me a hand out of this pod?"

"Yes, Commander."

Alexandra chose a set of fatigues that were loose enough for her to wear and didn't have Alan's energy clinging to them.

From there, they examined the ship's supplies and went through the tiring process of inspecting each container in the storage bay and inventorying its contents. Alan had up-to-date weapons of various designs, ammunition, games from the handheld to the holographic, and seeds.

"Wonder why he wanted all these seeds?" Alexandra asked, puzzled.

Two stomachs growled, as if in reply.

"That's a clear signal for a break," Alexandra said.

While the two sat in the cockpit eating their packaged meals, Alexandra tried to figure out what they were going to do for eight months.

"I suggest we ride out most of the trip in the pods. Boredom and being cooped up in this small craft will do some nasty things to our minds, otherwise. But first, we need to check the data banks. I know I'm not going to like Alan's idea of entertainment."

Vanstar nodded. "I went through his program files. They're not for normal people, and I cleared a number of them."

"Have you ever been in one of these life pods?"

"No, Commander."

"Are you going to be okay with it?"

"I'll be fine."

Alexandra watched the colors of Vanstar's energy field change, grateful that she was seeing another side of this soldier.

"Tough it out like a Black Rose?" she said, teasing.

"In the Black Rose, we never knew who the enemy was. Getting in a life pod was giving up control of your life. We were just lucky Chaney didn't want us out of action for any length of time. He wasn't a nice guy, and with the exception of the Black Rose, he treated his employees as expendables. I guess he saw us as some kind of warrior class. It didn't stop him from sending us into some pretty messy situations, though.

"Once your squad, the Degas, was gone, Central Command decided they liked the idea of dropping a squad in the center of the enemy's camp and letting them work their way out, as you trained the Degas to do. The Black Rose felt honored to take up the role, and we were strongly motivated to succeed."

Alexandra was surprised with by the length of Vanstar's conversation, and the compliment she had given the Degas. "Honored? Whatever for?" she asked softly. "We didn't kill the enemy. We just stole whatever supplies we could, set off alarms, and pretty much ran as fast as we could."

Vanstar gave a rueful laugh. "You made us look bad. We were supposed to be the meanest and the most daring, and here was a group of misfits no one wanted, doing the impossible, creating havoc and dismay within enemy lines, and surviving. We admired you. Did you know the Black Rose raise their first drink to the memory of the Degas squad? Not just because of you, but for what the squad represented. Against all odds." She took a deep breath. "I'm really sorry about that last drop, Commander."

Alexandra waited expectantly for the tightness and the heavy feeling of guilt that often accompanied the memory, but it didn't come. "They were great soldiers, Vanstar. It's good of you to remember them. I hope you continue doing so."

"Yes, Commander."

Alexandra studied Vanstar, looking for the old insubordination and distrust, but found none. She saw only an embarrassed smile, and nodded in return.

Both rose, without anymore being said, and headed for the communications closet.

"Well, let's see what he has in this library that's not obnoxious, violent, or repugnant." Alexandra tapped one title on her screen. "Arnica. This might be useful. Then again, by the lack of content info, I think I won't select it after all." Her finger moved to another, while Vanstar deleted the obviously inappropriate content.

"You know," Alexandra said, glancing at Vanstar, "there's no way to know what he tampered with, even if we put each one through a sieve. I think I'd rather have a quiet ride for those eight months."

"I agree, Commander."

"That settles it then. We'll have silence for our trip. Let's move on to the logs. I want to check the pod specs and maintenance records to see if it's safe for us to use them. And while the diags are running, we'll see where this trip is taking us."

Retrieving the pod data was quickly done, and then Alexandra programmed the ship's computer to run diagnostics and test scenarios on each pod to determine how safe they were. Then they searched the database for any information they could find on their destination.

Vanstar was leaning over Alexandra's shoulder, looking at the screen.

"That's a castle," Vanstar said in awe.

"Yes, a castle updated with the latest and greatest gadgets of two years ago, when Alan's people headed out there."

"Two years ago?"

Alexandra pointed at the small date stamped on the right corner. "It's also got a moat with nightmares running around in it. I notice he doesn't have any small villages surrounding his retreat, but there's a river right here and a lake nearby." She didn't want to think about what might have become of anyone who had been there first.

"I think I need some physical activity about now," Alexandra said. "Would you care to join me for a workout?"

"Wouldn't mind at all, Commander."

"Incoming message," the computer's voice announced as Alexandra and Vanstar warily circled one another. They were tired after only thirty stan minutes of aggressively testing each other's defenses. The women scurried to the bridge and plopped into the chairs expectantly.

"Go ahead," Alexandra said.

Admiral JoCastao's face came on the screen.

"Greetings. I'm glad to see you're both well. We received your transmission, Lieutenant Vanstar."

"Admiral JoCastao," Alexandra said.

"Your ship's under full thrust, so we can't intercept or pull you in, and I won't ask you to do anything crazy when the situation doesn't warrant it."

Alexandra nodded. She had no intention of doing anything like getting into a life pod and being ejected into the wake of the ship, even if ordered to do so.

"We're sending a ship, *Catching Butterflies*, to pick you up, though it hasn't left the shipyard yet. Since it's a lot faster than that yacht you're on, we have time to assemble an appropriate crew. They will assist *Emperor's Last Chance*, which was sent to Arnica a year ago to find out what Alan's advance guard was up to. Those two ships have orders to subdue Alan's soldiers, assess the damage they've caused, and see what needs to be done to correct it.

"Within the data flow you're receiving now is the latest information on Arnica sent by *Emperor's Last Chance*. It was received a few weeks ago, so it'll be old news by the time you arrive, but it's a start. *Catching Butterflies* and *Emperor's Last Chance* have official duties and limitations. Therefore, we need you two to do some information gathering.

"You should know that two generations ago, a number of colonists, unsanctioned by either the Collective or GCFC, headed to Arnica. Commander, you're hereby ordered to do what is necessary to neutralize any damage the colonists have caused. Any questions?"

"Admiral." Alexandra cleared her throat, embarrassed to be asking a personal question, "Is Colonel Zohra all right?"

"Your lifemate? Yes, she'll be joining you. She's in *Rouster*, following at a slower pace. But we're hoping *Catching Butterflies* will overtake Colonel Zohra and give her a ride the rest of the way. You should all arrive at Arnica about the same time. Her orders are to join you on this mission. I emphasize that we must know what's going on with the colonists."

Alexandra's face colored at the public acknowledgement of her relationship, but she was relieved that it had been officially noted. That would make their lives easier.

Her thoughts returned to their new assignment. Something about the colonists was bothering two galactic governments enough to order a covert investigation in addition to the official presence.

"What about Alan, Admiral?" Lieutenant Vanstar asked.

"Colonel Zohra captured him on *Rouster* and had him transferred to a patrol ship, which was to return him to Century City for trial. That ship was boarded by smugglers and then blown up. Our rescue ships were too late to save the crew, but we inflicted heavy damages on the band that attacked them. Unfortunately, we have no way of being certain that Alan perished."

There was a moment of silence. At this distance, Alexandra couldn't sense whether Alan still lived. *So, that particular thorn will remain in my side, for now.* Alexandra shuddered, but then remembered that Alan wasn't anywhere near her now, and might never be again. She couldn't suppress the smile that warmed her face as she thought of who *was* following her.

"Safe journey, and safe return. Your Sisters already miss you, Lieutenant Vanstar, and Commander Montran, I still plan to award you your command bars myself."

"Thank you, Admiral. I appreciate your confidence."

The transmission ended. Alexandra turned to Vanstar, barely able to contain her excitement.

"Commander?"

"We're going to a whole new galaxy, and Colonel Zohra will be joining us. No pesky orders that change with every shift in the wind. No personnel files to update. No politicians to deal with. Let's get to it, Lieutenant."

Glossary and List of Characters

ADDM: Adjustment and Decontamination of Disturbed Minds. A private collection of schools set up to reeducate violent children of the privileged classes in GCFC territories. Implanted chips monitor subject progress and enforce the program's rules.

AEG: A'mort Environmental Garb, a suit used for entering hostile environments.

Aglauros: Major General of the House of Athena, and Zohra's adopted mother. Chairwoman of Hekate's Inner Circle.

Alan Fermin: A wealthy sociopath who became fixated on Montran.

Ald: Montran's robotic bathing room attendant on Merker's Outpost.

Alexandra Harriet Montran: Lady by birth and inheritor of Clan Montran titles and responsibilities. Educated at a monastery in her early youth to train her empathic abilities. Later, she enrolled in a military academy against her family's wishes.

Bach: Montran's robotic butler on Merker's Outpost.

Brothers of the Shadow: A warrior fraternity.

Captain Miller: Commanding officer of the Spartan Black Rose Squad which was sponsored by Lord Chaney and deployed by him to Merker's Outpost.

Centurions: Policing arm of the Collective government.

Charles: Personal attendant to Guardian of Merker's Outpost.

Collective: Group of planets whose inhabitants believe violence begets violence, and who seek peaceful methods to ensure good relationships between all planetary members.

Copoc: Intelligent species with four legs, six arms, and four fingers.

COR: Catu's Ortual Rstr. Equipment used to measure environmental variables and to diagnose and prescribe treatment for the injured.

Council of Rings: Governing body placed in authority over the two main galactic powers, Collective and GCFC.

Daughters of Athena: From the House of Athena, one of many women warrior organizations. Most members enter when still children. Shield Maidens of Athena are a specially trained group of women, skilled in various arts from healing to war.

Eugene Decker: Petty Officer Third Class on *Spinner's Tale*, and Alan Fermin's spy.

Galactic Central Command: Subcommittee of the GCFC that oversees military and police deployment, action and recruitment.

GCFC: Galactic Committee of Families and Communities Once an elected body of stewards and representatives of their continents and planets to the Galactic council, now members are selected on a hereditary basis. This change was due to the expense involved in training a child all her or his life in the duties and responsibilities of these positions.

Gedaliaha: Wieldworlds holy woman, and one of Montran's mentors.

Guardian: Overseer of Merker's Outpost. A Copoc scientist who became a disembodied sentience resident in the planetary computer system. All overseers of portals that link to other planets are called Guardian.

Hekate's Inner Circle: A group of female warriors and healers that work, usually covertly, to promote the Council of Rings' mandate of peaceful coexistence among all planets. These warriors for the Goddess do not necessarily practice violence, but they protect themselves when necessary and undergo deep soul searching before and after assignments that require taking another's life.

Hinterwield: The harshest of the five Wieldworlds. Used by the GCFC as a prison colony. Adults who have committed violent crimes are sent here.

Houses of Aphrodite: Houses of pleasure for all the senses. Working there is considered honorable employment.

House of Athena: A group of women who offer their lives to serve and protect the honor of women in all cultures. If they pass crucial tests for honor, attitude, ethics and valor, they may become Shield Maidens.

House of Jeborhara: Healers' house on Velta IV, where Zohra was born and spent the first four years of her life.

Jina Gari: Spartan Sergeant Major, also known as JG. Undercover identity of Zohra, Shield Maiden of the House of Athena and member of Hekate's Inner Circle, planted as a covert agent in the Black Rose Squad.

L'uenbeng Merker: Formerly a Copoc scientist, Guardian of Mer and owner of Merker's Outpost. As a scientist, he built laboratories and residences within the planet. All products of his laboratories are of high quality and ecologically sound. His work is intended for use by the general public, and is not sold to the military.

Lord Hadrian DeMonte: Montran's older cousin, who took over the Demonte house seat on the GCFC. Head of the covert organization Naboths's Vine.

Lord Milford Chaney of Dlephae: Leader of the smugglers based on Merker's Outpost, and miners' representative on Dlephae. A GCFC committee member, he holds important positions and is known for his brutality. He is also a pedophile.

Magewield: One of the five Wieldworlds. Inhabited by a telepathic species who revere two-spirit people. Homeworld of Rene, who became Sharon Teal.

Maud: The only biological agent of Guardian of Merker's Outpost, whose appearance has been modified to closely resemble Montran's.

Megan Vanstar: Sergeant, member of the House of Athena, covert agent in the Black Rose Squad.

Merker's Outpost: Part of the vortex highway of Portals, or gateways to other planets. Contains five underground cities: *Century City, Lair, WaterLand, Ilo, and Wanluf.*

Metradames: Metrapeople who have been programmed to satisfy their owners' sexual urges.

Metrapeople: Mindwiped individuals who are then subjected to reprogramming of consciousness. Basically slaves, they are subject to the whims of their owners, who may have them programmed for specific functions.

Metrasoldiers: Soldiers from violent cultures, kidnapped by Alan Fermin and turned into his personal army. Implanted biochips force them into servitude.

Naboth's Vine: An organization that works to change corrupt political systems, without the use of violence if at all possible.

JoCastao: Collective Rear Admiral, senior flag officer on *Ziggy* and Montran's commanding officer.

Rene: Two-spirit shaman born on Magewield. Body altered to the female gender at puberty, to reflect her feelings of herself. Underwent metradame programming in order to help stop the metrapeople business. As Dr. Sharon Teal, she was Montran's lover.

Rue Despario: An agreement between the two galactic powers that allows the emergency exchange of military personnel. Lord Chaney used it to remove Montran from Collective service and press her into GCFC duty until he could imprison her on Merker's Outpost.

Serpent's Tooth: A union of smugglers, thieves, and other criminals that operates outside of the mandate of the Council of Rings.

Sheila: Lord Chaney's metradame bodyguard. Became a metradame in order to go undercover as an agent for Naboths Vine.

Spartans: Military arm of the GCFC. Still use deadly force as part of their policy and training.

Tanjmi: A Collective special forces group trained to hunt down dangerous criminals and bring them to justice.

Tolec: One of Lord Chaney's private guards, skilled in extracting information from reluctant informants. Nicknamed the Painmaker.

Varina Chaney: Lord Chaney's daughter by his only wife. Varina sees all her half-sisters (Chaney only produced daughters) as threats, and goes about eliminating them. She is the only one of Chaney's daughters who is not the result of rape.

Zohra: Once a well known galactic athlete, she then enrolled in a military academy. From there, she went into covert operations for Naboth's Vine. Changed her appearance and took the name Jina Gari, or JG, for an undercover assignment in the Black Rose. Daughter of Lord Chaney.

I. Christie and Sara

About the Author

I Christie is a homegrown Southern California native. Her father's parents emigrated from the Azore Islands to Fall River, Massachusetts. Her mother was a WWII war bride from France. Her whole life, I Christie has been a reader, writer, gardener, artist, and athlete, excelling only in reading. During the course of writing a dissertation, her love of writing became an obsession. Once finished with graduate school, Christie devoted her energy to developing as a writer.

Christie lives in Long Beach, California, with Sara, a tall girl who is a golden lab/greyhound mix; Cleopatra, a white blue-green-eyed cat; and three calico sisters: Calie, Cagney, and Lacey. There are also the parakeets and finches that never cease to fascinate the three sisters.

Christie's favorite downtime activities are taking Sara for a run at the dog beach and playing catch with the three sisters. Cleo rules the house.